SOMETHING WICKED

ALSO BY FALON BALLARD

Change of Heart

All I Want Is You

Right on Cue

Just My Type

Lease on Love

SOMETHING WICKED

A NOVEL

FALON BALLARD

G. P. PUTNAM'S SONS
New York

PUTNAM
— EST. 1838 —
G. P. Putnam's Sons
Publishers Since 1838
an imprint of Penguin Random House LLC
1745 Broadway, New York, NY 10019
penguinrandomhouse.com

Library of Congress Cataloging-in-Publication Data
Names: Ballard, Falon, author
Title: Something wicked : a novel / Falon Ballard.
Description: New York : G.P. Putnam's Sons, 2025.
Identifiers: LCCN 2025010276 | ISBN 9780593854679 hardcover | ISBN 9780593854686 ebook
Subjects: LCGFT: Fantasy fiction | Romance fiction | Novels
Classification: LCC PS3602.A621125 S66 2025 | DDC 813/.6—dc23/eng/20250307
LC record available at https://lccn.loc.gov/2025010276

ISBN (international edition) 9798217178971

Printed in China
1 3 5 7 9 10 8 6 4 2

The authorized representative in the EU for product safety and compliance is Penguin Random House Ireland, Morrison Chambers, 32 Nassau Street, Dublin D02 YH68, Ireland, https://eu-contact.penguin.ie.

To my agent, Kimberly Whalen,

who has always believed in this book,

and always believed in me

Nought's had, all's spent,
Where our desire is got without content.
'Tis safer to be that which we destroy
Than by destruction dwell in doubtful joy.

—*Macbeth*, act 3, scene 2

AVON
VENEZIA
KALMAR
STRATFORD CITY
SCOTA
TALIA
N
W
E
S

SOMETHING WICKED

Yesterday I overheard Diana talking in the hall. I know I shouldn't have listened, she would be upset with me if she knew I heard her private conversation, but I couldn't help myself. I don't know who she was talking to, but she described this vision she had, a vision about Harry. He did something terrible, but it wasn't really his fault. I know it couldn't be his fault because Harry would never do anything bad to anyone. And then she Saw Harry with a crown on his head.

I wouldn't normally care too much about Diana's visions, but I'm almost entirely sure I've seen the same thing.

I don't want Harry to do anything bad.

Is Harry going to become the king?

—THE JOURNAL OF
CASSANDRA TRIUR, AGE TWELVE

1

CATE

A CLOUD OF THE deepest blue, edges of midnight bordering on black, fills the room as the man thrusts one final time, his grunt of release echoing around the spacious suite.

I latch on to the threads of color with my Gift, even as I come down from a climax of my own, finding the darkest hues of his grief, the color so saturated it becomes tangible, and I pull. Gently at first, then more firmly, twisting the strands, folding them up into tiny little pieces. Pieces I can then tuck away in the hidden recesses of his mind, allowing him to find a brief respite from the sadness enfolding him. I compress his grief, like a sponge wrapped in a tight fist. Eventually it will expand once again, the sadness refilling him, but for a short while at least, this man will know peace.

When I finish packing up his sorrow and have buried it deep enough so it will no longer disturb him, I stroke my hands down the expanse of his bare back. He tucks his face into the groove of my neck and cries while I soothe him, his nakedness now more emotional than physical. I don't take offense. Many of my clients end up in tears after a session with me; usually it's a sign I've done my job well.

Eventually, those tears subside, and he pushes aside the gauzy golden curtains draping the bed and rises, dressing quickly, leaving payment by the door before showing himself out. I make it clear to my clients that they never need to feel shame concerning what happens in this room, but some handle the rush of emotions easier than others. I have seen Charlie often since he buried his wife and child a year ago, casualties of an Uprising attack, and he has never been one for pillow talk.

I wait for the door to close behind him before I slide out from between the scarlet silk sheets covering my massive walnut four-poster bed. Fishing my dagger from underneath the pillow, I fasten its sheath around my upper thigh and slip it back into place, my thumb rubbing the smooth curve of the ruby buried in its hilt, a habit I've had since Harold gifted me the blade on my eighteenth birthday. It provides comfort more than a line of defense. I pocket the small handful of coins the man left in the gold elephant-shaped bowl that rests on my dressing table. I don't bother counting because it doesn't matter how much I earn. I'm not doing this for the money, or at least, not solely for the money.

The light in my suite of rooms is dim and sensual, the flicker of the candles muted by the lush crimson walls. I turn up the gas lamps ensconced on the walls once the man has left, lightening the space.

In the brighter light, I examine my face in the gilded mirror above the dressing table, ensuring my makeup is still impeccably done—it is, not even a smudge of lip paint out of place since I don't allow my clients to kiss me on the mouth—and slip into my robe. It's the same scarlet as my lips, and long; the silky sleeves are lined with soft feathers. The honey waves of my hair cascade down my back, a little mussed but still thick and shiny. Despite the toll that using my Gift takes on my body, I still look flawless.

I think about donning one of my costumes and joining the final performance of the evening—which actually takes place in the earliest hours of the morning—but I don't have the energy. Instead I stride to the golden bar cart that lives in the corner of my suite, pouring two fingers of whisky into a cut-glass tumbler and almost collapsing at my two-person table.

There has been an increase in demand for my services since the beginning of the Uprising two years ago, and while I try to never say no to genuine inquiries—determined to assist as many people as I can—I'd be lying if I said I wasn't exhausted, emotionally as well as physically. My clients might leave our sessions sexually satisfied with their emotions abated, but even when I'm able to find pleasure of my own, it doesn't counterbalance the heaviness of bearing their feelings or the strain on my body. I'll need to soak in a bath with one of Bianca's healing tonics before I think about seeing another client.

"How many have you seen tonight?" My twin sister Andra opens the door separating our adjoining rooms, helping herself to my booze and joining me at the table.

"That was my fourth." I take my first sip of whisky, letting the alcohol burn down my throat and warm my belly. Whisky helps my recovery, but the need to stay sober during appointments outweighs the benefits, and I don't imbibe until I've seen my final client of the day.

She grimaces, the frown pulling down on her perfectly full lips. "It's too much, Cate."

"They need my help." And I've never been one who could stand by and let people suffer. Andra has always considered this one of my biggest flaws.

"Was it good for you, at least?" She shoots me a sly grin over the rim of her crystal goblet. Andra only requires rest after using her Gift, but that doesn't stop her from stealing my gin whenever the mood strikes her.

I roll my eyes. "You know that's not the point." I swirl the remaining whisky in my glass, letting the richness of its scent fill my nose and fortify me. "Have you checked in with Harold at all lately?"

Andra's eyes, the same color as the light shining through my whisky, the same color as mine, flash with some sort of perturbance. "I'm still having a block where Harold is concerned. I haven't been able to read anything in his future for weeks now."

I sigh, throwing back the last of my drink. "Something tells me the lack of Sight does not bode well for what's to come."

Andra frowns, but there isn't much real worry in it. She has the undying optimism of a younger sibling who's never had to worry about much in her life, even if the age difference between us is a mere few minutes.

The two of us have been living here at La Puissance—Stratford City's premier pleasure club—since we were kids. When our parents abandoned us shortly after Andra's Gift revealed itself, we were left as wards of our home province in Scota. Sent to an orphanage for Gifted children, we quickly learned that being a ward, particularly a Gifted ward, meant being neglected. When that neglect turned to abuse, I convinced Andra we needed to run away. We snuck off into the night, making our way from Scota to Avon's capital city. For a while we lived on the streets, depending on strangers for food and a little coin now and then. Because we're both Gifted, we were unable to find any sort of work without sponsorship, and who was going to sponsor two neglected children? I thought we might be on the streets forever until Diana found us. She and Harold took us in, gave us a place to live, and, more importantly, gave us a safe place to explore our Gifts.

Andra started having visions when we were just four years old, but we were too young and inexperienced to know what was happening to her until several years later when we met Diana, the Seer who was a den mother of sorts at the club until her death not long ago. Diana helped Andra hone her powers, helped her turn her Gift into a beneficial tool. Neither of us even remembers the parents we spent our first four years with, and we haven't spent more than a few days away from the club since. It's our home, and our sanctuary, a sanctuary for all the Gifted in Avon, or at least, as many Gifted as are legally allowed. The discriminatory laws limit the number of Gifted who are allowed to reside in one location and make it almost impossible to find legal work. Luckily, in Stratford City, the laws against Gifted aren't typically enforced.

My own Gift didn't appear until later, when I came of age and had a torrid fling with one of the bartenders. It was his first time as well as mine, and when he finished after a few seconds and the room exploded in a riot of color and elation, I thought that was what happened for everyone. It wasn't until I relayed the story to Diana that she informed me most people do not experience a kaleidoscope of color and an avalanche of emotion during intercourse. Between Diana and some of the other Gifted members of the club, we discovered the true nature of my Gift, and from then my goal was to harness it in a way that could provide relief to those who truly needed it, which is what I have been doing for the past seven years. Growing up at La Puissance, I always knew the option to be a courtesan was open to me but never pressed upon me. When the nature of my Gift was revealed, it felt as though it was meant to be.

I push my chair back from the table and rise, untying the belt of my robe. I step into a simple dress, the black cotton soft against my skin, and turn around for Andra to lace me up. "Are you going back out on the floor tonight?"

Andra shakes her head and swigs the last of her drink before doing up the ties on the back of my dress. "I've told enough fake fortunes for the evening."

The patrons of La Puissance love Andra's "visions"—the ones she sells that magically foretell everything the client wants to hear. Sometimes what they want to hear matches the reality of what she sees for them. But usually not. It doesn't stop club patrons from returning to her again and again, taken in by her snappy wit and charming smile. None of them have any idea what she's truly capable of, and I've always aimed to keep it that way. Having a Gift of any kind is frowned upon; having the kind of visions Andra has is downright dangerous.

"Come with me to the kitchens, then. I'm starving."

Our footsteps are hushed over the ragged and dingy crimson carpet lining the hallways of the upper floor of La Puissance. Down below, raucous laughter and clinking glasses and live music still permeate the air, the loud brass of the horns competing with the incessant thumping of the drums and the shouts of glee. The lower level of La Puissance is all glittering colors and bright sounds; it stands in stark opposition to the upper levels, which are all about decadent silence. The closed doors we stride by are thick enough to hide the sounds of pleasure emanating from within, but it's no secret what is happening behind them. The evening may no longer be young, but the club is nowhere near ready to say good night.

We make our way to the end of the hallway, down the back staircase, and into the kitchen. The club hasn't exactly been rolling in resources since the Uprising began, but the age of the building shows more here than anywhere else, even in the dim light of the gas lamps. There's a group of women in various stages of undress crowded around a worn wooden table, the surface covered with scratches and burns, initials and doodles etched into every available inch. It's not a big kitchen, but that doesn't keep us all from gathering here when we have free time.

The wood-burning oven keeps the room hot, even in the coldest months of winter. Eliza, the head cook, is permanently red-faced and sweating and can usually be found yelling at one of her assistants to work harder and move faster. But she dotes on us girls, the women who make La Puissance the most sought-after pleasure club in all of Avon. Not all the workers at La Puissance are Gifted, just as not all are courtesans, but everyone here is treated equally and has been for as long as we've lived here.

Eliza arrived at the club the same year as Andra and I. She was in an abusive marriage in Venezia and was forced to leave everything and everyone she'd ever known behind to escape her husband's violence. We all grew acclimated to our new lives together, and though she would never admit it, I'm her favorite. When she sees Andra and me making our way through the cooks and servers dashing about the cramped space, she immediately hands me a plate of bread, cheese, and fruit, like she had it waiting for me.

I sink into my usual spot at the table, between Bianca and Andra, across from Meri, Rosa, Helen, and Tes. The seven of us have been here so long, I don't remember a time in my life when they weren't a part of it. All Gifted, all abandoned by our families. All without anywhere to go or any way to make a living if it weren't for the generosity of Harold MacVeigh.

Meri reaches a hand across the table, nabbing one of my strawberries and popping it into her mouth. "Did you hear the latest?"

I shake my head as I smear a stripe of soft cheese across the warm and crusty bread. Meri is an infernal gossip, and I know she will report the latest whether I want to hear it or not. A fellow

Gifted with the ability to cast beautifully realistic illusions, Meri charms everyone who visits her bed, and many who only wish they could.

"Supposedly the Uprising leaders are meeting tonight to accept the monarchs' surrender."

My hand freezes, the bread halfway to my mouth. This is not Meri's typical gossip.

"The monarchs are going to surrender?" Rosa voices my question before I have the chance to. Her big brown eyes widen as she tosses her long black curls over her shoulder, wrapping her thick robe tighter around her lithe figure. Rosa hails from Talia and has never adjusted to the cooler weather of Stratford City.

Tes purses her lips. "That's what everyone is saying." Her blue eyes darken with worry, and I know she is thinking of her close childhood friend, the prince of her home province of Kalmar. As far as I know, the two haven't seen each other much since Tes came to live at the club when she was seven, but they still exchange letters, and I know she still cares for him.

I reach across the table and pat her hand. "I think this is a good thing, Tes. If the Uprising wins, it means we get our rights back. Plus, it means an end to the fighting, which is better for everyone."

"That's probably what spurred the conversation of surrender—I heard the latest Uprising attack killed hundreds." Meri shudders, the glitter on her dark brown shoulders shimmering with the movement. She's still in her performance costume—a tight red corset covered in rhinestones—even though the rest of us have changed into more comfortable clothing, cotton dresses and robes, or in Tes's case, pants and a tunic. "If the letters from home are any indication, if the fighting doesn't stop soon, there might not be much of Talia left to fight over."

"I, for one, am certainly ready for the violence to be done." Bianca, a Gifted with healing powers, tucks a strand of her wild red curls behind her pale, freckled ear. Her voice is quiet.

"Me too," Andra mutters, with something more than the usual concern lacing her voice.

I study my sister, wondering if she's told me everything about what she's Seen lately, making a mental note to question her about it later, when we're alone. "Well, if the rumor is true, it can only mean good things for us, right?"

One of the major tenets of the Uprising has been to restore the rights of the Gifted. For more than two hundred years now, we have faced discrimination and lived with senseless laws limiting our rights. Laws that were justified to the citizens of Avon because we could be considered "a threat to public safety," but laws that have truly done nothing but oppress us. And while not every province enforces the laws with the same fervor, being Gifted is still seen as being less than in every corner of Avon.

"Here's hoping." Helen, a Gifted who can read people's memories, raises her goblet of red wine to the center of the table and the rest of us clink our cups against hers, the sound swallowed up by Eliza's shouts as she prepares another course.

I make my excuses soon after finishing my evening snack, leaving Andra and the rest of the women behind as I make my way back up the stairs to Harold's office.

I knock on the mahogany door and am granted entry a second later. Sliding into one of the leather armchairs in front of his heavy wood desk, I adjust my skirt so my skin doesn't stick to the fabric and my legs are covered. The room is dim, lit only by the two sconces on the wall behind the desk and one flickering lantern resting precariously on a mountain of papers.

"How was your night?" Harold doesn't meet my eyes as he asks the question, his attention focused on the stacks of paperwork in front of him. He's shucked the top hat and bright red coat he dons as our master of ceremonies and rolled up the sleeves of his white button-down shirt, his bow tie hanging loose around his neck. No one really knows for sure how old Harold is. His golden-brown hair has tinges of gray at the temples, but it wasn't until recently that I began to notice the lines etched on the pale skin of his forehead.

"Good. Charlie is still suffering from his grief, but I think I managed to alleviate at least some of it. Lady Amanda is still not doing well, but there were fewer tears when we finished this evening."

Harold nods but doesn't respond, his eyes flitting from paper to paper, his brow furrowed.

"Harold?" I repeat his name until he finally looks up from the stacks of sheets. "Is there something wrong?" Maybe the rumors about the end of the Uprising being in sight aren't entirely true. No one but me knows of Harold's involvement, his financial backing and the advisement he offers to the rebel group. If the Uprising is as close to victory as Meri thinks, I would expect him to look much less stressed.

For a second I think he might ignore my question, but then he heaves a resigned sigh and gestures to the mess of his desk. "La Puissance is in trouble, Cate."

It's an unexpected answer, one that makes the cheese and fruit and whisky in my belly sour. "What kind of trouble?"

"The money kind. What other kind is there?" He drops his pen and lets his head sink into his hands. "Ever since the Uprising began, things haven't been the same around here."

"What about the rumors that the Uprising is almost over, that the monarchs are getting ready to surrender?" I'm fishing for information, for confirmation that the nightmare of the past two years is almost done, even if I know the effects of the rebellion will be felt for years to come.

Of course, I've noticed the general state of disrepair that seems to be spreading like a plague throughout the club. Broken fixtures, carpets that need to be replaced, gold filaments gone brassy and tarnished. I guess I attributed the poor conditions to the ongoing rebellion and assumed that now that the end is in sight, the club could return to its former state of opulent beauty.

Harold's bushy eyebrows rise. "How did you know the monarchs are preparing to surrender?"

I smile sweetly, taking the question as confirmation. "You know I know everything."

He sighs but doesn't give me the satisfaction of admitting I'm right.

"The club will recover once everyone has the chance to settle back into daily life, Harold. I wouldn't worry about it too much."

He shakes his head sadly. "I don't know that it will be enough, Cate. I don't know if we have time to wait for everyone to recover from the strikes and violence and upheaval. Even if the new decree is signed tomorrow, it will take months, or even years, for actual change to be enacted."

A dark pit opens in my stomach. "What are you trying to say?"

Harold slides a piece of paper across the desk. "I'm saying if we don't take some drastic action, find some kind of miracle, there's a good chance I'm going to have to shut down La Puissance."

I know how much it pains him to even utter those words because it pains me just as much to hear them. The ache in my stomach is a pure physical response at the mere thought of losing the club. This isn't just a place where our clients come for a bit of fun. La Puissance is our home. It's our refuge.

So many of the Gifted—all of whom are women and girls—have landed on Harold's doorstep after being kicked out of our homes or abandoned by our families. There are no laws prohibiting having Gifts, or even using them, but being Gifted makes it difficult to find work, and illegal to bear children, limiting marriage prospects. Many a girl has found herself on the street after discovering her Gift, finding her new ability to be unwelcome in her home. But we always found a home and a family here. I don't know what we will do if that sanctuary is taken from us.

My eyes run over the sheet full of numbers, but my brain doesn't absorb much of the information. It doesn't matter what the numbers say, La Puissance cannot be shut down. "Do whatever you need to do to save this place, Harold."

"Cate—"

"I mean it. You know how important it is. Do whatever it takes." I stand, as if the action can somehow stop this news from pressing down on me.

Harold sighs and rises, coming around the desk and taking my hands in his. "I promise, no matter what happens, I will make sure you and Andra are cared for, Cate."

I nod, knowing the truth in his words like I know my own name. Harold would never let any harm befall us.

For many years, we, the rulers of the provinces of Avon, have governed our individual provinces as we see fit. Today, we stand united in making this decree. The Gifted have lived among us for as long as any of us can remember. They have been advisors, mothers, teachers, healers, and even friends. But we can no longer ignore the imminent danger they pose. How can we allow one group of people to amass an array of Gifts that may one day be used to destroy the very kingdoms your monarchs are sworn to protect? Such danger will no longer be permitted.

From this day forth, no woman deemed to possess a Gift will be allowed to bear a child.

From this day forth, no more than ten Gifted may gather together in any one location.

From this day forth, in order to seek employment, any Gifted woman must have the sponsorship of a gainfully employed man.

From this day forth, no Gifted shall own property or operate a business.

From this day forth, the power entrusted by you in your faithful monarchs will be protected.

Signed,

King Claudius I of Kalmar

King Capulet III of Talia

King James I of Scota

King Jacob II of Venezia

2

CALLUM

THE BLOW TO my gut catches me by surprise, folding me in half.

"Good form," I mutter when I finally catch my breath, pulling myself back to standing.

My younger sister, Dom, raises an eyebrow. "That's the third time I've caught you unaware today. Don't tell me you've been slacking on your training?"

I press my shoulders back, attempting to stretch my muscles and ease a bit of the ache. "Of course not. It's more important to be on top of—"

"—our game now than ever before." Dom lowers her voice as she finishes my sentence in a false approximation of my tone.

I gesture for her to return to fighting stance. "Have I mentioned that once or twice?"

"An hour? Yes, yes you have." She squares her padded fists in front of her face. "Since the beginning of the Uprising, I think you've told me at least a hundred times a day."

I duck her first punch and strike back with a quick jab. "The past two years have been filled with nothing but violence, Dom. It's my duty as your brother and your general to look out for you." The title of general might not truly be earned, since my father refuses to let me fight on the front lines against the Uprising for fear of losing his heir, but I hold it over Dom anyway. Dom has been allowed to fight, though she focuses more on protecting Scota, directing her battalion of soldiers to act as guards when the fighting veers too close to innocent citizens, rather than launching any offensive action. If anything, she should be the one training me.

She aims for my ribs and, when I spin away, connects instead with the side of my head. "Don't forget that you're my prince, if you want to lord one more title over me."

Shaking off her blow, I sweep my leg, catching her behind her ankles and knocking her to the ground for the first time this session. "I've always hated that one." I offer her my hand, hauling her up. "And besides, once the Uprising accepts the monarchs' terms of surrender, it will no longer be relevant."

"Well, if Father has anything to say about it, we'll be calling you president before too long." She begins unwrapping her fists, signaling she's done with torturing me for the day.

I grimace and begin doing the same. "How can I lead a united country when I don't agree with its newfound principles?"

Dom levels me with an intense stare. "You cannot be serious, Callum."

"I'm dead serious, Dominique."

She rolls her eyes at me and sticks out her tongue.

We both toss our discarded wrappings to a nearby attendant and duck out of the ring our father had installed in one of the many unused ballrooms of the Scotan Castle. The Reid line has lived on these grounds and ruled over Scota for hundreds of years. If the monarchs do decide to surrender—which they most assuredly will—and give in to the demands of the violent rebels who have been wreaking havoc on the provinces of Avon for the past two years, we will likely be turning over all our land and holdings to the new government.

The new government that has yet to secure a leader or any semblance of rules or policies. The new government that the people are supposed to put their faith in without any kind of answers as to what happens next. The new government that is going to allow dangerous individuals free rein, with no regard for public safety.

I have tried to be sympathetic to the Uprising because overall, I don't truly disagree with them. I've spent enough time on diplomatic missions in other provinces to know that life across Avon is only good for one group of people: the wealthy. While we here in Scota have made several reforms in recent years to redistribute wealth, it's a process that takes time, and one our fellow provinces have chosen not to partake in.

But while I support reforms, it's hard to accept that my family's legacy will be a sacrifice on the altar. My father—and his before him, and his before him, dating back centuries—has led Scota with fairness and equality. Our citizens are well cared for, our Gifted population well managed, and if anything, Scota should be the example for the rest of Avon. Instead, my father, the current king, will be asked to hand over his leadership position to a group of people who are set on ignoring history.

There is a reason laws exist regulating the Gifted and their powers. Those laws have kept our citizens safe for over two hundred years. And now we're expected to go back to the way things were, when the Gifted infiltrated the leadership councils of every monarch in Avon, exploiting their positions and using their powers to cause harm.

The Uprising might have what it takes to overthrow the monarchial system, but so far they have proven they have no business establishing a new system of their own design.

Dom and I stride down the long hallway from the ballroom toward the dining room. The gas lamps throw shadows on the walls, though barely any light shines in from the large windows as the early-evening sky is nothing but gray clouds. Scota's perpetual gloomy weather is an apt reflection of my mood.

Our uncle Alex meets us in front of the towering walnut doors of the formal dining room, his nose wrinkling as he takes in our sweaty training clothes—simple linen tunics and cotton pants. He's dressed in a smart three-piece suit, though I'm surprised he didn't don a full tuxedo and tails. "Not going to bother to bathe before dinner?"

Dom rolls her eyes. "It's just the four of us."

Alex tugs on his lapels. "Doesn't mean we can't dress appropriately."

I clap him on the back as a servant opens the heavy door for us. "It's the end of times, Alex. Soon we will be fending for ourselves out on the streets, at the mercy of the Gifted. Who cares what we look like?"

Alex's lips purse for half a second before he schools his face. "All the more reason to enjoy these last moments of civilized dining."

Dom and I exchange a glance and don't bother to hold in our laughter. Alex is my late mother's younger brother, and only ten years older than me. He's always been more like a brother than an uncle, though his taste for the finer things in life can be a bit exhausting.

Our father already waits for us, seated at the head of a table much longer than needed. In years past, the table has housed fifteen, twenty, thirty extra people for meals—leaders from other provinces, but more often citizens from every corner of Scota—but since the beginning of the Uprising, only the four of us frequent meals.

Servants still bustle around the room, filling our wineglasses and serving dishes, even though the grand parties have shrunk mightily.

I let my eyes wander around the room, drinking in the sight of it while I still can. The tall windows are framed by heavy gold brocade drapes. The furniture is all made of rich wood, the darkness offset by the cream fabric-covered walls. Portraits hang, covering almost every inch of available space, generations of Reids looking down at us while we eat.

I avert my eyes, as if these former leaders might somehow shame me from their gilded frames. Are the former rulers of Scota watching their carefully crafted legacy crumble to dust?

My father clears his throat and raises his crystal goblet, though I'm not sure what there could be to toast to. "To family," he says simply.

We all echo his toast. I gulp red wine, letting the rich liquid swirl in my mouth before swallowing, enjoying the burn.

We eat in silence for several minutes. Unsurprisingly, it's Dom who breaks it. "Was an agreement reached?"

She directs the question to our father, though I don't believe any of us are hopeful we will receive much of an answer.

"Yes." His response is resigned, making it clear he doesn't want to discuss it further.

I set down my sterling silver cutlery. Dom and Alex follow suit. My father may not want to discuss it further, but he doesn't have much of a choice. We deserve to know what happened, what the monarchs have agreed to. We deserve to know how the rest of our lives are going to play out. I understand that the violence has reached levels that cannot be ignored, that innocent people are losing their lives because of the Uprising's attacks, but I still cannot stomach the thought of surrendering to them.

My father's fist tightens around his own cutlery before he lets the pieces fall to the table with a clatter. "I suppose I can only delay this conversation for so long." He gives each of us a long, searching look. "We have come to an agreement with the Uprising. The newspapers will be announcing the formal surrender tomorrow. I know it is not what we wanted, but I do believe we made the right decision. The latest attack—" His mouth purses into a tight line. "Well, let's just be grateful it was on Talian soil and not Scotan."

I scoff, the sound echoing around the mostly empty room. "How can you even say that surrendering is the right decision? Isn't now the time to fight back harder?"

He shoots me a withering look, making me feel like an insignificant child. "You do not even know the terms."

"Is one of the terms that the Gifted will regain their full rights and privileges?"

"Yes."

I sit back in my chair. "Then I don't need to hear anything more."

Dom looks between the two of us, hesitating before she tries to make peace. "I know it might sound unbelievable, but I do think the Uprising has good intentions and is going to do their best to create a unified country where every citizen can thrive."

I think highly of my younger sister, and therefore refrain from calling out her naïveté. Though my silence does the job well enough.

"I, for one, would be interested in hearing about the terms," Alex ventures after a minute of awkward silence.

Father refills his wineglass. "The monarchs agreed to relinquish our claims on our individual provinces. We will give up both our land holdings and our titles."

I have to fight back the triumphant smile when Dom blanches at that news. How will she feel when some Gifted sympathizers, or even the Gifted themselves, move into her bedroom? Take over the boxing ring and tear down the artwork and destroy hundreds of years of family history.

"And the Gifted?" I ask through clenched lips, hating that I have to.

"The laws regarding the Gifted's ability to bear children, gather in groups, own businesses, and work without a sponsor will be rescinded as soon as the new government secures their place."

"How will the new government be selected?" Alex questions, his eyes darting to me.

"They have not determined that yet. But they did concede one point to us."

I bite my tongue to keep in my sarcastic retort because so far these terms seem wholly weighted in the Uprising's favor. I cannot help but feel like we should have fought harder before giving in.

"Though I and the other current monarchs will be ineligible for any position in the new government, our descendants will not be similarly barred."

Dom and I exchange looks, the implication in this news clear. I have been primed to take over leadership of Scota from the moment I was born. Scota doesn't forbid women from inheriting titles, unlike the other three provinces, but I was born first, and Dom has never shown any interest in leadership. If one of us is going to work within this new government, it's going to be me.

Truthfully, I want nothing to do with this new government, would leave Avon altogether if I thought it would make my life easier. But Father said the laws regulating the Gifted won't be officially rescinded until the new government is in place. Which means there might be hope still left.

"However it is the Uprising decides to select a new leader, we all know what needs to be done." Father picks up his knife and fork once again.

Dom's and Alex's eyes land on me.

Father spears a bite of roasted meat on his fork, with more fervor than required. "I can admit, I do not know what comes next, but what I do know is that we will do whatever it takes to protect Scota and protect this family's legacy."

I swallow thickly, burying my gaze in my plate of food, even though I no longer have an appetite. Ruling not just Scota, but the entire country of Avon? Running a new government full of people whose ideologies don't match with mine? "I do not know if I am up to the task."

Father swirls the wine in his glass, his outwardly calm appearance hiding whatever true emotions he feels about losing his title and legacy. "There is no doubt in my mind that you are the leader Avon needs, Callum, and you must be prepared to do whatever it takes."

"What if whatever it takes is something I'm not willing to do?" I know I sound like a petulant child, but I want him to give me more. I need him to show me that the loss of life as we know it is as devastating to him as it is to me. I need to know that he thinks this is truly the best course of action for Scota, that he's not just rolling over to play dead.

He leans his elbows on the table, pushing his plate out of the way. His dark eyes meet mine, piercing. "Are you telling me you wouldn't do anything to keep this family's legacy? To protect the citizens of Scota? To build a society where all citizens of Avon can be cared for and prosper and live in safety?"

Heat flames my cheeks as shame flows through me. "You know I would."

"Then let this argument be done. Whatever the decision might be, whenever it is to be handed down, you must be ready to act, son."

I push back my chair, needing to escape the heavy stares from my sister and uncle. My father has already dismissed me, waving for a servant to come clear my plate.

Dom catches up with me in the hallway, her shorter strides rushing to keep up. "I'm going to head over to La Puissance tonight. Maybe you should join me, help take your mind off things."

"The last thing I need is to spend my evening with a bunch of Uprising sympathizers. I can't believe you patronize such an establishment. The gold you spend there goes directly to funding our enemies, to providing room and board to the Gifted." The little food I managed to eat curdles in my stomach.

She grabs my elbow, yanking me to a stop in the grand foyer, my shoes squeaking on the pristine marble floors. "Your bias against the Gifted is truly wearing thin, brother."

"I'm not biased." The defense is automatic, even if we both know it's not true. But we have laws regulating the Gifted's use of their powers for a reason. We know why such laws are necessary, better than anyone.

"She was an outlier, Cal. The rest of the Gifted are not like her." Her voice softens, as it always does when we broach this subject.

Dom was six when our mother died, I was ten. Mother was tossed from her horse and a Gifted healer was brought in to save her. For a short while, it seemed like her Gift would work, but at the last minute, something changed in her. Rather than healing my mother, the Gifted woman sat by and watched Mother choke on her last breaths. She listened as my father begged her to do something, as I sat in the corner and sobbed. And she did nothing. When my mother's chest stopped rising, her heart gone still, the Gifted stood calmly, looked to my father, and said, "The penance has been paid."

I didn't understand what her words meant then, and I was too afraid to ask. All I knew was the chill that raced through me as she delivered them so calmly, as if sitting by and watching my mother die meant nothing to her.

Now I know that the woman was attempting to make some kind of statement, lodge some kind of protest against the restrictions in place against her kind, even though they were enacted long before my father took power. All she really did was prove the need for those very laws.

I shrug off Dom's hand, forgoing the easy escape in favor of turning back toward my rooms. "Do what you wish with your own time, Dom, but don't expect me to come along. Don't expect my coin to fund the people trying to destroy everything this family has built. Some of us have responsibilities to think about instead of focusing on our own pleasure."

I don't have to see her to know my words have scored a direct hit; the soft intake of her breath is enough to let me know. I regret the insult immediately, but I don't take it back, striding up the stairs as quickly as possible. Putting distance between us, between all the things I can't bear to think about.

DEATH TOLL BEGINS TO CLIMB AS THE UPRISING PRESSES FURTHER INTO AVON'S FOUR PROVINCES

Authorities from Venezia and Talia have reportedly asked for military support from Kalmar and Scota in light of the Uprising's most recent attack. The Uprising's forces were able to strike two of Avon's four provinces on the same night, taking both Venezian and Talian leaders by surprise.

Though the Uprising officially declared war on the four provinces of Avon one year ago, it has not been until recent months that violence truly began to erupt and escalate.

"We have tried all peaceful means of communication," said Uprising leader August Sotello in a statement this morning. "The leaders of Avon have chosen not to respond. Because of their inaction, we will be forced to resort to less subtle means of making our point."

There is no word yet on the number of casualties, but at least several hundred lives have been lost so far.

3

CATE

HAROLD'S DIRE WARNING is all I can think about for the several days that follow. Even the official word of the monarchs' surrender isn't enough to distract me. What will happen to Andra and me if the club is forced to close? What will happen to Meri and Tes, the rest of the girls, Gifted and not, who call La Puissance home?

In many ways, living in the club has kept us sheltered. Our location in Stratford City, the center of Avon, has kept us from having to endure the horrors of most of the fighting during the Uprising, as most of the violence was focused on the monarchs. Living here has also kept us insulated from extreme enforcement of the laws against the Gifted. While none of the monarchs can claim kindness toward their Gifted populations, Scota has at least stopped the senseless murders encouraged in some of the other provinces, and they don't kill the pregnant Gifted like they do in Talia and Venezia. If the club closes and we are forced to return to our birthplaces, what will that mean for the girls from the more dangerous provinces?

Despite the Uprising's victory and the promise to restore our rights, these things take time, and we will not be afforded protections overnight. Neither will prejudices long held magically disappear.

I'm so lost in my thoughts, wallowing in the possible scenarios and their implications, I don't see Bianca rush into the kitchen, where I've been too busy thinking to eat much of my breakfast, my tea and toast already gone cold.

"Cate, come quickly. It's Andra." Fear lines Bianca's green eyes, and she doesn't need to elaborate or ask twice.

I'm out the door before she's finished her sentence, racing up the creaking wooden back stairs to the room next to mine. I shove through the door and find my twin sister curled up in a tight ball on the chaise longue, rocking so violently I'm surprised she hasn't fallen to the floor.

"Cool water and a towel," I command Bianca, grasping one of Andra's chilled hands in mine. "It's okay, I'm here. I'm right here." I whisper soothing platitudes, smoothing back her sweat-soaked hair from her sticky forehead.

Bianca hands me the requested items, then bolts from the room. She knows what's coming and doesn't want any part of it. She also knows enough to keep anyone else from entering the room.

Dabbing Andra's clammy skin with the damp towel, I continue to whisper. "I'm here. You can let it out now. I'm here."

Her grip on my hand tightens, and when her mouth opens, it's not my sister's voice that rings out. Her words are guttural and ragged, several octaves deeper than her usual tinkling pitch. "Things bad begun make strong themselves by ill. What's done cannot be undone. Foul whisperings are abroad. Unnatural deeds do breed unnatural troubles." Andra's body spasms, her limbs releasing their tight grip as she collapses flat on her back on the chaise.

"Shhhh, shhhh. You're all right." I dip the towel in the cool water once more, wringing out the excess before placing it on her forehead.

Her chest heaves with stilted breaths for several minutes before returning to its natural rhythm. Her eyes remain closed, but her voice returns to normal, though her words come out in the barest of whispers. "What did I say?"

I hand her a glass of water. "Nothing that made any sense."

She opens her eyes so she can take small sips from the cup until she is able to pull herself into a seated position. "Nothing has made any sense lately. Not since . . ."

I wait for her to finish her thought, but when she doesn't, I don't push her.

Not all of Andra's visions are as violent as this one, but lately they have been more and more unpredictable in both nature and outcome, like her command over her Sight is slipping. She hasn't had Sightings like this since we were kids, back before she knew how to control and harness her Gift. The whole thing turns my stomach.

"I miss Diana," she says softly, and I squeeze her hand gently.

What I wouldn't do for a bit of Diana's insight and wisdom in these moments.

Andra hesitates, sitting up cautiously, her mouth opening like she has more to say but doesn't want to say it.

I sit next to her on the chaise, wrapping an arm around her shoulders. "Do you want to talk about it?"

"It's the same vision every time, Cate." Her voice is heavy with worry, so unlike the bright chatter I'm used to hearing from her.

Fear stirs in my belly. "What did you See?"

"Blood. And a dagger." She swallows thickly. "And Harold."

That fears grips me from the inside out. "Harold is going to die?"

She shakes her head. "He's wearing a crown."

My brow furrows because it doesn't make any sense. Harold isn't royalty, but even if he were, the monarchs have just been overthrown. No one will be wearing a crown from this point on.

A quiet knock taps on the door and after a beat, Bianca's head pokes into the room, her red curls a cloud around her face, pale with worry. "I'm sorry, I know this is bad timing, but Harold is requesting we all join him in the main salon."

Andra and I exchange a heavy look. Harold doesn't gather us all together unless there is some kind of major situation. Given the dire warnings that just spewed forth from Andra's vision, combined with what I know about the state of the club, I don't know that I want to hear what Harold has to say, don't know that any of us are ready for even more upheaval.

Bianca joins us at the chaise, taking one of Andra's hands in hers. "Nothing physically wrong with you, then," she declares once her healer's Gift has managed a full assessment.

"Come on." I rise, pulling Andra to standing next to me, and paste on a wide smile. We are the same height, the same coloring, though Andra has always been lanky where I am nothing but curves. "Let's go see what the big fuss is." I inject my voice with a levity none of us feels.

The main salon is already crowded with people when we arrive. Many have congregated on the stage, and just as many clutter the small café tables circled around it, where each night our patrons await our dazzling performances. A few are perched on the balconies that rim the room, leaning over the tarnished gold railings. It's early enough in the day that we all wear our casual clothes—cotton dresses and linen tunics and plain trousers—enjoying the comfort before we don our intricate and bold, and sometimes restricting, costumes for the evening. The main hall of La Puissance is vast, and in the nighttime hours teeming with people and booze and music. I've always loved it during the day, when our voices echo around the empty space, when the natural light shines through the skylights.

The stage is the focal point of the main salon, framed by heavy, mottled crimson curtains and lined with gas-powered flames that have caught more than one frilly skirt on fire. Wide enough to hold a chorus of twenty girls, today it looks like a gaping maw, dark and empty and vast.

Bianca, Andra, and I find an empty table and slide into the waiting seats. It looks like every member of the club, from performers to bartenders to musicians, has gathered. As my eyes take in the group—people from every province, a vast array of skin tones and accents, as many Gifted as permitted, even more with no Gifts to speak of—something fierce and protective surges through me. Things might look bleak, but I know there is nothing that can tear this group, this family, apart. Meri, Tes, Rosa, and Helen find seats at the table next to us, and from the tense smiles we exchange, I can tell none of us knows what to expect.

A hush falls over the room as Harold enters. He's dressed in his finest tuxedo, the one he normally wears only when important patrons are dining in his box at the club, complete with top hat and his fanciest cane. And he's not alone.

A tall woman, hair as dark as the ebony keys of the piano, eyes a bright amber, accompanies Harold as he strides confidently into the room. Her face is stoic and not a single hint of emotion shows as she takes in the room, takes in the group of us waiting. Her long black dress is as severe as her features, her corset tight, fabric covering her from the top of her neck down to the tips of her fingers. Never has a woman looked so thoroughly out of place in La Puissance.

Harold claps his hands together for silence, though the buzz and chatter ceased immediately when he entered. "Friends, my darlings, thank you all for being here this lovely afternoon." A wide smile breaks across his face and with it, a sense of ease spreads through the room. If Harold is beaming like this, whatever news he has to tell us cannot be bad.

At first, I relax with the rest of the crew, but when I take in Andra's face, something leaden drops in my stomach. She looks as though she's seen a ghost; what little color was left in her cheeks after her vision has been drained away. I reach for her hand and her ice-cold fingers squeeze mine in a silent warning.

"I know this may come as a surprise to some of you." Harold's eyes find mine but flit away before I can latch on. "But I have been feeling lonely for some time now, wondering when or even if I might ever find that perfect person with whom I wanted to spend the rest of my life." Harold reaches back, joining his hand with the woman's. She doesn't smile. "And I'm delighted to announce I have found that woman. And we have been married."

An audible gasp echoes around the room with his pronouncement. Andra's fingers are holding mine so tightly I fear I might lose circulation in my hand. My hand automatically drifts to the dagger at my thigh, not sure what the threat she senses is, but wanting to be ready for it.

"My dearest darlings, it is with greatest pleasure that I introduce you to my new wife, the Lady MacVeigh." Harold says the words with such a flourish that applause breaks out, leading to raucous cheers and cries of congratulations.

Those around us leap out of their seats, rushing to grant hugs and handshakes to the new happy couple. No one at my table moves, Bianca having sensed that something has gone seriously wrong.

"Look the innocent flower but the serpent under it," Andra whispers to no one in particular.

My eyes turn from my sister back to the front of the room, where

Harold and his new bride have begun to distribute glasses of champagne. I find Lady M's eyes easily as she is staring right at me.

No. It's not me her eyes are locked on. It's my sister.

Andra's face goes an even starker white and she sucks in a sharp breath.

Lady M's eyes drift from Andra to me. Her expression morphs quickly, hiding her shock with a smirk so devastating it chills my blood.

Dear Mother and Father,

When you come to my chambers to wake me this morning, you will find my room empty. You have likely realized I am no longer here, seeing as you have found this letter. I have been cautioned against even leaving this missive, but I could not abandon our home without letting you know that I am going to be all right.

I will not be back. Do not attempt to look for me. I will not write you again after this letter, and I ask that you destroy this once you read it. I am likely being overly cautious, but please humor me.

I know I am not offering much here, but I want you to know that I will be safe, and most importantly, that I will be happy. I have found my heart's true purpose, and I must follow that path, wherever she leads me.

I will think of you often, and always be grateful for the loving home you have given me. I hope I may provide the same for my own children one day, should I be blessed enough to have them.

Please do not worry. I am where I'm meant to be.

Your son, always,

Harry

P.S. I am sorry for taking Grandfather's dagger, but I believe he would have wanted me to have it. I promise to keep it in the family, always.

4

CALLUM

I KNOW FROM THE moment I stroll into the breakfast room that something is wrong, a feeling enforced by the three sad pairs of eyes that turn to me the moment I walk in.

My stomach sinks and I know without even having to ask that the decree has been issued, the Uprising has finally deigned to decide how the next ruler of Avon will be chosen. And it's not good.

Alex wordlessly hands me the morning edition of Scota's newspaper, the bold black letters large enough to be seen from across the room.

I take the paper, falling into my chair. My hands automatically go through the motions of pouring tea, adding sugar, stirring in a splash of milk, while my eyes absorb the details.

FIRST PRESIDENTIAL CANDIDATE QUALIFICATION ANNOUNCED: MUST KILL CURRENT MONARCH

The words of the article below the damning headline blur along with my vision. I never expected anything good from the Uprising, but this, this is low, even for them.

I force my eyes to focus, my mind soaking in the rest of the news like it's a slow-spreading poison.

Delegates from the Uprising have been meeting since the monarchs' surrender to come up with a just method of determining the candidates for Avon's first election, one representing each of the four provinces. Many ideas were considered, and this morning the Uprising leadership has announced a decision. In order for a candidate to secure the chance to represent their province in the presidential election, that candidate must assassinate the current monarchial ruler of their province.

"For hundreds of years, the monarchs of Avon have suppressed, degraded, murdered, and stolen from their citizens. They have oppressed the Gifted and put the needs of the wealthy over the needs of the majority. Now is the time for atonement to begin," said a member of the Uprising who wished to remain anonymous.

Though this decree may seem to be stoking the flames of violence—a position in direct opposition to the Uprising's call for peace among Avon—there are strict guidelines in place. The killings must take place within a specified time period to be announced. Each province will have their own designated period. And only the reigning monarchs are to be targeted.

"There must be no violence struck upon innocents," claimed our source.

I toss the paper across the table, not caring where it lands. The silence hangs in the air, heavy with unsaid words.

"I won't do it." I break first, needing all of them to know in no uncertain terms how I will not be a party to this ridiculous plan.

"You must." The declaration comes from my father, as I expected it would. I search for a sign of his anger, for surely he must be furious at this so-called decree, but his face remains smooth and calm, like his death warrant hasn't just been signed by a group of upstarts playing pretend at how to rule a country.

"This is not the way to begin an election that is supposed to signal a time of peace, of fostering unity and equality." I force myself to focus on the logical, tangible reasons why I cannot possibly go through with this plan. "This goes against everything we're supposed to be striving for in this newly united Avon. I certainly never trusted the Uprising, but they have been preaching peace for two years, all the while killing innocent people."

"You cannot deny that the monarchs have done the same thing, Callum," Alex says quietly.

"That might be true of the others, but not us." I loop my fingers through the handle of my teacup, because I need something to hold on to so I don't run out the front door and directly to Uprising headquarters to handle this injustice in the only way they seem to understand. "I've said from the beginning that allowing the Gifted any sort of privileges would only lead to more violence, and here they are, proving me correct from their very first decree."

Alex doesn't meet my anger with his own, which only irritates me further. "This is not about the Gifted. This is about the new government setting the tone for how they want to rule this country."

"With violence and bloodshed."

"With reparations."

"So you are satisfied with this decision, then?" I aim anger at him because it's easier than dealing with any of the other emotions roiling through me. The grief, the fear, and buried deep within me, the slowly building dread. Though I will do everything in my power to find another way. Any other way. One parent was already stolen from me by the Gifted; I refuse to let the other fall by my own hand.

Alex's eyes flit toward my father but dart right back to me. "I am not happy, and I will mourn the loss of James like I mourned my own sister, but I understand why they made this decision. It isn't just about you, or the Reids, or even Scota. It's about what's best for Avon."

"Killing people is what's best for Avon?"

Dom, sitting to my right, places a calming hand on my forearm. "You can't really blame people for wanting some kind of vengeance, Cal."

"It's unfortunate that Scota must be lumped in with the others." Alex offers this tiny bit of compromise. "But in the rest of the provinces, this decree will not be seen as unjust. Or unwelcome."

I tighten my grip on the handle of my cup and turn my attention to the one person who should be on my side. "And you have no thoughts on the matter?"

My father turns his weary eyes to me. His face bears the marks of a lifetime of service, and it strikes me for the first time how old he has grown, how tired he looks. His hair is now more gray than red; we no longer share that defining attribute. "I have only one thought on the matter."

"I won't do it."

His fists clench, the only outward sign of emotion he shows. "Then you are a fool and a coward, and not the man I thought you were."

Dom sucks in an audible gasp.

The handle of my teacup snaps in my hand, the rough edge digging into my palm, a stinging sensation letting me know I should let go before drawing blood, but I can't seem to force my fingers to uncurl.

I push my chair back from the table. "I'm sorry to be such a disappointment."

Tossing the broken shard of porcelain into the fireplace, I push out of the breakfast room and head directly for the front door.

Dom catches up to me as I head for the stables, running to keep up with my angry strides. "He didn't mean that, Cal."

"We both know he absolutely did."

For my entire life, I have admired my father. That admiration has only grown as I've gotten older. I've seen other fathers lie and plot, seen other sons betray and backstab, and I've always been grateful that our relationship would never have to suffer any of those indignities.

Life hasn't thrown us Reids many setbacks, at least not since the loss of Mother, and while I've been grateful, I never realized how it might have colored our relationship, this ease with which we've been able to make decisions in the past. We don't know how to disagree with each other, and now, with the stakes so high, is not the time to try to learn.

I stop short, before reaching the stables at the edge of our property, letting a small copse of trees shield me from spying eyes back at the estate.

Dom gives me the silence I need to process my thoughts, plopping down in the shade, her back resting against a large oak.

"It's not just that I don't want to do it," I finally admit as my brain shifts through the anger, allowing other emotions to rise to the surface. "It's more that I don't think I can, Dom. I can see the logical points. If I don't do it, someone else will. Father has lived a long and prosperous life and he would love nothing more than to pass on to the next in an act of sacrifice for Scota." So many things make sense on paper, but the truth of them stifles the breath in my chest.

"But?"

I sigh, sliding down next to her, preparing myself to reveal this weakness I don't think I could voice to anyone other than my sister. "But I don't think I could live with myself. I think the guilt would eat me alive." The back of my head hits the trunk of the tree, unfortunately not hard enough to knock some sense into me.

"What is there to feel guilty about if you are doing what Father wishes?"

"I'd still be taking his life, Dom. Only for a mere chance at being elected. There's no guarantee I would even win." I run a hand through my hair. "And what if I went through all of that, actually went through with killing our father, only for the act of it to drive me so mad with grief and guilt I couldn't function as a ruler anyway? I don't know if I have the strength." I let my eyes fall closed, as if that could block out my thoughts. "It isn't worth the risk."

"Isn't it, though?"

I turn my head to face my impertinent sister. "How can you ask that?"

"How can you not?" She studies me with her piercing blue eyes, looking so much like our mother that it chokes the breath out of my lungs. "Living a cautious life won't protect you, Cal. And living a risky life didn't kill her."

"Except it did."

Our mother was vivacious. Full of life, always ready to try something new and go for what she wanted. Many times her risks paid off, like when she pursued our father despite him being the next king and her being the daughter of a farmer, until that final time when it didn't.

"You know, you would make a strong leader yourself, Dom.

Look at how your soldiers respect you, follow you. You would have no problem getting elected and whipping Avon into shape."

"I know I could have a head for politics if I really worked at it, but I don't have the heart for it, you and I both know that." She pulls her eyes from mine, directing her attention to the cloudy gray skies above us. "And even just the thought of . . ." Her voice drops. "Please don't ask me to do it, Cal."

Shame heats my cheeks for even suggesting it. I can't stomach the thought of killing my father, so instead I place that burden on my sister? Father's insult grows more and more true by the second. "I would never place that upon your shoulders, Dom. I know what it will do to me and I would never want that for you."

"If you knew you could do this without the guilt driving you mad, then would you?"

"Of course." I lie easily.

Dom picks at the grass underneath us, pulling out small tufts and letting them float off into the breeze. "I think I might have a solution."

I laugh humorlessly. "Something that will make me feel no guilt for murdering our father?"

"Not something. Someone."

My stomach turns. "Absolutely not, Dom."

She tosses a fistful of grass in my lap in some kind of childish protest. "Callum, be serious. This is something you have to do. I understand that it might take you some time to accept it, but we both know there is no other choice. And we don't know when this predetermined period is going to begin. You need to be ready. And there is someone who can help."

"A Gifted?"

She sighs and rolls her eyes. "Yes, Cal. A Gifted."

"You know I won't let them anywhere near me, Dom, and yet you expect me to allow one of them unfettered access to my mind?"

"Lady Caterine—and all of the Gifted at La Puissance I've encountered for that matter—is not like that. She has a reputation for helping people."

"So did the healer that killed our mother."

Dom sighs again, this time pushing to her feet. "We both know that's not what happened. But if you want to allow your stubborn prejudices to color you against a whole group of people you don't even know, then you are not the man I thought you were. Maybe Father was right, maybe you really are a coward. When you're ready to grow up and accept that there's more to this world than your limited view of it, come find me." She stalks away from me, kicking up clouds of dust in her wake.

I bang my head against the tree, harder this time, trying unsuccessfully to knock some sense into it. I know Dom is only trying to help. Maybe I should give her plan a chance, at least explore the idea. But the thought of putting myself anywhere near La Puissance is enough to make me want to retch.

This is exactly what the Gifted want. They will regain their rights, infiltrate our leadership, divide families. The plan isn't even fully enacted and yet they are already winning.

I am allowing them to win.

There has to be some way around this, some kind of loophole we can find and exploit. There has to be another solution aside from killing my father and entrusting my mind to a Gifted.

I'm not a coward, but I also refuse to be an idiot. I know in my heart I can be the kind of leader this country needs. I can find balance and restore order. Maybe Dom is right and I'm letting my prejudices color my reactions. And maybe what I really need to do to secure my position is exploit the Gifted the same way they are exploiting me.

Alex,

I know you contacted me at great risk to yourself. I appreciate your bravery. Having a man on the inside like yourself would be invaluable to the Uprising and we welcome your knowledge, insight, and perspective. We are currently gathering funds and organizing our troops. We do not think it will be long before we are ready to move on the rulers of Avon. I know that, personally, that may be difficult to hear, but I also believe you know it is for the best.

I look forward to our partnership.

Sincerely,

August Sotello

5

CATE

"HOLY FUCK, LADY Caterine," Lady Amanda, one of my favorite and more regular clients, groans.

The air around me explodes in a deep, dark pink as Lady Amanda cries out her release. I continue to stroke her while I search for the threads, the fear and betrayal and grief that normally accompany her orgasm. But today I find nothing but peace and happiness.

I grin up at her. "You left him."

Her own grin echoes back. "I did."

I laugh, sliding off the bed and slipping into a robe. "Then why did you come back?"

Lady Amanda shrugs, her lithe body stretching, accentuating her gorgeous figure. "I missed your mouth, what can I say?"

I snort, tossing back my long waves and wrapping them into a loose bun. "That's the nicest thing anyone's said to me in a long time, my lady."

Lady Amanda perches on her elbows. "You know I don't bother

with that honorific nonsense. Especially not now. Titles are a thing of the past, are they not?"

So far Lady Amanda—I suppose simply Amanda now—is one of the few nobility I've encountered who doesn't seem to mind her new change in station, probably because it hasn't affected her net worth. With the Uprising's victory officially declared, life across the provinces has begun to see change. Minor ones, because laws that have existed for over two hundred years are not so easily swiped from the books. The Gifted have not magically been granted our full rights overnight, but there is a tinge of hope in the air that has brought on a new kind of lightness.

But despite our comfortable relationship, I don't typically talk politics with my clients. So I flash Lady Amanda a wink. "I suppose it's a good thing my title was bestowed upon me by myself. No one can take it away."

She laughs, pulling the silk sheets up to cover herself, making no move to vacate the bed. "I am dying—no pun intended—to see how this candidate selection process shakes out."

I grimace, trying to hide my frown by turning toward the mirror over my dressing table. "It does seem a little odd, don't you think? That the Uprising preached peace at us for two years, and this is the way they choose to determine the first leader of our united country?" It's a thought I've voiced often since the announcement was made, to everyone from Harold to the newspaper delivery boy. So far I seem to be alone in my worries that encouraging murder isn't the best way to begin a new chapter in Avon's history.

"I wouldn't worry about it too much. The commoners love a little violence now and then."

It's a stark reminder of the gap between us. Lady Amanda has never had to worry about where her next meal comes from or if she'll have to spend the night on the streets. Even with her affection for me, I will always be a commoner, and she will always be nobility, even without the title to prove it.

"But that's enough of that dreary talk." She pats the silken sheets of the bed, tugging the fabric down so her breasts are on full display. "Why don't you come back over here and I'll leave you a little tip."

My eyes travel over the expanse of her bare skin, tempted by the offer. "I wish I could, but I've got a meeting with the big boss."

"Why must the responsibilities of real life always get in the way of the fun?" Lady Amanda pouts, even as she rises from the bed and reaches for her dress. We help each other don our clothes, cinching corsets and doing up the long lines of buttons on the backs of our dresses. Hers is a sumptuous midnight blue velvet, mine a dark gray with an elegant black collar and cuffs. Normally I wouldn't dress up for a meeting with Harold, but things have changed since Lady M has taken the helm of La Puissance.

"The club has been looking well," Lady Amanda remarks, almost as if she can read my thoughts.

"It has." I don't elaborate, not wanting to get into any part of this conversation with anyone, let alone a client.

She tucks a heavy handful of gold coins into the pocket of my dress, using the moment to draw me closer and place a soft kiss on my neck. "Is it all right if I continue to see you, Lady Caterine?"

I reach down, taking her hand in mine. "We both know you no longer need my services, my lady."

"Maybe not your Gifted services, but I certainly appreciate your *other* services."

"My lady . . . Amanda, you know my goal is to provide whatever help I can, but the truth is, you don't need me anymore. And there are others out there who do. If you would like to continue to benefit from a sexual arrangement, there are several girls here at the club who would love to meet with you." I squeeze her fingers gently before letting our hands separate. This part of the process can be difficult for many clients, but it's actually one of my favorite things, when the work I have done for them reaches its final payoff.

"Something tells me there's no one out there quite like you, Lady Caterine."

"Well, of course you're right about that."

We laugh and separate in the hallway, her heading down the grand staircase—it's been buffed and painted and repaired and is once again worthy of the descriptor "grand"—while I make my way to Harold's office, my feet treading over the plush new carpet, so soft under my feet it's like walking on a cloud. It's late, but the main salon is still full of people, the sounds barely contained in the theater. I still have time for more clients, but the day has been a long one, and I would rather end on a high note.

I will miss working with Lady Amanda. She was as kind as she is wealthy, an unusual combination, even if she was a little out of touch.

I tap on the thick mahogany door at the end of the hall and wait for Harold to grant me permission to enter. It's an action I've taken on so many nights before this, but nothing about our visits feels the same anymore. Now, not just Harold greets me from behind his massive desk; he is joined by Lady M.

On the surface, her addition to the club has brought nothing but positives. Repairs have been made, electrical lighting has been installed on the stage, new girls have been offered refuge, and the main salon is full to the brim every night. Everyone at La Puissance—including Harold—is prospering. The girls, and everyone else who lives and works at the club, seem to love Lady M, showering her with praise and gratitude whenever she blesses us with her presence.

And for her part, Lady M does seem to be trying to acclimate herself to the club. She has begun dressing in less severe clothing, and though I still have yet to see her smile, she dotes on the girls in a way we haven't experienced since we lost Diana.

But I can't shake the memory of the way she looked at Andra, like my sister was something to devour. Something to bleed dry. No one else seems to share my trepidation—I've made small mentions to several of my closest friends that are quickly dismissed as ludicrous—but something is keeping me from fully trusting our new benefactress. I keep hoping that with time I will come to see the goodness the others see in her. So far, the only feeling she stirs in me is unease.

Perhaps it's the way her golden eyes always seem to pierce right through me, as they do while I take my position in one of the chairs in front of the desk. My hands clasped in my lap, back straight, ankles crossed. When Lady M is present, I sit like a lady.

"You are looking well, Cate." Harold begins with a warm smile on his face.

I force myself to return it, even though he has to realize mine is strained. "Thank you, Harold. You are looking well yourself. As is the club." I tilt my head the slightest bit in Lady M's direction, all the thanks I'm willing to offer, though I am happy to see fewer lines on Harold's face. His smile genuine, his eyes brighter. Even his golden hair seems shinier.

"I'm happy you've noticed the improvements, Lady Caterine. They have certainly helped put La Puissance back on the right path." Lady M's voice is as cool as her eyes. She still doesn't smile, but the corner of her mouth tilts up just a tad.

"And what path is that, my lady?" I place an emphasis on her title, one that, like mine, has been bestowed by herself, one that she insists everyone at the club continue to use.

"The path to prosperity. I expect great things are in store for everyone here at La Puissance."

"Indeed."

"You have been living here at the club for many years, correct, Caterine?" Lady M doesn't give me a chance to answer. "And in that time, you have paid Lord MacVeigh a paltry sum to cover your living expenses."

My eyes narrow. "I have contributed to the finances of the club in many ways, my lady. Including bringing in multiple loyal and dedicated patrons."

"Patrons who also tend to pay a paltry sum." She flips through her stack of papers.

I open my mouth to retort, but she cuts me off.

"Yes, you have several clients who are able to pay fully for your services, Lady Amanda for one. But you also see a number of clients who can barely afford to leave a single gold coin."

I grit my teeth. "Those clients need my help even if they can't afford to pay full price for it."

"Hmm." Lady M taps the end of her pointed nail on the desk. "So perhaps one of the reasons the club was struggling so much financially was because members like you were making full use of the club's amenities while charging insufficient rates to cover the loss."

I don't respond to this remark because I don't have a response. Working at La Puissance has never been about making money. Yes, there is money to be made, and several of the girls make plenty of it. But that has never been my aim, and no one has ever taken issue with that. We've always covered each other, found a natural balance that never needed to be questioned.

"There will be no more losses here at La Puissance, Caterine. This guarantees that." Lady M slides a piece of paper across the desk.

I study the sheet of paper, the words blending together and blurring my eyes, my brain unable to parse the meaning. "What is this?"

"It's a contract, Cate." Harold chooses this moment to speak up. "It solidifies our partnership, the relationship between you and the club."

"What does that mean?" I was unaware that after almost twenty years of living here our relationship needed to be further solidified.

"It means that you—and every one of the members of the club—are now responsible for bringing in a certain amount of revenue annually to offset the cost of your room and board, your place here at the club, and the protection we offer you." Lady M folds her hands in her lap as her eyes bore into me, watching me try to make sense of the words and figures on the page.

"This says here that if I don't meet my annual quota, the unpaid debt rolls over into the next year." My chest clenches, and any sense of calm bestowed upon me by my session with Lady Amanda dissipates. "And if I don't make my quota for two consecutive years, I may be asked to leave the club."

"That's correct."

"But that means if I don't make enough money this year, I start the next year already in the hole. Making it all but impossible to ever climb out of it." My stomach starts to turn the more of this so-called contract I read. "And if I don't find a way to make up the difference, I'm going to be forced to leave? To lose my sponsorship?"

"That won't be an issue for you, darling. You'll meet your quota in no time. People will be lining up to pay for your services, especially once you begin to advertise your Gift more widely." Harold leans forward, his arms resting on the desk. "Besides, the Gifted laws will be rescinded before losing your sponsorship could even be an issue."

I don't bother to remind him that I don't say yes to all prospective clients, depending on who they are and what they want from me. I also don't advertise my Gift for a reason. To most, I'm just a prized courtesan of La Puissance, not a Gifted who can manipulate emotions. Clearly the way things used to be done no longer matters.

"And what if I refuse to sign this?" I can't imagine a life without the club, but I also can't imagine willingly handing over this amount of control to anyone—not even Harold.

"Then you will no longer have a home here." Lady M's cold eyes meet mine, a hint of a malicious spark in them, like she is daring me to take that option. "And that sponsorship you're so afraid of losing in the future may become a real problem. It may take several months for the old ways to be fully erased from the law books. If you were to find yourself out on the street now, with no job and no man to vouch for you, I hate to think what might happen."

Clearly Lady M knew about my Gift before this meeting. Harold told her, and if he told her about my Gift, it stands to reason she also knows about Andra's. My stomach tumbles, thinking of our most precious secret in the hands of this woman who I know, deep down, cannot be trusted.

"Now, we don't need to even think about that. Of course you'll sign, Cate. This contract isn't just about money, it also offers you the security of our protection." Harold taps the bottom of the page, the tiny sliver of the contract that covers what the club will provide.

"Yes. Don't you want to keep the protection La Puissance has always so kindly afforded you? At least until the government is able to offer their new plan for the Gifted?"

"I need some time to think about this."

"Take all the time you need, darling."

"As long as you have an answer to us by the end of the day tomorrow. If you don't want your spot here at the club, there are many others who would be happy to take it. We are still only able to offer our sponsorship to ten Gifted at one time, and if you don't wish to be one of them, well . . ." Lady M's lip curls again, and I can't help but wonder if she's trying to smile and her face is incapable of the movement.

My eyes flit back and forth between Harold and his new wife. Is this really what Harold wants? To tie us all to the club this way? Harold has always cared for us, treated us like family; does he really see no issue with holding a debt over our heads and forcing us to perform like trained animals?

I excuse myself from the office without a word of goodbye, the contract clutched so tightly in my hand I can feel the paper wrinkling.

As I make my way back to my suite, my mind holds on to the look in Lady M's eyes. She knows she has me trapped, knows she is going to get exactly what she wants. What I can't figure out is why she wants it.

Meri and Tes come out of Tes's room as I'm rounding the corner, both with wide smiles on their faces, like they haven't a care in the world.

Before I can consider if the hallway is the best place for this conversation, I hold up the damning piece of paper clutched in my hand. "Have you both been told about this?"

Meri squints her brown eyes, as if she might be able to read the fine print through my clenched fist. "Is that your contract?"

Tes's head cocks to the side, her short blond hair falling across her face. "Did you not sign it already?"

Nausea swirls in my gut. "You both signed?"

Meri nods. "I did in the office when they presented it to me."

I swallow my incredulity and try to temper my reaction. "You didn't even take the time to consider the terms?"

Tes shrugs. "What's to consider? I'm not leaving La Puissance. And Lady M is right. It isn't fair for us to take full advantage of the club's generosity without paying it back in kind." She gestures to the new carpets and freshly painted walls. "None of this would have happened without Lady M's funds and she's just trying to make sure we never fall into hardship again in the future."

"But don't you think it's predatory? Making us sign over our lives like this?"

Meri looks at me like I've grown an extra head. "Predatory? You think Harold would ever agree to something that put us at risk?"

I shake my head, though I'm starting to question Harold more and more. In my heart of hearts, I cannot truly fathom a world where he put his girls in any sort of danger.

Meri and Tes push past me, making their way to the main staircase. Tes claps my shoulder as the two brush by. "Just sign the paper, Cate. Stop making everything so difficult."

I make my way back to my rooms, churning over the words of two of my dearest friends. Maybe they're right.

Signing away my life is a terrifying thought, but is giving up the protection of the club even worse? Can I leave behind my friends, my family, and strike out on my own? And what about Andra? She, more than any of the other Gifted, needs to be surrounded by people she can trust. Her Gift is too valuable for us to be out on the streets without the safety the club affords us, especially given the uncertainty of the times.

This contract presents a major problem, and yet, I know my friends are right and I have no choice but to sign it.

We moved into the club today. Its official name is La Puissance, but it seems like most everyone refers to it as "the club." Diana introduced me to everyone, and Harry too. He made fast friends with the bartenders and everyone already seems to love him.

The girls here seem nice enough, I guess, even if some of them weren't exactly what I would call welcoming. Diana made sure to point out the other Gifted girls who live here. I can't wait to talk to them more about their Gifts, to learn how to harness my power, how to best use it to my advantage.

This truly isn't what I expected when I asked Harry to run away with me, and certainly not what I expected for the first year of our marriage, but I can't help but feel like we were meant to end up here, like La Puissance was always meant to be our home.

—EXCERPT FROM THE JOURNAL OF GRECIA MACVEIGH

6

CALLUM

IT'S BEEN A week since the announcement and I still have not come up with a viable solution to the problem. Alex's acceptance and Dom's suggestion cycle through my brain, equal parts frustrating and intriguing.

But it's my father's words that repeat the most often, that linger, that fester, enough to make me consider the unthinkable. The word *coward* dances behind my eyes from the moment I wake until the moment I sleep, permanently etched in my brain. I have never let my father down before, and yet every morning when he greets me across the breakfast table, there is shame in his eyes, shame aimed at me. I know I should be making this easier on him, but I cannot bring myself to give him the one thing he truly needs: my word that I will be the one to take his life from him.

The idea Dom proposed is so preposterous, I tend to dismiss it the second it flits through my mind. But it has begun to linger there, the more time has gone on. I still do not think the Gifted should regain their rights and privileges, think that not regulating their Gifts can only end in disaster for all of Avon. And yet I'm just selfish enough to wonder how I might use this Caterine's Gift for my own benefit.

And so one night, I dress in my best, a tuxedo with tails and a top hat slick enough to make Alex proud.

I don't tell anyone where I'm going, commanding a carriage to drive me into the city. After about two hours, the grassy green knolls of Scota give way to the cobbled streets of the capital, the wheels of the carriage clacking over the rocks. I watch from the window as we pass by Scota's prosperous farms, the emerald fields rich and vibrant, and move into Stratford's dingy streets. Trash litters the cobblestones and the smell of sewage seeps through the carriage doors. More than one person is perched along the streets, tucked under blankets that do little to shelter them from the elements.

What could the country look like if all four provinces lived by Scota's model? Perhaps peace and prosperity for all is possible. If it is, I might be the only one able to achieve it.

The carriage turns a corner and rolls to a stop. We've left behind the slums of Stratford and arrived in what feels like a different world, though I know we are only a few streets away. Here, opulent townhouses tower over a road that is smoothly paved and lined with gilded carriages. The street in front of the club is crowded with patrons waiting for entry, their jewels glinting under the bright lights adorning the front of the building. So much wealth while only blocks away, there is so much need. It churns my stomach, and for a second, I think of asking the driver to turn around and head back home. But I've come this far, I might as well explore my options.

Bold red letters lined with more lights announce our arrival at La Puissance. I step from the carriage and make my way through the chittering crowd. Laughter and joy surround me as I slip the doorman a handful of gold coins to expedite my entry. The noise is overwhelming, so different from the calm, country evening air of Scota. My brain buzzes, and I struggle to focus as my senses are overloaded. Rich perfume erases any lingering hints of sewage from my nose. The only thing brighter than the colors are the diamonds. The wave of sounds that overtakes me is enough to drown out even my darkest of thoughts. For a second, I appreciate how easy it could be to get lost in La Puissance. It's not an entirely unwelcome feeling.

The moment I set foot in the lobby, carpeted in plush crimson with an immense golden staircase at its center, I'm greeted by a stunning woman in a glittering red corset, the skirt of her dress cut high in the front and flowing down to the floor in the back. A giant feather tops her head, along with a massive gemstone that sparkles like her smile.

"Welcome, my lord. Is this your first time visiting La Puissance?"

I nod, refusing to be charmed by this gorgeous creature, determined to reveal as little of myself as possible.

She tucks her hand into the crook of my arm, gently pulling me away from the front doors and farther into the club. Opulence is everywhere, from the dripping jewels adorning the women to the ornate gold railings and balustrades. Costumed people are draped on chairs and across the railings like further ornamentation. Laughter rumbles around me, the air vibrating with it. In one corner of the lobby, a small group of people crowd around a woman, barely dressed, with a sword lodged in her throat. She pulls it out slowly and her audience erupts in cheers as she licks the blade and smiles.

My escort pauses just long enough for me to watch a man pull the sword eater into his lap before she leads us through a wide doorway and utter madness greets us on the other side. The cavernous room is packed full of people, their shouts and giggles competing with the live band performing onstage. The music is loud, thumping, the horns wailing out notes I've never heard before. There's a dance floor, but nothing happening is like anything I've ever seen at a society ball. In twos and threes and fours and fives, people writhe against one another, their bodies pressed so tightly together it's hard to tell where one ends and another begins. Most of the men wear tuxedos, but several are wearing skirts and dresses, some bare-chested and glistening with sweat. Most of the women wear next to nothing, but some are dressed in evening gowns, others in tuxedos. It's as titillating as it is shocking, and my mouth goes dry. I'm surprised to find myself wanting more, the urge to insert myself into the undulating masses catching me off guard.

Across the room from the stage, a massive bar takes up an entire length of the wall, crowded with even more patrons. Balconies ring the room, people shouting from above to their friends down below. Several doors line the hallways on the second level, and it doesn't take much imagination to picture what happens behind them, though the sound of the music drowns out any hints.

The woman watches me while I take it all in. She takes pity on me, chuckling and leading me toward the bar. "What's your poison, love?" She has to lean in close to be heard, and she doesn't pull away.

"Whisky," I yell back so she can actually hear me.

The woman hands me a glass, pressing it into my hand while at the same time pressing her breasts into my arm. "You are quite attractive, my lord."

I notice she still makes use of honorifics, even though the Uprising has officially done away with all titles—one of the few things they've managed to accomplish quickly. I don't bother to mention the correct title would be *Your Highness*, shoving the hand bearing my signet ring deep in my pocket.

I take a bracing sip of the drink, not sure how to let this woman know that despite her beauty I'm not interested.

But she clearly has experience enough to read me like a book. She laughs again. "Stick around, the show's about to begin. You don't want to miss Lady Caterine." She blows me a kiss as she turns to leave me alone at the bar. "Come find me if you change your mind!"

I nod, though we both know that I won't.

I am, however, grateful for the information she's provided me. Lady Caterine is set to perform soon. It'll be the perfect opportunity to observe her.

Strolling through the room, I keep my head down. I've already recognized nobles—former nobles, I suppose—from Venezia and Talia, and I would be a fool to think no Scotan citizens are among the crowd. The last thing I need is for someone to recognize me.

I slip into a seat at one of the spindly black café tables arranged in front of the stage, pulling down on the brim of my hat and sipping cautiously from my drink. A whole bathtub full of whisky wouldn't be enough to soothe my nerves, but the searing down my chest at least gives me something else, something concrete, to focus on.

Without warning, the room goes dark, a pitch black so deep it envelops the massive space.

Rather than inspiring panic, the room explodes in raucous cheers. The people clearly know what's coming.

Soft strains of music fill the air, and the crowd falls into a hushed silence, like the entire room is holding its breath. I find I'm holding mine, too.

The music gets louder, and faster, and a spotlight kicks on, aimed at the red velvet curtain hiding the stage. The crowd cheers and screams again as a single gloved hand emerges from the gap in the curtain.

It disappears after a quick twist of the wrist. A second later a foot emerges, encased in a gold strappy shoe that looks more like a weapon than footwear. The curtain pulls back ever so slowly, revealing a shapely leg sheathed in some kind of sheer sparkly fabric.

The leg disappears, and for one long minute there's nothing but the cries of anticipation from a ravenous crowd.

The next glimpse we get is of the most perfectly round backside I have ever seen. It's encased in more sparkles, black and shimmering under the lights of the stage.

The crowd erupts at the sight.

The curtain closes once again, and the audience groans at the loss.

The music grows louder and faster still until it comes to a sudden halt, the lights blacking out once again so that for a single second, the room is enveloped in silent nothing.

Then the music begins again, slow and low. The curtain begins to part, one inch at a time. And the lights rise, revealing Lady Caterine. Her golden hair shines under the lights, her curves highlighted by the sparkly tight black fabric that barely covers her. Her brightly painted lips smirk, and though I know it's not possible, it feels like she is looking directly at me.

She plays the tension in the room masterfully, holding her pose until the frenzy in the room peaks.

The room explodes, people going wild as Lady Caterine begins to dance. She moves across the stage with a natural grace, like she was born to be here, entrancing this room of people. Entrancing me.

The crowd jostles me, pushing closer to the stage as if drawn to Lady Caterine like magnets, but I barely notice.

I haven't moved since Lady Caterine revealed herself to the crowd. Haven't been able to breathe since taking in her gorgeous face and the sumptuous curves that my hands itch to explore.

Lady Caterine, the Gifted woman who could very well hold the fate of the country in the palm of her hand, is the most beautiful woman I have ever seen.

My heart stops in my chest, my breath caught in my lungs. A single word echoes through my head.

Mine.

And I know beyond a shadow of a doubt that I am well and truly fucked.

THE TIME HAS COME: FIRST WINDOW OF ASSASSINATION ANNOUNCED FOR THE SCOTAN PROVINCE

The dust has barely settled in Avon, and now it seems the time has come for what is likely the greatest act of sanctioned violence in the country's history. But it is not our place to judge the Uprising's decree—though many citizens of Avon may have differing opinions, it is the firm belief of this writer that we all want one thing for this new united nation: a life of peace, prosperity, and equality for all.

We know the people will have a voice and a say when it comes time to elect our first president of Avon. What we do not yet know is who the four representatives, the four candidates, will be.

It will not be long, however, until we know who will be representing the province of Scota in the election. The killing period for the former king of Scota, James III, will begin in one week, and will last for one week following.

King James III, like most monarchs, is not without his flaws. However, we here at the *Stratford City Tribune* will be keeping him and his family in our thoughts during what will surely be a most difficult time.

7

CATE

I SPOT HIM DURING my performance. I used to get lost in the feeling of being onstage, the entire room's eyes on me. The audience would become a blur of cheers and applause, the adrenaline too thick in my blood to allow me to focus on anything but the sensation of performing. Now I use the time to try to find my mark for the evening.

He's handsome, this one, but that's not what draws me to him. It's the fine cut of his tuxedo. The expensive watch chain hanging from his pocket, and the gold ring circling his finger. It's the stunned look on this face as he watches me dance, letting me know this is his first time. He looks at me like he's never seen anything like me before. And if he's never visited La Puissance, then he hasn't. A fact I plan to take full advantage of.

I absorb the applause when my number concludes, letting the crowd shower me in an adoration that bolsters my already high confidence.

They're eating out of the palm of my hand, and my mystery

man's mouth still hangs open in shock. I wonder if I can take him for the full amount I need to make tonight's quota, work him so well I only need to see one client this evening. Based on his wide eyes, he probably doesn't have much experience with pleasing a woman, but I can be patient if the price is right. Besides, my own pleasure has become a non-issue; with Lady M's new contract firmly inked with my signature, my only goal now is to make enough money to protect myself and my sister.

The amount of money I've been tasked with bringing into the club is exorbitant but still within the realm of possibility. I've had to stop seeing clients like Charlie who barely have two gold coins to rub together and start catering to the wealthiest patrons of La Puissance. And I've had to begin spending most of my time in the bedroom, leaving little time remaining for performing onstage. For the foreseeable future, I'll be sticking to my one solo act, using it to rope in the biggest fish in the club, and devoting the rest of my time to paying off first my debt and then Andra's.

Andra has also been tasked with a high debt, but since she peddles fake fortunes, she tends to collect fewer coins. The only way for her to bring in the amount required would be to begin hosting actual readings, provide visions that prove to be accurate. It wouldn't take long for word of her Gift to travel, and she could become a target for those who seek power. Rather than risk discovery, she is continuing on as she always has and I will make up the difference for her.

When my number comes to an end, the crowd roars, tossing flowers and coins, even some small jewels, onto the stage and I sashay to the wings, blowing kisses as I leave. Backstage, Rosa helps me out of my costume and into a long, red satin dress; cut low and tight, it's a dress that tends to get me whatever I want. And tonight, I want him, the man who was so enthralled with my performance that I was able to pick him out of the boisterous crowd. I want him and his money. I hoist the sumptuous crimson fabric up to my waist, returning my dagger and its sheath to their rightful place, running my thumb over the scarlet jewel set in the hilt as if it can bring me some kind of luck.

"That's an interesting piece."

I don't need to see her to identify her—her voice alone sends a chill racing through me. But I turn to face Lady M as I drop my skirts. "Harold gave it to me."

"Such an intricate design. And that jewel. It reminds me of one I used to have." Her golden eyes bore into mine, unreadable but undeniably cold. "Harold must care about you very much."

"Harold cares about all of us very much. One of his best qualities is how much he cares for people." It's a quality he instilled in me, the desire to help others, though as of late I haven't been able to act on it much. I push my shoulders back, though even at my full height, I am still several inches shorter than Lady M.

She takes a step closer to me. "The problem with caring for others is that it makes it so easy for them to take advantage of you."

I ignore her insinuation. "If you'll excuse me, I need to get to work. I have a quota to meet, after all." I smooth down the satin of my bodice and turn for the stairs.

Her hand clamps around mine, her pointed nails digging into the soft flesh of my arm. "I think deep down, you are an intelligent woman, Caterine, even if you do degrade yourself. So let me make this clear. I know who you are, and I know what you can do. More importantly, I know what your sister can do. You do not want to find yourself as my opposition."

I yank my arm from her grasp and pray she can't somehow feel the rapid beating of my heart. I refuse to let her see the fear chilling my blood. "Stay away from me. Stay away from my sister." I turn on my heel and race down the short flight of stairs leading from the backstage wings to the entrance of the main salon. I pause before the door, taking a moment to still my breathing and drop my mask fully into place before I push out into the waiting crowd.

When I enter the main salon, the crowd swarms me, but I brush them off with smiles and waves. My eyes catch on the guards posted around the room, dressed all in black, standing still as statues. They've been here since we all signed our contracts. Lady M claims they're for our protection. I can't help feeling they're more likely to protect her investment than our well-being. I ignore their looming presence and head directly for the bar, my eyes sweeping the room, looking for a tall man with impeccable taste, determined to push all threats from Lady M from my mind. Tonight I'm going to make my quota *and* enjoy myself, just to spite her.

Instead of finding the wealthy newcomer, my eyes land on one of the club's most handsome, and flirtiest, regulars.

"Lady Caterine." Maro Violaine pushes off the bar, closing the distance between us. His long dark curls are artfully disheveled, in a way that makes me think he spent an hour in the mirror before stepping out of his grand estate.

"Maro." I reach for the glass of whisky clasped in his hand, taking a long sip, leaving a perfect red imprint of my lips behind on the crystal.

"I hear congratulations are in order."

I raise one eyebrow, watching his face closely for any hint at his meaning. "Oh?"

He flashes me his signature grin. It's charming and disarming and allows him to get his way in just about anything. "Your new benefactress. The club has had quite the makeover in the past few weeks."

"Right." So much for pushing Lady M to the back of my mind.

Maro takes his glass of whisky back. "You're not a fan?"

I don't say anything, not because I don't want to, but because Maro's father is one of the most powerful men in Talia, and even if Maro is considered the black sheep of his family, I can't have him running to Daddy and spilling all of Harold's secrets. So I shrug and flash him a coy smile of my own. "The club has surely benefited from her patronage. We are lucky to have her."

Maro chuckles at my obvious lie. "I'm sure you are, Cate. Always a pleasure." He tosses back his drink, leaving the empty glass on the bar top before disappearing into the crowd.

I never know quite what to make of that man.

Leaning over the long mahogany bar, I flag down one of my favorite bartenders. "Hey, Jimmy!"

Jimmy grins and automatically pours me a whisky. "Great show tonight, Lady Caterine, as always."

"Thanks, love. Have you seen a new guy anywhere? Tall, handsome, looks very rich and slightly scared?"

Jimmy laughs and cocks his head toward the end of the bar.

And there he is. His back faces the room, missing all the action still happening onstage. Definitely a first-timer. He's hunched over his drink like he doesn't want anyone to notice him, which given his height and the breadth of his shoulders is practically impossible.

I slide down the bar until I'm perched right next to him, a sliver of space separating our elbows, resting on the bar top. "Not enjoying the show, my lord?"

The man grunts, his eyes fixed on the golden-brown liquor in his glass.

He doesn't answer, so I turn my body, letting my breasts graze his biceps. I lower my voice. "Perhaps there's something I could show you in private that would pique your interest." Normally I would let the tension linger between us a little longer, flirt for a few more minutes before propositioning him, but something tells me this man isn't one for games.

He shifts then, and his eyes find mine. They widen with recognition, and for a moment we just stare at each other.

I knew he was handsome. I could see that even when I was dancing onstage in front of the crowd. But up close, this man is beyond handsome. His jaw is sharp and clean-cut. His eyes are the brightest blue. His hair tumbles in copper-colored curls that I suddenly long to run my fingers through.

He's beautiful. It's the kind of face a girl could fall in love with. Or at least, the kind of face any girl but me could fall in love with.

And yet a single word darts through my mind.

Mine.

A shiver races up my back and somehow seems to embed itself under my skin. There's a buzz, an itch I've never experienced before, a longing that feels rooted deep inside my chest. I want to reach out and touch him. But I push the urge down and ignore it, focusing on the task at hand.

I recover first, from this seemingly unbreakable eye contact. I remember who I am, and why I'm here. I clear my throat, dragging a single finger along my collarbone. His eyes follow my touch before drifting down to the swell of my cleavage, exactly as I knew they would.

I tamp down on my grin because this is too easy. "I don't think I've seen you at La Puissance before, my lord."

He throws back the remainder of his drink. "First time. And I'm not a lord."

My heart sinks a bit because I'd pegged him as a wealthy patron and my judgment isn't usually off. But then my eyes rove over him again. His clothing doesn't lie. He may not be a lord, but new money spends just as well as old money. I trace that single finger along his forearm. "Perhaps you would allow me to show you the ropes? My private suite is right up the stairs."

He clears his throat and steps away from me, though the action looks as if it pains him. "That won't be necessary. I don't think I'll be staying much longer. Or returning."

I arch an eyebrow. "Did we do something to offend you?"

He shakes his head. "Quite the opposite, I'm afraid, Lady Caterine."

Both eyebrows rise this time. "I'm afraid you have me at a disadvantage. You know my name, but I don't know yours."

He flashes me a sad smile. "I believe that's for the best. Good night, Lady Caterine."

Before I have time to protest, he turns and leaves.

I stand blinking at the empty space where he stood a moment ago, shock and something like regret roiling through me.

He said he wouldn't be coming back, which means I won't be seeing him again. And for some reason, that makes me incredibly sad. That itch under my skin kicks up until the sensation almost burns.

Because of all the funds I could have gleaned from him, of course, I reason.

But I don't have time to wallow. The night is getting on, and I haven't yet brought in a single customer. I'm still getting used to this new mindset—searching for funds instead of people who might need my help—and I can't pretend to enjoy the hunt. So when an obviously wealthy man approaches me, flashing a leering smile and a pocket heavy with gold coins, I don't consider sending him away.

It doesn't take long before we're naked in between my cool silk sheets. The man is fumbling and quick, clearly not caring one bit about my comfort or pleasure. Turns out, when I share an emotional connection with my clients, they are more likely to care about my pleasure in return. But my pleasure doesn't matter anymore, what matters is keeping my sister safe.

I close my eyes as he pushes into me, willing my brain to travel elsewhere for the next few minutes. Instead, an unbidden image pops into my mind. The man from the bar. His shy smile tugging on his perfect lips. The bright blue spark in his eyes. I imagine his hands tracing gentle lines over my bare skin. His lips tracing the same path. I let out a breathy sigh.

"You like that?" the man grumbles, yanking me out of my pleasant vision.

The air in the room turns a putrid sort of puce as he heaves one final thrust and groans in a way that could give off the impression he's dying. Luckily, I don't think that's the case.

"Oh, that was wonderful," I cry, keeping my voice light and pure so he doesn't notice the lie. I hold the man in place, not that he's made any effort to remove his weight from smothering me. In this case I don't mind since I'm not done with him yet. I push any thoughts of handsome men from my mind and focus on the task at hand.

The man mumbles something unintelligible into my neck. Whatever it is, it must be good because the green thickens and darkens around us. Not that he can see it.

I have to search hard for the correct emotions, for so long that the green starts to dissipate, and the man starts to pull away. Snaking my hand in between our bodies—his slick with sweat—I stroke him until both he and the color harden, until I find the string I need to pull on. Rather than tuck this emotion away, folding it up into a tiny box, I expand it, inflating the man's stilted sense of generosity.

I wait until I've expanded his sense of charity to the fullest before I put on my breathiest voice. "I don't know about you, my lord, but things have been so hard for me since the Uprising." I continue my gentle strokes, though he's begun to soften in my hand.

He pulls far enough away to look at me. He doesn't make eye contact, but his gaze roves over my face and down to my chest. "I was under the impression you were one of La Puissance's top performers."

"I am." I shrug, not bothering with false modesty. "But even I have been seeing a downturn." I sigh, as long and dramatic as I can manage. "I might have to find another line of work if things continue this way."

The man frowns, putting even more space in between us. His eyes trace my naked body before he climbs out of bed and dresses, his attention never returning to me.

Shit. I must have messed up somehow. I'm still not used to using my Gift to take advantage of my clients, and I've had some trouble pulling the right emotional strings with the right amount of pressure.

The man pauses by the door, looking at me one final time. "We can't have you leaving La Puissance now that I've finally found my way to your bed, Lady Caterine." And with that he dumps the entire contents of his pockets into my elephant-shaped gold bowl.

I keep my eyes soft and innocent, overcome with gratitude. "Oh, thank you, my lord. I cannot tell you how much I appreciate you." I sit up and clasp my hands in just the right way, pressing my breasts together.

"You can show me. Tomorrow night."

Fighting back the grimace, I nod like there's nothing I would rather do, wishing I could turn back the clock to the way things used to be, but no part of me feeling sorry for taking advantage of the man as I have.

THE FOLLOWING MORNING, Andra comes to my room as I'm getting dressed for the day.

"Just in time to help me." I gesture to the buttons along the back of my burgundy velvet dress. It's one of my more demure pieces, despite the sumptuousness of the fabric, tight in the bodice, but flowing into a wide skirt. The neckline dips low, but the cap sleeves provide a small amount of coverage.

She raises her eyebrows but obliges. "This is quite a look for midday."

"Lady M has requested my presence at a meeting."

"Perhaps you should try to hide at least some of your disdain for the new lady of the house."

I snort. "Haven't you heard, ladies no longer exist?"

She snorts right back, popping the final button in place. "I'll keep that in mind, *Lady* Caterine."

"We missed you at breakfast this morning." I head toward the mirror above my dressing table to check my lip paint.

For a second, Andra's face pulls into a tight grimace, but by the time I turn from our reflection, she's smiling. "I wasn't hungry."

I take a moment to study my sister, noticing the hint of a shadow underneath her eyes. "Is everything all right?"

She doesn't get the chance to answer before there's a knock on my door.

Lady M doesn't wait for permission, opening the door and pushing into my room. Her eyes rake me over and she gives one single, imperious nod. "Our guest has arrived." Her eyes flit to Andra, whose cheeks pale under the weight of her gaze.

It's a small enough reaction that no one but me would notice, but I don't have time to inquire further with my twin before Lady

M is ushering me out of the room and down the stairs. I make a mental to note to stop by Andra's room later and figure out what's going on.

For now, I walk slowly down the grand staircase and into the formal sitting room, trailing behind Lady M. An unfamiliar young woman stands with Harold, glasses of whisky in each of their hands. The gold brocade curtains have been pushed back to let in the daylight, though the gas lamps and candles are still lit for ambiance. Heavy wood accents the room, from the massive fireplace to the masculine furniture, lending an air of oppression to the space. It's one of my least favorite rooms in the club, one I avoid whenever possible. Of course this is the room Lady M chose.

The unfamiliar woman turns as I enter, her bright eyes roving over me, though her head-to-toe perusal feels more appraising than salacious. She's gorgeous, with strawberry-blond hair and blue eyes that immediately bring to mind the handsome stranger from the night before. I wonder if I will continue to see him everywhere, and for how long. It is unlike me to linger on someone who clearly had no interest in lingering on me.

Harold steps forward. "My dear Caterine, may I please introduce you to Her Royal Highness Dominique Reid, Princess of Scota?"

Everyone in this room knows that Dominique is no longer a princess, not technically anyway, but that doesn't stop me from dipping into a low curtsy.

"Your Highness. It is an honor." It's a lie, is what it is. Scota might pretend to have the best version of royal leaders, but I have personal experience with the so-called benevolent ruler of my home province that proves otherwise. I will never forget that it was as a ward of the province under her father's rule that my sister and I suffered, forcing us to flee to the streets as children young enough to barely survive on our own.

But I wipe any traces of those memories from my face.

The princess tosses back the rest of her whisky in a very unprincesslike manner. "We both know I'm no longer a princess, and even when I was, I didn't bother with any of that nonsense."

I arch one eyebrow, trying and failing not to be charmed by her candor. "You look familiar, Your Highness. Have you been to La Puissance before?"

She grins and it brightens her already shining eyes. "Several times. I have always enjoyed watching you perform. And please, call me Dom."

"Her Royal Highness has come to us with a most interesting proposition, Lady Caterine." Lady M, as usual, directs the conversation. She doesn't seem to catch—or care about—the way Dom grimaces.

I gesture to an emerald-green velvet divan. "Shall we sit so I can hear all about it, Dom?"

The four of us settle, Lady M and Harold on armchairs, Dom and I on the divan, though I note she leaves as much space between us as possible. Maybe I've misread the spark of flirtation. Or maybe whatever it is the princess has to ask requires propriety.

"How may I be of service to you?" I clasp my hands in my lap and gaze at her as demurely as I'm capable of.

"I'm actually here to inquire about your services on behalf of my brother."

"Oh?" My interest is piqued, though I try to keep my feelings under wraps. Not much is known at La Puissance about King James's would-have-been successor. Unlike the other provinces' princes—and apparently, his sister—who frequent the club regularly, he has never blessed us with his presence. "And what can I do for your brother?"

"Callum."

"Callum." His name rolls off my tongue, something about it sticking just slightly in the back of my throat.

Dom looks between me and Harold and Lady M. She turns to the latter. "Might I have a moment alone with Lady Caterine?"

Lady M begins to protest, but Harold places a bracing hand on her forearm. "Of course, Your Highness. Whatever you need."

Harold helps Lady M to rise, but she is slow to exit. "We'll be right outside," she throws over her shoulder, "should you need us for anything."

The door clicks shut behind them, and I turn to the princess. "Don't worry, they can't hear anything that we say—or do—in here. All the rooms at La Puissance are soundproofed, for obvious reasons."

Dom flashes me another one of those slightly wicked grins. "Unfortunately, I don't think we'll be partaking in any loud activities today, but it does help to know we won't be overheard."

I scoot an inch closer to her, still unsure as to what she could ask of me. Especially if we won't be partaking in any "loud activities." "Now. Let me have it. What could I possibly do to help the prince and princess of Scota?"

Dom clears her throat and sits back in her seat. She is dressed in leather breeches and a billowing tunic and the movement pulls her pants tighter, showing off the lean muscles of her thighs. No crown rests on her golden red waves, but she does wear a green-and-navy brooch, the Reid crest displayed on the collar of her shirt. "As I mentioned, I am here on behalf of my brother. He needs your assistance, but the matter is somewhat delicate."

"I am a vault. Anything you tell me—and anything that happens between me and your brother—will be handled with the utmost discretion."

"I appreciate that." Dom taps her fingers on the arm of the divan. "My brother needs sex lessons, Lady Caterine."

I blink several times, as if the movement can clear the confusion from my brain. "Your brother needs sex lessons?"

A teasing glint flashes in her eyes, but it's gone before I can fully decipher her intentions. "Well, to be totally honest, because he is my brother, I don't know much about his experience with women—and I'd like to keep it that way. But I do know that he doesn't spend nearly enough time out of the house. He refuses to accompany me when I spend evenings away from the estate. He's never even been here, as far as I know."

"And so you are worried about his romantic abilities?" Something doesn't seem to be fully adding up, and I still can't seem to wrap my mind around what the princess is actually asking of me.

Dom's cheeks flush. "It's not just that."

I sit in the silence, waiting for her to elaborate.

"My brother, he is a good man, Lady Caterine. The best, really. And these past few months, few years really, have been hard on him."

I'm not keen on the sympathy building in my chest for the prince, but it's clear from Dom's speech that she cares about her sibling very much, a feeling I can relate to.

"And now . . . and now . . ."

I place a gentle hand on her forearm. "It's okay. You don't have to say it out loud."

And now her brother, Callum, is going to have to deal with the loss of their father. I never had a real father of my own, but I imagine how I might feel if I knew Harold had no more than a few days left to live. I would be devastated.

Dom's voice falls. "I'm worried about my brother. How he is going to handle things, how he is going to cope."

My fingers tighten on her arm. "Is this really about sex lessons, Dom?"

She straightens, pulling her shoulders back and facing me head-on. "Yes. It's also about letting my brother find some relief from the tension that seems to be eating him alive. Can you do that, Lady Caterine?"

I stop myself from immediately agreeing. Something about this woman and her obvious love for her brother is pulling at my heartstrings, but now is not the time to ignore the opportunity that sits before me. "Does your brother know you are here, Your Highness?"

She shakes her head. "No. Callum was not exactly open to the idea of coming to you for assistance."

I arch my eyebrows. "Is he prejudiced? Against courtesans, I mean?" Though she hasn't come right out and said it, I know the princess is asking me to use my Gift on her brother. But on the off chance she doesn't know about my true talent, I am surely not going to be the one to tell her.

"Not prejudiced. Just untrusting. I think it might take a few lessons before he is able to really open himself up to you."

"It will be hard to teach him if he does not trust me." My Gift only works when my clients allow themselves to be fully vulnerable.

"I do not think it will take him long, Lady Caterine. I think if anyone has the power to reach him, it might be you." Each of her words is weighted, heavy with double meaning.

I nod, crossing my legs primly at the ankle, ready to get down to brass tacks. "How many lessons would you like to arrange?"

She meets my gaze head-on. "I would like you to be available to my brother—and only my brother—for the next week, my lady."

"A full week of my time is going to cost you, Your Highness."

"Name your price."

My breath catches in my chest, but I fight to hide the excitement I know must be visible. "Fifty thousand gold marks." It's an exorbitant amount—enough to pay off not just my debt, but Andra's as well.

"Done." Dom holds out her hand. "I will have the first half delivered tomorrow. You'll receive the rest at the conclusion of the week."

I wrap my fingers around hers, making the connection that the conclusion of the week is the day after the Scotan killing period begins. I squeeze a little tighter, as if I can imbue enough sympathy in that single grasp to make up for the fact that her father is about to be killed, even if I'm not sorry about that fact itself. "Pleasure doing business with you, Dom."

She drops my hand and rises.

I stand, ready to see her out.

Dom pauses just before I can open the door. "Sometimes he comes off brusque, my lady, but I promise, you'll never meet a kinder man."

I nod, warmed by her loving words. "I promise to do everything I can for him."

"Expect him tomorrow for his first . . . lesson." She reaches for the door herself, nodding to Lady M and Harold, who wait just outside.

Harold rushes to show her to the front entrance.

I make to leave the sitting room, but Lady M blocks my passage, herding me back inside and shutting the door behind us. The last thing I want is to be trapped alone with her hard-as-amber eyes and cold mouth. She ushers me back over to the divan, pushing me down and then folding herself, sitting much closer than Dom did. Uncomfortably close. The hairs on the back of my neck rise as I take in the glint of excitement in her eyes.

"Tell me exactly what she asked of you," she demands.

I think about refusing, but I know she is going to notice if the same man—the same former prince—is coming to my room for days in a row. "I am going to be providing the prince of Scota with sex lessons. I'm to be paid forty thousand gold marks for a week of my time." I lower the number, knowing forty thousand marks is enough to pay out our contracts. I'll keep the extra ten for myself, just in case.

"Do you realize the opportunity before you, Caterine?" Her whisper is hushed but no less fierce than her normal tone. The possessive glint in her eyes makes my stomach turn.

"The opportunity to clear our debt and then some in a matter of a week? I'm aware." I brush my skirts and move to stand, but Lady M reaches out and holds me in place.

"You will have access to Callum Reid, the likely candidate for the Scotan province, under your power, Lady Caterine."

"How do you know he's the likely candidate for the Scotan province?"

Lady M rolls her eyes, like I'm a small-minded fool. "You really think he isn't going to even attempt to take the position?"

From everything Dom just told me, I can't imagine Callum Reid being the kind of man who could murder his father, but then again, there isn't much I would put past the royals.

I attempt to tug my arm from her grasp. "None of that is any of my concern. Callum is a client and I will treat him as I would any other."

Her pointed nails dig into my bare skin, and I don't like that this is becoming a habit. "You will do more than that."

My eyes narrow. "Just tell me plainly what it is you want from me, Lady MacVeigh."

"I want you to act as a spy. Bring me information about Callum's plans. When he plans to kill his father, where, and how." Her eyes glitter with something bordering on malevolence, and I can practically see the wheels spinning inside her diabolical mind. "Better yet, you could make that man fall in love with you in a matter of hours. Think of what we could do then."

The joy I see in her eyes at the prospect freezes the blood in my veins. "Why would I do that?" All I care about is his money. Or his sister's money, in this case. Callum Reid means nothing to me.

"So we can thwart him, obviously. Why should a Scotan heir be the voice of the people? Why not someone who could truly bring new representation to our government? Wouldn't you rather see someone like Harold leading Avon?"

"Is that something Harold is considering?" He's never before expressed any interest in politics, at least not beyond his involvement with the Uprising, content to run the club and lead our found family.

Lady M nods, her lips pulling into the closest thing I've seen to a smile. "Isn't that something you would want for him? For all of Avon? For Harold to finally come into the kind of power he truly deserves?"

She has me there, and she knows it. I can think of no one I trust more than the man who has cared for so many for so long. Harold would be the perfect Scotan candidate, a fair and just leader who knows better than most the difficulties the common people—the Gifted, particularly—face. He has overcome challenges and hardships most couldn't even dream of. And I would do just about anything for Harold, a fact Lady M knows well by now, given how quickly I agreed to sign my contract, even if I do find his recent decisions to be questionable.

My contract. Perhaps I can walk away from this situation with more than just money.

"I want to be released from my contract. Andra too. Permanently." Just because I might want to assist Harold doesn't mean I won't wring every advantage I can from the situation. I still can't imagine leaving the club, but if the time comes when we need to, I don't want there to be anything standing in our way. Something tells me by the time this whole thing is over with, I might need to make a clean break, and though the mere thought rips away a chunk of my heart, for my sister's sake, I need to be prepared for the worst. "If you do that, I'll make Callum Reid fall in love with me and help you with whatever you need."

Lady M pretends to think about it for a minute before offering me a single word. "Done."

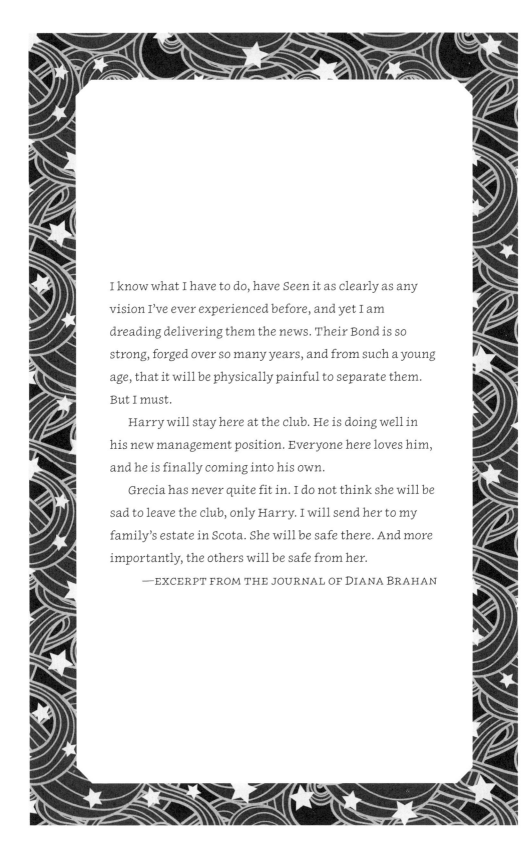

I know what I have to do, have Seen it as clearly as any vision I've ever experienced before, and yet I am dreading delivering them the news. Their Bond is so strong, forged over so many years, and from such a young age, that it will be physically painful to separate them. But I must.

Harry will stay here at the club. He is doing well in his new management position. Everyone here loves him, and he is finally coming into his own.

Grecia has never quite fit in. I do not think she will be sad to leave the club, only Harry. I will send her to my family's estate in Scota. She will be safe there. And more importantly, the others will be safe from her.

—EXCERPT FROM THE JOURNAL OF DIANA BRAHAN

8

CALLUM

"HAVE YOU THOUGHT any more about your father's proposition?" Alex dismounts his horse in front of the stables, handing the reins off to one of the waiting stablehands.

I had been about to dismount myself, but now I reconsider. Perhaps I should dig my heels in, giving my horse the signal to hightail it away from here. I would love nothing more than to escape this conversation. But I sigh, jumping from the horse and passing off the reins. "You know I have thought of little else."

It's not entirely true. My thoughts over the past day have swung back and forth between the need for me to murder my own father, and the gorgeous face of the woman I am supposed to trust to help me.

I'm not sure which line of thinking has been more disturbing.

"Is there a reason you do not want to become the Scotan candidate?" Alex removes his riding gloves, shoving them in his pocket before turning to walk back to the estate.

"Aside from the fact that in order to do so I need to kill my father?"

"Aside from that, yes."

I glance at my uncle, but he does not mean the words in jest. Alex has always been insightful. He comforted me when my mother died and gave me advice before the first time I bedded a woman; he has seen me through every phase of life.

"Something is keeping you from accepting this responsibility, Cal." He comes to a stop under a large tree, the canopy of leaves shading us from the midday sun as it peeks through Scota's ever-present clouds, as well as any prying eyes that might be sweeping the grounds of the estate. "And I don't think it has as much to do with killing James as you might want us to believe."

It might have something to do with the person I would need to trust once the act was done.

It also might have something to do with the insecurity I feel deep in my bones, an insecurity I couldn't acknowledge to anyone else other than Alex.

"It is one thing to think about ruling Scota. I was born for it, bred for it, have been preparing for it my whole life."

Alex nods, letting me know he is listening, but he does not interrupt.

"But it is another thing entirely to think about presiding over all of Avon. Not only that, but to be the first one tasked with bringing the four provinces together. It is a job I am not sure I am equipped to handle." A weight lifts off my shoulders, the act of admitting this fear already alleviating it.

"You would make a good leader, Cal." Alex slings an arm around my shoulders. "You have the experience and you're one of the most even-keeled people I know. This country is going to need someone kind, someone levelheaded, someone intelligent. You have all of those qualities in spades."

I scoff, turning away from him so his hand is forced to drop from my shoulder. Something about the physical touch chafes instead of comforts. "I am not sure that I do."

"Is this about the Gifted?" he asks after a quiet moment.

My shoulders stiffen. My opinion on the Gifted and my thoughts on them regaining their rights under the new regime haven't shifted so greatly since I saw Lady Caterine perform. But the thought has crossed my mind: Maybe I have judged the situation harshly.

Though maybe that is Lady Caterine using her Gift. She brushed up against me when she approached me at the bar. Perhaps she knows exactly who I am, what I intend to do, and is attempting to use her Gift to stop me.

"You know, your mother was a fierce advocate for the Gifted." Alex takes a step forward, forcing me to look at him.

"And look where it got her."

"I do not believe that someone as smart as you, Callum, can truly base your opinion of an entire group of people on the actions of one single person."

"I believe that when that one single person kills your mother, it's understandable."

He shoves his hands in his pockets, likely to keep from reaching out to strangle me. "Your mother believed that the Gifted had been oppressed for much too long. She believed that all citizens of Avon deserved equal rights. It is part of the reason why we do not enforce the laws against the Gifted here as strictly as they do in the other provinces."

"And you agreed with her?"

"I still do, Cal. And I think deep down in your heart, if you let yourself move beyond the past, you would too."

I shake my head. "The Gifted want me to move beyond the past?

Fine. How about what they are forcing me to do in the present? They already stole one parent from me and now they want me to murder the other."

"That is not the work of the Gifted but the decision of the Uprising."

I snort. "You and I both know they are one and the same." I run a hand through my hair. "Perhaps you are right, Uncle. Perhaps I am the right leader for this new united nation of Avon. And perhaps the first thing I will do once elected is make sure the Gifted never have the power to hurt anyone else the way they hurt my mother."

Alex places his hands on my shoulders as if to hold me back, though I made no move to strike him, would never. "It's okay to be upset, Callum. This is a terrible situation, and you've been given an impossible choice. It's understandable to be mad about it."

I wish I believed him. But I don't have time to be mad. I don't have the right to be mad. My father can be mad, my sister can be mad, even Alex can be mad. But it's not a luxury I can allow myself to sink into. Too much is riding on me, riding on this decision I don't think I have the strength to make.

"Do not patronize me."

Alex sighs, patting my cheek and ruffling my hair as if he wants to do exactly that. "I hate what this has done to you. There is the possibility of so much good that can come from this, but it isn't fair that you have to be collateral damage. I wish there were another way."

I let my anger simmer down to something closer to anguish. "What would she tell me to do, if she were still here?"

Alex's eyes, the same blue as mine, the same blue as my mother's, pierce through me. "She would have told you to follow your heart, and as long as you do that, everything will work out as it's meant to."

Everything will work out as it's meant to. Sounds like a bunch of trite nonsense to me.

I leave Alex under the tree, striding across the grassy green lawn of the castle grounds. I don't know where I'm going, or where I'm supposed to end up. It feels like I don't know much of anything these days, and despite his best intentions, I'm not sure Alex helped me gain any clarity on the matter.

I would be naïve not to realize that the other provinces have not been so lucky as Scota. I have heard stories that turned my stomach, seen the evidence of the economic disparity that plagues the other provinces. Maybe assassinating the monarchs of those provinces is the closure the people need to move on and focus on a new future. A befitting punishment.

But that is not the case here, and I do not know how to come to terms with it.

I wind up back at my suite of rooms, sinking into an armchair in front of the stone fireplace. It is still early afternoon and the flames have not yet been stoked. The light shining through the windows provides its own kind of warmth. I only have a few minutes of peace before a knock on the door pulls me out of my thoughts, perhaps just in time.

Dom enters the room without waiting for permission, heading directly for the decanter of whisky sitting on the small wooden table in the corner. She pours two glasses, handing one to me before sliding into the seat across from mine. "You should drink that before we have this conversation."

I'm too weary to argue with her, too lost in my own thoughts to worry about what she could possibly be here to tell me that requires bracing myself with liquor. I just toss back the contents of the glass, enjoying the burn.

Dom takes a dainty sip from her own glass. "I went to meet with Lady Caterine this morning."

My hand, halfway to reaching for the bottle for a refill, freezes. Her face has haunted my dreams—both waking and asleep—ever since my visit to La Puissance. The only time I'm not thinking about her is when my mind is consumed with the impending death of my father. "What could you possibly have to discuss with Lady Caterine?"

"I went to La Puissance with the goal of trying to get a read on her. And to ask her for a favor. Well, a favor I'm paying for, so really, asking her if she was up for a job."

"Spit it out, Dom. What did you ask her to do?"

She takes the bottle from me and refills my glass. "I've arranged for you to spend the week with Lady Caterine."

I choke on my drink. "I'm sorry, you did what?"

"There is less than a week left until . . . you know . . . and if you are going to need Lady Caterine's assistance to deal with the aftermath then that means we have one week for you to learn to trust her."

"You've gone mad," I mutter, knowing full well she can hear me.

"This needs to be done, Cal. There isn't much I can do to help you with this situation, so I decided to do this." On the outside, she is nothing but blustery confidence, but I know her well enough to see the pain in the depths of her blue eyes, and I wonder what all of this is doing to my sister—watching me struggle with this decision and being powerless to help.

"So what, I'm just going to spend the week hanging around La Puissance? Joining their dance rehearsals and palling around with scores of the Gifted?" The thought doesn't sound as terrible as it once might have, not if it means seeing Lady Caterine again.

"Lady Caterine is going to be giving you sex lessons."

Whisky comes flying out of my mouth. Luckily Dom is quick enough to duck.

"Sex lessons? You asked her to give me sex lessons?" I picture the woman I watched glide around that stage, her knowing smile and lush curves. I think about my sister telling that majestic woman that I need sex lessons. My entire body flushes with heat and shame, and perhaps underneath all of that, maybe a tinge of excitement.

Her eyes meet mine, the blue twinkling with mischief. "You brought this on yourself, Callum. You are resistant to what needs to be done. Don't blame me for finding a way to make this situation work."

"There wasn't a slightly less humiliating reason you could've come up with?" I grumble. It doesn't escape me that it's been a long time since Dom had anything close to humor in her eyes, and how grateful I am to see it, even if it is at my expense.

"She's expecting you in her suite tomorrow evening. She doesn't know the full extent of what you might require of her."

Well, there's that small bit of relief at least. She doesn't yet know I'm being pressured to murder my own father.

"Use this time to learn to trust her, Cal." She swigs the remaining whisky from her glass. "And if nothing else, maybe let her relieve some of your stress, if you know what I mean."

I glare at her, because I know too well what she means.

Dom heads for the door, but she hesitates for a brief minute. "Lady Caterine's Gift is powerful, but specific. She can't manipulate your emotions unless you . . . finish . . . in her presence. So if you are feeling wary, abstain from release and you'll be fine."

"How am I supposed to relieve my stress if I can't—" My question is cut off by the door slamming in my face. "Why couldn't I have been an only child?"

I down the remaining liquor in my glass. Then I finish the small amount left in the bottle.

Sex lessons.

My stomach flutters, the mere thought of my hands on Lady Caterine's curves enough to set my emotions whirling. Embarrassment floods through me, but I'd be lying if I said there also wasn't a hint of anticipation. A whole week to be spent in Lady Caterine's bed. My skin begins to itch, like something spiky is coursing through my veins. My blood begins to heat, before it rushes to my cock, the mere thought of Lady Caterine wrapped in silk sheets enough to make me hard as granite.

Then the reality sets in. A whole week in Lady Caterine's bed without allowing myself to orgasm lest she manipulate my emotions without my consent.

A week that will likely end with me stabbing my father in the back.

Will this be the best week of my life, or the worst?

Alex,

I have not yet received word from you regarding your nephew's decision. You swore to me you would handle it and we are running out of time. If things are going to go according to plan, Callum must be the candidate representing Scola. I thought this was one thing we both agreed on.

Please provide a progress report immediately.

Sincerely,

August Sotello

9

CATE

I ASK THEM TO meet me in Bianca's room so we're on neutral territory. The ink has long dried on our contracts. The guards seem to be watching our every move. Lady M hovers over every facet of the club, focused on only one thing: bringing in enough coin to satiate her needs. She is using me to collect information on the royals of Scota. I can only imagine what she might have asked of the other girls.

Surely by now the rest of the Gifted at La Puissance have realized the danger she poses to life as we know it. Andra and I might have a way out thanks to my little visit from Dominique Reid, but the others are not so lucky. If my remaining time here at the club turns out to be limited, if it proves we need to make a quick escape, I need to make sure my friends are safe. I need to make sure they are seeing what I'm seeing as far as Lady M is concerned.

I need to make sure Harold is safe, as well. And the only way I can think of to do that is to show him how much hurt she has caused his darlings. Harold might love his wife, but he loved us first, has loved us longer, and I have to believe if I can present him with evidence of her wrongdoings, he will not take her side.

Bianca's room is smaller than mine, the bed not as commanding or opulent. When clients come to Bianca's room for services, they are looking to be healed, not pleasured, and the space reflects her more spartan needs. A large shelving unit dominates the space, tinctures and glass bottles lining the dark wood. We sit around the small dining table—Bianca, Tes, Meri, Rosa, Helen, and I. I tried to collect Andra from her room on my way here, but she wouldn't even open the door, claiming she needed to rest. I should ask Bianca to check on her later, but first, I need to prepare my case for Harold.

I clear my throat. "You know how much I love all of you."

Tes rolls her cherubic blue eyes—the only angelic part of her—at the sentiment, and the rest of them shift uncomfortably in their seats, like I'm a schoolmarm about to scold them.

But I don't let their reactions deter me. I skip over the heartfelt emotions and cut right to the point. "Things have changed since we signed our contracts, and I know you must have noticed. I know we've always sought to use our Gifts to help our clients and provide a service for our community, but I can't be the only one who's had to scale back on appointments with those who truly need me in favor of those who can pay me the most."

No one says anything for a minute. Tes is the first to work up a response. "My clientele hasn't shifted much."

I force back an eye roll of my own. Tes's Gift of bending metal doesn't exactly lend itself to charity, though she will often offer her skills to building houses throughout the city, assuming they will provide options for those who have a lower income, and for those Gifted who are in need of shelter. I turn to Rosa and Helen. "What about the two of you?"

Helen shrugs, but her throat bobs as she swallows, belying her casualness. "I've still been able to make time to help victims identify their attackers." Her ability to read memories has often been useful to those who have suffered a crime. Helen's olive cheeks turn a light shade of pink, and I wonder if her relationship with Stratford City's law enforcement has changed. I wonder which victims—and which attackers—are getting the benefit of her time now that Lady M is in charge of managing it.

Rosa straightens in her seat, her thick black hair falling over one shoulder in a cascading wave. "I'm still seeing all my old clients in addition to my new ones." It sounds like a brag, but we can all see the dark circles under her eyes, the dullness in her normally luminescent golden-brown skin.

"You're only sleeping for four hours a night," Bianca points out. It's unlike her to speak so boldly, so I know she must be worried about Rosa. The two often work together, as Rosa's Gift allows her to suppress specific parts of the mind, including pain receptors.

Rosa opens her mouth to argue with Bianca, but I hold up my hand. "I don't want this to turn into a fight. We're all on the same side here. I just wanted to check in and see how you all were faring under this new system." I really want them all to tell me I am right. Not just because I want to be right, but because I need them to see what Lady M is doing to us, and to the club.

"Lady M isn't wrong, Cate." Meri finally speaks up, having bitten her tongue for far longer than normal. "We have been living here for mere pennies, bringing in such a scant amount that we can barely cover our own room and board."

"But we didn't come here for wealth," I argue. "We came here to have a safe home, and to help people when we can."

"We're still doing those things," Bianca says, though she doesn't sound totally convinced. "We all just needed a little shift in perspective."

I look around the table at the women I have considered my best friends for most of my life. Not one of them meets my eyes. "So you are all happy, then? With how everything is going?"

"I've been able to send money back to Talia, in addition to paying down my debt here," Meri tells me. "Things are still rough there." Her voice softens, and I know she is thinking of her home province. "It's different for you, Cate. You and Andra have been here for so long. You don't have the connections back in the provinces that the rest of us do. Of course we want to help our clients, but we also want to help our families."

The others nod, and it's a stab directly in the heart.

Because these women are my family. I hadn't realized they didn't consider me theirs.

I sit back in my chair. I had hoped to come here and gain some allies. Not that we're waging a war, but the truth of the matter is I don't trust Lady M and I certainly don't trust her motives.

But maybe I've been reading this situation all wrong. Maybe the one they should all be wary of is me.

BIANCA COMES TO my room a few hours later, an hour before Callum Reid is scheduled to arrive for his first lesson, to help me into my dress, pull the laces on the corset that transforms my already generous figure into nothing but ample curves.

"Have you seen Andra today?" I grip one of the posts of my bed as Bianca yanks on the ties at my back.

"Not today, but I've been busy seeing clients." There's a hint of something in Bianca's voice, something that makes me want to poke and prod, ask her if she still thinks Lady M is the best thing to ever happen to La Puissance, despite what she insisted on earlier today. Maybe away from the rest of the girls she'll be more open with her feelings.

But I don't push the topic just yet. Bianca wants to see the good in everyone.

Bianca finishes lacing me up and helps me step into one of my favorite costumes. The bodice is all gold glitter, sparkles covering my chest and torso, leading down to a frilly gold skirt that's short in the front and long in the back, showing off my shapely legs.

She tucks a gold-and-diamond-studded comb into my hair, which I've pulled up into an elegant updo. "Do you know how you're going to handle him?"

I shrug, as if I haven't been pondering this very question. I didn't tell anyone—even Andra—about my ulterior motives in meeting with Callum Reid. Everyone thinks he's coming to see me because I'm Lady Caterine and my reputation precedes me. No one knows my plan to make him fall in love and spill state secrets.

I have mere days to make Callum Reid trust me enough to reveal his plans for the Scotan killing period. If I were anyone else, I might be concerned. But once I have His Highness under my spell, once he finds release at least once in my presence, I can twist his emotions and make him trust me. I don't think it will take more than a day or two before I have Callum Reid positioned exactly where I want him: falling at my feet and head over heels in love. The thought sends a quickly-becoming-familiar shiver racing down my spine.

Bianca smooths the skirt of my dress. "I hope you know what you're doing."

"Of course I do." I push my shoulders back and my chest out, studying my reflection in the mirror above my dressing table. I line my lips with my signature red paint, letting it act as a shield of sorts.

Bianca blows me a kiss and leaves me alone with my thoughts. I might feel confident about my ability to manipulate Callum Reid, but I can't hide the irritating feeling in my chest that none of this is going to go how it should. I may not have the Gift of Sight like my sister, but my intuition is rarely wrong.

And speaking of my sister, I haven't seen her since yesterday morning. I haven't had the chance to tell her the good news—that in just a few days we'll be free of the control Lady M is trying to exert over us. I had been hoping to see her this morning, to see if she could give me any hints as to what might be headed my way. But I guess I'll have to go into this first meeting with Callum Reid without her guidance. The thought sends another flight of butterflies through my stomach, not the good kind.

A knock sounds on the door and I force myself to take several deep breaths before opening it, the expansion of my lungs almost spilling my breasts over the swooped neckline of my costume.

I let the costume act as a reminder. I'm playing a role here, and no matter how terrible or insufferable Callum Reid turns out to be, I must stay in character.

I open the door with that resolve strong in my gut. Only to have the wind knocked out of me.

Callum Reid stands in front of me, dressed in a classic tuxedo, perfectly tailored to his impressive frame. He's tall and broad, with the kind of arms that could sweep a woman off her feet. His copper-colored curls are longish and slightly disheveled, as if he's been running his hands through them; he twists a top hat in his hands. But it's his eyes that arrest my breath. A light, bright blue that doesn't hide his emotions: nerves, and a hint of excitement.

I find my voice first, though I can only manage two scant words. "It's you."

A sheepish, not-quite smile pulls on his lips. "I wasn't sure you would remember me."

Of course I remember. Not many handsome strangers turn down a night with me. Even fewer linger in my mind long after they've left the club. But I can't let him know how often he's been on my mind since our brief encounter. I force myself to stand up straight, give the impression of confidence even if I'm not feeling it in the moment.

I sweep my arm, gesturing for him to enter. "Welcome, Your Highness." At least he wasn't lying when he told me he wasn't a lord.

His near smile fades as he steps into the suite. "I shouldn't need to remind you that titles are no longer required, Lady Caterine." He twists my name in his mouth, as if to remind us both that it has always been meaningless, always been fake.

"Well then, welcome back to La Puissance, Mr. Reid."

He crosses to the center of the room, his eyes sweeping over every inch of the space, like he's on some kind of tactical mission, taking in the details, the sumptuous fabric draped across the bed and across the four posts surrounding it; the crimson chaise piled high with pillows; the small dining area and accompanying golden bar cart; the dressing table littered with headpieces and jewels and makeup. "Just Callum will suffice."

"As you wish, Your Highness." I give his title a twist of my own, smirking at the furrow of his brows. The man wears his emotions all over his face. Handsome and easy to read; perhaps this week will be fun after all. "So . . ." I perch myself on the edge of the bed, crossing my legs so the full expanse of my thigh is visible, up to the cut of my hip.

Callum's eyes trace that leg, from ankle to hip, and the tips of his ears turn a darker red than his hair. I will not even need two full days with him if he is this affected by the sight of my thigh.

He catches me catching him and I grin. "So, Your Highness, you are in need of some guidance? Of the sexual persuasion?"

He grimaces, the flush spreading to his neck and cheeks. I remind myself that he is a royal so I don't find his blush to be adorable. "I don't know that I would say I am in *need* of said guidance."

I cock my head to the side, exposing the long line of my neck. "Are you a virgin, Your Highness?"

"Callum. And no."

An unexpected bolt of jealousy hits me right in the chest, at the thought of Callum in someone else's bed. And before I can dismiss it, that itch returns, this time with waves of heat behind it.

He doesn't seem to be lying. I might not have him as vulnerable as I truly need him to be in order to manipulate his emotions, but I can usually tell when someone is hiding the truth.

I steady my breathing as I watch Callum Reid fight a war within himself. I watch every bit of it play out over his face and in his eyes. This man really needs to get better at shielding his emotions. But he comes to some sort of conclusion and turns to face me head-on, though he keeps his eyes averted. "I am aware that I will need to marry soon, my lady, and it is my wish to learn how to please my future wife. And I choose to learn from the best."

I push off the bed and close the distance between us. I find myself needing to be close to him, to breathe him in, to feel the heat of him. Surely because I know the mission at hand requires it. "You are certainly right about that, Your Highness. Are you ready to begin?"

"I would be lying if I said I wasn't just a little nervous." Bold of him to admit such a thing just a few minutes after meeting me.

"That's okay. I figured tonight we could start with something easy."

His blue eyes finally meet mine. "I would appreciate that."

Now I'm the one shoving down emotions. Those eyes. They have some kind of hypnotic power. They make me want to press my lips to his or breathe him in deeply or spill all my secrets. But I don't let myself look away. Instead, I drag a finger along the glittered edge of my neckline. Callum's eyes can't help but follow it as it traces a path, and I'm spared the fire of his direct eye contact.

So far this man seems nothing but genuine, and if I allowed myself to think about it, I might feel guilty about what I plan to do to him over the course of this week. Of course, this whole bumbling-shy-prince façade could be an act. I won't truly know until I bring him to climax.

Fortunately, I don't think that will be too difficult. Adding an extra swivel to my steps, I cross the room, bending over to check my lip paint in the mirror. "I do have a couple of rules before we begin."

"Of course." He swallows, his throat bobbing.

I want to rid us of the space between us and lick it.

The thought startles me and I keep my back to him, watching his reactions in the reflection. "I don't kiss on the mouth. And I won't touch you without your consent. I expect you to do the same."

"Of course, my lady," he repeats. The honorific I hear every day sounds wholly unique when it comes from him, affects me unlike any two words ever have before despite the teasing lilt of it.

"Good. We'll start with dancing." I spin around, letting my skirt swirl around my legs.

"Dancing?"

I close the distance between us, raising my hand, placing it right over his chest without making contact, until he nods his permission for me to touch him. "Dancing is an intimate act we perform fully clothed and a good precursor to the most intimate act we perform fully . . . not clothed." I let my gaze burn a trail down his chest, all the way down to his crotch.

But Callum doesn't so much as flinch. His hand finds my waist, settling into the curve. "I never thought of it like that."

I hold up my other hand, letting him curl his fingers around it. "Then you must have been dancing with the wrong partners."

"I don't doubt it, my lady."

10

CALLUM

THE POSITION WE hold is not foreign to me—dance lessons were required when I was younger, the skills seen as necessary for a man of my station.

But I have never had a dance quite like this one. Even standing still, this dance already feels like the most erotic moment of my life. And not to say that I haven't had erotic moments—I wasn't lying to Lady Caterine, I'm no virgin. There's just something about being in her embrace, her sunlight-through-whisky-colored eyes on mine, that hypnotizes me. She gets under my skin. Quite literally, in fact; my veins are on fire.

Lady Caterine flicks on her phonograph and steps back into my embrace, pressing our hips together as she guides me in the dance, a tango that is equal parts quick steps and sensual movement. I clutch her to me as we move around the small space of her suite, my steps never faltering. If she is surprised by my skill, she doesn't show it on her face, but she does pick up the tempo, throwing more complex moves into the mix as we continue to glide around the room.

"Tell me about yourself," she says, her calf curving around mine for half a second before flicking back to its original position.

"I'm sorry?" I keep my concentration on the movements, focusing on not missing a step, which is harder to do with her wrapped around me. Just that touch brought to mind an image of Lady Caterine's legs enveloping me, tight around my torso, our cores pressed together.

"It's one thing to learn to please a woman, but before you can please her, you have to win her over. So tell me about yourself. Woo me." She smiles, her steps never faltering, her breath never stuttering.

The truth is I don't usually have to get to know people, because most people I encounter already know plenty about me. Add to that, I'm not sure how much I can reveal to this woman. I'm supposed to be earning her trust and learning to trust her, but the truth is she is a Gifted with the power to manipulate emotions. I would be a fool to give her any information she can't find out herself.

"I have a younger sister" is what I finally come up with. It doesn't even occur to me that Lady Caterine has already met said sister, the haze in my brain keeping me from fully functioning.

She purses her lips, like she isn't quite sure how to respond to that. "Do you two get along?" she finally asks.

"We do. She annoys me to no end, of course, but we've become friends as we've grown older. She's the most formidable person I know. We lost our mother at a young age, and I know that can't have been easy for her, because it wasn't easy for me. I really admire the woman she's become." I bite my tongue to keep myself from expounding further. One seemingly simple question and I'm already spouting off my innermost thoughts, letting her see more of me than I should.

Lady Caterine's forehead creases and her eyes bore into me as if she can gaze into the very heart of me. "Sounds like you care for her very much."

"I do." I don't reveal any more than that, and the fact that I care for my sister shouldn't make me feel as vulnerable as it does. It should be expected that I care for her. I home in on the physical sensations surrounding me so I don't find myself trapped in the emotional. I slide my hand a little farther up Lady Caterine's back, until my fingers can stroke the bare skin between her shoulder blades, the need to feel her skin under my palm almost overwhelming. "Do you have any siblings, my lady?"

"A sister as well. We're twins." Her breath catches when my fingers graze her back.

I pretend I don't enjoy flustering her, somewhat mollified that I am not the only one affected. "You mean to tell me there are two of you?"

She laughs, her grip on my hand tightening. "Andra is the better of the two of us, in every way that matters."

Her laughter bolsters me further. "I don't think you give yourself enough credit, my lady."

"You don't know me very well, Your Highness."

I lower my head so my lips are a millimeter from the curve of her ear. "I would like to change that." The truth comes out of me unbidden, as if my brain has been swept away by the music and her eyes and the softness of her skin, like there is some force greater than the two of us dancing around the room. I forget who she is and why I'm here, forget my own name when she looks at me with raw desire flaming in her eyes.

She leans in, for just a second, letting my lips brush her delicate skin. Then she seems to come back to herself, putting space between us and reinforcing our original position. She studies me for another intense moment, as if she is trying to make sense of me. Something shifts, hardens in the depth of her honey-gold eyes.

It shakes me back to the present moment. My arms return to

their original hold, locking into place as if that could prevent me from falling under her spell again.

"You move well," she says as she spins behind me, her hand draping over my shoulder and resting on my chest.

I take her hand in mine, spinning her back into my embrace, determined to rise to her unspoken challenge. I will not let her see how the feel of her hand on my chest makes my heart jump. "I have always been a quick study, my lady."

"The tango is a dance of passion, and a dance of control." She presses her back to my front, sliding down my body slowly, her hands dragging over my thighs. Her grip on my legs is nothing short of tactical warfare. "Are you confident in your abilities on the dance floor, Your Highness?"

She's goading me and given the position of her hands at the moment, she knows the effect her body is having on mine.

I grasp her wrists, twirling her once before gently yanking her back to standing, noting her surprised gasp with just a hint of pride. While I have her in my control, I tug her closer, draping her arms over my shoulders, watching those golden eyes for any hint she is as affected by the closeness as much as I am.

She hides it well, but it's there. The flicker in her gaze, the catch in her breath.

It's a victory. And a reminder. I must keep my guard up; I must remain focused on the task at hand.

Her fingers tease the curls at the nape of my neck. She shifts her hips and a wicked smile pulls on her lips when she feels me, the hardness brought on by this erotic movement we're spinning across the floor. Her hands slide down my chest, to my waist.

I'm drunk on her, drunk on whatever this is between us. Her citrus scent and her closeness and the feel of her body beneath my hands. If her fingers moved lower, I wouldn't stop them. She's pulled me under her spell with nothing but a few spins and turns, a few measly minutes of conversation. Maybe I really am as weak as my father and sister have suggested.

The song ends and silence scratches across the room.

The breath returns to my lungs like I've been swimming under water and finally broke through to the surface.

I put a few steps of space between us, remembering Dom's warning and what I absolutely cannot let happen in this room. Remembering who Lady Caterine is and what she stands for. Remembering what she has the power to do, and why I can't let her get too close. Chances are she's already exerting that power, and I'm letting her. It's the only explanation for the urge I have to touch her, take her, make her mine.

She's breathing heavily too, her chest rising and falling like it's fighting to burst free from her corset. I can't look away. "Not bad for your first try." She turns away from me, starting the music from the beginning. "Let's go again."

It feels like another challenge, and I don't know why but I can't let her win. I chalk it up to the fact that if I am going to ever ask her for what I truly need from her, she needs to not only trust me but also respect me.

But only a fool would believe my actions in this suite have anything to do with the greater mission. All I see is her.

And so I pull her into my arms, leading her in the steps, our bodies pressed together until the room is hazy with sweat and wanting, until I feel almost frantic with needing her.

After our fourth tango, Caterine pulls away from me before the final note has flourished, heading straight for the bar. She pours herself a half-full glass of whisky and downs the whole thing in one gulp.

"Are you all right, my lady?" I try to keep the smugness out of my voice, but I don't try very hard. Whatever this undefined game is that we're playing, I've won.

"Fine," she says sharply. "I think that's enough for this evening."

"Not even going to offer me a drink?" The balance between us seems to have shifted, and I can't lie—I'm enjoying seeing her caught off guard.

She turns away from me, tension visible in the set of her shoulders. It takes a minute, but her stance softens and when she spins back around, it's like I'm being greeted by a different person, her mask smoothly settling into place.

"My apologies. Pick your poison, Your Highness."

"Whisky, my lady."

She pours the drink and hands it to me. Our fingers brush, and the spark makes her grimace, but she hides it.

We clink glasses and sip, and she watches me from underneath her thick lashes.

"Where did you learn to dance like that?" She sidles closer to me, never dropping eye contact.

I swirl the whisky in my glass, focusing on the golden-brown liquor so I don't drown in her eyes. "I took many dance lessons when I was younger. All part of the required training for the next in line for the throne."

She arches one eyebrow but holds back the sarcastic retort I can read in her eyes. "What do you hope for the future? What are your goals, Your Highness? Now that you're no longer in line for the throne."

Between the alcohol and her eyes and the feel of her body underneath my hands, I forget myself and give her another honest answer. "I think I could have been a good leader, my lady. Could be still. I'm sure you have many preconceived notions about me, based on who I am and where I come from, but I want to help people. I care about creating a society that is more equal than the one we are currently living in."

She sucks in a breath, and I realize immediately the mistake I've made, the possible future I might have just hinted at. Lady Caterine doesn't know my father wants me to kill him. It would be dangerous for anyone to have insight into our plans.

Suddenly the entire evening feels like a mistake. I'm opening myself, breaking down walls I don't break down for anyone, and all for a Gifted who has the ability to manipulate emotions. Dom said her Gift can only be used when finding sexual release, but maybe she was wrong. Maybe Lady Caterine is nudging into my brain as we speak. It's the only explanation, really, as to why I can't shield myself from her.

I swallow the remainder of my drink, setting the empty glass down on the table much harder than I've intended, annoyed that she is taking advantage of my openness and furious with myself for letting her. "I should be going."

I fumble my hat and coat as I throw open the door.

"Will you be back tomorrow?" she calls after me.

I spin around, just outside the doorway. I want to tell her no, but I can't. "You will see me again tomorrow, my lady."

She flashes me a soft smile, and I'm filled with the urge to press my lips to hers.

But that's not allowed, even if it were advisable, which it most definitely is not.

"I'll see you tomorrow, Your Highness."

I all but sprint away from her, out of the club, into my carriage, banging on the roof so the driver knows to hurry the hell up.

Tonight I will fall asleep dreaming about the way my hand fit the curve of her hip and how her fingers trailed along the nape of my neck.

But tomorrow night I will need to do something different, get my head on straight before I even think of stepping foot back in the club. She might have infiltrated my mind tonight, but I won't let it happen again.

Or this woman may very well be the death of me.

My dearest Harry,

I know these past few years of our marriage haven't been easy. I was unsure when Diana moved me out of the club, but even though I miss you with every fiber of my being, I do believe it was the best decision. I've learned so much living here, and I've grown as well.

I am happy here, but I'm happiest when you come visit me. Being with you, Harry, has always brought out the best in me. And it can get lonely here all by myself sometimes.

I know it may not be the way we envisioned it when we were children, but we did always plan to have a family one day, and I think I am ready to become a mother. I've harnessed my Gift and am able to control it now, and I want nothing more than to bring a child into this world. Our child, Harry. With your hair and my eyes and all the love we could give her.

I know you will try to tell me the laws forbid it, but I am safe here in Scola. They haven't prevented Gifted pregnancies for years now. I am protected, and I won't let anything happen to me, or our baby.

It is time. I'm ready. I look forward to your next visit.

All my love,

Grecia

11

CATE

THE MINUTE THE door closes behind him, I let out the deep breath I've been holding in.

I reach for the ties of my corset, needing my lungs at full capacity. I practically tear the clothes from my body, slipping into a robe and collapsing into one of the chairs around the table. My skin is on fire, but the cool comfort of the silk robe does little to soothe it.

I look down at my hip, thinking for a minute that his hand might have left some kind of imprint with how hot his skin burned against my waist. I could feel the heat even through the layers of fabric cinching me together. The heat between us was everywhere. I find myself in the arms of a new partner frequently, and many times the attraction I convey is feigned. But I didn't have to fake anything once Callum Reid swept me into his arms, pressed his hips against mine. Let me feel how much the attraction was reciprocated.

And even worse than the attraction, he told the truth. When he spoke about his sister. When I asked him what he saw for the future, and he spoke about equality for the people, he told the truth.

The air around us had turned a peaceful blue, the same damn color as his stupid eyes. He revealed a bit of himself in that moment, allowed himself to be vulnerable, and with that exposure showed me an honest piece of himself. I can only twist and manipulate emotions after my partner has achieved release, when the vulnerability is thick enough for me to latch on to, but when a person shares an honest bit of themself with me, I can discern the truth of their words and their intentions. And Callum Reid's intentions are as pure as the blue of the ocean waters surrounding Avon.

Not that it matters. The man may have kind eyes and an impressive bulge, but that doesn't take away from my main goal here. Get enough money to buy out our contracts, get the information Lady M requires, and make sure my sister is safe. Callum Reid is nothing more than a means to an end. The man may seem charming and kind, but it was under his father's rule that my sister and I were abandoned and abused and neglected. Which means I need to keep my guard up. I need to treat him like any other client and keep him at arm's length. Especially since I already know I plan on betraying his trust.

I wish the thought didn't already turn my stomach with shame.

I POUND ON Andra's door the next morning, my worry transforming to fear the longer it takes her to answer. I haven't seen her in almost two days, and I can't even remember the last time we went so long without a conversation.

My worst suspicions are confirmed when Andra finally opens the door.

It's only been two days, but in that time, my sister appears to have aged ten years.

"What in the bloody hell is going on?" I demand, taking her

firmly but gently by the elbow and guiding her to a seat on her chaise longue.

She shrugs out of my grip. "I'm fine, Cate."

The dark circles under her eyes, the way her thick golden hair hangs lank and greasy in front of her face, and the weight she seems to have lost would say the opposite.

I sit next to her, placing a comforting arm around her and softening my tone. "Andra. You know there is no use in lying to me. What has happened? Where have you been? I've been worried sick."

She rests her head on my shoulder. "I've been with Lady M."

My whole body tenses, ready to spring to a fight and cut anyone and everyone down, but I fight my every instinct, remaining calm for Andra's sake. "What have you been doing with Lady M?"

"She's been having me read. Multiple times a day."

I force myself to loosen my grip on Andra's arm. "What has she been asking you to See?"

"Everything I can about the election."

I suck in a breath. Between my spying and my sister's visions, it seems like Lady M—and maybe even Harold—is preparing for something big. "She isn't giving you time to recover in between sessions?" It's not really a question because the answer is clear on Andra's face.

"It's not just that." She hesitates, pulling away from me, putting space between us.

I grip her hand. "Andra. You know you can tell me anything."

Her eyes, the mirror of my own, meet my gaze and so much fear is layered in them it steals my breath. "Something is happening to my visions when I'm with Lady M."

"What do you mean?"

"They're stronger, somehow? I've never felt anything like it. It's like they're being amplified. I See more and the visions are clearer and more specific, but each reading also takes more from me. I'm completely drained after each one."

My brow furrows. I've never heard of any Gifted's power being amplified before. I don't even know how such a thing would be possible. I do know that Lady M is using and abusing my sister's Gift, and the sooner I can get her away from here, the better. I've been avoiding the truth—that we will need to leave the club, escape before word of Andra's Gift gets out. It's heartbreaking, but it's time to face it.

"Well, I have some good news." I tuck a strand of oily hair behind her ear. "I've taken on a special client, and I'll be earning enough money this week to buy out both of our contracts, with enough left over for us to move away and start fresh somewhere else."

Andra doesn't react with the overwhelming joy I expect. "You want to leave La Puissance?"

"No, of course I don't. But you know how I feel about Lady M, and that was before I knew what she was putting you through the last two days. She can't be trusted, and these contracts are bordering on diabolical." I take her hand in mine. "Andra, we need to get out of here while we can. Something is not right."

Andra turns away, her gaze on something far off that neither of us can see. "The things I've been Seeing, Cate." A shiver runs through her.

I tighten my grip, debating whether to ask for more details. But the light in her eyes is so dim, I don't want to cause her pain by reliving what may be the darkest of her visions. "All the more reason to leave. I don't think La Puissance is going to be safe for us for much longer."

Judging by the state of my sister, it's not safe right now. But we'll just have to tough it out for a few more days. We've survived worse.

Which means I need to do whatever I have to do to get the information Lady M needs from Callum Reid. Despite what his eyes and the feel of his hand on my waist might do to me, the man is a mark and nothing more.

CALLUM ARRIVES SO late that night, for a minute I think he might not be coming. The thought brings a weird combination of relief and disappointment. I need his money and his information. But I'm not sure what's worse: continuing to get close to him as I know I must, or the eventual betrayal that will come from said closeness.

A knock sounds on the door just a few minutes before I plan to write him off for good and when I open it, he stands in front of me with a sheepish smile on his face. A smile that could very well break down the defenses of a weaker woman.

Luckily I'm not a weaker woman.

"I apologize for my tardiness."

I gesture for him to enter. "I wouldn't have been surprised if you decided not to come back."

"Oh?" He hangs his hat and coat on the rack near the door, shooting me a curious glance over his broad shoulders.

"I know how hard it is for men to admit when they need help with something." I'm purposefully pushing buttons, or looking for buttons, rather, testing to see if he'll give me some kind of adverse reaction. So far Callum Reid is perfect—too perfect—surely he must have a flaw, and tonight I hope to find it. If the man is an asshole like the other monarchs, turning him over to Lady M won't be so bad. "Especially asking for help with something as delicate as intimacy." It's a reminder to both of us as to why we're supposedly here.

"I need help with a lot things, my lady. It would be foolish to believe otherwise."

I close my eyes for half a second, using the brief respite from his earnest face to remind myself what the end goal is here.

"Shall we dance?" Callum unfastens the buttons at the cuffs of his sleeves, rolling up his shirt to bare his forearms, covered with a light smattering of freckles and golden copper hair and roped with muscle. He's dressed more casually tonight, in black pants and a black shirt covered with a red brocade vest.

And how am I supposed to focus on finding his flaws with forearms like that. I swallow thickly. "We won't be dancing tonight, actually."

"What's the plan, then?" There's a hint of fear in his eyes.

That fear bolsters me. I have the upper hand here. Callum Reid is already under my thumb; all I have to do is keep him there. I pull back my shoulders. "Undress me, Your Highness."

The color drains right out of his face, leaving him even paler than he was before. "I'm sorry?"

"That's tonight's lesson. Undress me."

"Is that really necessary?" He asks the question like I'm not gifting him with an opportunity plenty of people have paid good money for.

I cross the room, landing right in front of him, tilting my chin up to meet his solid blue gaze. "Ladies' garments are tricky, and nothing kills the mood faster than having to call a servant in to help remove your partner's clothes."

"Can't you just explain how to do it?" His voice rises in pitch, and I wish I didn't find his hesitation so charming.

"You are going to have to put your hands on me at some point, Your Highness." I spin around, my back to his front, peeking at him over my shoulder. "Now, take off my clothes."

He sighs and I don't feel his hands on me for a full minute. But then his fingers take to the buttons lining the back of my dress, popping each one quickly, like he has done this in the past.

I don't know why the thought of his hands undressing other women bothers me, but it does.

"Good. Now, it's important to remember that undressing can be a form of intimacy all on its own. Slide the dress off of me and let your hands explore the skin that's revealed as you go. Take your time, make this part of the seduction." I'm grateful I don't have to watch him while I deliver my directive, certain that one glance from those eyes or a hint of a smile on his perfect mouth might send me into a state of combustion.

He hesitates again, but then his warm hands land on my upper back, slipping underneath the silky fabric of my dress and sliding it off my shoulders. His fingers linger on the trio of freckles on my right shoulder and I have to bite my lip to stifle a gasp.

I'm even more grateful he can't see my reaction—a reaction I shouldn't even be having. But the gentle trace of his fingers over my bare arms sends a burst of heat through me.

The dress pools around my hips, the swell of them preventing the fabric from falling fully to the floor.

I peek over my shoulder again. Callum's eyes are locked on my bare upper back like it's the most erotic thing he's ever seen. And surely it can't be, unless he was lying to me about having previous partners and is somehow just really good with buttons, and yet I almost want it to be. Reaching back, I take his hands in mine, guiding them to my hips.

His thumbs stroke the lace-covered skin there and I have to hold in a gasp. He pushes the fabric of my dress down and I kick it away from my feet.

I turn to face him, dressed now in just my corset and panties, garter belt, hose, and shoes. A fair number of items providing not a whole lot of coverage.

Gently pushing Callum back so he is seated on the chaise, I lift one foot and place it on his thigh. Channeling the character I only slip into for the most offensive of my clients, I fit a mask firmly over my face, determined not to let him see me sweat. I point at the buckle of my strappy gold shoe, afraid that if I open my mouth to speak, nothing will come out. He obliges, slipping the heel from my foot.

I cover one of his hands with mine, dragging it slowly up the curve of my calf until it's resting just below the edge of my hose.

When I pull my hand from his, he drags his fingers higher up my leg, landing on the dagger sheathed at my thigh.

"Do you always wear this?" He runs a finger over the hilt, tracing the intricate patterns carved into the metal, lingering on the ruby-red gem, and my skin burns.

"Sort of a necessity in my line of work."

He tilts his head up so his eyes meet mine. "How often do your clients try to take things too far?" There's no judgment in his question, only curiosity, and maybe a hint of anger.

"Not often anymore. There are strict rules here at the club. And I have a reputation." I flash him a wicked grin.

He chuckles. "I'm sure you do." He traces along the leather line of the sheath, circling my thigh before returning his fingers to where I'd originally placed them. "Do you perform often in the main salon? In the shows?"

"I used to, though now I stick to just one number an evening. I love being onstage." I don't know why I answer him, and so honestly, except the way his fingers trace delicate swirls on my thigh seems to have hypnotized me. "Unclip here," I instruct in a soft whisper, pointing to my garter. "And here."

I don't have to guide him any further after that.

His hands slide the delicate hose down to my ankle, pulling my foot free before gently placing it back on the floor. "If you love it, why only one performance a night?" He reaches for my other leg, performing the same ministrations and leaving me breathless once again.

"You are a quick study," I say, bringing him back to his feet.

He grunts and I want to swallow the sound.

His hands still, as if he knows I'm ignoring his question.

"My time is better used elsewhere these days. Working here used to be more than a job, but things have changed lately." I need to stop talking, stop sharing these unbidden thoughts, but those blue eyes pull me in and I find myself wanting to tell him everything.

"You enjoy what you do?" he asks without a hint of judgment.

"For the most part. At least, I did." When I was actually helping my clients instead of just milking them for every cent. "What about you, Your Highness? What occupies your days?" I take his hand in mine, guiding it to the laces of my corset.

I immediately realize it was a mistake to wear a corset that laces in the front instead of the back, as now I have to watch as he toys with the ribbons. I have to breathe in his woodsy sage scent and not let it show how much I want to bury my nose in his chest and inhale.

His eyes meet mine and they are blazing as hot as my cheeks. I can't wait to be released from the fabric because surely the corset is the reason I can no longer catch my breath.

"I used to spend my days preparing to lead the Scotan province." He tugs on the end of the bow and begins maddeningly slowly releasing the laces, never removing his eyes from mine. "Meetings with members of the community, the occasional diplomatic trip to visit other provinces, learning everything I could about my land

and my people so I could hopefully be an effective and compassionate leader."

His answer surprises me. Not because the information itself is unexpected, but because Callum Reid seems to genuinely care about what was to be his future leadership role. And the air around us is a clear blue. He is once again being truthful, open, and honest.

But if he did spend so much time studying the state of the Scotan province, then surely he knows about the atrocities some of his citizens face. Sure, Scota may not have people starving in the streets, but just because they are provided with a place to live doesn't make it a good or safe place to live. The Gifted in Scota may not be hunted and killed like they have been in some of the other provinces, but that certainly doesn't mean they are treated fairly. And if he knows about the places like the orphanage Andra and I were forced to flee, where we were overworked and underfed, why doesn't he do anything about it? Unless he's not the compassionate man he's pretending to be.

Somehow, I find that thought difficult to accept.

I focus my attention on the deft way his fingers pull at the strings of the lacy fabric, using my doubts about his character as a shield. Neither of us breathes until the ribbon finally springs free and the corset parts. I catch it before it falls, tossing it to the side.

Callum's eyes are no longer on mine. No, they trace over every inch of exposed skin, leaving a trail of fire burning in their wake. Over my collarbone and down the dip of my waist and the curve of my hips and the softness of my stomach. Along the edge of the one tiny piece of fabric still left on my body. Back up to my voluptuous breasts, heavy and aching, my nipples peaked.

His hand rises, like he might reach out to cup one of my breasts, stroke his thumb over my nipple. And fuck if I don't want him to. If I don't *need* him to.

Instead I arch a brow in a silent challenge and his hands drift lower, his thumbs hooking in the edge of the lace, dragging my panties down my legs until I am fully bared before him.

He takes a step back, seemingly forgetting the chaise is behind him. The move knocks him into a seated position, bringing him eye level with the patch of golden curls at the apex of my thighs.

My eyes flutter as I think about his mouth finding me there.

I force myself to take in the person in front of me, remembering who he is and why he's here.

I put some much-needed space between us, crossing to the bed and perching on the edge, ignoring the urge to slide onto his lap. The urge to cover his mouth with mine. I ache for his touch in a way I've never experienced before, but I cannot let my body take control of my brain. Crossing my legs, I level Callum with a stare. "Ready for part two?"

"No," he chokes out.

I laugh, and it's genuine. "Stand up, Your Highness."

He obeys and my eyes fall directly to his pants and the very clear evidence of how much tonight's lesson is affecting him.

"Woo me. And if you do a good job, I'll take care of that for you." I let my eyes linger on the massive erection straining the bonds of his pants. I need him vulnerable again if I'm to find out the kind of information Lady M is expecting from me, and taking care of the impressive-looking bulge should give me the chance I need. The sooner I can be done with Callum Reid, the better.

His hand flies to his cock, as if to hide it. "That won't be necessary."

"I'm sorry?" There is no way this man is rejecting my advances for the second time.

"I don't need you to . . . that is to say, I'm perfectly capable . . . I won't be needing those services from you, my lady." His hand presses hard on his erection, like he can't help but try for a little relief.

I uncross my legs, watching his eyes linger on what I've revealed. "Letting you leave this room looking like that would be very bad for business, Your Highness. Think of my reputation."

He grimaces, dropping his hand. "I appreciate that, but I will not be swayed. I'm here to learn how to please a woman. I won't be distracted by seeking pleasure for myself."

My seductive smile freezes on my face.

He doesn't want me to touch him? This has never happened to me. Ever. Which can only mean one thing.

He knows what I can do, the kind of relief I can provide for my clients. Dom hinted that there might be a need for my more innate talents, but she never came right out and asked about using my Gift. But clearly Callum already knows what I can do. My abilities aren't exactly a secret, but I also am very choosy about who I share them with. Before Lady M came along, I only used to twist the emotions of those with whom I'd built a relationship, one of mutual trust and respect, and for purposes I found worthy. The men I've been manipulating for money to try to earn my way out of my contract don't know what I can do when they find release with me—they wouldn't be fucking me if they did. They are merely interested in one night in Lady Caterine's bed, some of them probably more interested in bragging rights than in me.

All my hackles raise to high alert, any connection we might have forged over the course of our conversations forgotten. I'm not sure how he was able to manipulate the truth I could see in his words, but clearly he has found some way to lie to me and make me believe it. And that makes him dangerous.

"What are you hiding, Callum Reid?"

His eyes dart around the room nervously, but they keep coming back to me. I'm naked on the bed before him, how could they not? "I'm not sure what you mean, my lady."

I tilt my head to the side, studying the man before me. From everything I've discerned, Callum Reid is good and honorable—my initial impression from Dom confirmed by his words and his honesty. Yet circumstances haven't exactly been kind to him. As much as I hate to admit it, Lady M may be right about Callum's intentions when it comes to his father. What else could bring him here other than an act so terrible he can hardly bear the weight of it?

"Do you know what I can do? What my Gift is?" I ask baldly.

His hesitation is less than a second, and yet it still manages to make him look utterly defeated. "Yes, I do."

"Is that why you came to me?"

Callum crosses the room to my privacy screen, grabbing my robe and handing it to me before returning to sit on the chaise. "I can't think straight with you looking like that." He flashes me a sheepish smile.

I fasten the robe around my waist and stay perched on the edge of the bed, leaving space between us. So we both can think straight. My head is a jumble. Nothing I know about Callum Reid is making any sort of sense.

Callum sighs, leaning forward, his elbows resting on his knees. "It was my sister's idea."

"Have I worked with her before?" I never forget a client, especially not one as beautiful as the princess, so I'm well aware Dom has never graced my sheets. But how much of our meeting did she relay to her brother?

"Not that I know of. But she heard what you can do, and she thought you might be able to help me."

"Help you with what, Your Highness?" I have a pretty solid guess, but I want to see how much he is willing to reveal. How much he actually trusts me. If he isn't going to let me touch him, then I'll need to find other ways to get him to open up to me, other ways to make him reveal himself.

"I can't tell you yet." He looks up, his gaze meeting mine. "But I promise I will. I wanted to spend this time with you before so you could get to know me, and so I could get to know you." He hesitates.

"Because you don't trust me?"

"Yes."

His frank admission makes me suck in a breath. "Because I'm Gifted?"

"My mother . . . when she died . . . a Gifted healer came. My father asked her to save my mother. She was a good woman, a fair and kind queen, but the Gifted refused to help her; instead she sat there and watched my mother suffer. A couple of hours later she was dead. The so-called healer seemed happy to see her pass." His mouth turns down and his eyes cloud with grief and, if I'm not mistaken, something that looks like shame.

"And so you have held that against every Gifted you've encountered since?" I try not to take it personally. At least Callum seems to have a good reason for his prejudice, just as the Gifted had a good reason to not save a royal life.

"Yes." He has the respect to look me in the eye.

"Do you believe the Gifted should regain our rights and privileges, Your Highness?" I force myself to deliver the question without choking on the words. It's an indignity to have to ask if I deserve to be treated the same as everyone else.

His hesitation is long. "I believe that regulating the Gifted has kept this country and its citizens safe for many years."

I laugh, though I find nothing humorous in his response. "I doubt many Gifted feel like they have been safe. But I guess our feelings don't matter as much, do they?"

At least the shame that falls over his face seems genuine. "I . . . I . . ."

"I am sorry for your loss, Your Highness." The words may sound like a common platitude, but I find myself genuinely meaning them, despite his admission. Perhaps I should return his honesty and openness with a bit of my own. But I owe this man nothing. He may need something from me, but he isn't willing to offer me basic human rights in exchange.

Callum rises, his strong thighs flexing beneath the fabric of his pants. "Perhaps it would be better if we ended our agreement." He must notice the look of fear I'm not quick enough to hide because despite his revelation, I still need him, need this week, if I am going to be able to clear my contract and put distance between my sister and Lady M. "You will still receive your money."

Unfortunately, money isn't going to be enough. I promised Lady M information, and with the way she is currently abusing my sister, I know she is not going to let us go without it. There is no way to escape La Puissance or Lady M's hold over us without more from Callum Reid.

I didn't make much of Lady M's request to make Callum fall in love with me, but it may be the only way. If he walks out the door now, nothing about my situation, or Andra's situation, will truly change. But I would be lying if I didn't acknowledge that there's something more worrisome happening in my heart as I take in Callum's words. The fear of never seeing him again—it chokes the breath from my lungs.

Which is ridiculous. It's been two days.

And yet I meet Callum at the door, placing a soft hand on his forearm. I let the neckline of my robe slip and fill my eyes, and my words, with honest hopefulness. "Please don't go, Your Highness. My services have been paid for, and I intend to fulfill them. I *want* to fulfill them."

"My lady, I . . ."

"Caterine is fine."

"Caterine."

I have to close my eyes for a second, the combination of my name in his mouth and the sincerity in his eyes too much for me to handle. "I would like to continue our lessons, Your Highness, and I would like to continue to get to know you. The real you. If you are amenable."

"Because you have been paid?"

I shrug coyly, fingering the buttons of his brocade vest, shifting from honest to flirtatious, moving back to safer territory. "Because I was enjoying our time together." I let my gaze drift lower. "And I think you were too."

"I think we both know I don't need sex lessons." His hand finds the dip in my waist and he pulls me closer, as if he can't help himself.

"That only persuades me further, Your Highness."

His fingers tighten. "Please don't call me that."

My hand travels up over the hard planes of his chest, wrapping around his neck. "Let us continue our lessons, Callum, let us spend this time together so, should the need ever arise for my other services, you already feel comfortable coming to me for help." It's all I can say without giving up the whole game. Maybe I can find a way for us both to come out of this with what we want. I can alleviate his guilt and make him see that he's wrong about the Gifted.

Maybe I can still get what I need from him.

"You would be willing to help me in the future?" He lowers his head, his breath warming my neck. "If I ever needed you, Caterine?"

All I would have to do is turn my head an inch to the right and my lips could find his. I long for the contact, ache for it. The thought of pressing my lips to his sends a shiver racing up my spine, that same shiver embedding itself under my skin until the urge to feel his mouth on mine is almost overwhelming.

"Will you let me touch you? Do you trust me enough for that?" I drag a single finger along the hard length of him, the bulge that hasn't softened, despite the heaviness of our conversation. "Not tonight, necessarily, but eventually?"

"I will." He covers my hand with his, pressing my palm to his thickness, his eyes fluttering closed.

"So you will continue with our lessons, then?" I run the tip of my nose along the exposed length of his neck, breathing him in. Every inch of him is intoxicating.

"I will, my lady." His head turns, his lips skimming the curve of my shoulder, over my trio of freckles. "And you will consider helping me when I need it?"

I can't help but feel I'm going to regret this. "I will."

I see the way the two of them interact, and it worries me. The way they are constantly reaching for each other, the way they seem to orbit around one another. But perhaps what is more worrisome is the way they behave when they are apart. I have observed both of them, together and separately, and there is no longer a doubt in my mind.

Harry and Grecia are Bonded, and it's a strong one.

I fear what might happen when they produce a child together. It could be our salvation. Or our downfall.

—EXCERPT FROM THE JOURNAL OF DIANA BRAHAN

12

CALLUM

I WAKE UP TANGLED in my sheets, sweaty and aching and so hard it's bordering on painful. I dreamed of Caterine; how could I not? The feel of her soft skin under my hands, her sharp intake of breath when I pulled her into my embrace. The knowing in her eyes when I hinted at why I might need her in the future, and the way she accepted it without pushing for more.

I wrap my hand around my cock. It only takes a few strokes and the thought of her perched naked on the edge of the bed before the orgasm overtakes me. I come hard and quick, Caterine's eyes, the curves of her breasts, the smooth line of her hips, in my head.

A knock on my door interrupts the lingering images of her. I hastily cover myself with the sheets. "Give me a minute!"

Once it becomes clear that whoever my visitor is plans to stay behind the door until I give permission, I spring from the bed, throwing on the first items of clothing I can find—an old cotton shirt and pants that have seen better days.

I find my uncle on the other side, and for once, he doesn't seem overly concerned with my wardrobe.

He raises a single eyebrow. "May I come in?"

I half-heartedly attempt to tuck in my shirt, gesturing for him to enter. "Of course."

He sits in one of the armchairs before the fire and I sink into the seat across from him, running a hand through my hair so it doesn't look like I just woke up. Alex has likely been up for hours, doing something productive, while I've been up in bed, fantasizing about a woman who has no place occupying my mind the way she has.

Alex leans forward, placing a leather-bound notebook on the table between us. "I know our last conversation got more heated than either of us would have liked."

I nod, acknowledging the sentiment, but not willing to apologize for it.

"I know what Dom has planned for you, Cal, and I know why you are resistant to it. Just like I know that you must become the candidate who represents the Scotan province."

I am not surprised my sister confided in Alex. I'm more surprised by his faith in me. "Even after everything I said about the Gifted, you still believe that to be true?"

"I do." He laces his fingers together. "Not because I agree with you on the matter but because I think you will have an open heart and an open mind when it is needed most."

"I do not see how my opinions will change, Uncle." Even as I say the words, I know they ring false. Lady Caterine has already managed to break me down, to sway me.

Alex nudges the book to my side of the table. "This belonged to your mother."

I take the book, my curiosity too strong to feign indifference. I open the emerald-green cover and find pages and pages of her handwriting, neat and precise, swirling with loops and flourishes that are at once fanciful and practical. "I do not see how Mother's diary is going to change anything."

"It's not her diary." Alex sighs, and he runs a hand through his hair. The motion is a mirror image of my earlier one, a sign of his frustration with me. Perhaps it's a genetic tic. "Your mother wrote many articles for the *Scotan Herald* while she was alive."

I nod, flipping through the pages, not reading any of the words, too transfixed on the idea of her hands touching the paper, leaving her mark for us. I remember Mother penning opinion pieces for the paper, though I was too young to ever read them when they were published.

"Your mother had strong opinions about the way the Gifted were treated, are treated, and she made those opinions known."

For a second, I want to believe that my opinions are being reinforced by my mother's beliefs, but then one of her headlines catches my eye. *It is well beyond time to reinstate the full rights and privileges of the Gifted citizens of Scota.*

"When she died, she was fighting for their rights, if not across all of Avon, then at least here in Scota."

I raise my eyes from the damning words, meeting my uncle's gaze. "And that still wasn't enough to save her. She went out of her way to fight for the Gifted, and they couldn't be bothered to do the same for her." If Alex thinks this is the way to sway me to his side, he is sorely mistaken.

He shakes his head sadly. "I had a feeling you might say that." He pushes back his chair and stands. "I'll stop trying to convince you that all should not suffer for the sins of an individual."

I start to hand him back the book.

"Keep it. Maybe your mother can get through to you." He slams the door of my suite behind him as he leaves.

His disappointment stings, but it's becoming a familiar sensation. I seem to be letting down everyone in my family lately.

I toss the book to the side, heading for my bathing chamber to wash up. I don't have plans to see Lady Caterine for several more hours, so I dress casually, but in clean clothes at least.

I vow to not give the book another thought, having no need to read the words my mother wrote in good faith, only to be betrayed by the very people she was defending.

But it calls to me, from the minute I step back into the sitting area.

My mother wrote in this book, filled it with her thoughts and opinions, in her own hand. I'll never again get to hear her speak to me, but I have her words, thoughts she might have discussed with me had she been able to watch me grow older.

The temptation, the need, is too great. I reach for the book, opening to the first page.

At first, it is difficult. I can almost hear her delivering these impassioned arguments, as if she were right here in the room with me. She manages to take this topic, one so sensitive, that leaves people so divided, and make it seem relatable and relevant. Her voice lingers as I fill my head with her thoughts.

> What right do we have to deny these women their right to a free life?
>
> I, for one, can never stand by the sanctioned killing of women who have done nothing but exist.
>
> Being a mother is the greatest thing I have ever done, my children the best gift I have received; how can I stand by and deny others the immense privilege of motherhood?

It isn't until a drop lands on one page, smudging the long-dried ink, that I realize I'm crying.

My mother considered me and Dom her greatest gift, and yet here I am, working against everything she believed in. Shame washes over me. I don't have to imagine what my mother would think of me in this moment. I already know.

I slam the book closed, partly to protect the pages from further damage, partly because I do not know if I can stand to read anymore.

My mother had a clear vision for Scota, for a united Avon. A vision she felt so strongly about, I have no doubt she would have given her life for it.

My skin begins to burn, with fear or with anger, I'm not completely sure what is driving me. I do know, somewhere deep in my bones, that there is only one way to soothe the ache.

The carriage ride to La Puissance is bumpy and seems to drag on for hours longer than necessary. My mother's words tumble in my mind until I know only one thing for certain: I must be the one to kill my father. I must be the one to lead Avon.

I must learn to trust the Gifted.

When I finally arrive at the club, the lobby is nearly vacant, only a few residents milling around. It looks different in the light of day, less opulent and more gaudy. No one rushes over to entice me, and the silence rings in my ears. We're outside normal business operating hours, but I'm hoping Dom spent enough money for them not to apply to me.

Caterine opens her door midsentence, like she was anticipating someone else. Someone who is clearly not me. I tamp down the jealousy sparking in my chest at the thought of her waiting for someone else to come to her chambers.

"Callum. I wasn't expecting you until this evening." She glances down at her clothing, which is remarkably similar to my own, cotton pants and a loose-fitting shirt. Her face is completely bare of makeup and her golden waves are loosely braided, hanging down her back.

She's never looked more beautiful.

I swallow thickly, pushing away the urge to sweep her into my arms and bury myself in her. "I'm sorry to just barge in, my lady."

"You did pay for an entire week of my time." She leans in the doorway, and it doesn't escape my notice that she does not invite me in. "Unfortunately, I was just on my way out."

"Oh?" She isn't dressed to be meeting clients, and Dom told me that one condition of their agreement was that Caterine entertain only me. "May I come with you?"

She raises one eyebrow. "You don't even know where I'm going."

I shrug. "I do not much care. As long as you are open to a little conversation along the way?"

She studies me for a second, and I must pass whatever test she is silently giving me because she nods, ducking back into her room to grab a canvas bag before joining me in the hallway, closing the door behind her.

I follow her down the back stairs and out onto the street. "My carriage is out front, if we are going somewhere far."

She laughs, leading me to a stable where two horses are saddled and ready. "I don't think it is wise to bring your carriage with us, Your Highness."

"Were you expecting someone else?" I gesture to the second horse as she mounts the first.

Her eyes darken. "Andra, my sister, usually comes with me, but she isn't feeling well."

I mount the waiting horse, his black coat shining under the midday sun. "I hope she gets better soon."

"Me too," she mutters, spurring her horse into a trot.

I follow in her wake as she leads us out of Stratford City. I haven't spent nearly enough time in Avon's capital, and so I try to absorb as many details as I can as we ride. Many of the city's roads are bustling, outdoor marketplaces and food vendors lining the cobbled streets. Just as many alleyways are dark and dingy, littered with trash. Beggars occasionally reach out a hand, but we are traveling too fast for me to offer much help. I make a mental note to bring more coins with me on my next journey to La Puissance.

If I am going to lead this country, I need to know it. And the people need to know me.

I am somewhat surprised when Caterine turns down the path I take to get home to Scota. I draw my horse next to hers. "Where are we going?"

She shoots me a look, nudging her horse to go faster now that we've left the city behind and have open country road and rolling green hills in front of us. "You'll see," she shouts over her shoulder.

I dig my heels in to keep up. The wind is icy on my face, the air cooling the farther into Scota we travel. It's bracing but also helps clear my head, and I'm grateful for it.

We ride for maybe two hours before coming to a stop in front of a stone building that looks like a strong wind might destroy the whole thing. I thought my travels had taken me to every corner of Scota, but I am unfamiliar with this location and which family might reside in this home made of crumbling gray stone. A light rain mists the air, and it lends to the feeling of hopelessness blanketing the structure.

Caterine jumps off her mount, tying the reins to a post before bringing over a bucket of water for the horses to drink from. She is clearly familiar with this property and the people who reside here. I wonder if this is where she grew up.

I tie my horse off next to hers. "Where are we, Caterine?" I don't doubt my ability to fend for myself should the situation turn dangerous, but I do need to know what I'm walking into.

"Just Cate here." She turns and begins walking toward the front of the estate, not bothering to answer my question.

I catch up in a few long strides. "Cate." Saying her name shouldn't send a shiver through me, yet it's enough to almost distract me from the question at hand. "I need to know where we are."

She comes to a stop with a sigh. "No one here is going to hurt you."

"That isn't what I'm afraid of." It's a little bit of what I'm afraid of, but I can't make myself say that to her.

She studies me for a silent second. "This is an orphanage. An orphanage for Gifted girls who have been abandoned by their parents."

I suck in a breath. "Oh."

"Yes. Oh." She begins walking again, at a much slower pace this time. "Should you decide to stick with me for the rest of today's journey, you'll visit one in Talia as well."

"You go all the way to Talia to visit an orphanage?"

"I visit the ones in Kalmar and Venezia too, they're just too far apart to get to all of them on the same day." Her hands wrap around the strap of her canvas bag, her knuckles going white with the tension in her grip. "I was born in Scota. You probably didn't know that."

"I didn't."

"My sister, Andra, and I were abandoned by our parents when we were young, probably when it became clear we would both turn out to be Gifted. I will not lie, Scota treats their Gifted better than the other provinces, but that does not mean the people are without their prejudices." She turns toward me, halting her steps once again, her eyes watching my face and taking in every one of my reactions. "We were sent to live here. This Scotan orphanage."

I swallow thickly, my throat closed up with foreboding. "I have visited many such places, Caterine. I'm glad to know that you were cared for."

She laughs humorlessly. "I doubt you have been to this one. Was it caring when the wardens denied us food if we didn't complete the hours of chores they assigned us each day? Was it caring for them to beat us if we dared to ask for a break or, heaven forbid, step out to use the toilets?" Her eyes dare me to contradict her.

I don't know what to say. I have never seen such things taking place in Scota, but I certainly don't pretend to know everything, couldn't possibly know everything that happens throughout the entirety of the province. And she's right, I have not been to this particular facility. I don't know the differences between an orphanage for Gifted children and one for "regular" children. "I'm so sorry that happened to you, Caterine. I assure you that had my father known of these atrocities, he would have done something to stop them."

She opens her mouth, ready to argue with me, but surprises me instead. "About ten years ago, the director of this orphanage was removed from his position. Things have improved since then, in terms of the quality of care the children receive. Though they of course would face difficulties when they come of age if it weren't for the Uprising, as they would not be legally allowed to work without a man to vouch for them. The Gifted don't have to fear for their lives in Scota, but that does not mean it is easy to survive."

I take her words to heart. We Scotans have allowed ourselves to feel morally superior to the other provinces of Avon—at least we don't hunt and kill our Gifted—but if we deny them the right to work and support themselves, are we really any better?

"How long did you live here?" I ask quietly.

"Almost three years. I knew we wouldn't survive much longer if I didn't get us out, and so we ran away one night and came to Stratford. We lived on the streets for a couple of weeks, begging for scraps and relying on the kindness of strangers to keep us safe. Harold took us in shortly after. Provided us with the home and care we should have received back in Scota. He took better care of us than anyone else ever did." Her voice hardens with resolve, as if relaying the story has solidified something in her mind. She begins walking again.

I follow her in silence.

She pushes through the wide wooden door without knocking.

The moment she crosses the threshold of the building, the stone floors cold and echoing, she is mauled, a horde of young girls of various ages attaching themselves to her legs.

The tension in her eyes immediately lightens and she laughs, reaching down for the smallest girl and hoisting her up to rest on her hip. The girls chatter over one another, their volume and pitch so high I can't parse out any of the words. Though it's clear these girls love her, and that she loves them right back.

An older woman with smooth warm brown skin and a head of dark curls strides purposefully into the entryway. "Girls! Give the poor woman room to breathe!" Her voice is sharp but kind, and the young charges immediately obey their mistress, giving Cate room and ceasing their chatter.

Cate leans in, exchanging a kiss on the cheek with the woman before setting the girl in her arms back on her feet. "Sorry I'm late." She throws a glance my way. "I got unexpectedly delayed."

My cheeks heat as the attention of the entire room focuses on me. I don't know how I am supposed to introduce myself, but luckily, Cate takes the decision out of my hands.

"This is my friend Cal. He wanted to come along today to say hi to all of you."

The girls eye me warily. I try not to look as intimidated as I feel.

"I like Andra better," one of the girls claims.

Cate leans down and whispers—not at all quietly—in her ear. "Me too."

"He is handsome, though," pipes in another.

"I suppose so," Cate says with a smile. She reaches for the hands of the two girls closest to her. "Well, what are you waiting for? Show me what you have been up to this week!"

The girls need no more encouragement, tugging her up the stairs and down the hallway, chattering audibly even once they've ducked inside one of the many rooms.

"Prince Callum."

Shit. Of course the headmistress of the orphanage knows exactly who I am.

I straighten my shoulders and reach out a hand. "Just Callum while I'm here, please. Pleasure to meet you."

She raises one arched eyebrow like she means to challenge that notion. "Amelia. I'm the warden of this care facility."

"Could I trouble you for a tour?"

Her second eyebrow rises to meet her first. "Of course. I have offered many times to host the royal family for a tour. No one has ever taken me up on that offer."

My stomach churns. It's a condemnation, and not a subtle one. "I apologize for that. But I am here now, and I would like to hear about what you do here, and how I might be of assistance."

Amelia turns on her heel and leads me through a stone arch, into the dining room of the building. There's a long wooden table in the middle, mismatched chairs along either side. "I take care of up to ten girls at a time here."

"Only ten?"

She shoots me a withering look. "Only ten Gifted are permitted to reside in one location at a time, are they not?"

I clear my throat, chastened. "Right." I suppose I never considered the law being applied to children, but it does make sense to limit the number of Gifted who can gather in one space. Otherwise they might be able to combine their powers and use them to overthrow law and order.

Though the Uprising was able to do that just fine on their own, without the Gifted army we've always feared.

Amelia continues her tour, leading me around the well-appointed, if old and outdated space. She points out the books and paper, the writing instruments and paints each child has in the makeshift classroom. "Cate has made sure we are always fully stocked on the supplies we need for the girls' education."

"Does the money you receive from the province not cover such expenses?"

She snorts, not bothering to hide her disdain. "I am lucky if I am able to cover food and clothing with the money from the province. There were many times in the past when we have been forced to ration food in order to last until the next shipment arrives. So no, our expenses are not covered by the royal family." Her mouth twists on the final word.

I swallow, fighting back the shame. "Forgive me, I was under the impression the orphanages in Scota were well provided for."

"I'm sure some of them are, Your Highness."

I nod, guilt roiling in my gut. "Point taken."

I listen for the rest of the tour, keeping my comments and questions to myself. Amelia does not hold back, telling me stories of the injuries the girls bore when she first arrived, and how her requests for aid are continually ignored. Cate said things had improved since Amelia took over; I hate to think what they were like before.

Cate comes back down the stairs right as the tour is ending, as if planned. The girls trail after her like a line of ducklings following their mother. She wraps them in hugs before opening her bag and handing a heavy-looking sack to Amelia. The two women have a whole conversation without exchanging a single word.

I offer a hand to Amelia. "Thank you for the tour. I will not ask for your forgiveness, but I will promise that your words have not gone unheard."

She returns my shake with a firm one of her own. "I appreciate that, Your Highness."

The reaction from the girls at my given title is immediate and intense.

Cate reacts quicker than I can, looping her arm through mine and tugging me toward the door. "See you next week, girls. Be good for Amelia and finish all your schoolwork!"

A chorus of groans follows us out the door.

Cate waits for me to speak as we slowly make our way across the overgrown field back to our horses.

"I do not know where to begin, my lady." My voice is hoarse, choked with emotion.

Cate sighs. "I will not pity you for not knowing what is happening in your own province."

"I will not ask for your pity. Or your understanding. I did not know, but I will make it my mission to be better informed in the future."

Cate unties her horse, stroking her neck a few times, pulling an apple from her bag to feed to her before mounting. "The day is getting on, I think I will save my trip to Talia for tomorrow."

I pat my horse, a silent apology for not having a treat to offer him. I throw my leg over the saddle. "Are things the same there? And in the other provinces?"

Any lightness bestowed upon her by the girls at the orphanage fades from her eyes. "No, they're not."

I raise my eyebrows in question.

"They are so much worse, Callum. Worse than you could even imagine. Here they might be short on supplies, but at least they have Amelia, who cares for them with love and kindness. The Gifted children in the other provinces are not so lucky." A sheen of tears fills her eyes, but she doesn't let me see them fall, kicking her horse into a gallop. She rides hard for a long while, and I do my best to keep up with her.

Finally, she pulls back on the reins, slowing her horse's pace.

I match mine with hers, waiting for her to speak. When she doesn't, I venture forth. "You are good with them. The children."

She looks over at me. "For a long time I wasn't sure if I would ever be able to have children of my own. So I gave the girls at the orphanages every bit of love I might have reserved for a child I might one day bear."

My chest aches at the thought of Caterine cradling a bundle of a newborn in her arms. At the thought of her being denied that gift for no other reason than being who she is. "You will make a wonderful mother one day, my lady," I say, and I mean it.

"Thank you," she says softly. She doesn't spur her horse back into a gallop, but she also makes no further conversation for the rest of our ride.

When we reach the stable at La Puissance, we hand off our horses to the stablehand and I wait for her to dismiss me, to tell me she never wants to see me again, that our lessons are canceled, money be damned.

Instead, she reaches for my hand, silently pulling me up the stairs to her suite of rooms. The sun is beginning to set outside, but it will still be several hours before the club opens for business. The sound of the bustle of preparations disappears when Lady Caterine closes the door to her rooms behind us.

She leads me over to the chaise, pushing me down before she goes to the liquor cart, filling two glasses with whisky. She knocks one back before handing the other to me. I do the same.

I want to ask her what she is thinking, the need to hear her thoughts almost a physical ache inside me.

But all she does is take my empty glass from me. It's as if the shot has fortified her somehow, as if being in this room has reminded her who we are and why we are here. She hasn't changed her clothes, but it's as though she has donned her costume and stepped out onto the stage. She is no longer Cate, the friend beloved by a bunch of orphaned children; she is once again Lady Caterine, a courtesan desired by the faceless masses. She leaves my empty glass on the table and then turns to face me, pulling her shirt over her head. She is completely bare underneath. Her thumbs hook in the waistband of her trousers and those come off a second later.

I understand exactly what she is doing, the wall she is erecting in between us. I know I should direct the conversation back to our journey. I should want to know more about the orphanage and how she was raised and what's happening in the other provinces, but I can't make myself care about anything other than the woman standing before me. I don't think this is unintentional on her part. She is bared fully, and I drink my fill of her. The force of her beauty physically knocks me back. Luckily I manage to catch myself. This new position—me leaning back, my full weight on my hands resting on the chaise—pulls at the fabric of my pants, making my bulge obvious.

Her eyes linger and my cock twitches underneath her stare.

Rather than noting the motion with triumph, she swallows thickly, walking backward until the round curve of her ass hits the bed.

She turns away from me, and I can't help but hope she needs the moment to collect herself. I'm desperate for some kind of sign that she is as affected by me as I am by her. Her back still facing me, her hands begin to explore the familiar territory of her body, tracing over every inch of naked skin she can reach. Even though I can't see most of what she is doing, it only entices me more.

She puts me out of my misery soon enough, spinning slowly, her hands cupping her ample breasts, her fingers stroking the soft skin.

"What are you doing, Caterine?" My voice is as raspy as if I'd inhaled the smoke of a hundred fires.

"You are here to learn how to please a woman, yes?" she asks, as though the past few hours have not happened.

"Yes, my lady." If she wants to pretend, who am I to deny her?

"So what better way than to watch a woman please herself?"

I choke on the air in my lungs. "I'm going to watch you . . ." I can't even say the words, the mental image alone enough to cause a tightening in my groin.

"Touch myself." The glint in Caterine's eyes lets me know she knows exactly what she's doing. And she's going to enjoy every minute of watching me suffer. Might even get off on it.

For some reason I don't hate that thought.

Her hands don't stop moving, her fingers pinching her peaked, pink nipples. The sight causes my hand to jump automatically to my cock. I'm aching for relief, but I'm still aware enough to know I can't find it—not yet anyway. Still, I press my palm against my stiffness, hoping to ease the ache.

It helps a little. At least until Caterine climbs onto the edge of the bed, spreading her legs before me.

I can't fight off the groan this time.

She is gorgeous and glistening, and the smell of her arousal is intoxicating. I want to close my mouth over her, drink in the scent and taste of her. I have to grip the edge of the chaise to keep from lunging across the room and burying my head between her thighs.

She lets her fingers dance along the edges of her pussy, her breath catching as she comes closer and closer to her folds. I watch her chest rise and fall in stilted breaths and it becomes clear that none of this is for show.

It might have started out that way, but she is aroused. Touching herself for me is arousing her.

Just the thought makes my balls tighten.

"Fuck, Caterine," I mumble, barely coherent.

"What was that, Your Highness?" She's as breathless as I am.

"Touch yourself," I growl. "At least one of us should be able to find release."

I half expect her to fight me, but instead her fingers find the swollen bud at the top of her pussy. She strokes lightly, like she is holding herself back.

We both breathe out a sigh of relief.

"Teach me, Caterine."

"What?" She gasps as her fingers dip into her channel before returning to the center of her pleasure.

"Isn't that why we're here? For you to teach me how to give pleasure? Tell me what to do." It feels good to be the one pushing her buttons for once. I revel in it, watching her war within herself, wanting to find pleasure while also not wanting to let me win.

Her hand stills and her eyes fall closed. I would give anything to hear her internal debate at this moment.

But when her golden eyes pop back open, she is determined and in control. Her power is one of the most sexual things I've ever seen.

"If you take nothing else away from these lessons, Callum Reid, let it be this." Her fingers resume their stroking. "This is the clitoris, and it is the center of a woman's pleasure."

"How should I touch a woman there, my lady?" I ask, as if I haven't been dreaming of stroking her there in every moment of my dreams, both sleeping and awake.

She stifles a groan. "Every woman is different."

"How do you like it, Caterine?"

"Soft at first." Her hips move, undulating beneath her as if searching for something. "Then harder, and with more pressure."

"Mmmm." The sound is the only acknowledgment I can muster. I dig the heel of my hand harder into my crotch, focus on the bite of pain, letting it ground me.

"When you use your tongue on a woman, start with gently licking her, swirl your tongue around the bud." Caterine's head falls to one shoulder, like she isn't capable of holding it up.

"Can I suck on it?"

"Yes." She slides two fingers inside herself, letting out a moan that almost makes me come in my pants. She brings her other hand north, rubbing while she fucks herself.

It's the single most devastating thing I've ever seen.

She closes her eyes, head falling back as her pace increases.

"Are you going to make yourself come, my lady?"

"Yes, yes," she gasps.

"Do it. Let me see you come."

She cries out a second later, her hips continuing to move as she rides the wave of her orgasm.

I fight with everything in me to keep from coming with her. The image of Lady Caterine bringing herself to orgasm will be forever imprinted on my mind, and I know it will be what I see when I close my eyes tonight and every night for a long time after.

She slips her fingers from her channel and before I know what I'm doing, I'm on my feet, taking her hand in mine, guiding her fingers to my mouth.

She doesn't stop me.

Pupils wide, she watches as I lick the taste of her from her skin. I swirl my tongue over the pads of her fingers before releasing them.

For a full minute there is nothing but the sounds of our ragged breaths.

"Can I touch you, Callum?" Her eyes drift down to the bulge in my pants. "Please?"

"I don't know if that's a good idea, my lady."

Her eyes meet mine. "You say you want to build trust, Your Highness. You must trust me as well. I give you my word that I will never manipulate your emotions without your consent."

"It isn't just that, Caterine." I lean against the bed, grasping a post to keep myself upright. "If I never know the wonder of you, it might make it easier to walk away."

Her eyes soften and she reaches for the waistband of my pants, slow enough so I have plenty of time to stop her. "Relieve yourself, then." She pops the button but doesn't move to release me from the bonds of the fabric.

But I do it myself. I free my cock, watching her reaction as it bobs against my belly.

She watches me with wide eyes, her tongue darting out, touching the corner of her lips.

I close my eyes and my hand wraps around my shaft, pumping slowly. My eyes flutter open when I hear her breath stuttering in her chest. Her pupils are wide, her gaze locked on my dick.

"What are you thinking, my lady?"

"I'm thinking how amazing your cock would feel inside me, with you thrusting so slowly I could feel every magnificent inch of you."

"Bloody hell, Caterine. If I buried myself inside you I might not ever come out."

She raises an eyebrow. "Promise?"

I choke on my laugh. It gets caught in my throat when her fingers once again begin to stroke that center of her pleasure.

"Watching you is turning me on, Your Highness."

"Watching you is going to make me come, my lady."

She wraps her calf around my hip, bringing me closer. Inches separate our bodies, the only place we are touching the press of her leg. My eyes drift from her frantic fingers up to the swell of her chest, heaving with stuttered breaths.

The orgasm builds low in my stomach, my balls painfully tight. "Fuck, Caterine, I'm going to come." I move to pull away from her, but her leg traps me in place. My release spurts across her stomach. I wring every bit of pleasure from my aching cock, and the groan that escapes me is so long and low that it borders on embarrassing.

"Callum," she whispers as a second release takes hold of her.

And it does something to me, the sound of her breathing my name as she comes. I pull away from her before she can say anything else.

13

CATE

THE ROOM EXPLODES in a cloud of rosy red lust when Callum finishes, so thick it almost chokes me. His response is so strong, I could easily tug his emotions in any direction I wanted. And I should, I should be twisting and turning, wringing every drop of pleasure and using it to my advantage.

I could make him fall in love with me with barely a twinge.

But I don't.

I promised him I wouldn't manipulate him without his consent—a lie—but now I can't imagine breaking my word.

I saw how he reacted at the orphanage; I watched him interact with Amelia, really listen to what she had to say. She conveyed more than enough to me with a single look in that entryway before we left. He listened. He cared.

It's why I brought him back here, why I stripped myself bare—of clothing at least—to remind us both why we are here, what this all really is.

The way he pulls away from me a mere second after finishing

makes me think he doesn't have much faith in my promise to not manipulate him without his consent. I try not to let that sting.

He buttons his pants and disappears behind the privacy screen. I hear the faucet turn on and I prop myself on my elbows, trying to catch a glimpse of him. I tell myself it's to keep my eye on him, but really, I just hate seeing him run away.

When he comes back, he has a damp towel in one hand and my robe in the other. He gently cleans my exposed skin, so tender it stops the breath in my chest. It's becoming a common occurrence when I'm in his presence.

"I'm sorry, my lady." He places the lightest of kisses on my stomach before rising and striding across the room like he can't get away from me fast enough. Callum Reid is one giant mass of contradictions.

I stand, slipping into the robe and knotting it at my waist. "You have nothing to be sorry for, Callum."

"I shouldn't have done that"—he gestures helplessly to the bed—"without your express permission."

I cross the room to him, placing a tentative hand on his shoulder. "Nothing that just happened was without my consent, Callum."

The look in his gorgeous blue eyes is nothing short of tortured. "I think I should go."

"Okay." I don't know why it burns, his constant need to put space between us, but it does. I shake my head, as if that can help clear from my brain the notion that Callum is anything more than a client. In reality he's nothing more than a mark. Just because he listened to Amelia doesn't automatically make him a good man, a good person. It certainly doesn't make him anything more than the means to an end for me.

He cups my cheek in his hand. "Is it okay with you if I come back tonight?"

I raise one eyebrow and force myself not to lean into his touch. "You'll be ready for another lesson in just a few hours?"

His hand moves to grasp the nape of my neck and his eyes fall closed as if he can't bear to look at me. "I'm ready for another lesson right now, my lady."

"Then why don't you stay?" I ask softly, before I can think of all the reasons why he shouldn't.

"I have some things I need to take care of. But I will be back." He presses his lips to my forehead before closing the distance to the door with a few long strides.

I lean in the doorway, watching him depart, pretending like I'm only interested in the view of his impressive backside as he walks away. In reality, I'm wondering why it feels like a piece of me is walking away with him. I reach an absent-minded hand up to rub at the ache in my chest.

Meri whistles; she and Bianca are striding down the hallway just in time to watch Callum leave. The two join me at my perch. "Who, may I ask, is that fine human specimen and why have I never seen him before?"

I gesture for them to join me in my room. It's still early evening, but I pour myself a whisky anyway. I need it. "That is Callum Reid."

Bianca shoots me a wary look, perching on the edge of my bed, but she doesn't say anything. She knows more about my arrangement with Callum than anyone, but she still doesn't know the whole truth of it.

Meri's eyes widen as she slides into one of my chairs. "Wait, you're telling me that incredible-looking man is the Prince of Scota?"

"Former Prince of Scota." I down my first glass and pour another, limiting myself to just these two. Apparently I need to be ready to "teach" again in just a few hours. The prospect stirs a confusing swirl of emotions in my chest.

"He is visiting you in the middle of the day now?" Worry lines Bianca's voice. I wonder if she is fearful of his motives, or mine.

"He did pay me for a week of my time."

Meri's eyebrows rise. "A whole week? What does he need a whole week for?" She leans on the table, ready for all the gossip.

"I'm giving him sex lessons." I arch my eyebrow right back, as if this is all a joke.

Meri wrinkles her nose, leaning back in her seat. "Does he need them?"

I swallow a large gulp of the amber liquid. "Nope."

"Hmmm." Meri looks back and forth, between me and Bianca. "I feel like I'm missing something."

I keep quiet. I used to tell Bianca practically everything, the rest of the girls nearly as much, but I've been holding back since that day in Bianca's room. If I tell them what Lady M has asked of me, what she is doing to my sister, and they don't believe me, it might destroy me.

Bianca's brow creases in worry. "Cate, what is really going on?"

"I'm doing what I need to do to protect myself and Andra."

"From the Reids?"

I shrug, not willing to contradict her, though despite everything, I don't feel like the former rulers of Scota truly pose a threat.

Meri leans forward, reaching for my hand across the table. "I don't like this, Cate. This is a former monarch, a man who will lose everything because of the Uprising. A man whose family is part of the reason Gifted have no rights. How do you know he's not setting you up for something truly terrible? How do you know he doesn't have ill intent?"

I squeeze her hand. "Despite all my better instincts, I think I trust him." If nothing else, I trust Callum Reid more than I trust Lady M.

Bianca's green eyes study my face. "You like him."

I pull my hand away from Meri as if that can hide the flush on my cheeks. "Don't be silly. He's a client."

Bianca shakes her head, a small smile tugging on her lips. "I know you better than that, Caterine. You are not nearly suspicious enough. You like him."

I down the remaining few drops of whisky clinging to my glass. "What does it matter if I do? He's just a client, it's not like there's any hope for anything more. I wouldn't want it even if there were." The lie tastes sour on my tongue, and I realize just how deeply Callum Reid has implanted himself in my life, maybe even in my heart. I shake the notion out of my head.

Meri shrugs. "Why not? Things are different now, Cate. He's no longer a prince. He could be with whoever he wants." She pushes her chair back. "I truly hate to miss out on the rest of this gossip, but I have a client meeting." She blows us kisses as she lets herself out, the door of my room clicking shut behind her.

Bianca levels me with a knowing look. "What's this really about, Cate? Has he done something to you?"

"It's not about him. It's about me."

Bianca's face softens and her smile holds no small dash of pity. "You deserve to be happy, Cate. It's not your job to take care of the whole world. The club is fine, the Uprising is over, Andra is—"

"Andra is being worked to death and the only hope I have of getting her out of the situation is to finish this job. Callum is paying for my services, just like any other client. And that's all he's going to be." My words are sharp, and I don't know if I'm trying to convince her or myself.

Bianca's teasing smile fades. "What do you mean Andra is being worked to death?"

I close my eyes, admonishing myself. "It's nothing."

Unfortunately, the door separating my and Andra's rooms opens just in time to prove me wrong.

Andra looks even worse than the last time I saw her, like she's managed to lose both weight and sleep over the past couple of days.

I jump out of my chair, crossing to where she hovers by the bed. "Andra? What happened? What's wrong? Are you okay?"

"I'm fine." Her voice is weak.

I guide her to the chaise and gesture for Bianca to get her a glass of water.

Bianca hands her the glass and kneels in front of her, her healer's eyes scanning Andra's face. "I don't think there's much I can do. There's nothing physically wrong." She looks at me, a thousand questions in her eyes, but I ignore her and them, focusing on my sister.

I sit next to Andra on the chaise. "Just a few more days and this will all be over."

Andra gulps down the glass of water and turns to me. "I Saw something."

Bianca and I exchange a worried glance. I put my arm around Andra and pull her toward me. "What did you See?" My first thought is that something horrible is going to happen to Callum, and it chokes me.

"It's Harold." Andra's eyes meet mine and the worry in my own is reflected. "He's going to do something and the consequences will be deadly."

"What is he going to do?" Bianca asks quietly.

"He's going to kill the king of Scota. To become the nominee for the province." She looks at me. "It's the same vision I had before, but sharper, clearer. I don't think there's any way it won't come to pass, Cate."

I suck in a short breath. The plans are fully in motion, then.

Lady M is going to take the information I provide and find a way to make Harold the victor. Harold is going to become the nominee for the Scotan province. It isn't that part that frightens me but the way he is going to have to go about it that does.

The Harold MacVeigh I know would never dream of committing such violence.

Violence against Callum's father.

The second realization hits me square in the chest. If Callum and Harold are both set on being the candidate for Scota, if they both have plans to assassinate King James, if Harold has the advantage of knowing what Callum's plans will be, what are the chances Callum comes out of this unharmed?

Bianca's eyes meet mine as she also slides the pieces into place.

"This has to be because of Lady M," I finally breathe into the stilted silence. "Harold would never have come up with this plan on his own." I stand quickly, knocking Andra off balance. "We need to stop him."

Bianca steadies Andra before standing next to me. "Do we?"

I gape at her. "Are you serious?"

"Think about it, Cate. Someone must kill the king of Scota and become the representative for their province. Why not Harold? We know where he stands, and he stands with the people, and with the Gifted. For all his faults, Harold is a good man. I'd much rather have him in charge than some arrogant former royal." She gives me a pointed look.

But the one thing I know that she doesn't is that Callum Reid is the opposite of arrogant. An arrogant man would not have listened to Amelia the way he did today.

I need to warn him.

I use every argument I can think of to justify telling Callum the whole truth, even though to do so would be betraying a man who has been like a father to me. Betraying the ideals I've held close my entire life. Until a certain blue-eyed prince showed up at my door.

"I need to go lie down for a little bit." Andra breaks me out of my thoughts, rising from the chaise and handing me her empty glass. Her eyes are so vacant it scares me.

And it's that look in my sister's eyes that reminds me what my true purpose is. I'm not here to serve Callum Reid. I'm not even here to serve Harold MacVeigh. I am here to protect my sister, and the best way to do that is by keeping my mouth shut. I can't tell Callum what I know, even if the thought of keeping this from him makes me physically ill.

I walk with Andra to her room, pulling the covers up under her chin and tucking her in like I did when we were kids.

"Cate," she calls just as I'm about to leave the room. "There's one more thing."

I pause in the doorway, dread pooling in my stomach. What more could there be? "What is it?"

"You're involved somehow. With the king's death. I can't see how exactly, I just know that you'll be involved. Be careful, please. Bonds aren't meant to be broken." She hesitates, her brow scrunching up. "And there's trees. Use the trees."

I nod, my throat so tight I can't offer her a real response, not that I would know what to say. Andra's final words might be nonsensical, but they don't erase what came before: I will be involved. I fear I already am. I shut the door softly.

Bianca is watching me with wide eyes. "You can't tell him."

"I know."

"Even if you do like him, even if he does turn out to be a good person, you can't tell him."

"I said I know, Bianca." The words lodge in my throat.

She studies me for a few long seconds before heading to the door. "I'll let you prepare for your next lesson."

Callum will be back in my room in a few hours, and if I have any hope of saving my sister, I'll have to keep this knowledge hidden. I'll have to look him in the eye, feel his hands on my skin, and know that his life and his legacy are both in danger, and there's nothing I can do.

My dearest Harry,

It seems like not long ago I was writing to tell you the good news. Now I must deliver the bad.

I lost the baby.

My heart is broken.

Please come see me soon.

I need you.

All my love,

Grecia

14

CALLUM

When I return from La Puissance, I move through the hallways in a daze, brushing off a request from Dom for a sparring session in favor of locking myself up in my room with a bottle of whisky. I sink into the armchair in front of the stone fireplace, my body satiated but heavy. I pour myself a drink, leaving the bottle within easy reach on the low wooden table beside me.

But I can't even enjoy the fine liquor; too many thoughts and feelings whirl through my mind.

I can't believe I lost control with Lady Caterine. I could barely make it a few days before giving in and losing myself in front of her. She promised not to take advantage of me, but I don't know if her word can be trusted.

No. That's not quite true. Things may be tenuous between us, but I don't think she would manipulate me without my consent.

The more I think about her, the more I trust her, find myself wanting to open up to her. Those feelings alone could indicate that she's already been twisting my emotions.

But she didn't twist anything at that orphanage. To think, what I saw today was the best of it. Caterine's childhood was spent in an even more dangerous situation. I cannot even imagine the horrors she hinted at for the Gifted children living in the other provinces.

I toss back the whisky I filled my glass with, pushing the bottle to the side.

Perhaps I have been wrong about the Gifted. Perhaps I have been wrong about everything.

Perhaps Lady Caterine is messing with my head.

Perhaps I'm letting her.

I roll the empty glass between my fingers, the raised edges of the crystal cutting into my palm when my grip tightens.

Am I really going to let the words of one woman deter me from what I have always known to be right?

It isn't just her words, an internal voice protests. It's the words of my uncle and of my sister. It's the words of my mother. It's what I saw with my own eyes today at that orphanage. Children who had been abandoned by their parents. An orphanage forced to rely on the kindness of its former charges in order to feed and educate children who have done nothing wrong.

I push out of the armchair and stride to my bathing chambers, running the tub full of cold water. A few hours remain before I need to return to La Puissance. And in those few hours, I need to decide what kind of ruler I am going to be. I need to decide what kind of man I want to be.

I ARRIVE BACK at the club later than I intended. I've been warring with myself, trying to find a single scenario where I don't come out of this completely fucked.

It's clearer now than ever that I must be the one to kill my father and represent the Scotan province in this election. Never did I imagine that decision would be the easiest one I would have to make.

Lady Caterine opens the door for me, dressed in nothing but a few scraps of lace, her silk robe tied loosely around her curves. Her face is painted, and I almost wish she'd left it bare. Something tells me it's more to her than just makeup.

Perhaps she has spent the hours we've been apart arguing with herself as well.

She guides me into the room, to a chair at the dining table, handing me a glass of whisky as I sit. "I want to hear more about you, Your Highness. I feel like you got to see a part of my history today. Now I want to have the chance to see part of yours. What is your father like, Callum?"

I nearly choke on the caramel-colored liquid, the question is so unexpected, her tone so cold and detached. "I'm sorry?"

"You've told me about your sister, even a little bit about your mother, but I haven't heard you mention your father much. What is life like under Scotan rule, from a royal's perspective? What is he like as a father, and a ruler?" She arches her eyebrow like the question is playful, though we both know it's anything but. I know the shifts that have taken place in my mind over the past several hours; maybe her thoughts have shifted as well.

"Have you been to many of the other provinces, my lady?"

She sits back in her chair, leaving space between us. "I have been everywhere, though never for more than a couple of days. When I venture to other provinces, it is usually to drop off supplies and money for the Gifted children. But I spend most of my time here in Stratford City."

I nod, not surprised. Most people don't travel between the provinces of Avon. One of the main reasons why it took so long for a revolution to succeed. One of the main reasons why Gifted are killed in some provinces but not in others. "I know you will think me biased, and I realize you faced some special circumstances, but life in Scota is not like what you may have seen in the other provinces."

"All provinces have their areas of peace and prosperity." She eyes me over the rim of her glass, as if she can discern my honesty with a simple gaze. "Special circumstances aside."

"True. And Scota certainly has some citizens who are wealthier than others. The difference is that those wealthy citizens take care of the poor."

"Take care of them? What does that mean to you? They provide them with a hot meal every once in a while? Toss a gold coin out the window of their fancy carriages?" Hostility laces through her voice, and I can't even blame her. After the things I witnessed today, the things she told me about, I would understand if Lady Caterine detested me. But I don't think hate is behind her line of questioning.

"No, my lady. The wealthy pay a hefty tax, and those funds are used to make sure all people of Scota are housed, fed, and provided medical care when needed."

She stares at me for a long second, a war waging in the depths of her amber eyes. "All people but the Gifted, you mean."

I turn my attention to the remaining liquor in my glass so I don't shrink under her honey gaze. "I will not pretend everything is perfect in Scota. Clearly we still have work to do. But I will stand by the fact that we approach the issues with the best of intentions."

"And yet plenty of Scotans were members of the Uprising, plenty of them support this new government."

"Did you talk with many of them?"

"Did you?" she challenges.

I study her for a moment, wondering if something greater happened while we were apart. Lady Caterine has always been sharp, but she has never before seemed angry. Is this simply lingering resentment from the cruelty she faced as a child, or is it a sign of something more? "I did. As a leader of Scota, I found it important for me to know why some of my people would want to fight for an organization set on disrupting life as we know it."

She sips her drink, her eyes still narrowed on me. "And what did they say?"

"That they wished for all people of Avon to have the freedoms and basic necessities we in Scota believe in."

She scoffs. "Do you disagree with them, with the Uprising and your citizens who joined it?"

I put down my drink and reach across the table, taking one of her hands in mine. The simple touch soothes my racing mind, steadies my pounding heart. "I don't. The Uprising has taken more from me than you might understand, Lady Caterine." I choke back the emotions rising in my throat as I think about what I still stand to lose. "But that doesn't mean I disagree with their most basic of principles. I hope for a future of peace and unity."

"And continued restrictions against the Gifted."

"I am beginning to rethink my position." I squeeze her fingers before pulling away. "Why are you set on thinking the worst of me, my lady?"

She throws back the rest of her whisky. "I'm not sure. Might make things easier, I suppose."

I don't ask for clarification, because I think I know all too well what she means.

She pushes back from the table with a sigh. "You didn't come here to talk. Let's get to tonight's lesson, shall we?"

I stay seated. "I enjoy talking with you, Lady Caterine. And if you prefer, we do not have to partake in a lesson tonight."

She bristles. "I plan on fulfilling my end of our deal."

"Your feelings are more important than any deal, my lady."

"Some of us do not have the luxury of feelings, Your Highness." She spits out my former title like it's sour.

I stand, crossing to her so only a few inches of space remain between us, my heart aching for the sadness—no, the indifference—of her sentiment. I cup her cheek in my hand, letting my thumb stroke her soft skin. Her lips part as I reach for her hip, tugging her closer. She might talk a good game, but we both know there are feelings here, lodged in this silent space between us. But if staying focused on the physical is what she needs, I'm happy to oblige. "What do you plan to teach me tonight, my lady?"

Her chest flutters, her breasts straining at the bounds of the lace encasing them. There's a quiet moment before she answers me. "Not so much a lesson tonight, as a test." She unties her robe, letting the silky fabric drop to the floor. "Earlier you watched me find pleasure at my own touch. Let's see how closely you were paying attention."

My eyes travel over the length of her body. Her lacy undergarment is cut high on her hips, cinching her waist and pushing up her glorious breasts. My cock starts to harden as I lean down, my mouth brushing the shell of her ear. "You know how closely I was paying attention, Caterine."

"Good." She swallows and I fight the urge to let my lips trace her neck, though I do give in to the temptation to brush them over the trio of freckles on her shoulder. "Then make me come, Your Highness."

15

CATE

I RELEASE THE STAYS of my lace bodysuit, letting it drop to the floor. I scoot back onto the edge of the bed, needing the space from him, yet wanting his hands on my body already, lying to myself about how much I ache for him.

He surprised me earlier with his frank apology, the way he seemed to take in my words and my story without insisting on his own version. At the orphanage, I could see how seriously he was absorbing the details, how the circumstances didn't sit right with him. It was easy to keep a wall up between us when this arrangement was about money and collecting information. But it was a foreign feeling—to be heard, to be understood—and it did something to the armor guarding my heart.

I wanted him to reveal something damning, something that would make it okay for me to betray him, but Callum Reid never seems to do what I expect him to.

I watch him from the perch on my bed while the same kind of

war flashes in his eyes. He wants me, but I can tell he doesn't want to. I want him to touch me, and I know how dangerous that want will turn out to be. For both of us.

"Am I allowed to use my mouth?" Callum crosses the room slowly before crowding into my space; my legs part around him, my thighs settling around his hips.

My nipples tighten at the question. I push any hint of sentiment away and focus on the task before me. I can't afford to let another chance slip through my fingers. "Hands and fingers only tonight."

"Very well."

Callum places his hand flat against my sternum, gently pressing me to lie back on the bed. I keep myself propped on my elbows so I can watch his ministrations. For educational purposes, of course.

I expect him to dive right in, but he takes his time. His fingers trace the edge of my collarbone before trailing down the center of my chest, avoiding my breasts altogether. His touch is as light as a feather over the plane of my belly, down one leg and up the other. His eyes linger on my face, watching when my breaths quicken, when I hold back a gasp. He notes the spots where his touch ripples through me and comes back to them again and again.

Finally he allows one hand to cup my breast. He doesn't squeeze or knead it like many men are apt to do. Instead he works those nimble fingers, grazing the sensitive underside before focusing his attention on my nipples.

I can't fight the gasp when he pinches one, rolling the bud between his fingers, using his free hand to provide the same delicious treatment to the other.

"Next time will you let me use my tongue, my lady?" His voice is hoarse, and a quick glance down lets me know he's as aroused as I am.

"I would be a failure of a teacher if I didn't show you how to please a woman with your mouth." My hips buck at the thought of Callum's head buried between my thighs.

"I can't wait to taste you, Caterine." He pinches my nipples, right on the border of too hard.

"You apparently don't require any lessons on dirty talk," I moan.

He doesn't seem to really need these lessons at all. Yet I forget to question why we keep up the pretense when Callum's hand skates down my stomach, cupping my sex with his large, hot palm.

"Sometimes you might need to provide lubrication if your partner isn't aroused enough," I warn, though I don't see how that could ever be an issue for him or his partners. I'm well beyond damp and we haven't even gotten to the good part yet.

Callum paints a single finger through my center. "You seem to be plenty wet, my lady."

I gasp at the touch, hips rising automatically, desperate for more contact. "Touch me, Callum. Please." I hate that I'm begging, but I also don't care if I find the relief I need. Today has been too full of emotions and I'm desperate for the physical release, the release I know only he can provide me.

Callum's finger dances over my clit, moving exactly how I like it. He teases me, his touches light and fluttering. Gradually his strokes become firmer, circling the sensitive bud until my hips are thrusting.

He pulls his touch from me right as I'm about to topple over the edge. "Not yet," he growls.

"I never expected you to be so demanding, Your Highness."

"You bring out a different side of me, my lady." He brings two fingers to his mouth.

I reach up and grasp them lightly. "May I?"

He hesitates for a long second before nodding his permission.

I take his two fingers in my mouth, careful not to smudge my scarlet lip paint, letting my tongue work over his skin. His fingers are surprisingly calloused and I suck them until Callum's blue eyes flutter shut, his own hips thrusting, looking for any measure of relief. Releasing his fingers with a pop, I guide them into me, groaning at the fullness.

"Holy fuck," Callum mutters, his cock twitching in his pants. "You are the sexiest woman I've ever seen, Caterine. I'm aching for you."

"Let me ease the ache, Callum. Please." My hand drifts toward the button of his pants, the need to touch him burning through me, not a single thought of manipulating him in the aftermath in my mind. I want him, only him.

He presses my hand to his hardness as his fingers move inside me and we release matching moans. I stroke him once, then twice, before he captures my hand in his, linking our fingers and raising my arm over my head.

"Let me feel you come, my lady. Then you can do whatever you'd like to me." His fingers continue to thrust inside me, curling around to find that perfect spot. His thumb massages my clit and the tension builds in my belly.

Callum is perched over me, and I want to pull his body down, pull him into me, see what those blue eyes look like when he reaches the pinnacle of pleasure, feel the fullness of him moving inside me. "Careful what you promise, Your Highness."

"I'm always careful, my lady." He lowers his head and mutters in my ear. "I've been dreaming about you, Caterine. Touching you, watching you fuck my fingers, burying my face between your thighs and never coming up for air. How fucking gorgeous you look when you come for me." The room shimmers with the crimson truth of his lust for me.

"Callum—"

"How good my name sounds in your perfect mouth. Fuck, Caterine. I spend all day wanting you." The air darkens, the crimson deepening to an almost black-edged lace, not thick enough for me to grasp, just enough to discern the truth. Nothing about his words is a lie. Callum wants me.

Just as much as I want him. The realization of our tightly wound connection is enough to push me right to the edge.

"Make me come, Callum."

He pulls back, his eyes searching for mine, watching my face as my body tightens around his fingers, as I call out for him to give me more. As he obliges.

The release rips through me and my lungs inexplicably tighten for the briefest of moments. For a second, I think Callum might find his own release with me. But as soon as he works me through the orgasm, he puts space between our bodies—mine naked and his fully clothed. This feels different from the other times he has run away. Like he is forcing himself to give me the space to decide what happens next.

I sit up once I've regained my breath, reaching for him, needing him. He comes to me after just a second's hesitation. I let my hand hover at the button of his pants. "Do you still want this?"

He leans into my touch and nods.

"Say the words, Callum." I need to hear them, need him to show me this bit of himself, to trust me the way I'm coming to trust him.

"Touch me, Caterine."

I kneel on the edge of the bed, bringing us to almost the same height. Running my fingers down the buttons of his shirt, I tug the bottom hem loose from his pants. After popping a couple of buttons free, he pulls the whole thing over his head.

I take my time drinking him in. The lean muscles of his chest, the ridges of his stomach, the trail of copper-colored hair leading into the waistband of his pants. My fingers follow the same path as my eyes, and he sucks in a breath at the light touch.

I press my lips to his chest, leaving behind a perfect crimson imprint. I mark him, a trail from his collarbone down to his stomach, the color fading as more of the paint is left behind on his skin.

He cups my chin in his hand and for a second I think he might kiss me. I think if he tried I would let him. "You're beautiful," he says instead.

I scoot closer to the edge of the mattress, my hand tracing his hard length through the cloth of his pants. "So are you."

16

CALLUM

HER FINGERS MAKE quick work of the clasp of my pants, and she shoves the fabric to the floor, leaving me in just my undergarments. I hook my thumbs in the waistband and lower them, watching her face as she watches me.

She sucks in a breath when my cock springs free, and I can't help but preen under her gaze. Her eyes drift up to mine. "You were really going to keep this from me?"

My cheeks heat, and I have to close my eyes to try to tamp down the flush I don't need overtaking my whole body.

She laughs and her hand slips into mine. With just a gentle tug, she pulls me down onto the bed. When my eyes open, she's perched over me like some sort of mythical goddess. Her golden hair tickles my chest, the citrus scent of her fills my nose, and how perfect—the thought crosses my mind—would life be if we could just stay in this bed forever.

I want more than anything to reach up and pull her lips to mine.

But Caterine has done nothing but respect my boundaries, and I will do the same with hers.

Instead I watch her fingers as they trail over the bared skin of my torso, as they skate around my body, touching me everywhere but where I need her most. Which I guess is payback for teasing her earlier.

Finally, her hand finds my aching cock, so tight with wanting I have to force myself not to buck in her grasp. She strokes me slowly, her thumb gathering the wetness at the head and smoothing it down over my shaft. Her skin on my skin is almost otherworldly.

I trail my hand down the length of her arm, needing to feel the softness of her under my palm, needing every part of us to be joined.

"Does this feel okay?" she asks, her pace still slow, like she wants to drag this out for as long as she can. Like she too wants to stay trapped in this pleasure-filled bubble for as long as we can.

"It feels incredible. You know it does."

She flashes me a wicked grin. "How about this?" She leans down, letting just the tip of her tongue trace the tip of my cock.

I hiss. "I thought today was hands and fingers only?"

"It was. For you."

Without further warning, she takes me in her mouth. My hips thrust of their own volition, but Caterine doesn't flinch. She takes me deeper and deeper until I hit the back of her throat.

I groan, fisting my hand in her hair. "Don't let me hurt you."

She releases my cock from her mouth, her fist continuing to pump me slowly. Her eyes meet mine and there's something more than lust there. "I know you won't."

I sit up, moving so I'm on my knees, my weight resting on my heels. "I need to touch you."

She studies me for a second before shifting her position, turning so that when her mouth returns to my cock, I can stroke her from behind.

The vibrations her moans send through my dick almost cause me to come on the spot, but she knows exactly when to pull back, exactly how to keep me from reaching the pinnacle. Her pussy is still dripping. I slide three fingers into her as she works me with her tongue, bringing me to the edge and pulling me back again.

I know without her having to say it that she won't let me come until she finds her own release, so I pump harder and faster, curling my fingers inside her while I thumb her clit. She whimpers as she starts to tighten around my fingers, but she never lets up. She takes me deeper, even as she cries out her release and my hips buck.

I lean back on one hand, the other still tight in her hair. My balls clench, and the familiar tingling starts low in my belly. "Fuck, Caterine, I'm going to come." I release my hold on her hair, pulling back slightly, giving her space to move away.

But she doesn't stop, sucking me deeper until the orgasm barrels out of me and I choke on her name. There's a tightening in my chest, my lungs compressing so for a second I can't breathe, but the sensation passes. In its wake there's only a certainty, a sureness about the woman kneeling before me.

Caterine's fist strokes me through the aftershocks, her tongue lapping at my cock, cleaning me of any remaining seed.

She places a kiss on the tip before straightening and sitting back, a shy smile on her gorgeous lips.

Neither of us speaks for several seconds, the air around us heady and hazy. I want to pull her into my arms and burrow under the blankets, tucking her in for safekeeping. I want to fall asleep with her head on my chest and wake up in the middle of the night to watch her at rest, at peace. I want to know that whatever is binding me to her isn't one-sided.

She stands before I have the chance to reach for her. She crosses to the bathing chamber and I hear the faucet turn on. When she comes back, she has a damp cloth in her hands. She pushes me back on the bed so I'm lying flat and carefully wipes the lip prints from my skin. She comes to the one on my chest last, the brightest one, stamped right over my heart.

I stop her hand. "I'm keeping that one."

Our eyes meet, and we exchange something heavy and unsaid.

"It won't last forever," she tells me.

We both know she's not talking about the lip print, but I can't make myself believe it, even if I know it to be true.

"I know. It won't last past tomorrow, actually." I rise from the bed and begin to dress as the harsh reality settles in.

"Tomorrow? Does that mean you're finally going to tell me what it is you really need me for?" There's a hint of knowing in her amber eyes, but it's gone as quickly as it comes.

I nod, stepping into my undergarments. "Yes. I hope that what I have to ask of you doesn't make you think less of me."

She watches me, perched on the edge of the bed with some unreadable emotion in her eyes. "I don't think I could ever think less of you, Callum. Whatever it is you have to do, I know you have a good reason for it."

"How can you know that after just a few short days?"

"You make it easy to know you, Callum Reid." She stands and slips into her robe as I finish dressing. "There is something . . ."

"Yes?"

She shakes her head to dispel the thought, taking a seat on the chaise longue. "Nothing. It's wild to even imagine it."

I sit next to her, covering her hand with mine and raising my head to meet her gaze. Somehow this simple touch feels more intimate than what we just did. "Am I an idiot thinking this is even going to work? Has holding you, touching you really made it easier to ask you to do this unspeakable thing for me?" I run a hand through my hair, tempted to yank it out in frustration. "Am I just deluding myself to think this is possible? Giving myself an excuse to keep seeking you out?" The need to see her, to touch her, is almost overwhelming, and yet I can't fully give myself over, can't let myself fall.

She scoots even closer to me, cupping my cheek with her free hand. "That was a lot of questions, Your Highness."

My shoulders hunch in on themselves. "I'm sorry."

"Don't be sorry." She takes my hand in hers, flipping it over so our palms meet, linking our fingers together. It's another simple touch, nothing compared to the way my hands skirted over her bare skin or the way my fingers pleasured her mere minutes ago. And yet it somehow means more. Feels like more. "I don't know if us spending this time together, being intimate with one another will make it easier for you to ask me what it is you need. And to receive whatever it is once you've asked."

I squeeze her hand and push the rest of my questions aside. I don't need answers, I need honesty. And to get honesty, I need to give it. I might be a fool, but if there is one lesson I'm learning this week, it's that no words should be left unsaid. "I'm sure you will think me an idiot for saying this, and I can't imagine it will be your first time hearing these words, but I feel like there is something between us, Caterine. I want you, of course. I can't imagine there are many who don't. But I also find myself wanting to tell you things and hear your thoughts. I find myself longing to just be in your company." It's the first time I've allowed myself to give voice to this feeling, this inexplicable link between us. The way that, even after just a few days, it's hard to imagine a time when she won't be in my life. "If I'm alone in this—"

"You're not." Her answer is quick and sharp, but laced with something soft. "You're not alone in your feelings, Callum." She hesitates before pulling away, slipping her hand from mine. "But feelings don't really matter. I don't plan to remain at the club for much longer, and you clearly have much bigger plans than anything happening in this room." She gives me a sad smile. "There is no future for us beyond what has been paid for, Your Highness."

I suck in a sharp breath, her words a direct punch to the gut. "Right."

She brushes a stray curl out of my eyes. "But I will help you with whatever you need, and I will fulfill my part of the contract."

"Sex lessons."

She shrugs with a coy raise of her eyebrows. "Or something more, if you'd prefer." She rises and stands in front of me.

Something more. The something more that I'm beginning to allow myself to want—the something more I've wanted since the moment I watched her dance across the stage of the club—is not the something more she is offering. It could never be what she's offering.

I want to press her further, but if I stay in this room for one minute longer, I might never be able to convince myself to leave. I hesitate on my way to the door. "Thank you. For everything today. Not just that," I gesture helplessly to the bed. "But for everything."

She stands on a tiptoe, pressing her lips to my cheek. "It was my pleasure. Quite literally."

I chuckle, but the sound is lacking humor. "I'll see you tomorrow."

"Tomorrow."

I stride out of the room and down the grand staircase, out to the cobbled street and into my carriage. Lady Caterine is everywhere.

Her scent on my clothes, her lips on my skin, the imprint of her mouth on my cock, and over my heart. She consumes me. And after tomorrow, after I take my father's life, everything will change. A sick feeling of dread washes over me, clinging more fervently than even the ghost of her presence.

I DON'T SLEEP that night.

Breakfast in the dining room is a silent affair, the four of us sitting with our thoughts without being able to share them.

Dom keeps her eyes on her meal, but every so often I catch her looking at our father, drinking him in like this will be the last time she sees him. I guess it might be.

Father tries to pretend nothing is wrong, reading the paper—the headline reminding us that the Scotan killing period begins at midnight—and eating his toast as if it were a normal morning. Not many people wake up knowing a certain day will be their last. Does that make it easier or harder, I wonder.

Alex watches me. Several times I catch him opening his mouth as if to speak, but he always shuts it shortly after. He knows there's nothing left to say.

I try to eat, but even the plain toast I choke down sours in my stomach.

Finally, my father rises. He looks at each of us, one by one. "I'm not one for big emotional speeches, but let me just take this moment to tell you all that I know this is the right outcome. For Scota, and for all of you. I ask that you feel no guilt for your actions; spend your time and energy instead on uniting Avon and bringing the ideals of our province to the country at large." His eyes flit between me and Dom. "I get to go be with your mother now."

Dom sniffles, though she tries to hide her tears.

I keep my back straight, forcing myself to be the kind of man my father thinks I can be, the kind of man I want to be.

He looks right at me. "I will see you tonight, son."

Wordless, I nod, my hands clenched in tight fists at my side.

He exits the dining room, leaving the three of us to sit in pained silence.

"I've arranged for a group of trusted guards to be posted around the castle tonight," Alex says, as though he is delivering a casual morning report, though I can hear the emotion hiding underneath his words.

"What for?" My voice is hoarse, choked on tears I won't allow myself to shed.

"To ensure that you are the one who . . ." He doesn't finish his thought, but his words slowly penetrate my mind.

"You think there are others who will show up tonight? Others who will want to kill him?"

Alex looks at me like I am a naïve child. "Yes, Cal. I think there might be others."

It has never occurred to me that there would be other Scotan citizens who might want the chance to rule Avon. It's another reminder of how out of touch I have been, and how much work I will have to do if I am elected. I don't want to be the kind of ruler who doesn't understand his own people.

Dom, unusually silent, lets out a quiet sob.

Alex hands Dom his handkerchief, but his eyes never leave me. "Do you have everything else you need?"

I swallow. I don't know what I need, honestly, other than to not sit in this room, in this house for the rest of the day stewing in my own misery. I push my chair back from the table and stand. "I need to get out of here."

Alex stands too, but I gesture him to stay put.

"I will be back when I need to be. I know what I need to do."

I squeeze Dom's shoulder, knowing I should stay and attempt to offer her some comfort, but there's nothing I can say to make today any easier.

Once I push my way into the hallway, I find myself following in my father's footsteps. The door to his study is already closed, but I knock and don't wait for permission to enter.

My father stands at the window, his gaze locked on the rolling hills of our estate grounds and the great mountains beyond. Sometimes I forget how beautiful Scota is with all of her lush greenery and rolling hills. I'm sure it's something he is going to want to remember.

"I hope you haven't come to tell me you've changed your mind."

I cross the room, joining him in front of the window. "You know I haven't."

"Good." He spares me a quick glance before his eyes return to the green and blue landscape outside. The sky is bare of clouds, for once, like the sun wanted to be here to witness his final day. "I know this is not an easy thing to ask of you, Callum. If there were any other way, you know I would take it."

"I know." I've spent many moments over the past few weeks fighting against his wishes, angry with him for even asking me to do the only thing that can be done. "I'm sorry I've made this more difficult than it needed to be."

He claps a hand on my shoulder. "I can't really be upset with you, Cal. In any other circumstances, it's all a king can hope for—a son who doesn't want to see him dead."

"I know we haven't always agreed on everything, and I know I have been hardheaded and stubborn. But I want you to know that I'm going to do everything I can to be the kind of leader who would make you proud." I swallow the emotion in my voice, but it doesn't stop the sheen of tears from springing to my eyes.

His grip on my shoulder tightens. "You have always made me proud, Callum. What I want, more than anything, is for you to be happy. And despite everything, this week you have been happier than I have seen you in a long time. I hope you will allow yourself to keep that happiness, even after I'm gone."

I hesitate before speaking again, not wanting to ruin this moment. But it could be our final one, and there are things I need to know. "I spoke with someone recently, someone who was born in Scota and abandoned by her parents."

My father's eyebrows rise. "Did she become a ward of the province?"

I nod. "She was sent to a Scotan orphanage. But it did not sound like any of the ones I have ever been to. The wardens were cruel and abusive to both her and her sister."

He turns away from me once again, a heavy sigh on his lips. "I wish I could tell you her recollections are untrue, Callum."

"So you knew this was happening? How many other orphanages were under similar rule?"

"Son, this is going to be a lesson you're going to need to learn and learn quickly. Leaders—no matter who they are and where they rule—are not all-powerful. We can't be everywhere at once, see everything happening. All we can do is put people we trust in positions of power and leadership."

"What did you do when you learned of this information?"

"I removed the wardens from their positions, fined them, and banned them from ever working with children again." He shrugs, but there is nothing easy or light about it, his shoulders sagging with the weight of responsibility. "There are going to be things you miss, Cal. You just have to fix them as soon as you become aware, and do whatever you can to make sure the same mistakes aren't repeated again."

I nod, taking my time to absorb his words, advice I will surely need should I take the helm as the leader of Avon.

My father clears his throat, a knowing smile on his lips. "Things are going well, then, with you and the Lady Caterine?"

If by going well you mean the very thought of her is enough to consume me, then I suppose so. "They are going as well as they can. I will be ready when the time comes."

"And you trust her enough to help you?"

"I do."

And suddenly, even though I know this very well may be the last conversation I will have with my father, I long for nothing more than to be far from this room. I long to be with her, in her arms. Only she can bring me the calm and peace I need before undertaking this task.

"Go," my father says, the knowing smile growing.

I turn to leave, but double back. Wrapping my arms around my father, my king, I wait until he hugs me back, knowing this will be our last embrace.

I force down the sadness and focus on the joy of it.

When he clears his throat and loosens his grip on me, I release him from the hug and leave him to his thoughts, heading directly for the front door.

I dressed casually for breakfast in a button-down shirt and vest, but I don't bother changing before heading outside to my awaiting carriage. The driver doesn't even need instructions.

There is only one place I could possibly go.

My dearest Harry,

I am writing to you with joyous news. I have come to be with child again, and something about this time is different, Harry, I just know it. This time we're going to have our baby, and she is going to be perfect.

Please come visit soon.

All my love,

Grecia

My dearest love,

I wish I could say I am filled with nothing but joy at this happy news, but I am worried for you, my darling. It's not just the restrictions that worry me, I know Scota is kinder to pregnant Gifted than most. But the midwife cautioned against any more pregnancies, told us one more loss might kill you. I can handle many tragedies, but losing you would be the death of me, Grecia.

Please be careful. I will come see you as soon as I am able.

All my love,

Harry

17

CATE

I LINGER IN BED long into the morning hours, waiting impatiently for Callum to come knocking at my door while at the same time dreading it.

Last night was the perfect opportunity for me to gather the information I needed from him. And I couldn't do it. His emotions were there, thick as the lump that's been permanently lodged in my chest. It would have been so easy to reach out and grab them, twist him into compliance. But I didn't. I couldn't, some invisible force keeping me from betraying him.

I still have nothing to bring to Lady MacVeigh and our time is running out. Today will be the last time I see Callum Reid before he has to kill his father. He still doesn't know that I'm aware of his plan. It's only the where and the how and the when still missing from the puzzle, information I should have gleaned from him by now. Information I'm not sure if I want to know.

Eventually I pull myself out of bed, dressing in simple day clothes. I need to see Harold, preferably without the shadow of his wife hanging over us. I hesitate before slipping my sheath around my thigh, but running a thumb over the familiar etchings on the dagger brings me comfort. Normally I don't feel the need to carry a weapon when the club is closed for business, but nothing about life here feels as it used to.

I approach the door to his office, holding back before knocking. I've been avoiding him all week, ever since my conversation with the princess. He's not a stupid man, I know he knows what this means for my and Andra's futures at the club. I just haven't been able to face him, say the words out loud. But it's time. I need to tell Harold that when this week is over, we'll be leaving and never coming back.

And possibly even more than that, I need to know what he plans to do with the information I'll be forced to gather tonight. And what are his plans for Callum in all of this? The rules state that no innocents may be harmed, but accidents happen, and I wouldn't put anything past Lady M at this point.

I place my hand flat on the mahogany wood. It wasn't long ago that I planned on spending the rest of my days at La Puissance. Couldn't imagine ever finding a place where I felt safer, more at home. But this place is no longer safe.

And when I think of home now, it's not a place that comes to mind, but a person, a pair of bright blue eyes and a head of copper curls.

My breath catches in my chest, and I pound on the door before I can let that thought run away with me.

Harold calls for me to enter, though I can barely hear his voice.

I push through the door, unsure exactly what I'm going to say. I hate this woman he brought into our lives to destroy everything he'd so carefully built. I hate that it has to be this way, and I hate him for ruining what was once my home.

But all that anger fades away the moment I see him.

Harold MacVeigh is a proud man, a handsome man. A performer and an entertainer and our fearless leader.

The man who sits before me is broken and bent. Quite literally, as he's slumped over his desk, his head held up in his hand.

I rush to his side, placing a hand to his forehead but finding no fever. "Harold, what's going on? What's wrong?" I go to move to the door. "Let me get Bianca."

Harold's fingers clasp around my wrist, pulling me to a stop. "I don't need Bianca. There's nothing wrong."

My hands fall to my hips as I stare down at the wreck before me. "Harold, be serious. Something is beyond wrong. Look at you." *Look at what she's done to you.* I manage to keep the words in, but I'm sure he can hear them anyway.

He lets out a long sigh and gestures for me to sit. "There's nothing physically wrong with me, how about that?"

"What's going on?" I ask again, Andra's dire prediction racing to the front of my mind. With everything going on with Callum, I haven't had much brain space left to ruminate on her vision, but now, seeing him here before me, I can't help but think that his current state must be tied to what she's seen, the atrocious act he is close to committing.

"I have to do something, Cate. Something that doesn't sit well with me. Something that has been haunting me."

"Then don't do it." I lean forward in my seat. "You don't have to do it, Harold. Everyone at this club will support whatever decision you make." Certainly no one would fault him for deciding not to commit murder.

"Even if it means the club closes?" His tired eyes meet mine. "I know you've managed to find a way out, but what about the others. Where do you think they'll end up if La Puissance shuts down?"

"So Lady M is forcing you to kill King James and if you don't she'll pull her funds from the club?" Just when I thought I couldn't hate her any more, though I probably should have foreseen this. Harold did what needed to be done for the Uprising, but he always preached for nonviolent means and certainly never participated in the violence himself.

"Yes." He seems surprised by his own admission.

I reach across the desk for one of his hands, noting how thin and frail he's gotten even over just the past few days. "Then let me help you, Harold. If all of this is causing you distress, you know I can help ease it."

I've never used my Gift on Harold. He's never asked, and our relationship has never veered into sexual territory. But Harold has done so much for me. If he needs my help, I'm willing to do whatever I can to provide it.

He yanks his hand away from me, shaking his head. "No. I could never . . . we could never . . ."

"There is another option, you know." I check over my shoulder, as if Lady M could have somehow materialized in the office without me noticing.

He sighs, the breath sounding ragged in his chest. "And what is that?"

"We both know Callum Reid is planning on becoming the Scotan candidate." I wait for Harold to fill in the blanks, but he just stares at me vacantly. I lean forward in my seat. "So we let him, Harold. Callum is a good man. He will be a good leader."

"And you've discerned this over the course of what . . . fifteen hours you've spent with him?" His voice takes on a tone he's never used with me before, like I'm a naïve fool.

"I could discern that much of him in less time than that." A small smile tugs on my lips at just the thought of him. "Callum . . .

well, he's everything we could want in a leader, Harold. He's everything."

Harold watches me closely, studying me so intently I shift uncomfortably under his gaze. The way he is looking at me, it's like he sees through to the heart of me. And like what he sees might hurt me.

"You need to be careful with him, Cate. Guard yourself."

I just barely manage to keep from rolling my eyes. "You know as well as I do that I don't need much time with a man in my bed to know his true character." I place my hands flat on the desk between us. "This isn't you, Harold. You don't want to rule this nation, and you certainly don't want to kill."

Harold sits back in his seat, letting the desk divide us. "The plan is already in motion."

My blood chills in my veins. "What do you mean? The window doesn't open until midnight."

"And come midnight, I will be waiting outside the Scotan Castle." He looks at me with sadness in his deep brown eyes. "There's nothing you can do, Cate."

"And what about Callum? How do you know he won't be there too?" I clasp my hands in front of me to try to still their shaking, a terrible feeling about to swallow me whole.

"Because he'll be here. With you."

"No." My head shakes back and forth, moving almost of its own accord. "Absolutely not. I won't do it, Harold. I can't even believe you're asking me to."

"She has Andra, Cate."

My already frozen veins crackle and snap. "What do you mean she *has* Andra?"

"I mean, she's taken your sister. Andra is no longer at the club. If you ruin this plan for us . . ." He doesn't have to finish voicing the threat for it to hang in the air.

Tears fill my eyes, clouding my vision and closing my throat. "You would let her hurt Andra, Harold? You're okay with harming my sister for this woman you just met? For a position you don't even want?" The betrayal stings, worse than any pain I've felt before. "Look at what she's done to you. Look who you've become."

Look at who *I've* become. I didn't even notice my sister was gone, I've been so wrapped up in myself. And in Callum.

"Cate, everything I'm doing, everything I've done, has always been to protect you. You need to trust that I'm doing everything I can for you and your sister."

"You never needed me to get information from him, did you? You just needed me to distract him, get close to him and keep him busy while you stab us all in the back." I shake my head, clearing away the tears to make room for the anger.

Harold's face is pained, his lips turned in a grim frown. "I thought you knew me better than that, Caterine."

"So did I." I press the heels of my hands into my eyes. "I have to go." I push my chair back so violently it falls to the ground, but I don't stop to right it.

"She will kill him, Cate." Harold's words stop me in my tracks. "I will ensure that no lasting harm comes to Andra, but I can't protect him. So if you care about him, you will keep him away."

I don't stop to acknowledge his warning, throwing open the door to the office and finding the last person I want to see on the other side. I swallow down my tears, determined not to let her see them. "Lady M." I brush past her, shivering at the slight contact.

She closes the door behind her, and I make a split-second decision.

There is an alcove to the left of Harold's office, mostly hidden as long as it's unoccupied. I duck into the shadows and find the metal latch easily. Before this room was an office, it was used for other activities, and all of our rooms have this contraption, mostly used for safety purposes, but sometimes, like right now, used for spying. I slide the thin metal bar, opening a slit allowing me to peer into the room.

Lady M sweeps into the office, her black skirts brushing the floor. Harold immediately vacates his seat behind the desk, allowing her to gracefully fold herself into his chair. He hovers next to her, ready to do her bidding, and my stomach roils.

"Will she do it?" Lady M's cold, emotionless voice penetrates the tiny hole in the wall, clear as day.

"I think so." Harold's shoulders sag, and I wish I could find some pity for him within my heart. But whatever happens next, Harold has brought down on himself.

"*Think* isn't good enough. I need to know that Caterine will play her part."

I lean a little closer to hear Harold's response.

The hairs on the back of my neck rise, but it isn't Harold's response setting my nerves on high alert. I reach for the dagger sheathed at my thigh, for reassurance more than anything else. But I'm too slow.

A hand clamps over my mouth, an arm thick with muscle snaking around my waist.

I fight, clawing at the hands and arms that bind me.

Until I hear two simple words, whispered against the shell of my ear. A voice I would know anywhere. "It's me."

I relax against his hold and Callum releases me, though the heat of him stays at my back. The weight of him is so reassuring I don't question how he found me, or why.

It takes a second for my brain to catch up.

Harold's voice slithers through the slit in the wall. "I told you, Cate is going to do what we ask of her. She—"

I react without thinking, slamming the metal partition closed. Callum cannot hear the rest of that sentence.

The metal makes a ghastly sound, loud and squeaking and unmistakable.

"Shit," I mutter, turning to Callum and taking him by the hand. "We need to go. Now." I tug him toward the light, out of the shadow of the alcove.

But the door to Harold's office is already open, the sound of footsteps thudding our way.

"What's going on?" Callum asks.

Instead of heading for the light of the hallway, the escape route back to my suite, I pull him deeper into the darkness, hoping the shadows are enough to hide us. Harold's final words to me run on repeat through my mind.

Lady M will murder Callum if he goes to kill his father. What's to stop her from taking him out right now, solving the problem before it becomes worse?

I have a split second to figure out how to save us both. "Do you trust me?" My back hits a wall; we've retreated as far back as we can go.

"Yes," he breathes, his weight pressing me into the darkness.

I let that weight comfort me, let myself feel, for just the briefest second, happy that he is here.

Happy isn't the right word, of course. Because he's here, and if I keep him here, if I do what Harold demands I do, Callum Reid is going to end up hating me. If I cost him the opportunity to do what he feels is best for his father and the country, he will never forgive me. The thought makes me sick to my stomach.

But what is the hatred of one man when compared with my sister's life, even if he is a man I've grown to care for? I would do anything to keep Andra safe, something Harold and Lady M both know.

They're putting me in an impossible position: Risk my sister's safety or betray a man who doesn't deserve it. Betray a man who, whether I can fully admit it or not, has buried himself inside my heart.

The footsteps grow closer, and I know we are not hidden enough. If Harold or Lady M steps into the alcove, they will see us. Harold will immediately know that I was listening to his conversation. And with Callum right here, what's to stop him from thinking the very worst—that I've betrayed him and told Callum everything?

I tilt my chin up, searching for the steadiness of Callum's blue eyes in the dark. "Kiss me," I breathe.

"What? That's against your rules, Caterine. I don't—"

I don't give him time to finish his sentence, pressing my lips to his and cutting off his protest.

He hesitates for only a second before kissing me back, his soft lips moving gently over mine. I sigh into the kiss, leaning into the warmth of his embrace, forgetting after just a second that this is a ruse, that his life could be at risk if we are discovered, as could my sister's. My hand fists in the fabric of his shirt and his travels to the nape of my neck, holding me tightly. As if I could even dream of pulling away.

I tease the seam of his lips with the tip of my tongue, swallowing the groan he releases like it's rich whisky. His tongue sweeps into my mouth and this time I'm the one letting out an unholy moan.

Callum's hands travel down to my waist, as mine tangle in his hair. His hips thrust into me and I relish his hardness.

I lose myself in him.

Until I hear Lady M's derisive declaration. "It's just another one of your whores."

Callum moves like he wants to pull away, address the claim, but I keep his lips pressed close to mine, desperate to hide his face and his recognizable copper curls in the shadows. I wrap my legs around his waist and his hands slide to cup my upper thighs. It's the distraction we need, so potent I even distract myself.

I don't hear Lady M retreat, but the sound of the office door slamming shut reverberates through the small space.

I gently guide Callum's lips away from mine, not wanting to separate from him, but knowing we need to move quickly.

His breaths are shallow as we part. "Are you okay?"

The fact that his first concern in this moment is whether I'm okay breaks something in me. I laugh. "Not really."

He tries to put space between us, but I keep him close, needing his solidness and comfort. "I'm sorry I overstepped."

I take his cheek in my hand and press a soft kiss to his lips. "You didn't. But there's something I need to tell you. Can we go to my room?" I know I can't tell him the whole truth, not really, but maybe if I put some time and space between me and Lady M and this new version of Harold, I might be able to come up with some plan that doesn't involve me hurting everyone I care about.

"Of course, my lady. Whatever you need."

I peek into the hallway, only emerging fully once I see that the space is clear. Tucking my hand into Callum's, I pull him along the corridor until we reach the safety of my suite. I put some space between us the moment the door closes and locks, darting toward the balcony doors.

Callum doesn't say anything, and he doesn't follow me, giving me the space I desperately need. My brain is a hurricane of thoughts. Callum is here. Lady M has my sister. Harold is going to kill the king. I might be the only one who knows everything.

And that kiss.

I don't kiss my clients.

Kissing Callum is a good reminder why.

I close my eyes and focus on my breathing. Something tells me kissing my other clients wouldn't be anything like kissing Callum. Kissing Callum was . . . earth-shattering and grounding all at the same time. It didn't satiate my need for him, only stoked it.

After a minute, I turn to face him. He's watching me with such tenderness in his eyes it almost makes everything worse.

He takes a few cautious steps in my direction, stopping just a foot away from me, his hand reaching for my waist. "Can I make a request before you tell me whatever it is you need to tell me?"

I nod, unable to form words at the moment, too many emotions and possibilities warring in my head.

He takes a deep breath. "I need the evening, my lady. This one final evening of nothing but you and me and this room." He scrubs a hand over his face, through the stubble that's grown over the past couple of days. "I need to lose myself in you. I need to escape, for just a little while longer. I need you to give me the strength I fear I might be lacking."

I know I shouldn't, shouldn't take advantage of his trust in me in this moment. I know how much he is going to hate me when the truth finally comes out, when he learns I could have put a stop to everything but chose not to. But when he looks at me with those eyes, I can't deny him anything. And so I nod again. "Of course, Your Highness."

He tugs me closer, angling his head so his lips can trace the line of my neck. "Can I have my final lesson, Lady Caterine?"

I take his face in my hands. "You can have whatever you want, Callum Reid." I can deny him nothing.

His lips brush mine, the faintest hint of contact. "Even this?"

I answer by pressing my lips to his.

The kiss is slow and unhurried, softer than the one in the alcove. He takes his time exploring, sucking my bottom lip before tangling his tongue with mine. His hands work their way into my hair, the waves soft and loose. When he tugs gently to expose my neck, I moan. His mouth moves everywhere, over the line of my jaw, down the curve of my neck, along the line of my collarbone.

His hands fist in the fabric of my tunic, drawing it slowly over my head. I wear nothing underneath, and his eyes drink me in like it's the first time. He sits on the edge of the bed, pulling me into the vee of his legs.

I run my fingers through his curls, nibble along his stubbled jaw while his hands skim over the bare skin of my stomach, tease the undersides of my breasts.

His mouth moves lower, leaving a trail of soft kisses over the mounds of my breasts, his hands cupping them, his thumbs sweeping just far enough away from my nipples to leave me panting.

He pulls away seconds before providing me with relief, pinning me with a teasing grin. "I thought this was supposed to be a lesson, my lady."

I try to direct his mouth back to where I want it. "You seem to be doing just fine without my guidance, Your Highness."

"Teach me, Lady Caterine. Tell me what you want me to do."

"I want you to put that glorious tongue to work."

"Here?" He swipes a lick between my breasts.

I guide his mouth to my aching nipple. "Here. Tease me, Callum."

He swirls the tip of his tongue over my skin. "Like this?"

My back arches, pressing me further into him. "Yes," I breathe.

He pulls the peaked bud into his mouth, sucking gently. "Like this?"

"Yes." My fingers tighten in his curls.

He grazes his teeth over my sensitive skin. "How about like this?"

"Yes, Callum, yes. More," I demand.

He chuckles and the vibrations buzz through my skin. But he doesn't tease me for much longer, his mouth moving between my breasts, tonguing, sucking, biting until I'm on the verge of release and aching for some measure of relief.

I pull him away from me, just long enough for me to undo the button at the waist of my pants and push them to the ground. Tugging him to standing, I rid him of his own pants and undergarments while he yanks his shirt over his head. He's hard and glistening, and I lick my lips thinking about taking him in my mouth again.

Callum surprises me by lying flat on the bed, pulling me down on top of him. Our lips meet again and there's nothing slow or soft about these kisses. They're messy and passionate and hopefully a good indication of what he can do with his tongue.

He grips my hips and shifts me upward.

"What are you doing?" I grab on to the headboard as he settles himself under me.

"What better way for you to show me how to please you than by letting you be in control?" He shifts my thighs so they're on either side of his shoulders, his hands running up my legs and around to the curves of my ass.

I hover over him, watching his eyes as he takes me in. His pupils widen and he licks his lips, and I don't know if there's anything more arousing than a man who is aroused by the sight of your pleasure.

He looks up, his gaze meeting mine.

I know what he's going to ask so I answer before he can get the words out. "Lick me. Put that tongue to work and devour me, Callum."

He groans and doesn't wait to meet my demands, his tongue tracing me open, exploring me. He's attentive and perceptive, as usual, homing in on the places that make me gasp. He dips his tongue into my channel and my hips buck. He grunts, pulling me closer, holding me in place as his tongue makes its way closer to my clit.

I cry out the first time he makes contact, already so sensitized and aching. No partner has ever made me feel this way before, so ready and so attuned.

"Show me what you like," he grinds out, easing his grip on my hips.

And I do. I work myself over his tongue, my eyes never leaving his gorgeous face.

I'm already climbing the peak, cresting the wave, the release building low in my belly. Then Callum sucks my clit. Gently at first, then not so gently. I come so hard I have to grip the headboard so I don't fall over. The orgasm rolls through me, wave after wave, and Callum doesn't stop, doesn't let up, until I pull away.

I'm panting, breathing as if I've just sprinted through the city being chased by a madman. I balance myself on his chest. He tucks his hands behind his head, a self-satisfied smirk on his face.

And he earned that smirk. So I let him have it.

I trail my fingers down his torso, shifting my weight lower. "You are a very quick study, Callum Reid."

"You're a very thorough teacher, Lady Caterine." He sits up, maneuvering me until I'm straddling his lap.

"My friends call me Cate."

"Are we friends now?"

"With how many times you've made me come? It's safe to say we are." I kiss him, tasting myself and deepening the kiss. "I think you've earned a reward for being such a good student." I reach in between our bodies, slick with sweat, and take him in my fist.

He covers my hand with his. "You don't have to."

"What if I want to?" I do want to, want to bring him this last bit of pleasure before I completely blow up his life. I want to see some spark of joy in those blue eyes for one final time. "What if I need this just as much as you do?"

18

CALLUM

HER BREATH CATCHES the moment the question slips out, like she didn't mean to ask it. Didn't mean to reveal herself to me.

I brush a kiss over her full lips and make sure my tone is light and teasing, bringing us back to neutral, because I know neither of us can really go there. We've found solace this week in our physical connection, and it is easier to come back to that than try to figure out if there could truly be something more here. "By all means then, my lady. I exist merely for your pleasure."

She rolls her eyes but pairs it with a kiss, before pushing me back to lying down and moving between my legs.

This time she takes her time, teasing me like I know she loves to be teased. Her tongue slides up the ridge of my shaft, circling the head of my cock before trailing back down again. I moan as she laps at my balls, sucking one into her mouth, releasing it with a pop before moving on to the other, her fist stroking me slowly while her mouth works.

"Caterine . . . Cate. You are so incredible." My hips buck, my cock searching for her mouth, needing even the smallest measure of relief.

She kisses the tip of my head. "I like bringing you pleasure, Your Highness. It turns me on."

I take the nape of her neck in my hand. "Are you already ready for more, my lady?"

Her eyes meet mine, the honey amber softening. "It seems like I'm always ready when it's with you, Callum. Like I can never get enough."

I swallow thickly but don't allow myself to fall further under her spell. "Glad to hear it." I sit up long enough to grasp her hips and spin her around, lying back down when her pretty pussy is settled back over my face.

She peeks over her shoulder at me. "It's supposed to be your turn."

"I like it better this way." Watching Caterine find pleasure with me makes me feel something close to invincible.

She doesn't protest further, finally taking my aching cock in her mouth. She moves slowly, gradually taking me deeper and deeper. The things this woman can do with her tongue.

No partner in my future is ever going to be able to compare. Not just with the way she makes me feel physically, but with how comfortable I've become in her presence. How at home I feel in her company, and in her bed.

I let my tongue find her center, keeping the pressure soft and gentle in case she's still sensitive. She lets out a moan with my dick deep in her mouth and I have to fight to keep from coming on the spot.

I've never engaged in this act with a partner before, too afraid in the past of looking improper, fearing rumors about the Prince of Scota and his demands in the bedroom. But with Cate, I have none of that fear. And so I let go of all doubts and just enjoy this. Bringing her pleasure, while she guides me to the strongest orgasm I've ever had.

It builds quickly. I don't even have time to warn her before I explode, but she doesn't seem to mind. Her sucks turn gentle while I come down, and I increase the pressure of my tongue, slipping two fingers inside her, feeling her tighten around me seconds later.

She cries out her release and it's the sweetest sound. If I heard it a million more times, it wouldn't be enough. That doesn't soften the blow of knowing I might never hear it again.

She shifts her weight off me, lying next to me on the bed, her feet at my head, her head at my feet. We both breathe heavily, as heavy as the silence around us.

I reach for her hand and she tangles her fingers in mine. I squeeze and dread the moment one of us speaks and this bubble is broken.

She sits up first and I reluctantly do the same. I wait for her to dart out of bed, and she does, but not before she places a soft kiss on my lips.

Caterine disappears behind her privacy screen, into her bathing chamber. The water runs for several seconds, and when she emerges, she's draped in her robe.

I gather my clothes from the floor and dress quickly, not wanting to be the only one in the room exposed.

She pours us both a drink, setting the glasses on the table. We sit, and still the room remains silent.

I open my mouth to make my final request.

She holds up a hand to stop me. "I know what you're going to say."

"You do?"

She sucks in a long breath. "You're going to kill your father so you can become the Scotan candidate."

There's no question in her voice.

"I know you probably think I'm a monster, Cate . . ."

"I don't." She reaches across the table and squeezes my hand.

I want to tangle our fingers together, keep her tight in my grip, but she pulls away before I can manage. "You don't think I'm a monster even though I'm planning on murdering my own father?"

She looks me directly in the eye. "I know what kind of man you are, Callum Reid. And I know having to do this must be ripping you apart. I can't even imagine. I know that just as clearly as I know you would never have come to this decision on your own."

I have to pull my gaze from hers because there's a sudden wetness building in my eyes. "How can you possibly know that?"

"Because I know you." She shrugs, sipping from her whisky like we're in the middle of a casual conversation.

"It's only been a few days."

"That's more than enough for me to have seen the heart of you, Callum. You are a good person. If this is the course of action you've decided on, then it's the right one."

I sit back in my chair. "So you know what it is I have to ask of you?"

She nods. "I don't think you have anything to feel guilty about, but if the guilt feels like it is going to consume you, then I will happily ease it." She hesitates for a second before throwing back the remaining liquor in her glass.

"But?"

"But I have a request." Her voice softens as her guard drops. It's not often Lady Caterine reveals herself. I've come to search for her in her rare moments of vulnerability, but they typically seem to catch her off guard. This time feels more deliberate.

"Anything, my lady."

She rises, untying the belt of her robe and letting the silky fabric fall to the floor. "Stay with me for just a while longer."

I focus my eyes on hers so I'm not distracted by the sight of her luscious curves. The golden brown is hazy with wanting, and with something else. Something deeper. But there can never be anything more between us; both of us know it. I would be a fool to even hope for it. And yet it's there, that hint of feelings.

I stand, sweeping her into my embrace, burying my face in the curve of her neck, lifting her easily, carrying her back to the silken sheets of her bed, where for a few more hours at least, we can keep pretending it's only us.

WHEN I WAKE, the night sky outside Caterine's window is black as ebony. This should startle me, I know, somewhere deep down, but the fact doesn't bolt me out of bed. Instead, I tilt my head, letting my eyes trace over the naked beauty tucked into my arms. Cate's head rests on my chest, her golden hair spilling across her shoulders. She looks peaceful and calm and so beautiful it makes my chest ache.

I run my fingers along her bare arm.

She stirs, turning into me first before pulling away, blinking the haziness out of her eyes. "What time is it?"

I shrug, as if time doesn't matter, as if I've forgotten what tonight is and what I'm meant to do. "Late."

She sits up, the sheet falling to her waist. "Fuck, Callum. You have to go." She pushes out of the bed, running to the window as if the night sky can tell her the time.

"It's fine, my lady. I still have plenty of time." Her frantic energy forms a pit in my stomach. I don't have plenty of time. Maybe an hour or two at most. I know what's waiting for me at home, and even though I'm in no rush to complete the deed, I promised my family I would take care of it quickly, before anyone else has the chance.

I rise from the bed, slowly making my way around Caterine's suite to gather my discarded clothing.

She whirls away from the window, rushing around the space and shoving said clothing into my hands. "I'm not kidding, Callum. It's already almost midnight. You need to get home."

I tug my shirt over my head. "A few minutes more won't kill anyone, Caterine." I wince as soon as the words are out of my mouth. "You know what I mean."

Her hands wring together as she wordlessly tries to get me to dress faster. "Shit. Shit fuck shit."

I raise one eyebrow as I step into my pants. "Something wrong, other than the obvious?"

Tears well in her eyes and the sight punches me in the gut. "You're going to hate me," she whispers.

I drop my shoe and cross the room to her, taking her shaking hands in mine. "Never."

"There's something you should know." She pulls her hands from my grip. "You are not the only one planning on killing your father."

A chill sweeps over my body before sinking into my veins. "What do you mean? And how could you possibly know such a thing?"

She crosses to the other side of the small space. "You obviously know of my abilities. Well, my sister, Andra, she has a Gift of her own."

"What kind of Gift?" One part of me wants to yell at her to say whatever she needs to say, and quickly. The other wants to linger in this state of not knowing for as long as possible.

"She's a Seer." Caterine wraps her arms around her middle, as if she's trying to hold herself together. "I guess I should start at the beginning. After the Uprising, the club was in a lot of trouble. Money trouble. Harold financially helped support the rebellion, and our business took a hit, leaving us on the brink of closing. Harold would rather die than see that happen, so instead he married a wealthy woman. Lady M."

My brow furrows in confusion. "I've never heard of her."

"She sort of just appeared one day. When she married Harold and took over partial control of the club, she put all of us under contracts, most at impossibly high sums, so high we'd never be able to work our way out of them." Her fingers tighten around her, her knuckles turning white.

"That's why you agreed to help me?" I knew she always saw me as a client, yet what she's telling me now makes her motives even more clear. Not that I can blame her.

She nods. "With the money your sister paid for your lessons, I could buy out not just my contract but Andra's as well." She makes some kind of decision, dropping her arms. "Lady M has been making Andra read for her, pushing her to See in a way that has worn Andra down, both physically and mentally. And today, right before you got to the club, I found out that Lady M has taken her and is keeping her somewhere."

"To get you to obey? She's holding your sister's life?" This Lady M must have asked something terrible of Caterine, and my stomach tightens as I think of what that could possibly mean. What she might have done. Might still be doing.

Caterine nods again.

"What did they ask you to do, Caterine?" My voice is low, brimming with barely restrained anger—if she did what I think she did, it's time to cut to the heart of the matter.

"Harold is going to murder your father under Lady M's orders." The words come out as faint as a whisper. "They told me to keep you here until after midnight, and if I didn't, if I told you what was going to happen, they would hurt my sister." She crumples into a chair, and I don't have the capacity to care that she appears completely drained.

"So you've known this entire evening that this terrible thing I have to do, this thing that has been torturing me for weeks, is going to be thwarted and you didn't bother to tell me?" I try to keep my voice level, but I don't succeed. The anger is a good mask for the total devastation ripping through me. I thought we had shared something special this evening. I came to her for help, and this entire time she was lying right to my face. No doubt manipulating me and my feelings for her.

No. Not feelings. There's no love here, only pure lust. It's her job to exploit that lust, and she played me perfectly.

"I'm sorry, Callum. I wanted to tell you, but what was I supposed to do, sacrifice my sister's life?" She crosses over to me, her hands clenched in fists at her side, not about to let my anger go unchecked.

"If it means saving the country from being ruled by people unfit for leadership, then yes, Caterine, that's exactly what you should do!" I'm being unfair, and I know it. God knows I would probably do the same in her situation, but I can't make myself justify her actions knowing the consequences.

She gets in my face. "I'm sorry I wasn't raised like that, Callum Reid! I will not apologize for doing what's best for the only person who's been there for me my entire life." She lowers her voice. "Besides, Harold does have the capacity to be a good leader."

"Does this Lady M? Because it seems like the two of them are a package deal. Is she the kind of person you want in control?" I shove my feet into my shoes, gathering my coat and heading for the door. "I don't have time for this argument, I may still be able to get there in time."

"Wait!" she cries, meeting me at the door. Her hands find mine, and I wish I had the strength to pull away, but my fingers latch on to hers like they were created to be connected. "Please be careful, Callum."

"You don't get to tell me that now, my lady."

A single tear rolls down her cheek, and for a minute I question everything. This tear, this night, everything that's happened in this room.

"Was any of it real?" I ask the question I don't want to know the answer to.

"Yes," she says fiercely. "I . . . I care about you, Callum."

I gently tug my hands from hers, grabbing my coat and slipping into the sleeves. "I thought I cared about you too."

She sucks in a sharp breath. "I earned that, I suppose. And I understand if you never want to see me again." Her voice breaks and falls to a whisper. "But please don't hurt him. He's the closest thing I've ever had to a father, Callum."

"You don't get to ask that of me either."

"I know." Tears flow freely down her cheeks now. "I will still help you, after. If you need my services, I'm here."

"Because I've already paid for them?"

She shakes her head. "Because you don't deserve this. You don't deserve any of this."

A million words dance on the edge of my tongue, but none of them are the right ones. So I nod, open the door, and walk away.

This pregnancy is going to stick, and she won't know until the time has already passed, but there's not one baby, but three.

I have Seen what she plans to do with them, Seen things no mother should ever do to her children. I know there is only one solution, but it is going to destroy her. I don't know what it's going to do to Harry.

But I must take the girls away from her. It is the only way for them to be safe. It is the only way for all of us to be safe.

—EXCERPT FROM THE JOURNAL OF DIANA BRAHAN

19

CATE

I ALMOST FOLD INTO myself when the door closes behind Callum, but I manage to hold myself upright, clutching to the edge of a chair so tightly it hurts. I don't know what I'm supposed to do in this moment, but I know I can't do nothing.

I fling open the door to my room, fighting my instincts to follow Callum and instead heading the opposite direction, toward Harold's office. Maybe there's still time to talk some sense into him. Maybe I can get through to him and stop this whole nightmare before it truly starts.

But his office is empty and a quick glance around the hallway reveals a heavy quiet that's unusual for the club. For the first time, I wonder just how many of my colleagues, my friends, might be involved in this plan.

After another furtive glance around the corridor, I pull a pin from my hair and slide it into the lock. I would feel guilty, but Harold was the one who taught me to pick locks in the first place.

I slip into his office and shut the door behind me quietly.

I don't even know what I'm looking for, but I know there must be something here. Something that might give me some kind of hint as to what Lady M's plan is, really.

I go for the ledgers first. The truth revealed in the numbers is bleak. The club really was on the brink of closure. If it hadn't been for the influx of funds coming from Lady M, La Puissance would've had to shut its doors months ago. I try to be grateful for this reprieve she's bought us, but I can't find it in me.

I put the ledger back in the exact spot I found it and open the bottom drawer of Harold's desk. A paper on top of a stack catches my eye. My contract. And Andra's right below it.

I remove the pile and sort through them. Various contracts for all the members of La Puissance, the sums ranging from manageable to exorbitant. It isn't until my second time flipping through the papers that I notice the pattern. Not all of us have a contract. Only those of us with Gifts. Me, Andra, Bianca, Tes, Meri, Rosa, Helen, and three others who just arrived at the club in recent weeks.

Lady M doesn't care about the club. She cares about us, the Gifted, claiming ownership over us, and by extension, our talents.

"What is she doing?" I mutter to myself.

Lady M is up to something that has nothing to do with the finances of La Puissance. But what is she doing? And why?

A sound from the hallway startles me out of my stupor. I gently place the papers back in the drawer and close it softly. I tiptoe to the door and press my ear to the wood. When I don't hear any further noises, I crack the door and peek into the hallway. It's clear, so I dart through, locking up behind me.

My eyes roam over the empty hallway and a chill creeps through my veins. It's still quiet. Too quiet. Even in the off hours, the club is full of people and chatter and laughter. The silence is so thick it's foreboding.

I jog down the corridor, past my room, searching for any sign of life, but I don't find any. No one is here. Which means they are likely all together. With Harold. On their way to kill a king.

A king Callum is also planning to kill.

I head back to the main staircase. I don't know who I'm going to warn, who I'm going to save, I only know that I need to be there.

I get to the front door, my hand wrapped around the handle, when I'm grabbed from behind. Reacting immediately, I kick out at my attacker, but another pair of arms latches around me, keeping me still.

It's two of Lady M's guards. I guess the club wasn't so empty, after all.

They carry me back up the stairs to my room.

"Put me down," I insist repeatedly, fighting uselessly against their hold on me. Their arms are banded so tightly around my chest, pinning my arms in place. I attempt to reach for the dagger at my thigh, but it's not there.

They ignore my cries, carrying me as though I'm nothing. I might as well be at this point.

One of them opens the door to my room while the other practically tosses me inside. The door slams and I'm reaching for the doorknob when I hear the lock click. Tugging futilely, I pound my fists against the wood, shouting for them to release me at once. But of course no one can hear my cries for help.

I'm trapped.

To all concerned parties,

We must come to a decision about the election. We all know who needs to be chosen as Avon's first leader; now it is up to us to figure out how to make that happen without raising the suspicion of the people. Many provinces are thirsting for violent retribution, but we must make sure we stay in control and give the heirs the greatest chance of moving forward. We will meet tomorrow to discuss your possible solutions.

In solidarity,

August Sotello

20

CALLUM

I JUMP OUT OF the carriage before it can reach the roundabout at the front of the estate, knowing the second my feet hit the ground that something is wrong. Dashing through the thick copse of trees at the side of the house, I head directly for Alex's cabin on the outskirts of the property. Whatever is happening inside our home, I know enough to know I shouldn't face it alone.

The door to Alex's cabin stands open, and my stomach turns at the sight. I sprint inside, searching for any sign of him. Or for any sign of a struggle. But the small space is deserted and nothing seems to be out of place.

I head down the tight hallway, finding the loose plank of wood in the corner of the floor. Ripping it up, I see that our emergency packs have been taken. In their place is a note dashed out in Alex's precise handwriting.

> I have Dom. We're safe. You know where to find us. Be careful, Cal, this is more than we bargained for.

A small bit of relief slips through me, but it's short-lived. If Dom and Alex fled, just how bad have things gotten? What am I going to be walking into, alone and unprepared? It will make it easier to fight, knowing my sister and uncle are away from the fray, but if things are as bad as Alex's warning implies, I might be outmatched anyway.

I crumple the note in my fist, tossing it aside and sprinting for the main castle.

I encounter the first would-be assassin steps from the estate. He slips into the back door and I spend a precious second wondering how he knew to enter from the rear for easier access to my father's chambers, wonder if this is someone we used to call a friend.

I increase my speed, following him on light feet. He's halfway up the staircase by the time I overtake him, my arm tightening around his neck, enough to knock him unconscious. The man wears a mask, and once he's slumped in my arms, I yank it off, revealing the face of one of our guards. A man sworn to protect the life of the royal family, and here he is, planning to assassinate his king. I drop the man's body, not caring that he tumbles down the stairs, coming to a harsh stop at the bottom. I hope he wakes to several broken bones. It's the least he deserves for his betrayal.

Making my way up the steps, I realize no servants or guards bustle through the halls or work in the kitchens. Normally an estate of this size is teeming with people. The silence is deafening. It sends a chill of foreboding through me.

I'm too late.

No. If my father were dead, I would feel it. I would know. I'm sure of it.

My footsteps slow as I get closer to the king's suite. I can see the open doorway from far down the hallway, but it isn't until I creep closer that I hear the voices inside.

"Just do it already," a woman's voice commands. There's a trace of familiarity in her tone, but I can't place it, can't figure out where I might have heard it before.

"I don't think I can," a man responds, his voice weak.

"You must!"

I lean forward, ready to spring into action, when a punch to my lower right side knocks me into the wall. I don't have time to reach for a blade, the assailant's fists flying at me. I duck a punch, grateful for Dom's sparring sessions for improving my form. The assailant is quick, but their punches begin to soften the more they throw. I bide my time, knowing I can last longer. I wait for the strike aimed at my head, catching their fist and using their momentum to twist an arm behind their back.

"The last thing this country needs is another one of you at the helm." The voice is high-pitched and feminine, unrecognizable, but laced with anger.

I slam her body against the wall, yanking both arms tighter behind her back. "Let's let the people decide that, shall we?"

She tries to throw her head back, aiming to connect with my nose, but a swift strike to the back of the head with the butt end of my dagger I managed to unsheath, and she's crumpling on the floor.

There's only a slim chance the occupants in my father's room missed all that commotion, so I stride forward, trying to quiet my footsteps.

"We do not have time for hesitation! We are not the only ones who want this!" The original commanding voice has gone shrill with panic and frustration.

A different voice chimes in, lower-pitched and strained. "I can't keep him under like this forever."

"He's going to wake up soon." Yet another voice, higher and breathy.

I turn on my tactical brain, leaning on my military training, so I don't do something rash and stupid. I've acted on my emotions enough for one evening. There are at least four people in the room, but from the sounds of it, my father is still alive. I hold on to that as I continue to make my way down the hallway, silently drawing a dagger from my boot to join the one already gripped in my hand.

"You must do as I instruct. This is the only way." The first woman's voice, fiercer now, angry.

"I don't want to hurt anyone. King James is a good man. He doesn't deserve this."

"You think he is so good and benevolent? He is a monarch, just like the rest of them. Merciless. Unforgiving. A liar and a cheat. Kill him, Harold!"

My breath stops in my chest. I'd somehow managed to forget the information Caterine bestowed upon me before I left. Managed to block out just who the would-be killer actually is. Harold MacVeigh.

I edge down the hallway, keeping my back pressed to the wall until I can peek into the room. Light spills out into the hall and I see the bodies of several others who wanted to kill my father and will no longer have the chance. Unlike the two I left behind, these would-be assailants are dead. Lady M and her companions were clearly more ruthless than I am; not once did I think there might be this many others gunning for the candidacy, willing to kill my father for the chance at power.

My stomach turns, the smell of blood thick in the air.

I force myself to steady my breathing and gather my wits. Edging around the doorway, I peek into the room. My father lies on his bed, his eyes closed. He shows no sign of struggle or injury. If I didn't know better, I might think he was taking a peaceful nap.

Harold MacVeigh leans over him, a dagger clutched in his trembling hand. His face is red and it's hard to know for sure from this distance, but it looks like tears are streaming down his cheeks.

A woman stands on the opposite side of the bed, her arms crossed over her chest, her gold eyes flashing with malevolence. Lady M.

"You are weak and foolish. This is your destiny. This is my destiny! You know what has been Seen. Slit his throat!" Her screeches echo around the room, and I recoil from the sound.

I can't see the other two from my position, can't see if any others perch around the perimeter of the room. I hate the idea of going in half-blind, but I can't wait much longer. Lady M's rage is growing, her anger flustering MacVeigh even more.

All I have going for me is the element of surprise. And so I use it.

I dart into the room, heading right for MacVeigh. I tackle him to the ground, pinning him beneath me and knocking the knife free from his grip. It barely registers that this dagger is familiar, that I've run my finger over the ruby buried in its hilt when it was attached to Cate's thigh.

A second later, I'm hit from behind, the wind pushed from my lungs as my body hits the floor. My attacker rolls me underneath her. Her fists pummel into my sides and I curl up, trying to protect myself. Her blows hurt, but they're accompanied by a deeper pain that reaches down to my bones.

Lady M is shrieking, but I can't make out any of the words as my attacker shifts her punches to my face.

Whatever hold she or her companion had on my father, though, seems to have dissipated when she turned her focus away. He heaves himself from the bed, kicking my attacker in the ribs, giving me enough space to shove her off me and jump to my feet.

"Run," I tell my father, slashing out with my dagger and connecting with the woman's shoulder.

She grunts but isn't deterred, coming at me again. I'm bigger than she is, but she's fast and her strength doesn't seem to be waning. I dart out of the way, but she crashes into my father instead.

I bring my knife down on her back, but she spins before I can do real damage. Hoisting my father from the ground, I shove him in the direction of the door. "Go!"

"I'm not leaving you." He glares at me and grabs for one of my knives.

I know we don't have time to argue, so I turn my back to him, placing myself in the direct line of the attacker.

The two of us have been able to keep her at bay, but it looks like Lady M's screeches have finally had an effect and MacVeigh comes at my father as the woman charges at me.

The room fills with the sounds of our fighting, grunts and cries as knives make contact. Thuds as we hit the ground and punches land. I can't pull my attention from my opponent for even a second, so I let the sound of the fighting behind me reassure me that for now at least, my father is still alive.

I manage to swipe a large gash across my attacker's belly, finally causing her steps to falter. Her hand moves to stanch the bleeding as she falls to her knees.

I use this time, spinning around to help my father just in time to see MacVeigh's knife raised over his head. Just in time to watch it plunge into my father's chest, that red ruby glinting in the firelight.

Everything goes still for just a moment, as if the whole world is frozen.

MacVeigh's eyes meet mine, and the shock I feel is mirrored in his expression.

Time seems to slow, as muddy and thick as my head.

I move toward my father, my steps stilted and slow. I still manage to catch him as he collapses to the floor, his weight pulling both of us down to the ground.

MacVeigh stands over us, the bloody knife held limply in his hand, crimson drops splattering the floor.

I hold my father, one hand supporting his head, the other uselessly trying to stem the blood spilling from his chest, as if I can somehow manage to push it all back in, as if I can rewind the clock. It coats my hand in sticky scarlet and I know the sight will never be erased from my mind, my hand covered in my father's blood.

"Callum." My name slips from his mouth, choked and gasping. A trail of scarlet dribbles down his chin.

I tear my gaze from the blood and meet his eyes. "I'm so sorry. I shouldn't have . . . I should have . . ." I press my forehead to his. Part of me is unwilling to believe I've let this happen. The other knows I need to make my amends before it's too late. "I'm so sorry."

His hand reaches up, grasping for my cheek. "No time for that." He sucks in a wheezing breath and another line of blood trickles from his lips. "Find a way. Protect Scota. You are the leader the world needs. Find a way."

My grip on him tightens and tears clog my throat. "I will."

"I love you, son."

The tears pour freely down my cheeks as his breaths stutter in his chest. "I love you too."

I hold him, watching his chest rise and fall. Watching his chest still. Watching as everything I've ever known for my whole life is ripped away from me.

A hand grips my shoulder, pulling me to my feet, forcing me to drop my father's body long before I'm ready to.

"You need to get out of here," MacVeigh whispers fiercely.

I turn on him, fury flooding every one of my veins. Deep down,

I know there is no one but myself to blame, but in this moment, all I can think about is this man killing my father. I pull my arm back, the one holding my knife, ready to plunge it into his heart just as he did to my father, and to my future.

My hand falters when a pair of pleading honey eyes flash in my mind.

Cate, and her final plea to me.

I drop my hand after a few seconds, my chest heaving. "I will kill you for what you've done." This isn't the time, or the place—I manage to convince myself the decision to spare him is mine and mine alone—but the promise is made, and I intend to follow through. Cate will have to understand.

She played her own role in the events of this evening, and she will have to understand that whatever Harold MacVeigh is to her, I cannot let the future of this country rest in his hands.

MacVeigh looks at me with something like sadness in his eyes. "I hope you do. But Lady M will be back soon, and if you are here when she arrives, she will kill you too. Go now, while you still have the chance."

I don't wait. I'm outnumbered and neither my brain nor my body is prepared for another fight. I head toward the balcony doors, knowing it's the quickest way of escape. I'm sure there are others still out there who plan on being the one to take my father's life. Little do they know, they're already too late.

"Callum," MacVeigh calls softly just as I'm about to slip through to the outside.

I pause, not understanding why I care to give this murderer one more second of my time.

"Take care of her. Of Cate. Protect your Bond."

I don't acknowledge his request.

I climb over the balcony railings, my body aching, but somehow managing to push through. I dash my way to the stables, taking the reins of the first horse I find and riding away. Leaving my only home, and my only remaining parent behind.

I MAKE IT to the safe house quickly, without facing any trouble on the road. Scota is eerily quiet tonight, like the whole province knows of the violence brewing in its castle and wants to be as far away from it as possible when it arrives. The green hills of my home province give way to the dark and dank streets of Stratford's lower quarter as I try to prepare myself for what comes next.

How will my people react when they hear the news that Harold MacVeigh is their candidate? Will they be happy to see my family hand over the reins to a nonroyal? Or will they be disappointed in me for abandoning them?

I'm not sure which option feels worse.

I slip my key into the lock of the dingy apartment along the river, knocking out a short and simple code on the door so Dom and Alex know not to attack me the minute I cross the threshold. I don't think about how I must look, sweaty and exhausted, my father's blood staining my shirt, bruises already beginning to bloom.

I'm still attacked as soon as the door opens, Dom flying across the room and into my arms.

"You did it," she whispers into my ear, taking in the evidence on my clothing, her voice choked with tears. I'm not sure if it's pride or devastation lacing her words. Probably both.

I set her on the ground and cross to the far side of the room so I don't have to look at her, to see my own disappointment reflected back at me from the depths of her eyes. "Not quite."

"Is he . . . you know?" My sister can't even bring herself to say the words.

"Yes." My hands clench into tight fists at my side.

"What happened, Cal?" Alex gives me space, staying near the tiny, filthy kitchen of the flat.

We found this space in an old tenement building during the bleakest months of the Uprising and have kept it ever since, an escape plan and our last resort. I suppose now is the time to be grateful we planned for the worst.

"Father is dead." The words slice through me like MacVeigh's knife sliced through his chest.

Dom approaches me, a tentative hand placed on my shoulder. "I know you feel the guilt now, Cal, but you have to remember that it's what he wanted."

"I'm not the one who killed him."

The words hang heavy in the air.

"What do you mean you're not the one who killed him?"

I turn to face my uncle, thinking it might be easier than looking at my sister. "I mean, I was too late. Harold MacVeigh took his life. He will be the candidate for the Scotan province."

Alex's face pales, his blue eyes bright against the starkness of his face. "Harold MacVeigh?"

I nod, watching out of the corner of my eye as Dom sinks into a rickety chair. Her eyes have clouded over, and her shoulders hunch like she can no longer hold herself upright.

I did this. I did this to my sister, to my uncle, to my people.

And for what? A few hours in the arms of a woman who sees me as nothing more than a job. Nothing more than a quick way to earn some coin and advance her position.

I know I should tell them the whole truth, how Lady Caterine cost me the one chance I had to salvage everything. But I can't make myself say the words. Not yet, anyway. It hurts just to think them; I don't know how I will ever be able to give them voice.

Alex's brow furrows as he parses out all the information and its implications. "Why would Harold do that?"

I shake my head. "I don't know. But from what I can gather, I think the real person behind it is his new wife, a Lady M."

"Does she have some sort of political aspirations?" Alex crosses the room, his fists clenched at his side.

"I don't think anyone really knows. Cate—Lady Caterine—only knew that she and Harold recently married and apparently her funds helped save the club from closing." Her name tastes bitter on my tongue and yet I have the urge to seek her out. Seek the comfort I know only being in her arms can bring me.

Alex catches my slip on her name, raising a single eyebrow, but he doesn't mention it. "Lady M doesn't give us much to go on." He begins pacing around the small perimeter of the room. "This isn't the way things were supposed to go," he mutters under his breath. "Who could have sent her?"

"You think another province is trying to sabotage our candidate? Is there anything in the decree to stop that sort of thing?"

Alex shakes his head. "I don't think so. But that isn't what happened here anyway. If Harold is the one who committed the act, then Harold is the candidate. There can't be any more killing at this point. Unless . . ." His eyes cloud over.

Dom and I exchange a look.

"Unless what?" I ask when Alex doesn't bother to finish his sentence.

Alex sighs, running a hand through his already disheveled hair. "There is something I need to tell you both. You're not going to like it, but I ask that you listen to what I have to say before making any judgments."

Dom grimaces. "Not a very comforting precursor there, Uncle."

"I know." Alex gestures for me to sit.

I lower myself carefully onto one of the wooden crates acting as chairs around the dining table. "Whatever you have to say, say it, Alex."

"For the past year, I have been working with the Uprising."

The declaration seems to have weight, clouding the already dank atmosphere.

I fear I must have been hit in the head at some point during the preceding hours, because certainly my uncle did not just say what I think he said. Certainly there is no way he, a man I have relied on for my whole life, just admitted the deepest betrayal like it's nothing.

Dom recovers her wits first. "Why would you do that?"

Alex leans against the old wooden table, shifting his weight so the whole thing doesn't collapse under him. "It became clear to me early on in the Uprising that this revolution was going to be different. The man in charge is too smart, too tactical for it to have been a failure. The reports we were receiving were bleak, and I knew there was a chance the fighting could have gone on for years, costing thousands of lives."

"So you went behind our backs and gave the enemy our secrets?" My head spins, and I don't know if it's the result of my injuries or this news. Either way, I can't get a handle on what's being said.

"I did it to protect Scota and to protect you both."

Dom gestures to my broken body. "It doesn't appear you did a very good job of that."

Alex sinks onto a wooden crate across from mine, his elbows resting on his knees, his head hanging down. "I see that. I thought we had things carefully planned. But someone along the way must have betrayed us."

"You mean someone aside from you?"

Alex meets my gaze for half a second before dropping his eyes again. "The killing of James was rigged. Or it was supposed to be anyway. There were Uprising soldiers stationed at the estate to protect James until you could get to him, Cal."

"I didn't see any Uprising soldiers, Uncle." Though there were a host of bodies littering the hallway outside my father's suite of rooms. But the other two I encountered certainly weren't trying to clear the way for me or they wouldn't have attacked me in the first place.

"Something went very wrong tonight."

"That's putting it mildly," Dom mutters.

Alex stands, new determination in his gait. "But we can fix this. I have been working with the Uprising."

"You did mention that already." The mere idea of it still churns my gut.

"That means I have a direct line to their leader. I can fix this." He claps a hand on my shoulder.

I wince, shaking off his touch. I'm not ready for that yet. "How in the bloody hell are you going to fix this? Father is dead at the hands of a madman, and we no longer can trust a word you say."

Alex's face falls. "I know it seems like that now, but you will see that I did this for all of us. I don't know how I'm going to make it right, but the killing period doesn't officially end for six more days, so we have time. I'll get a message to August, and we will figure this out."

Dom shoots me a questioning look. I nod for her to continue. "If you think there is a way to correct this course of action and give Callum a chance to represent Scota, then you should do so. But it won't make up for what you did, Uncle."

He nods, his lips pulling down. "I understand. I know how this all must feel right now, but I hope you will come to see the reasons behind my actions, and how my goal was always to secure Callum the leadership position we all know he is meant for."

I don't feel meant for much of anything in this moment, and I don't have the strength to be angry. I also can't immediately accept his words as truth. It's been a day full of betrayal, and I can't even trust my own thoughts in this moment.

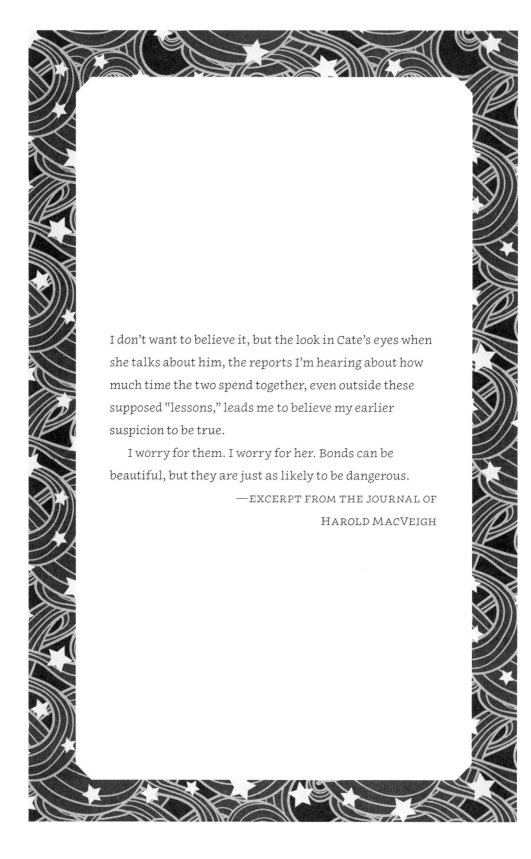

I don't want to believe it, but the look in Cate's eyes when she talks about him, the reports I'm hearing about how much time the two spend together, even outside these supposed "lessons," leads me to believe my earlier suspicion to be true.

I worry for them. I worry for her. Bonds can be beautiful, but they are just as likely to be dangerous.

—EXCERPT FROM THE JOURNAL OF HAROLD MACVEIGH

21

CATE

THE GUARDS ARE posted in front of my door from that point on. Food is delivered three times a day, still warm and hot and delicious, the only difference being that I'm forced to eat alone in my room, a room I'm not allowed to leave. But it means Eliza is still here, which gives me hope that some of my friends are still here. Eventually they will have to wonder where I am, and when they come and find me locked in my room, surely then they will know Lady M is the one behind all of this.

The door separating my room from Andra's has been permanently shut. I heard the banging from my side of the room and when I went to push through the door, I found it wouldn't be budged. I know she's not in there anyway, that there is much more than a door separating us, but it still feels like a link to my sister has been severed.

No one else has come to see me, or at least, no one has been able to make it past the guards.

It's been three days, and I have no idea where my sister is. No idea what happened to Callum. Who killed King James. Where my friends might have gone—or been taken.

The urge to see Callum again, to try to explain, to hold him close, itches under my skin. Worse than the loneliness and the uncertainty, the ache for him is physical. I need him in a way that would be frightening if I allowed myself to think on it too much.

The morning of the fourth day, the door opens and instead of a tray of food sliding across the floor, an actual person strides into the room.

Not strides. Limps. Practically falls into the room.

I didn't think it was possible, but Harold looks worse than before.

The sight of him sends a wave of conflicting emotions crashing through me. Harold is safe, and that news brings no small measure of relief.

But what about Callum? If Harold is here, what are the chances Callum is still alive?

I rush to Harold's side, helping him into a chair. "Where's Andra? What happened with the king? Why haven't you seen Bianca? Callum, Harold, what happened to Callum?" The questions fall from my lips faster than he could possibly answer them.

Harold grimaces, shifting in the chair until he lands in a comfortable position. "A drink would be lovely, thank you, Cate."

I glare at him, though I heed his request, pouring him a measure of whisky. I would take some for myself, but I'm running low and something tells me the guards won't be replenishing my stock. I hand Harold his glass and sit opposite him. "It's been more than three days, Harold. I did what you asked, and it's been three days and I still have not seen my sister."

"Andra is fine." He sips the whisky, wincing as it goes down.

"And Callum?"

"Callum is fine too, as far as I know." He holds up a hand to pause my next interruption. "Why don't you just let me speak, Cate?" He swigs the remainder of his drink, setting the glass down with a sigh. "I killed King James. Callum was there, but he escaped. Andra is safe, so is Bianca, so is everyone else."

"Where is she, Harold?" I don't feel nearly as comforted by his assurances as I want to be. How can I trust his word?

"I can't tell you." He hesitates for a second. "But Andra is in a safe place, one that I know well."

My brow furrows, tucking that piece of information away for later. I push out of my chair and stride across the room. "Look around, Harold. I've been trapped in this room for days with no word. You've taken my sister and my friends from me. We used to be a family. And now all of a sudden you're out here committing murder and kidnapping. Is she worth it?"

"You have to trust that I know what I'm doing here, Cate. Everything I'm doing is for all of you, everyone at La Puissance." Harold's shoulders sink in on themselves. "Besides, I couldn't stop it if I tried."

"What does that mean? You can take control again, Harold. We will all stand behind you. If money is the problem, we will find another way to raise the funds."

He shakes his head and it's sad. "We're Bonded, Cate. Grecia . . . Lady M and I. We've been Bonded since we were kids. I can't go against her."

My mouth falls open in shock. "Bonded?"

I know the basics of the term, but I've never known anyone who was part of a Bonded pair. All I really know is that it would be almost impossible for them to be parted, maybe impossible for one to live without the other. Suddenly everything that has happened begins to make a lot more sense.

Harold nods and his eyes find mine, staring deeply, as if he truly needs me to hear and understand. "When a couple Bonds, Cate, the need for each other is insatiable, indescribable. We can't be apart from one another for long, or it causes physical pain."

My stomach roils, not just because of what this means for Harold, but because the sensations he's describing sound familiar. But it can't be. We can't be. "But you just met."

His lips pull tight, his hand clenching into a tight fist on the table. "We didn't just meet. We didn't even just get married." He runs a hand over his beard, his normally neatly trimmed facial hair gone scraggly. "There is so much you don't know, Cate."

I reach across the table for his hand. "So tell me."

"I can't."

I shake my head, wondering what happened to the fierce leader who would have given his life to protect those in his care. "What exactly is your plan, Harold?"

"You know I can't tell you that either. But you also need to know I'm doing this for your own good."

I scoff, gesturing to the room I'm being held captive in. "Forgive me if I find that a little hard to believe right now."

Harold pushes out of his chair, the movement seeming to send waves of pain through his frail-looking body. "You don't have all the information, and if you can't take my word, then I don't have anything more to say to you." The change from sad to angry is instantaneous and I wonder if this is an effect of the Bond. Is he starting to take on her character traits? Is that common for Bonded pairs?

Panic darts through me. I need him to stay. This is the most human contact I've had in days, and right now, Harold is my only link to the people I care about. "Wait, Harold. Please. I did what you asked of me and I just want to see my sister. Let me see her and I will do whatever you want me to do."

His voice softens, but his words are sharp. "None of this would have even happened without your sister."

I freeze, hoping I've misheard him. "What do you mean, Harold? Andra is a victim in all of this."

He shakes his head sadly. "She told her what she Saw. If only she had kept it to herself."

I cross to his side of the room, grasping his bony forearms in my hands and just managing to stop myself from shaking him. "What did she See, Harold?"

He meets my eyes, shadows haunting his. "She told Lady M that a MacVeigh would win the election. Her vision is what set this whole thing in motion."

I drop Harold's arms, the contact overwhelming me. "Lady M was forcing her to read for hours at a time with barely a break. Of course she told her what she Saw. You cannot possibly blame her. Please just let me see her!"

The man I once considered a father, the man who took us in, sheltered us, raised us as if we were his own, looks at me with not a single hint of emotion in his dark brown eyes. "I don't think I can, Cate. I wish I could, but I just can't."

And without a backward glance, he opens the door and walks away.

It isn't until later that I notice the slip of paper he's left behind. It's a crude drawing, a map of some kind, and I can't help but wonder if this is his small act of rebellion, of standing up to the woman who's taken control of his life. Now I just need to figure out what to do with it.

HOURS MORE PASS without a hint of word from anyone. I eat my food and sit in the silence and think about all the ways I fucked up.

If I had been paying closer attention to those around me, maybe I could have stopped all of this before it got out of hand.

But more than anything, I think about the Bond. Is that what this is, this undeniable tie between Callum and me, this physical ache in my chest and coursing through my limbs at the absence of him? And if so, do I owe it to Callum to try to break it, if such a thing is even possible? Does he deserve the chance to live a life free of me?

Sometime after dark, the door to my room opens, the soft glow from the hallway lighting a stripe on the carpet.

I sit up in bed, the effort of the small movement proving to be exhausting. I should care who's coming into my room in the middle of the night, but I can't seem to find anything more than indifference.

"Cate?" a familiar voice whispers.

"Bianca?"

"Why are you in bed?" She rustles around near the door, finding a gas lamp and turning it on.

"It's nighttime."

"It's only seven o'clock, love."

I shrug. Time has lost all meaning over the past couple of days.

Bianca crosses the room, perching at the foot of the bed. "How are you?"

I shrug again. I don't have the energy to tell her *I told you so.*

"Harold told us all you've come down with the flu and to stay away so we don't catch it, but I'm not picking up any signs of illness." Her brow furrows, and she turns on another light, one that shines over my face.

I wish the warmth didn't feel good, but it does. I turn toward it.

Bianca sucks in a breath as she fully takes me in. "What's going on, Cate?"

I open my mouth, but it takes a few moments before the words come out. Once they start, I couldn't stop them if I tried. I tell Bianca everything—Lady M's demand for me to make Callum Reid fall in love with me, the contracts, the threat against Andra, and the guards posted at my door. The conversation with Harold and the utter hopelessness of the past few days. How I messed up everything, for my sister and with Callum. I leave out the possibility of the Bond. It's too fresh, and too personal.

She listens in complete silence, reactions playing across her face.

"Cate, you poor thing," she says when I've finally finished. "I had no idea. None of us had any idea."

This sliver of information stokes a small fire in the center of my chest. I'd allowed myself to begin to think they had all abandoned me. I reach for her hand, grasping it tightly in mine. "You have to tell everyone, B. You have to make them see what she's doing."

She flexes her fingers, forcing me to loosen my grip. "I can try, Cate, but I don't know that it will do much good."

I flop back onto my mound of pillows. "I don't understand how no one can see how evil she is."

"There's something about her. Using my Gift when she's around, it just feels effortless. As easy as breathing. It's like it becomes tangible. It's almost intoxicating." She lowers her voice, turning her head away from me in shame. "But I never imagined she would be keeping you locked in your room."

"Let alone what she's done to Andra." Just the words turn my stomach. The thought of my sister in the clutches of that woman while I'm here, trapped and unable to help her.

"Lady M needs Andra, she won't hurt her." Bianca's attempt at reassurance falls flat.

"You've got to help me, Bianca. Please."

She nods resolutely. "I will. I promise."

I have no choice but to trust her.

HOURS AFTER BIANCA leaves me alone in my locked room, the rattling of my balcony doors wakes me.

I'd been dreaming about Callum. Again. Finding solace in the warmth of his embrace, even if that embrace only existed in the depths of my mind.

I know it is likely I will never see him again, that the only version of Callum I will get to hold and kiss and touch is the one that lives in my dreams.

Callum Reid has no reason to come back to me now, now that he doesn't have to suffer the guilt from killing his father.

The rattle sounds again, and I climb out of bed and creep over to investigate, my hand reaching for the dagger at my thigh. But it's not there, of course; it's been missing since before the guards trapped me here. It's silly, but without the familiar warmth and weight of it at my side, it feels like a piece of me is missing.

Clearly no one is guarding the balcony, however.

The rattle persists, and I yank the curtains to the side, fists poised at the ready as though they could actually hurt someone trying to break down the door.

There's a man standing on my balcony. I start to back away, ready to call for help. But then the man steps into the light, silver beams of moonlight dancing through his copper curls.

I drop my fists.

A second later, I unlatch the doors.

He doesn't come in, both of us keeping several feet of space between us. A treacherous river separates us, and yet I want nothing more than to dive right into the dangerous waters and cross it.

My eyes flit over every inch of him, drinking him in. Hovering over the bruises coloring his face, noting the way he seems to be favoring his left leg, watching the breaths wheeze in and out of his lungs. "There are guards. Outside the door to my room. The doors are thick, but . . ."

Callum's brow furrows. "Guards? What for, Caterine?"

"Probably to keep me from going to find you." The truth flies from my mouth before I have the chance to stop it.

He sucks in a breath and the sudden move causes him to grimace.

"I guess they didn't consider you might come to me." I cross over to him, taking his hand and leading him into the room, knowing he won't enter my personal space without my permission. I guide him into one of the chairs around the dining table, pouring him a glass of whisky before I head into my bathing chamber. I grab one of the bottles of tonic Bianca made for me to ease the aches that come with my job, along with a soft, clean towel.

Callum is sipping from his glass when I return, wincing as the alcohol stings the cut on his lip.

I unscrew the lid from the bottle, dampening the cloth. Placing myself square between Callum's legs, I take his chin in my hand, tilting his face so I can examine the damage.

"They're a couple of days old already. They've been treated." His voice is hoarse, like he has been talking either too much or not at all.

"I figured." I press the cloth to the cut on his lip first. "This will help more than any of your remedies can." Pulling the cloth away, I watch as the cut starts to heal and make a mental note to thank Bianca. "It doesn't do as much for bruises, but it should still provide some relief."

Callum's fingers drift to his lip, tracing over where the cut used to be. "Thank you."

I finish tending to the most obvious of his wounds before sitting in the chair across from him. "Should I bother asking how you are doing?"

He drains the remainder of his drink. "I think you can probably guess the answer to that, my lady." The term holds no teasing lilt, no longer ringing of endearment. Now it feels meant to keep the distance between us.

I fist my hands in the silk of my robe to keep from reaching for him. But he's here, and that has to mean something. "I'm so sorry, Callum."

"I didn't kill him. MacVeigh, I mean. I could have killed him, and I didn't. Even though . . ."

"Why didn't you?" I whisper when he fails to complete his thought.

His eyes meet mine, and they are blazing with an unfamiliar emotion, something hard and guarded, so unlike the open man I've grown to know. "Why do you think?"

I blink back the wetness that springs to my eyes. "I never wanted for any of this to happen."

"I know."

"I wanted to tell you everything. And I would have, I would have betrayed Harold if it meant saving you. But they had my sister. They still have my sister." I choke out the words. "I've wanted more than anything to see you, and to apologize. I didn't think you would come back."

He reaches across the table, not taking my hand, but leaving his there for me to make the decision. "I've wanted more than anything to see you too. And you don't need to apologize. I understand why you did what you did. You aren't the only person close to me who betrayed my trust." He huffs out a humorless laugh. "Maybe I've been the problem all along."

I take his hand, lacing our fingers together. Something tense inside me eases at the contact. "What do you mean?"

"My uncle has been working with the Uprising this whole time."

I suck in a breath. "Did he know about the killing period? Before it was announced, I mean?"

Callum shrugs, and it looks as if the weight of the world rests on his shoulders. "I couldn't bring myself to ask."

My heart aches. Even with his faults and prejudices, Callum has proven to be nothing but good and kind, openhearted and open-minded. He didn't deserve that treatment from his uncle any more than he deserved it from me.

Neither of us says anything for a long minute. I focus on the warmth of his hand wrapped around mine, the comfort of his thumb swiping over my knuckles. It's a comfort I haven't earned, and yet I relish it just the same.

"Take off your shirt."

His eyebrows jump. "I'm sorry?"

I gesture to his ribs. "Let me see your other bruises, I have something that can help." I can do this for him, if nothing else.

He obliges, gingerly removing his cotton shirt, wincing with the pain of the movement.

I lean over to examine his mottled skin, breathing in the woodsy sage scent I've missed over the past few days. "Come with me."

I lead him into the bathing chamber, filling a tub with warm water and adding another one of Bianca's tonics. I gesture for him to climb in. I know I should turn around so he can remove the rest of his clothing in privacy, but I can't seem to force my eyes away. I drink in every inch of him, knowing full well this could be the last time.

He doesn't seem to mind my attention, dragging his pants and undergarments over his thick thighs, never breaking my eye contact.

I suck in a breath at the sight of him, just as beautiful, even if he is slightly worse for the wear. "I'll just be out there, let me know if you need anything." I move to cross back into the main room, but he grabs my hand.

"Stay. Please." He squeezes my hand before climbing into the tub, a moan of relief escaping him as he sinks into the hot water.

"Whatever you prefer." My mouth goes dry. It almost hurts to look at him.

"I'd prefer if you'd join me." It almost sounds like a challenge, as if he knows I can never back down from one of those.

Baring myself to him right now will only lead to more heartache. And yet I can never seem to deny him. I untie my robe, letting the silky black fabric fall to the floor, leaving me completely bare. Callum's eyes linger, tracing me from head to toe.

"Has it really only been four days?" he mutters.

I climb into the tub, settling across from him. His legs rest on either side of mine, and my body flushes, either from the heat of him or the heat of the water. I rest my hands on the edge of the copper tub, not knowing if I have permission to touch him.

But good lord do I want to touch him. I knew how much I missed him, knew how the ache of missing him has been gnawing at me. But now he's here and I don't know what he wants. I don't know why he's come. I just know I don't want to do anything to scare him away.

"How do you feel? Your bruises, I mean?" It feels like the safest question.

He leans his head back against the rim of the tub. "Whatever magic you put in this water, I'm grateful for it."

"I'll let Bianca know."

"Bianca." The name hangs in the air between us. "Was she there?"

"I don't know."

"There were two of them. I fought one. She distracted me while Harold killed my father."

My lungs tighten. "I'm so sorry, Callum." I can only pray Bianca wasn't the one in the room with him, but in the end, I'm not sure it really matters. Someone close to me is the one responsible for taking his father's life.

"I don't blame her."

I breathe a small sigh of relief.

"There is only one person responsible for the travesty that happened in that room."

I hold my breath, waiting for him to mutter my name, to end whatever this is between us for good.

Callum tilts his head up, meeting my gaze. "Me."

"Callum. No. Nothing about what happened in that room is your fault."

"I should have been there. I should have been ready the moment the time turned. I was so worried about my own feelings, I left my family and my people in a vulnerable position. I can't blame anyone else for my own lack of courage and foresight."

I reach for his hand, needing contact with him before the guilt overwhelms me. "You are one of the bravest people I know, Callum Reid. And you would have been there if it weren't for me."

"I made my own decisions, Caterine. I wanted to be with you. I needed to be with you." He laughs bitterly. "I'm a coward and a fool."

I inch my way closer to him, making sure to keep plenty of space between us. "I could help you with that, you know."

He runs a hand through his hair, water dripping through his curls and down his cheek. "I don't deserve to feel better, Cate. I did this, and now I have to live with the consequences. If I had been there, instead of . . ." He doesn't finish the thought because he doesn't need to.

The shame burns through me. I push my way to standing, the water dripping from my bare skin as I make to exit the tub. "I'm sorry, Callum. If anyone is to blame, it's me."

He takes my hand again, gently tugging me down, pulling me closer, positioning me so I straddle his lap. "I shouldn't have said that. There is nothing you could've done differently. I was so focused on you, on us, I couldn't see anything else."

I think about Harold's words. About the Bond. Maybe it is true. Because being here in Callum's arms, even with everything uncertain still swirling around us, I feel almost at peace.

"Do you regret it?" I brush a damp curl from his face, letting my fingers linger over the quickly fading bruises on his cheek.

His arm wraps around my waist. "I could never regret you, my lady." He presses his forehead to my collarbone, his shoulders sagging. "It feels so good to be in your arms again, Cate. It's the first time in four days that I feel like I can breathe."

"I know." I dance the words over the shell of his ear. "I thought it was going to be easy to let you go."

His arms tighten around my waist, pulling me closer to him, pressing our cores together. "I knew it would be impossible to let you go."

I take his cheeks in my hands, forcing him to look me in the eye. "Where do you want to go from here, Callum?"

"You mean other than to bed?" A hint of a grin tugs on his lips.

I roll my eyes, even though I delight in this hint of humor brightening his face. I tangle my fingers in the curls at the nape of his neck. "I will take you to bed, Your Highness. I don't like to leave my clients unfulfilled."

His eyes darken. "Am I still a client?"

"Do you wish to be something else?" I shift my hips the slightest bit, rolling against his stiffening cock.

His hands find my hips, shifting me away. "I wish to be a lot of things, Lady Caterine, but none of the things could ever be good for you."

I raise my eyebrows. "That sounds a lot like you're trying to make my decision for me, Your Highness." Though I know I should let him pull away, let him keep this distance between us, especially if it's what he wants.

"What decision is there to make, Cate?" Any hint of lightness has disappeared. "What could I offer you at this point?"

I press my lips to his cheek. "You, Cal. You could offer me yourself." I brush a kiss over his forehead. "And you could let me be the one to decide if I think you're enough." I kiss his other cheek before dragging my lips to his ear. "And I do." I turn my head, this kiss landing at the corner of his mouth. "I don't know much about what is going to happen over the next few days, or the next few weeks, or the next few months." I kiss the opposite corner. "But I do know that with you by my side, I think I'm ready to find out." I brush my lips against his in a barely-there kiss. "But if you're not ready to find out, then let me have tonight. Let me comfort you and bring you pleasure and help you escape, even if it's just for a few hours."

He cups my cheek in his hand, his thumb tracing along the edge of my jaw. He doesn't say anything, doesn't deny or accept my offer. He just brings his mouth to mine, in a kiss that burns me to my core.

His free hand finds the nape of my neck, holding me to him as he plunders my mouth, our tongues and teeth mingling and clashing as he pulls me closer and closer, until I'm not sure where my limbs end and his begin.

He hoists me without notice, stepping out of the tub and placing me gently on the ground. He grabs a clean dry linen from the stack by the bath and wraps it around us both. It's hard for the cloth to do its job when neither of us is willing to part from the other for long enough to dry our dripping skin.

We stumble into the other room, cloth long forgotten, mouths never parting. I discover the eternal paradox of never wanting to stop kissing Callum and wanting to move my mouth to every other part of him. Kissing him feels like coming home and exploring the world, new adventures and old comforts.

We fall onto the bed, Callum's hard, hot length covering me, enveloping me in a warmth that has always been missing from my life, a warmth only he has been able to provide.

He breaks the kiss first, but I don't complain when his mouth trails down my neck. "Fuck, Caterine. How does four days without you feel like an entire lifetime?" He mutters the words into my skin, not pausing for any kind of response.

A lifetime of you could never be enough. I think the words but don't say them out loud, still unsure of where this could possibly go, what I should do. All I do know is I have Callum here in my bed, and I don't want to waste the time we have together, even if it already hurts to even think about parting.

I drag his mouth back to mine, my fingers skirting down the ridged plane of his stomach, through the golden copper hair leading me downward, until they're wrapping around the thickness of his cock.

He groans, his hand covering mine, stroking with me, but a second later pulling me away. "I'll never last with you touching me like that."

"We have all night, you know."

"I plan to take full advantage."

He grasps both of my wrists in one hand, bringing my arms over my head as his mouth works its way down to my chest. He places a single kiss over my heart, his eyes meeting mine for a brief moment. His lips brush across my sensitive skin, his tongue licking at the peaked buds of my breasts. Releasing my hands, he continues to move down my body. I tangle my fingers in his curls, directing him right where I want him.

There is no teasing tonight. Callum's tongue traces me open, swirling my clit before sucking it between his lips. My hips buck and I tighten my hold on him, taking my pleasure against his mouth. My skin burns, the flush spreading outward from my core.

He gives me everything I need, and I take everything he offers, working me until I fall apart beneath him, until my cries echo around the room and I thank god for thick walls.

He kisses a trail back up my body, finally bringing his mouth to mine in a languid, sensual kiss. His cock strokes my sensitized folds, and I need nothing more in this moment than to feel him inside me, to let him become a part of me.

I push him gently, rolling him to his back and perching over him. Straddling his hips, I stroke him as I bring him to my entrance.

His hand reaches out, halting the motion.

I meet his eyes, terrified I've somehow taken things too far.

"Don't try to ease my pain. Please, Cate. Promise me." His voice is a broken whisper, his eyes a pleading shade of dull blue.

"I would never manipulate your feelings without your consent, Callum. I promise you." I would promise him anything if it meant bringing back the light to his eyes.

He leans up, kissing me deeply while I sink slowly down over him, taking him inch by delicious inch. I still once he's fully seated inside me, breaking the kiss and letting my body adjust.

Letting my heart adjust. It's so full, I fear it might burst.

Callum falls back on the pillows, his eyes traveling from where our bodies are joined up over the bared expanse of my skin, finally meeting my gaze. His eyes are light again and a hint of a smile tugs on his lips.

22

CALLUM

SHE SWIPES HER thumb over my bottom lip as she begins to move, her hips rolling slowly, rocking over me.

I've dreamed of what it would be like to be buried inside her more times than I could count. Somehow the reality is better than anything I could have ever imagined.

She braces her hands on my chest. I run my hands up the soft skin of her arms, slipping them down to cup her breasts, watching her breath catch as my fingers pluck and pinch her nipples.

Her head falls back as she begins to thrust harder, taking me deeper. "God, Callum. It's never . . . I've never . . ." Her words trail off, ending on a gasp as my thumb slips in between our bodies, stroking her swollen clit.

Her fingers dig into the skin of my chest, and I hope her nails leave a mark. I hope there is some kind of physical reminder so when I wake up in the morning and wonder if it was all a dream, I know it actually happened.

Cate claimed to want me by her side, that we could face whatever is to come together. But I know that standing next to me as I do what needs to be done is no place for her. I know that once she knows what I have to do, she won't want to see me again. I know, even as I experience the greatest pleasure I have ever known, that this will be the only time she invites me to her bed.

And so I grip her hips, stroking into her until I feel her walls tighten around me, until she calls out my name, until the force of her orgasm leaves her breathless and boneless.

I flip her over, smooth the hair from her face. Kiss her slowly, my tongue dancing with hers. I want to take my time, make this sacred moment last for as long as possible, but my body has other plans.

Cate's heels dig into my lower back, pressing me closer and deeper, and the familiar tightening grips my lower belly. I pull away from the kiss as I thrust, my heart pounding with a matching intensity. I want to see her when I come.

She reaches up, cupping my cheek in her hand, in a move so tender it's almost out of sync with my frantic thrusting. Our eyes meet and my chest caves in as I explode inside her, as she cries out again, as she presses me even deeper, her hips rocking up to meet mine.

There doesn't seem to be an end as wave after wave of pleasure rolls through me.

"Don't stop," she whimpers, and I don't dream of denying her.

She finally releases her grip on my lower body, her legs flopping on the bed. I pull out of her slowly, begrudgingly. I think I would bury myself inside her forever if she let me.

Her lips reach for mine and I give in to the kiss. It's the single best kiss of my life, and yet I can't help but feel like it was a mistake to come here.

I wanted her to hear it from me first, the plan and what I intend to do. But then she had to go and heal my wounds and examine my bruises with a look of worry in her eyes. It was the look of someone who cares, and I couldn't help but let myself hope that she somehow might care about me. Might have missed me as much as I've missed her. Not just the inexplicable chemistry we share physically, but our conversations and the way she somehow makes me feel totally and completely at ease with myself.

There is something greater here between us, something I cannot name or explain, but something that should be unbreakable. If we were anyone but who we are.

I stay perched over her, not wanting to leave this fragile bubble of peace we've created in her bed. I know that once I break away from it, it will signal the end for us. Just the thought feels like my heart has been ripped from my chest.

"Callum." Her hand returns to my face, tilting my head so our gazes meet.

"Not yet," I mutter, pressing my lips to hers in hope that I can delay the inevitable.

"You don't even know what I'm going to tell you."

I drag my lips down to her jaw, nibbling along the line of her neck. "I know it means we have to start thinking again, and I'm not ready yet."

She places her hands flat on my chest, not pushing me away, but coming close enough.

I flop over onto my side, resting my head on my hand so I can still stare down at her.

She mirrors my position, once again forcing my eyes to her face. "I had a talk. With Harold."

"Oh." I shift my hips, subtly putting a few more inches of space between us. "Did he tell you what I said?"

Her brow furrows. "No. He reminded me that I need to trust him. That we're family and he's always taken care of me."

I slide farther toward the edge of the mattress, but Cate grabs my wrist, holding me in place.

"Will you just listen to me, please?"

I sit up, turning my back to her. "I know what you're going to say, what you're going to ask of me, and I don't blame you, Caterine, truly I don't. But I don't want to taint what just happened here, color my one memory of us, with the knowledge that I have to disappoint you. Again."

"Hey." The bed shifts and then she's standing in front of me. Still naked, and still the most gorgeous creature I've ever laid eyes on. "First of all, you have never disappointed me." She wiggles her way to stand between my thighs. "Second of all, who says there is only going to be one memory of us?" She places a soft kiss on my lips. "And third of all, if you would just shut up for a second, you might not hate what I have to say."

I raise my eyebrows. "My apologies, my lady."

She takes my face in both of her hands. "I know what we have to do, Cal. I know I need to get my sister back. And I know you have to kill him." She bites her lip and a sheen of wetness springs up in her amber-colored eyes. "Harold begged me to trust him, and I want to, really I do, but how can I after everything that's happened?"

I soothe her bitten lip with my thumb and give her the space she needs to continue.

"Lady M has taken my sister, taken your father's life. And Harold has gone along with her, every step of the way. We can't let them get away with it, no matter what his excuse is. He may have once been the only man I ever trusted, but now . . ." She sniffles, digging her fists into her eyes.

I want nothing more than to hear the end of her sentence, to think that I might be the man she can trust now. But I know that's not the case.

"There's a part of me that thinks Harold wants it this way."

My brow furrows. "What do you mean?"

She shakes her head, as if needing to clear some vision from her mind. "I think there might be a small part of him that realizes he made a mistake, marrying Lady M, giving her access to Andra and the rest of us here at the club. I want to believe he has some regrets for what he's done, and what he's allowed her to do."

I don't know that I believe that, not after Harold MacVeigh has been keeping Cate prisoner here, but I don't want to steal this last bit of hope from her. I slide my arm around her lower back, pulling her closer into my embrace. "Cate, do you know where MacVeigh is right now?"

She nods, her teeth once again digging into her plush lower lip.

"Will you tell me?"

Her lips purse, but she nods again.

A sigh of relief trickles out of me. I tug her down onto my lap, burying my face in her neck.

"There's more," she whispers.

I put just enough space between us so I can see her eyes.

"Andra had a vision." She sucks in a long breath, the internal struggle written all over her face. It's a stark difference from the Cate who so easily hid her emotions when we first met, who masked every one of her feelings.

"What kind of vision, Cate?" I stroke my hand over her bare back, hoping the motion soothes the torment she is so clearly experiencing.

"It's not much, and it didn't make any sense to me at the time, but now I think I know what it means."

I try to tamp down the excitement I can feel rising in my chest. If Andra had a vision, that means there's a way we can actually do this. Not long ago I never would have trusted the word of a Gifted, let alone a so-called vision from one, but here I am about to put my faith in not one Gifted, but two.

"What kind of vision, Cate?" I repeat.

She looks at me, her whisky eyes wide. "Trees."

Just when I think there's nothing Diana could throw at me that would surprise me at this point, today she arrived at the club with the biggest shock of my life.

For eight years now, I've forced myself not to think of my daughters. Diana assured me they would be safe, well provided for. She told me that taking them away from Grecia was the only way to ensure their survival.

The two little girls who stepped into the club today didn't look well provided for, and they certainly were not safe before Diana found them.

They are perfect little combinations of us, my golden hair and Grecia's amber eyes. Even though life hasn't been easy for them the past couple of years, they are strong, and smart. Cate is stubborn as all hell, Andra as sweet as pie.

I have loved them from the moment I knew they existed. Never once did I think they would come to live with me, and I wouldn't be able to acknowledge them as my own.

But that doesn't matter. I will show them love and care, even if I must live without the title of Father.

I asked Diana about my third daughter, but she waved away my questions and told me to focus on the daughters who are here in my life, and not worry about the one who isn't.

Seeing them, I can't help but think about what our life could have been like, what kind of mother Grecia might have been. What I do know now is that she must never know our daughters are here, with me. Especially given what Andra is capable of, and what Diana has Seen.

—EXCERPT FROM THE JOURNAL
OF HAROLD MACVEIGH

23

CATE

WE DRESS IN silence. The air in the room is heavy with tension and wanting and things still left unsaid. Callum stills my hands before I can slip into my dress. He kneels before me, wrapping a sheath around my upper thigh, replacing the dagger I haven't worn in days with a new one. His fingers linger, tracing along the sensitive skin. He places a single kiss on my inner thigh before helping me step into the long cotton dress. I haven't laced myself into a corset or donned a feathered headpiece in several days. So much of my long-worn costume has slipped away since meeting Callum Reid. If there was any doubt truly left before, it is gone now. We are Bonded, linked, our lives forever intertwined. But I still want him to have a choice, if such a thing is even possible.

"I need to say something before we leave." I don't look at him as I practically whisper the words, afraid that I will lose all of my nerve if I feel the force of his blue eyes on me.

Callum, his back to me as he buttons his shirt, noticeably stiffens, his shoulders tensing. He takes a second before he turns around. "I don't blame you, Caterine."

My speech, my declaration, sits ready on the tip of my tongue, but his unexpected response confuses me. "What?" is all I can manage to utter.

He crosses the room, slowly, narrowing the gap between us. "I don't blame you if you've changed your mind about what you said. Before." He gestures helplessly to the bed.

"What did I say?"

"You know, the part about standing by my side." A shadow darkens his eyes. "I understand why you would no longer feel that way and I don't blame you."

I step closer to him, reaching for his hand. "Sometimes you say very stupid things, Your Highness."

His mouth parts in shock, but I don't let him speak.

"What I was going to say is that I would understand. If you no longer wanted me by your side." I hold up my hand to stop any sort of protest, but none seems to be forming. My stomach turns, but I knew this was coming. It's why I wanted to be the one to say it, so he wouldn't have to. "I know who I am, Callum. And I know who you are going to be." I lace my fingers through his. "You are going to be the first elected president of Avon, a man who is going to lead this country to the unity and the equity it so desperately needs. And we both know you can't do that with me by your side." I squeeze his hand and gently release it, as if that can somehow release the hold he has on me.

But he doesn't let me pull away, tightening his grip. "Are you trying to tell me that you don't wish to be with me, Cate?"

"It's not about what I want, Callum. It's about what's best for Avon. And what's best for you."

He arches a single eyebrow. "I seem to recall you admonishing me for trying to make your decisions for you, my lady."

I grimace, fighting uselessly against the tie that binds us. "This is different."

He tugs me closer, wrapping our joined hands behind his back, pressing us together. "Answer the question, my lady. Do you wish to be with me? To be my partner, my friend, and one day, when I have earned it, my wife?"

I choke on the unexpected emotion rising up in my throat. "In a perfect world, of course I would want that." I attempt to pull away again and this time he lets me go. "But we don't live in a perfect world."

"I thought the whole purpose of the Uprising was so that we could make a perfect world."

"We both know that you will never be elected with me—a Gifted courtesan—by your side." I refuse to allow shame to heat my cheeks. I am not ashamed of who I am or what I do, but I'm also not naïve enough to believe that everyone else will feel the same.

"If I cannot be elected for the person I am—and that includes loving the people I love—then I don't want to be elected at all." He stops just short of touching me, but the heat of him is everywhere.

"Then your father will have died in vain."

He sucks in a breath and I know the blow has landed. Callum is a good man, the kind of man who would fight for me. And I know I am not strong enough to continue to resist him.

"So this is it, then? You want me to walk out of those doors and never return?" Hurt and anger lace through his voice, punching me right in the chest.

"This isn't about what I want, Cal." I straighten my shoulders. "I will help you with the plan. Against Harold. So we can get my sister back." The words curdle my stomach, the acid burning up my chest. "And then I will let you go."

His arm snakes around my waist, pulling me into his embrace. He leans down, his lips skirting the line of my neck before brushing the shell of my ear. "And if I refuse to let you go? If I *can't* let you go?"

"I have faith that you will put the needs of this country before your own needs." I try to turn away from his mouth but instead find myself turning in, leaning into his embrace.

"What about your needs, my lady?" His mouth moves to the line of my jaw. He kisses my cheeks, the corner of my mouth, tracing the same path I dotted along his skin only hours earlier.

"My needs do not matter," I mumble, letting my own lips linger on the unshaven skin of his neck. He still smells the same, an intoxicating mix of woodsy sage.

"They do to me." He doesn't give me a chance to respond, his lips pressing to mine with soft urgency. "I spent four days without you, Caterine, and I spent most of them not wondering about the fate of this country or grieving the loss of my father. I spent them wondering about you. Worrying about you. Longing for you. I will not let the opinions of ignorant people keep me from the woman I love."

My breath stills in my chest, and I blink rapidly to clear the wetness from my eyes before I allow myself to meet his gaze. There is nothing in the depths of the blue other than truth and love. "You know I love you as well, Callum Reid, which is why I won't let you give up everything for me."

He smiles and places another soft kiss on my aching lips. "And you know me well enough by now to know that I'm not going to let you give up on this, give up on us."

I close my eyes, sinking into him as his lips press to my forehead.

I tuck myself deeper into his embrace, burying my face in his chest. His arms wrap around me, the strength and the warmth buoying me, deluding me into entertaining the possibility that there could ever be an us, that were it not for the Bond, he would still choose me. Choose us.

"You can't get rid of me so easily, my lady." His lips find mine again and this kiss is neither soft nor sweet. It's possessive and searching and it burns me from the inside out. Callum kisses me as if this is his last chance to convince me, as if he needs to prove the strength of his love.

It fills me up and empties me out and all I can do is lean in for more. I need more of him. All of him. Everything he is willing to give me.

My hands fumble with the belt at his waist, but my fingers eventually work the buckle before moving on to the button of his pants. He grips the long skirt of my dress, tugging and pulling until it's up around my waist.

I find the edge of the bed, his cock in my hand. He pushes into me, hard and quick, and I know I can never truly give him up. Can never live without this feeling, this feeling of being whole. Of being cherished and treasured and loved. Even though this coupling is rough, the way he looks at me, the way he strokes my cheek and kisses my forehead is nothing short of tender.

He loves me. And I love him.

And whatever happens next, the two of us are inextricably linked.

"You are mine, Lady Caterine." The declaration rumbles out of him like a growl.

I feel that tightening tension low in my core, his words and his thrusts a heady combination. "Say that again," I gasp.

"You are mine. And I am yours."

His lips crush down on mine, a bruising kiss that sparks a wave of pleasure that rolls through me. His mouth swallows my cries and he grunts his own release seconds later, the two of us falling off the cliff and tumbling into each other's arms.

WE LEAN OVER the edge of the balcony and it becomes immediately clear why there are no guards stationed here: One would have to be an idiot to attempt scaling it, and even more of an idiot to try to make it down.

"I'll go first." Callum swings himself up and over the edge, his grip on the metal railing so tight it turns his knuckles white.

"I don't think I can do this," I whisper as I watch him start his descent.

He pauses when there's just enough space for me to make my own way over the balcony. "I'm not going to let you fall, Caterine." I hesitate for another long minute before he looks up, his eyes soft. "Think of your sister, my lady."

It's the exact right thing to say—maybe the only thing to say—to convince me. I swing a leg over the edge, the cold metal digging into my fingers.

"Don't look down," Callum advises. "Just listen to the sound of my voice."

I let him guide me, platitudes and encouragement buoying me as I steadily climb down the metal railing, latching on to the wooden trellis attached to the side of the building, and finally landing on the ground.

"I knew you could do it." Callum places a single kiss on the top of my head before taking my hand in his and pulling me into a run.

Callum leads me to a dingy-looking building on the edge of the river. Everything is dull and muted, except for the smell, a cross between days-old trash and water-soaked sewage. It seeps in everywhere, buried deep in the yellow-tinged walls of the small apartment where Callum's uncle Alex and his sister Dom wait for us.

"Lady Caterine," she says, wrapping me in a warm hug while Callum and Alex huddle in one grimy corner of the room. "Nice to see you again. I had a feeling you might be the woman able to bring my brother to his knees." Her smirk is wide and her blue eyes—twins to Callum's—dance.

I mirror her cheeky smile. "I've heard lots more about you since our meeting, Dom."

"Either all of it is true or none of it." Her insightful eyes take in everything and my original impression of her—that she is one formidable woman—is solidified. Dom's voice loses its cheerful teasing as she surveys me. "I imagine things have been rough for you lately, my lady. I know this place is lacking in comfort, but it's safe. You will be protected here."

I nod, not doubting her sentiment, but also not fully trusting in the words. What does safe even mean if my sister isn't here?

Callum and Alex break away from their corner, joining us in what appears to be some kind of dining area, though there's only a broken-down table and a few banged-up wooden crates to sit on.

Callum immediately reaches for my hand, lacing our fingers together. Dom notices and her smirk returns.

Alex notices and grimaces. "Lady Caterine. Nice to officially make your acquaintance."

I nod tightly. "You as well." It may be the highest degree of hypocrisy, but I don't know if I can forgive him for betraying Callum as easily as Callum has. I squeeze his fingers. "What's the plan?"

Alex's eyes move around the small group, assessing each one of us. "I've been speaking with some friends inside the Uprising, on the leadership committee." He directs this amendment to Callum, guilt obvious in the blue eyes they share. "Though there is nothing explicit mentioned in the decree about what happens if a potential candidate kills the current candidate, it seems like they will have no choice but to honor Cal's place should he be the one to kill Harold. We didn't plan for things to go this way, so amendments are being written. I imagine the next killing period will have stricter rules and a shorter time frame to mitigate some of these unfortunate events."

"If only they had thought through their ridiculous decree before enacting it," I mutter.

"Right." Callum's fingers tighten around mine. "Hopefully things will go more smoothly for the next province, but that doesn't change what needs to happen here."

"Cal mentioned Andra has Seen something that could help us?" Alex's tone shifts, focusing on the task at hand.

"Yes. We know where Harold is staying." I hesitate before delivering the next bit, knowing how it might sound to someone who doesn't know Andra, doesn't understand how her visions work. "And we know how to get there. And how to get in."

Alex raises his eyebrows, Callum looks hopeful, and Dom looks like she's ready to march into battle.

"We'll go disguised as trees."

All three of their faces morph into identical confused expressions, even Callum's, with his earlier warning of what was to come.

"Trees?" Dom finally asks. "How does one dress as a tree?"

I take in a weary breath. "The place where Harold is hiding out is buried in a small copse of trees outside the city. It's well guarded and well hidden. He spent time there when he was younger, and I know how to find it." I don't mention the map Harold left for me, keeping his small rebellion as a secret between us. "The easiest way to sneak in is to use the trees as a disguise."

Callum's face morphs yet again, this time fully considering the plan. The tactical leader in him is crunching all the angles and it doesn't take him long to arrive at a conclusion. "It could work."

"It will work." I try to imbue my voice with some of the confidence the royals all seem to possess. "Andra's visions don't always make sense at first glance, but they are always true."

"If you say it is so, then I believe it, my lady." Callum nods, and the others quickly follow suit.

It's a simple statement, but it does something to the hollowed out cavity of my chest. Little by little Callum seems hell-bent on filling it.

"So we disguise ourselves as trees, sneak in, take him out, and then what?" Dom asks.

"Then we get my sister. And then we get the hell out." I infuse my words with all the ferocity I can. "Harold might have been the one who did the actual killing, but Lady M is the one who poses the danger. Avoiding her is essential."

"She is only one woman," Alex points out. "Between me, Cal, and Dom we could handle her if needed. Maybe it's better to eliminate her now, while we have the chance."

I shake my head. "She is not just one woman. She has a whole squad of Gifted club members on her side. And I don't want them hurt."

"If they are on her side, then they are also enemies, are they not?"

I shoot Alex a glare. "They are on her side because she holds their lives in her hands. They don't have a choice, and they deserve the opportunity to make one."

Alex looks like he wants to argue the point further, but Callum silences him with a single look. "The three of us will get in, complete the job, and get out before we have to deal with Lady M or any of her . . . colleagues."

“There are four of us, Your Highness.” I shoot a look of my own his way.

“Cate, you are not equipped or trained for something like this.”

“My sister is in there. I’m going. Let’s not waste time arguing about it.”

It only takes one more pointed look before he’s nodding. “Fine. Everybody clear on the plan?”

Alex nods his acquiescence.

Dom rubs her hands together. “So when do we go? Later to-night?”

I shake my head. “Tomorrow at the earliest. We’ll need the time to fully prepare our disguises. And we must go at the darkest of night.”

Alex heads for the door. “I will begin gathering supplies.”

“I’ll help.” Dom squeezes my arm before following her uncle out the door.

Callum and I follow right behind them, the four of us gathering sticks and twigs and bowls full of mud. If anyone were to spot us, I don’t know what they could possibly think, but it seems the neighbors prefer to keep to themselves anyway. A couple of hours later, we have everything we need. The only thing to do now is sleep, try to rest, and prepare for the following night.

After a short dinner of bread and hard cheese and a couple of bruised pieces of fruit, Callum and I meet in the one tiny bedroom, Alex and Dom camping out in the living room on two shabby cots.

I fall into Callum’s arms the moment the door closes behind me.

“It’s all going to work out, you know,” he tells me, brushing the hair back from my face.

“All of what is going to work out?”

“Everything.”

“How can you be so sure?” I press my forehead to the hard plane of his chest, absorbing the sound of his heartbeat and letting it steady me.

"Because we're here, and we're together."

"That is ridiculously idealistic, even for you, Your Highness."

He takes my face in his hands, brushing a soft kiss over my lips. "Something tells me I need to be idealistic enough for the both of us."

I snort. "That's certainly a word no one has ever used to describe me."

"Then I will keep believing until you no longer need me to." He kisses me again, this one just as soft, but a lot more lingering. "Are you sure you are okay with this plan?"

"Am I sure that I have no problem with you killing the man who basically saved my life?"

Callum's perfect lips pull into a grimace. "I hate thinking about it like that."

"I know. I'm sorry." I run my thumb over his bottom lip, turning his grimace into a pained smile. "I know you are only doing what needs to be done. And I know that to you, Harold is the man who killed your father. And honestly, as long as I leave with my sister, I don't care about Harold anyway. I never thought he would become the villain in my story."

"I think we both know there is really only one villain in this scenario, Cate."

"Lady M."

Callum pulls me closer into his embrace. "We are going to have to deal with her at some point. I don't think she's just going to roll over because she's lost her candidate."

This time it's me who grimaces. "I know she won't. Hopefully we can make it to the election and secure you a win before we have to think about how to handle her for the long term."

His voice quiets. "What if I don't win, Cate? What if we go through all of this pain and heartache only for me to lose?"

"We're not going to think like that. You are the best person for the job. And the people will see that."

"I hope you're right, my lady."

"I usually am." I press a quick kiss to his lips. "Now, come on. We need to get some rest before tomorrow night."

We tuck ourselves into the tiny bed, the sparse mattress providing little comfort. But Cal's embrace provides more than enough warmth, and despite the litany of worries running through my mind, in his arms, I fall into a peaceful sleep.

My dear Harold,

It is still hard to call you that, you know. I remember the day I first saw you on the streets of Stratford City. Young and in love and with so much life ahead of you.

So many things have changed since then, but I have known one thing about you, Harold MacVeigh, and it is one thing that has not ever changed. You have a good heart. You love well, and you would do anything for those who come to find a place in your heart.

I ask you to remember any love you might have had for me in the coming days. I do not have much longer left on this earth, and there are many things I need to tell you. Things about your wife, and most importantly, things about your daughters.

I have made a lot of decisions throughout my life, and while I have regrets, this is not one of them. I did what I did to protect you, and to protect those precious girls, to protect the entire country of Avon.

I have Seen what is coming, Harold. You will have to trust in me one last time.

Your friend, always and forever,

Diana

24

CALLUM

WE LOOK RIDICULOUS. The four of us—me, Cate, Dom, and Alex—have dressed from head to toe in black. Branches and leaves are attached to our clothing, and each of us carries a large bough that can be used to shield our faces. What little skin is not covered by sticks and cloth has been coated in mud.

It isn't until we approach the copse of trees Cate has led us to that I start to see how this might actually work. Dom takes a few steps into the thick grove and all but disappears. Alex follows, but I hang back, needing a minute alone with Cate. Before I murder the man she once thought of as a father.

"If you think I'm giving you a good-luck kiss with all that gunk all over your face, you are sorely mistaken, Your Highness." She adjusts one of the leaves on my shirt, though we both know she just needs an excuse to touch me.

"If you think I'm letting us enter this forest without kissing me, you are sorely mistaken, my lady." I loop my arm around her waist and pull her to me with no resistance. "Cate . . ."

"Callum . . ."

I clear my throat. Neither of us knows what's going to happen next, and if, god forbid, this is the last time we see each other, I can't leave anything unspoken. "Have you ever heard of Gifted people becoming Bonded to their partners?"

She sucks in a breath, tilting her head back to look me in the eye. "Have *you* ever heard of Gifted people becoming Bonded to their partners?"

"Dom told me about it." It was what spurred me to sneak into Cate's room that night, the thought that there might be some greater explanation for what I feel, why it was so easy for me to overlook the way she lied to me.

"And do you think . . . is that what you feel . . . ?"

I press my lips gently to hers. "Just the thought of separating from you, Cate, I can't imagine a greater pain. We were apart for four days and I thought I might combust from the sheer need to feel your skin on mine."

A sigh trickles from her lips. "I was almost hoping you wouldn't feel it, that it was all in my head."

I pull back from her, just the slightest bit. "Why would you say that?"

Her eyes meet mine, and there is guilt layered over the wanting. "You didn't choose this, Callum, and after everything that's happened because of me, I can imagine how being tethered to me like this would be difficult for you."

I cup her cheek in my hand. "Even if we weren't Bonded, I would choose you, Cate. Every hour of every day. You have to know that it's true."

"But—"

I cut off her protest with a kiss. Maybe if my words can't convince her, my actions can. I pour every bit of me into the kiss, leaving her gasping when we finally part. "If anyone should be looking to offer a way out, it is me, my lady."

"Do not apologize one more time for doing the thing we know you have to do."

"I wasn't going to say that, I was going to say . . ."

She shakes her head. "No. We're not doing that either. We're not saying farewell like there's a chance one of us won't come back."

I swallow the thick emotion that's sprung to my throat. "I wish there was another way."

"I know you do." She rises on her toes, placing a soft kiss against my waiting lips. "Right now, we need to get in there and save my sister and this province's hope for the future."

"I love you, Cate."

"I love you too, Callum."

We creep into the thick branches and leaves, side by side. I should probably be worried for her safety, but I know she can take care of herself. I know she will do whatever it takes to find her sister. And I know she will do whatever it takes to come back to me, just as I will do for her.

We meet Dom and Alex on the outskirts of the grove of trees, the two of them already scouting the best path to take deeper into the woods. Closer to Harold MacVeigh. Closer to vengeance.

I must be the one to lead Avon into the future. I know it as surely as I know Cate is the other half of my soul. And I will fight for that future, just as I would fight for her.

Alex and Dom take off in opposite directions and return minutes later, though those minutes feel like days.

"There is a clear path to the right. Only a couple of men on watch." Alex's voice is low and threaded with urgency.

“Guards surround the place, but it looks like they’re heavier on the left.” Dom’s eyes—the only part of her I can really discern aside from her teeth—have that light in them, the light that says she’s itching for a fight.

“We’ll go right. Remember, Alex is with me; Dom, you’re with Cate.” I turn to head in the direction Alex has scouted.

“I think I should go in with you,” Dom protests in a whisper from my left side.

“Absolutely not. If things should go wrong”—I lower my voice—“I need you there to protect her.”

“They’re not going to go wrong, brother. The future has been Seen.”

I pull my lips tight. I trust Andra because Cate does, but that doesn’t necessarily mean I believe everything she Sees will come to fruition. And I know enough about Seers to know that visions are not always as they seem.

Still, I also know how to get my sister to do what I want her to do. “I don’t trust her safety with anyone but you, Dom.”

A hint of pride shines in her eyes, and I would feel guilty except I mean every word.

Once we make our way through the outer ring of trees, the hideout is easy to find. It’s a small stone building that looks like it was built hundreds of years ago. It probably was.

We make our way to the back of the building, skirting several guards, our disguises serving their purpose better than I could have anticipated. The night is chilly, with the promise of rain in the air, and the guards stick close to the building where it’s warmer. There is little light this deep into the woods, the only luminescence coming from the sliver of moonlight peeking through the clouds high above us. Between the lack of light and our disguises, we blend in easily.

We approach the small fortress on quiet feet. I don't know if it's Andra's vision or sheer luck keeping us safe, but this almost feels too easy.

No sooner does the thought pass through my mind than a pair of guards circles the building, a mere fifteen feet away from the four of us. We all instinctively freeze, and our ridiculous getups do their job. Even though it goes against every instinct I have, I close my eyes, not wanting there to be even a hint of white visible among the darkness that encapsulates us.

I breathe in, quietly, slowly, honing my senses so my hearing can pick up on the slightest movements around me. Nothing but still silence from my companions. The guards, however, haven't spotted us and continue on with their conversation like they would on any other occasion.

"What do you think actually happens inside there?" one questions the other.

"I don't think we want to know. There are only two reasons to bring a steady stream of young girls into your home, and neither is any good. Sometimes it's better to collect your coin and not ask questions."

What the bloody hell is Lady M doing inside this fortress?

Dom nudges my elbow, and I nod. Squinting, I watch for the guards to turn their backs, face away from where we currently stand. My muscles start to cramp from the stillness, but the second the guards are diverted, Dom and I pounce. A couple of swift knocks to the back of the head and they both fold over easily, unconscious.

Cate's sigh of relief is audible, and as we continue our path to the fortress's entrance, she takes my hand, squeezing tightly.

I make eye contact with Alex a few moments later. He and I break away from Dom and Cate, ducking into a shadowed archway.

I try not to let my mind linger on what they are going to do. Worrying about their mission will only impede my own. I focus on the reason why I'm here, what I need to accomplish.

Pushing open a heavy wooden door, Alex and I slowly creep into a darkened room, leaving our handheld boughs of leaves by the door to better aid our escape. The room appears to be an ancient-looking kitchen, dusty with disuse, a stone hearth and worn floors and sconces lined with unlit torches.

I find a hallway, unsheathing a dagger from behind my back before creeping along the stone-lined walk, Alex silent behind me. My steps are light and almost soundless, but I still take caution as I round a corner. Another room sits off to my right, the door partway open, flickers of light beckoning me forward.

Signaling for Alex to wait here in the hallway, I edge into the room. At first glance it's empty, save for a small bed and a fireplace filled with sputtering flames. The décor is sparse, a single aged tapestry hanging on one wall, blankets a worn shade of ivory that used to be white, lumped on the bed.

But when my eyes adjust, I recognize the lump as a sleeping form.

It's fitting, really. MacVeigh planned to kill my father when he was in some kind of Gifted-induced sleep, and now I get to repay the favor.

I cross the room in a few silent steps, angling my view to make sure this is the right person I'm about to murder.

The word turns something in my stomach, but I know there's no time for that kind of thinking. He's left me with no choice. I must do this if there's any hope for the future.

Once I confirm that the man lying in the bed is in fact Harold MacVeigh, I raise the dagger higher, lining up to plunge the knife directly into his heart. It would probably be quicker and quieter to slit his throat, but somehow it seems the more violent of my options and I don't know that I can stomach the outcome.

My hip leans into the mattress, and MacVeigh stirs with the shifting weight. I pull back, waiting to see if he'll wake, ready to strike at a moment's notice.

His eyes flutter open, and my arm moves before I can even think about it.

A weak, bony hand juts up to stop me. I could easily shake him off, but something about the weary look in his eyes stops me.

"Callum Reid." Harold's voice is strained, broken. Nothing like the man Cate has told me so many stories about. Nothing like the man he was even just a few days ago, valiantly grappling with and ultimately overcoming my father. "I knew you would come." He can barely get the words out, as if some kind of invisible force is choking the breath from his lungs.

I adjust my grip on the knife. "I told you I would."

"As I told you I hoped would be the case." He shifts on the bed, dropping his hold on my wrist and hoisting his body into an upright position. It takes longer than it should. "I am not well, Callum."

"What is she doing to you?" I keep the dagger ready, but I can't help but feel like I owe him this chance to say what he needs to. Like I owe it to her.

"We don't have time for that now. There is much you need to know, so much only I can tell you."

I adjust my grip on the knife, not fully trusting that this isn't some kind of ploy to catch me off guard. "Then you better start talking."

"I need to see Cate. She needs to hear it from me."

"Cate is busy right now. Rescuing her sister. The one your wife has taken hostage." I press the tip of the dagger into his fragile skin, a thin line of blood breaking through.

"She is not just my wife. Grecia and I are Bonded. Have been since we were kids." He grimaces. "It doesn't excuse what I did, what I've been party to, but I didn't have a choice, not really."

My mind whirls with the implications of what he's saying, not just what it means for Cate's past, but what it could mean for our future. "Being Bonded doesn't take away your free will."

Harold leans forward, almost as if he craves more pressure from the blade of my knife. "Perhaps not for someone like you, Callum Reid."

"You know then, about Cate and me?"

He nods, his head lolling. "I'm glad she has you."

"She will always have me."

"She will need you. When she finds out the truth." His hand grips my arm once again, but this time his grasp couldn't stop a small child it's so weak. "Please, Callum. I don't have much time left. I need to see my daughters."

The word hangs between us and my stomach tightens. "Your daughters?"

"Please." It's all he manages to get out before he collapses, falling half out of the bed.

I reach for his neck, checking for a pulse. It's there, but it's weak. We don't have much time. I scoop Harold MacVeigh into my arms. He's so frail it's easy to carry him. I push my way into the hall, no time to worry about anything other than getting Harold to Cate.

I might have entered that old stone building prepared to kill the man Cate sees as a father, but if what Harold hinted at is true, she deserves a chance to hear the story directly from him. I couldn't live with myself if I let the opportunity be stolen from her.

Though the last few years have turned out differently than I expected, I would be a fool to pretend they have been anything other than perfect. Watching the girls learn and grow, being there to see my daughters turn into brilliant, kind, thoughtful young women, has been the greatest gift of my life.

I suppose I should have known they would turn out to be Gifted. I am determined now more than ever to make sure my daughters have more rights than my wife. I never want them to go through what Grecia had to. Maybe things would have been different for us if Grecia had always been allowed to embrace her true self.

As it stands now, I find myself avoiding Grecia, though the cost is high. I still burn for her, ache for her in a way that physically hurts, but so much has happened. She changed after the girls were taken from her—after Diana told her the babies had died. And now I find it nearly impossible to be in her company. Not just because of how she's changed but because I know I am keeping the greatest secret from her. Her daughters are alive, but for their own safety, I must keep them from her.

How can I be expected to look my wife in the eye knowing what I know?

—EXCERPT FROM THE JOURNAL
OF HAROLD MACVEIGH

25

CATE

WISHING IT WOULDN'T be a death sentence to light a flame so we could see our surroundings, I lead Dom through the darkened hallways of this castlelike fortress.

"Do you know where you're going?" she whispers fiercely, the first sound either of us has dared to make since we entered the stone building.

I shake my head, knowing she can't see me but not wanting to risk making any more noise, continuing to feel my way along the corridors. I don't know where I'm going, not really, but I know I'm going to find my sister, and for now, that's all I need. I let my intuition guide me through the darkness. Andra and I have been together since before we were born. We have never spent this much time apart, and I vow to never let her slip from me again.

If I hadn't been so focused on Callum, none of this would have ever happened. I should have manipulated him the first time he came for me, gotten the information I needed, and escaped La Puissance before Lady M ever had the chance to take my sister.

And yet I can't force myself to regret it. I will save my sister. I will make sure Callum secures his spot as the Scotan candidate. Only then will I allow myself to think about what comes after. I'm still not convinced a future with Callum is the right thing for him. But I pray we both live long enough to make that choice for ourselves.

I drag my fingers along the rough stone edges of the walls, using touch to guide me. The silence holds no sounds of fighting or skirmishes, no one raising any kind of alarm. I let that soothe my fears for Callum.

At this very moment, he might be watching the life drain from the man who, up until recently, showed me nothing but kindness and love.

What a difference a few months makes.

My instincts pull me toward a shadowed alcove, a quiet and hidden space, surely, but certainly not big enough to act as a hiding place for a human being.

Dom reaches up and grasps the sconce above us, an unlit candle tucked inside. The stones behind it creak as a small slit opens, just big enough for us to slip into.

"Good call," I tell her once we're on the other side of the wall.

"The Scotan Castle has a couple of hidden passageways. They're important for royals, so we can escape if there's an ambush. Of course, Cal and I mostly used them to sneak into each other's rooms, usually with the aim of scaring the hell out of the other." The smile is audible in her voice, even if I can't see it on her face.

There is somehow even less light here, and I'm wishing we had thought to grab the candle from the sconce. I reach back for Dom's hand, and she grasps mine tightly. We make our way along the curved stone wall, keeping it at our backs so we have some semblance of direction.

I don't know how long we walk; time seems to lose all meaning in the black hole of the passage, my eyes never fully adjusting.

Eventually we come to a shard of light peeking from below the seam of a wooden door.

Dom presses her ear to the wood, but it's too dark for me to make out any of her signals. Without warning, she rams her shoulder into the door and it springs open, flooding the hallway with light.

I rush into the room, my eyes immediately landing on the crumpled form of my sister. "Andra!" I cry out, fear gripping my heart when she doesn't stir. I fall to my knees at her side, searching for a pulse, a breath in her chest.

"She's alive."

I whirl around to catch the owner of the pained and breathless words. Bianca sits chained to the wall, her face bruised, her dress in tatters. Her thick red curls hang around her face, tangled and matted.

Dom checks Bianca over for injuries. "She seems to be okay, other than the obvious bruises."

I cradle Andra's head in my lap. "What happened to my sister?"

Bianca meets my eyes, but whatever she sees there pulls her gaze away. "Lady M . . . well, it was as you said, Cate."

"Yes, I know that part already. Tell me what happened, Bianca!"

She sighs, blinking away tears, but I'm too focused on my sister to hold much pity for her in the moment. "Lady M is a Gifted."

Dom sucks in a sharp breath and she shoots me a weary look. "Did you know about this? What can she do?"

Bianca shakes her head. "It's like nothing I've ever seen before. Nothing I've ever even heard of. She can amplify our Gifts." She hesitates. "Or she can block them."

"She was amplifying Andra's Sight?" Dom forms the questions better than I can. I can barely think straight through all the rage clouding my vision. This woman turned my sister into a shell of her former self. And I let her.

Bianca nods. "She burned her out, I think. Andra collapsed yesterday and she hasn't regained consciousness since."

"What happened to you?" Dom asks with more care than I manage to stir up in the present moment.

"I tried to tell the other girls, the La Puissance girls, what was going on."

This grabs my attention. I look over Bianca's wounds. "Our friends did this to you?"

She shakes her head, wincing at the movement. "No. Lady M's other girls. They came to my room late last night."

Dom and I exchange a weary look. There are other girls, Gifted presumably. This is worse than we anticipated.

"Where is Lady M right now?" Dom takes Bianca's cuffs in her hands, looking for a way to unlock them.

"I don't know," Bianca mutters. "We should have listened to you from the beginning, Cate. I'm sorry it took me so long to believe you."

"There's no time for that now." I set Andra's head gently back on the ground, pulling a pin from my hair and handing it to Dom. "Here."

Dom takes it and immediately begins working on the locks. "We need to get to Cal. He could be facing Lady M right now."

"She won't be alone," Bianca warns.

"How many are with her?" Dom asks as the cuffs around Bianca's wrists clatter to the hard stone floor.

I flinch at the sound, but it's Bianca's response that makes my stomach roil.

"All the rest of the girls from the club." She hesitates, rubbing her wrists.

“And?” I push her.

“I’ve seen many others since we’ve been here, but never all at the same time.”

“How many?” Dom repeats, her voice cold and cutting.

“I don’t know. At least twenty.”

My stomach heaves once again and for a second I think I might throw up at the thought of Callum and Alex facing off against Gifted who are having their powers amplified, Gifted we don’t even know. They could have powers we’ve never even dreamed of. “We need to go.”

Dom twists the pin, freeing Bianca’s ankles, the cuffs dropping with another echoing clatter.

Bianca immediately moves to Andra’s side, her hands hovering over her seemingly lifeless body. She looks at me. “She’s going to be okay. Just exhausted and hungry.”

Dom is already halfway out the door. “We need to go now, Cate.”

I shove my hands under Andra’s body, attempting to hoist her into my arms. I don’t make it very far before the door of the room slams open, the wood splintering with a crack when it hits the stone wall.

I cover Andra’s body with mine. She moans and it’s faint, but at least it’s a small sign of life.

I don’t have time to give thanks.

Lady M storms into the room, three women I’ve never seen before trailing in her wake. She points to Dom without saying a single word. Dom reaches for her sword, but before it’s out of the sheath, she’s clawing at her throat, gasping for breath.

I push Andra into Bianca’s arms, dashing for Dom, catching her as she collapses. Her weight drags us both down to the cold floor. “Dom! Dom!” I cry helplessly, no idea how to fight off an attack I can't see. Dom continues to scratch at her own throat, her gaze wide and wild. My eyes rove frantically over the Gifted flanking Lady M, but each of them stares stoically at Dom, giving me no hint as to who is responsible for stealing the air from her lungs.

Ripping the dagger from the sheath at my thigh, I lunge for the nearest Gifted, but before I can move two steps, my limbs become so heavy that crossing the few feet separating me from the person hurting Dom seems like an insurmountable task. Still, none of them flinch, none of them so much as blink.

"Bianca! Help Dom, please!" I struggle against the weight dragging me back, fighting to gain even an inch.

Bianca is quiet behind me.

I turn, pivoting away from Lady M and her small army. As soon as I do, I regain full range of motion. I stumble, crashing hard on the ground at Dom's side, my knee connecting painfully with the stone floor.

She's still, no longer choking and gasping for breath. Her lips are a sickly shade of blue, her eyes closed.

I meet Bianca's eyes. They are filled with tears I know match mine. "No." The single word comes out on a whisper, as if the air is being squeezed from my own lungs.

"I'm so sorry, Cate." Bianca reaches for me, but I shrug away from her embrace.

I blink several times, as if I can clear away the image in front of me. As if I can blink back time.

This is all my fault. If we hadn't come here, if I hadn't dragged Callum and Alex and Dom into this, none of this would have happened.

Maybe Callum was right all along. Maybe the Gifted are cursed and evil. Maybe we don't deserve to live unrestricted lives. Because look what can happen.

I stand on shaky legs, my knee still throbbing, moving toward my sister. I don't have the strength left in me to lift her, so I shield her from Lady M. Bianca stands at my side, and though I don't know if I will ever be able to truly forgive her, I'm thankful for her presence in this moment.

For the first time since she told me to make Callum Reid fall in love with me, I look Lady M in the eye. "I will kill you for that."

She smirks. "You're welcome to try."

I lunge for her, but once again, one of the Gifted standing at her back stops me. She doesn't even need to lay a hand on me, and I'm struggling to move. "Let me go!"

Lady M laughs, the sound low and grating. "Why would I do that?" She strolls closer, staying just far enough away that I can't reach her thanks to these invisible bonds. "No, I think I have you right where I want you, Lady Caterine."

"Then let my sister go. Let Bianca take her somewhere safe. She's no use to you in a state like this anyway." I gesture helplessly to my sister, still lying broken on the chilled stone floor. Bianca crouches by her side, but Andra hasn't shown any other sign of life since her stilted moan.

Lady M's head cocks to the side as she studies me. "You are not in a position to be making demands here, Caterine. Do not think that you or your sister are escaping my grasp again. I finally have you right where I want you, right where you belong." Her amber eyes flash, and a chill races through my veins, a sense of foreboding like I've never felt before gripping my chest.

"Tell me what you want."

"I have what I want."

"Just because you have us here does not mean we will do what you say."

She laughs again, and this one sounds genuine, and cold. "I

know exactly how to get you to do what I want. How do you think I've been forcing Andra to See?"

She gives me a second of silence, but I will not give her the satisfaction of a response. Lady M crosses further into my space, and I feel the weight around my chest tighten, holding me back so I can't punch her in the face like she deserves.

"That's the thing with sisters. All I had to do was threaten you, and Andra was a willing little puppet. She did whatever I asked because she knew her actions were protecting you. Just as I know you'll do whatever I ask to protect those you love." Something almost resembling a smile tugs on her lips. "Like that boyfriend of yours who's attempting to kill my husband as we speak."

I yank on the invisible force holding me back, fighting fruitlessly, doing everything I can to make it to the door. To Callum. "Do not touch him. I swear, I will kill you myself—twice over—if you lay a hand on him."

She throws her head back with that chilling laughter. "My dear Cate, I think I have made it more than clear that I do not have to lay a hand on anyone to hurt them. Others are more than happy to do the dirty work for me."

Tears cloud my vision, from anger and fear and desperation. Not Callum. I cannot let her hurt him. "Please. Do not hurt him. Tell me what you want me to do, and I'll do it."

She circles me, her steps slow, her eyes never leaving my face. "Just what would you sacrifice to keep your little boyfriend safe, I wonder?" She nudges Andra with her toe. "Your sister?"

I grimace, not about to give her an answer. I don't know what I would do if she made me choose between the two of them, and I'm not about to find out.

She stops behind me, leaning in over my shoulder. "How about your love?"

I swallow the lump of tears crowding my throat. "What do you mean?"

"I'm feeling generous tonight. I will let your sister live, I will let your best friend live. I will let you live." She stalks around me, the skirt of her long black dress brushing over Dom's lifeless body like she's nothing more than a speck of dirt on the floor. "I would say I would let his sister live, but I think it's too late for that. Pity." She stops moving once she's back in front of me, her eyes full of a familiar golden fire. "And I will let Callum Reid live."

A breath seeps out of me, but I'm not stupid enough to get my hopes up.

"All you have to do is convince him to leave."

My brow furrows. Convince him to leave and she will let him live? I blanch at the wrongness of it. Why? How? There is no way Lady M would let him escape alive, so why would she even offer this bargain?

Because he will never leave me here. And she knows it.

I don't understand the full scope of the sick game she is playing, but I do know there is no way Callum is going to leave me behind. "He won't leave without me."

She shrugs. "The fun part is watching you try to figure out a way to convince him."

The woman is sadistic, but if this is the only way to save Callum, I need to take it. No matter his military experience, he and Alex are no match for even just the three Gifted in this room, and I still don't know how many others there are or what their powers might be.

"I have an idea!" Lady M says brightly after a few moments of quiet. "Tell him you don't love him!"

My heart instantly rebels at the very suggestion, thumping in my chest so loudly it echoes in my ears. "He wouldn't believe me."

She takes my chin in her hands, her touch at first a soft caress, before her grip tightens, her nails digging into my skin. "Make him believe you. Part of your job is to make your clients believe you want them, yes? So how hard can it be to make a man believe the opposite?"

My chest aches with an emptiness I don't know that I'll ever recover from. Hurting Callum might destroy anything good left inside me, but if it's what it takes to save him, then I know I don't have much of a choice.

"Fine." The invisible pressure holding me back fades and I pull back my shoulders. "If you vow to let them live—Bianca, Andra, and Callum—I will do as you ask."

She claps her hands together. "Wonderful!" Her hand latches on to my elbow and she yanks me from the room. "Ladies, make sure our guests stay put until I return."

The three Gifted part around Lady M as she drags me from the room and out to the main hallway. The torches have been lit, bright enough for me to see Callum, his back to us, at the end of the hall.

He's alone, and the tension in his shoulders is enough to let me know that nothing this night has gone according to plan.

Lady M loosens her grasp enough to make it look like the two of us have joined arms like we're the best of chums. She leans down to whisper in my ear. "Showtime!"

26

CALLUM

I SHOVE AN UNCONSCIOUS Harold MacVeigh into my uncle's arms the moment I step back into the hallway. "Get him to the safe house and get him a healer, as quickly as you can."

It's a testament to his trust in me that Alex doesn't question my instructions. He nods, turning for the entrance. "I take it you're going to find them?"

"I can't leave without her."

He doesn't bother trying to argue with me, heading back the way he came on quick and quiet feet.

I make my way farther into the stone fortress, listening for any sound of Cate, for any sound of my sister. For anyone at this point. I know Lady M is still here, with her army of Gifted likely surrounding her. I stick to the shadows, hoping to avoid them at all costs, mostly because we don't know what they are capable of. But also because I know that hurting them will hurt Cate, and I've already done enough of that.

The air is musty and damp, like the rains have been seeping in and making a home among the blocks of the walls. I hit a corner and shift to turn around, to head in a different direction, the shadows so thick they are a trap unto themselves.

A voice from behind halts me in my tracks. "I was wondering when I was going to get to see you again, Callum Reid."

My blood chills, but I stand up straight, pulling my shoulders back. If I interpreted Harold's words correctly, this woman is more than just the person standing between me and my future. She is also Cate's mother.

My stomach roils at the very possibility, turns even further when I imagine how Cate is going to handle the news.

A flare of light brightens the hall, and I have to shield my eyes from it. When I lower my hand, I see her before me.

Lady M is not alone.

Cate stands next to her, their arms linked together like a true mother and daughter. For half a second, I wonder if Cate already knows, if she has been in on it the whole time.

But there is no happiness in Cate's eyes, only anguish. Anguish she is trying to hide, feelings she might be able to keep from another. Not from me.

Something here has gone seriously wrong. Everything tonight has gone seriously wrong. But there is one way I know it will all be right.

Lady M takes a step back and I rush for Cate, scooping her into my arms. When we are together, there is nothing more that can hurt us.

"Thank god you're all right." My hand finds the back of her head, swiping soothing strokes that are as much for her comfort as for mine. She's here, I'm touching her, she's alive. "Where's Dom?"

She burrows herself into my embrace, and I know deep in my gut that the worst thing has come to pass.

Even when I thought everything had gone wrong, I hadn't considered this.

My hold on her tightens, but after she doesn't respond, I shift her away, moving my hands to clasp her elbows, keeping us connected but allowing me to look her in the eye. I need to hear the words out loud before I can believe them. "Caterine. Where is my sister? Is she safe? Did you find Andra?"

She visibly fights back tears that are clouding her eyes. "I'm so sorry, Callum."

Not Dom. Not days after Father.

I have no one left.

The air is sucked from my lungs, and I don't know if I will ever breathe again. It's too much. A person is not made to endure so much pain, so much heartache. And it's all my fault.

The urge to crumple is nearly overwhelming. What a relief it would be to drop to this cold stone floor and let Lady M end me, right here and right now.

But Cate would never forgive herself. She will inevitably come to the conclusion that she is better off without me, a man who brings nothing but ruin and destruction to those he loves, but right now, she still has faith in me. I can see the sliver of it in her golden eyes, and I can't be the one to destroy her, at least not yet.

So I take a page from her book and shield myself with a mask. I tuck the news about my sister, the sting of my uncle's betrayal, the loss of my father, into a tiny dark corner in the back of my mind. I wipe my face of all emotions, putting on an impenetrable air that no one, not even Cate, can breach.

She is the one person I should never have to don a mask in front of. And yet here we both are, hiding our true selves from one another.

"We should go. We need to leave, Cate." The words are hushed and harsh. I don't know how long I can make this performance last, and I refuse to give Lady M the satisfaction of seeing me break.

"You should go, Callum." She steps away from me, gently pulling her hands from mine.

My brow creases, confusion marring this flawed mask I've dropped into place. "I'm not leaving without you."

"There is no more reason for you to stay." She smirks, tilting up the corner of her perfect lips, lips that have trailed over every inch of my body. "The ruse is over, Callum."

My hands clench into tight fists at my sides. "What the hell are you talking about?"

She laughs, too high-pitched. "We both know that's all this was. You came to see me under false pretenses, I made you fall in love with me to make sure you weren't the one to kill your father, and now the game is up."

"False pretenses? What are you talking about, Cate? You know that's not what this is." I lower my voice, a stark reminder we are not alone here in this damp hallway. I'm not willing to give Lady M any more than she has already taken from me. "We're Bonded."

She throws her head back with laughter, and it's vibrant and boisterous and rings completely false. "You believed that?" She reaches up to pat my cheek. "Oh, you are a dear one, Callum Reid."

I push her hand away and even though her words are stinging barbs, I miss the touch of her instantly. "Are you really going to stand here and tell me that all of this has been for nothing? My sister died, and it was all for nothing?" My voice cracks, and the tears I've been fighting back spring into my eyes. The mask is slipping and I know I don't have much time left to get out of here before I completely lose it.

Cate swallows thickly, like she is fighting back tears of her own. "I think it's best if you leave," she whispers.

Something is not right here. I don't know what game she is playing, but I know that what we have is not all in my head. Yes, Cate makes a living pretending to be interested in her clients, but what we have is different.

It has to be.

I look her dead in the eyes, knowing she will never be able to do what I'm about to ask of her. "Look me in the eye and tell me you don't love me, and I will leave right now and never come back."

Her breath stills in her lungs, her eyes flickering with a hundred different emotions.

She can't say it. I know she can't. It would kill me to even think it.

She pushes her shoulders back. "I don't love you, Callum. I never did."

What's left of my heart shatters.

I nod, dashing my clenched fists across my cheeks to clear away my tears. It's time for me to go. Who knows how long it's going to take me to fully process the events of the day, but the one thing I do know is I don't want to be in the presence of Lady M when the emotions rise to the surface.

Then I remember that Cate is not the only one keeping secrets.

I lean in, as if to give her one final hug. I don't think I can bear it, her citrus scent igniting something inside me, but I know she needs to hear this, even if I owe her nothing more. "Harold is alive. Alex has taken him back to the safe house. You might not want anything more to do with me, but I think you might want to hear what he has to say." My eyes dart behind her, to where Lady M is watching. I make my next words loud enough for the whole stone fortress to hear. "I knew I should have never put my faith in a Gifted courtesan. I was right about you all along."

A small part of me hopes my words cut her as deeply as hers did me. But the thought of hurting Cate doesn't make me feel any better. If anything, it only widens the hole in my chest where my heart used to be.

I'm leaving it with her.

I turn on my heel, stalking out of the fortress without a look back.

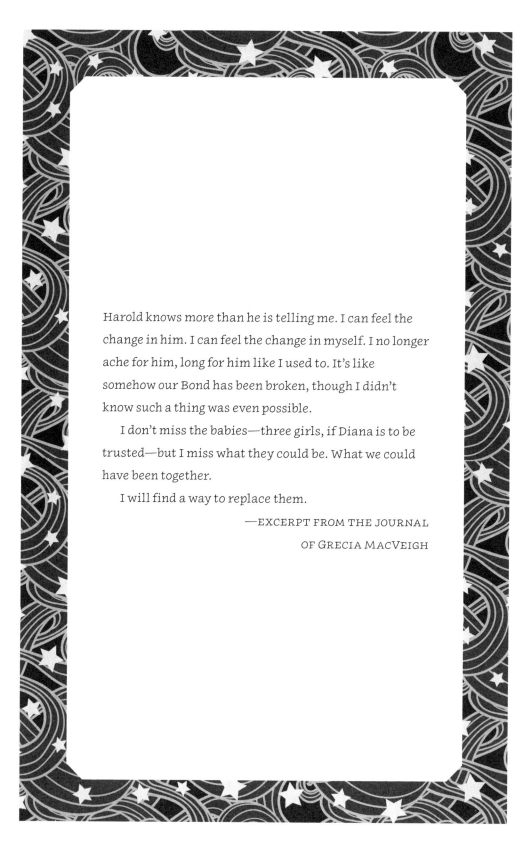

Harold knows more than he is telling me. I can feel the change in him. I can feel the change in myself. I no longer ache for him, long for him like I used to. It's like somehow our Bond has been broken, though I didn't know such a thing was even possible.

I don't miss the babies—three girls, if Diana is to be trusted—but I miss what they could be. What we could have been together.

I will find a way to replace them.

—EXCERPT FROM THE JOURNAL OF GRECIA MACVEIGH

27

CATE

CALLUM WALKS DOWN the hall, away from me, and I know this is likely the last time I will ever see him. So I don't pull my eyes from him, soaking in every single second of his presence, even as he grows smaller, the dim light of the hallway eventually swallowing him whole.

My arms wrap around my chest, as if to cage my heart behind my ribs when it really has been ripped from me; Callum has taken it with him, and I don't know if I will ever get it back.

"Nicely done."

A shiver races up my spine as Lady M closes in on me from behind.

"I have to admit, I wasn't sure you had it in you." She takes my elbow in her grip once again. "I hope I don't come to regret leaving him alive, but if the time comes when I need to dispose of him, I shall. For now, everything is going according to plan. Harold is dead. I will represent Scota in the election, and the prophecy will finally prove true."

I have to swallow multiple times before I can make my voice work. "What prophecy?"

"The one dear Andra Saw. About me finally coming to power as I was always meant to. The one with a crown, and a Gift, and a pair of golden eyes."

"Presidents don't wear crowns." It's ludicrous that that is the detail I push back against, given everything that just happened, given the mess of my current emotions, but it's all I can think of.

Her mirthless laugh titters, echoing around the empty hall. "Once I'm president I will have the power to do whatever I want, even make myself a queen." She snaps her fingers, and a young woman with pale skin and soulless eyes appears. She must have been standing in the shadows the whole time. "Take our dear Caterine back to her chambers with the others."

I don't fight against the grip of the Gifted girl. "You promised you wouldn't hurt us."

Lady M raises one eyebrow. "I know what I promised, Cate. Callum Reid walked out of here alive. Bianca is alive. So is your sister."

"You need to let us go so we can help Andra."

Lady M holds up a hand, and the girl dragging me down the hall pauses. "You will stay here until I no longer have use for you."

"And then?"

Lady M doesn't answer, shooing me away. The Gifted tugs on my arm, but she doesn't have to pull hard. I need to be back with my sister. She is the only one I have left.

IT'S IMPOSSIBLE TO tell how much time passes as we sit in the dank, cold room somewhere in the depths of the stone fortress. Andra has not awoken. Dom's body has been removed. Bianca and

I sit in opposite corners, eating when food is delivered and rotting in the silence the remainder of the time.

We've had four meals across the span of who knows how many hours—it's impossible to keep track of time when there is no sunlight, only darkness—when Andra finally stirs.

At first, I think I must be imagining it, that I've been staring at her motionless body for so long I've finally cracked and begun to hallucinate.

But then Bianca rushes to her side, and I know she must have seen it too.

I crawl to my sister, knowing I will get to her faster without trying to stand on stiff limbs. "Andra?" I place a hand on her forehead, her skin clammy and burning at the same time.

Andra's eyes crack open, just a slit, and for the first time, I'm grateful for the dim light in the room. Her eyes open slowly, unfocused, the golden hue burnished with fatigue.

"Don't try to talk," Bianca says softly, smoothing back the hair from her face. She reaches for a cup of water, holding it to Andra's lips.

She sips slowly, her gaze sharpening until it finally lands on me. "Cate," she croaks out, her voice hoarse with disuse.

I can't stop the tears and I don't bother trying to hold them back. I throw myself on top of her, practically smothering her, but I don't care. My sister is alive. It is the only thing that has gone right since Harold killed the king.

Bianca gently pries me away from my sister, a soft smile on her face. "She needs to breathe, Cate."

I nod, wiping at my eyes. "Sorry."

Andra sits up with Bianca's help. "Tired. And so hungry."

It's been a few hours since our last meal, but we don't know when the next one will arrive. I head right for the door keeping us trapped in this room and pound on it. It takes a full minute of incessant banging before it opens.

"We need food. Now."

The Gifted guarding the door frowns. "You just ate. It isn't time for your next meal."

"Andra is awake. My sister needs to eat. Lady M wouldn't want her weakened further."

Her brow creases, and for a second, I allow myself to see her as a person instead of one of Lady M's minions. How did she get here? Why is she helping Lady M? Was this her choice, or is she as helpless as we are?

Eventually, she nods, calling over another Gifted, who races down the hall after a whispered conversation.

My stomach sinks with dread. Surely she's run off not to get Andra the food she desperately needs to recover, but to tell Lady M she's awake. How long do we have before Lady M is forcing Andra to See for her again?

I sit down next to my sister, looking around the room as if a weapon is going to magically appear. As if I'm going to suddenly discover a secret way out of here that I haven't noticed after staring at these walls for hours on end.

I don't know how, but I know I cannot allow Andra to try to use her Gift. Not until she has had enough time to recuperate. Something tells me Lady M won't have the patience to wait.

It doesn't take long before the heavy wooden door slams open.

I hold my breath, but it isn't Lady M waiting in the hall, but another unknown Gifted, a tray of food in her hands. I jump from the floor and snatch it from her, like she might take it away if I don't grab it quickly enough.

"Lady M says she will be down shortly."

I carry the food over to Andra, holding the tray steady so as not to spill a drop. "She needs more time to recover. She cannot try to See yet."

The Gifted shrugs. "Tell that to her."

The door closes before I can deliver a retort. Bianca takes a bowl of soup from the tray, holding the spoon to Andra's mouth. I prop myself behind my sister, holding her frail weight upright so she can eat.

For several long minutes, there's only the sound of slurping. Bianca feeds her slowly, and I know there's a good possibility the food won't stay in Andra's stomach after going so long without. I rub soothing circles on her back, hold her cup of water to her lips, and care for her like I haven't since we were children.

Eventually, Andra pushes the tray of food away. Her head sinks down onto my shoulder, and I want to let her rest, know she still needs time, but time is something we don't have the luxury of.

"Can you See any way for us to get out of here?"

She stiffens, her shoulders going tight. "I don't know. Everything is just blackness."

Bianca glares at me. "Don't try to read, Andra. Right now you need to focus on regaining your strength."

I know she is right, just as I know that we need to get out of here, and I don't see how we do that without some kind of help.

Andra's eyes are drifting closed when the door opens once again.

Lady M stands in her usual black dress, the fabric swallowing her from head to toe. Her amber eyes glint when she sees Andra, awake and sitting up. "Welcome back."

I shift my sister behind me, not that I have much chance of shielding her if Lady M is determined to make her read. "She needs more time."

Lady M ignores me. Her head tilts to the side, her eyes so deeply focused on Andra I would swear they began to glow.

Andra gasps and I turn, tucking her into my embrace. Her hands fly to her head. "Harold is alive." It's all she manages to choke out before collapsing in my arms.

I turn my glare on Lady M. "What don't you understand about she needs to rest? Look what you've done!" I know there's no chance she didn't hear what Andra said, and yet I do my best to distract her.

But Lady M cares not for what I have to say. Her eyes narrow. "Harold is alive."

"You would think you would want that for your husband," I choke out.

She doesn't bother to respond, sweeping out of the room, gesturing for one of the guards to close the door behind her. It shuts with a damning thud.

I gently lower Andra to the ground and look helplessly at Bianca. She hovers over my sister even though we both know there's nothing she can do for her.

"I don't think it's as bad this time. She probably just needs more rest." Bianca rearranges Andra into a more comfortable position before looking at me. It's the first time our eyes have met since we've been locked in here, and I see so much in their bright green depths. Fear and anger and so much sadness. "What do we do now?"

It's an impossible question, one I have no answer for.

AT SOME POINT, I fall into a restless slumber. I only know this because at some point, someone attempts to rouse me, whispering my name and shaking my shoulder, until I slowly crawl out of the numb haze enveloping me.

As soon as I see my sister lying motionless on the cold stone floor, as soon as I remember the look in Callum's eyes when I told him I don't love him, as soon as the vision of Dom's lifeless body floats behind my eyes, I wish I could fall back asleep.

"Fucking hell, Cate, if you don't wake the fuck up right now I am going to gut you myself." Tes's voice is harsh and instantly recognizable.

I sit up, rubbing the sleep and disbelief from my eyes. "Tes? What are you doing here?"

"Saving your ass," Meri replies from across the room, where she is helping Bianca stand, her muscles cramped from so long on the hard stone.

"I don't understand."

Tes scoops her arms under mine, yanking me to standing. "We're getting you out of here."

"Who's we? And why?" I hate that my first instinct is to be suspicious. Of course my friends should want to help me escape the tyrannical woman who's holding me hostage, but they haven't exactly been on my team in this battle.

"All of us from the club." Meri leaves Bianca resting against the wall before going to help Rosa hoist Andra from the floor. Once Rosa has Andra situated in her arms, Meri returns to Bianca's side. "We don't have much time."

Tes tugs me toward the door, but I drag my feet. "Why should we trust you now?"

The three women exchange a look. "We overheard Lady M talking," Tes finally admits. "We heard her plans to kill Harold."

I nod, a sad wave of understanding cresting over me. "So you'll come to his defense, but not mine. Not Andra's."

"We didn't know how bad it had gotten," Rosa says quietly.

"I tried to warn you."

"We know," Tes says harshly. "But would you rather fight over who was right, or get out of here and get some help?"

That question, at least, has an easy answer. I make for the door, leaning on Tes when my limbs start tingling as they awaken.

When we reach the hall, Tes doesn't move toward the front of the stone fortress, instead making her way in the opposite direction, leading us down halls that echo with silence.

"Where is everyone else?" I whisper when I spot an archway leading to the outdoors.

"We're staying here," Tes replies, her voice tight.

I stop in my tracks. "What do you mean you're staying here? I thought you realized what's going on."

"I don't think you realize what's going on, Cate. She's building an army. She's gathered enough Gifted to be able to wipe out a battalion of seasoned soldiers in mere minutes. She doesn't know we know her plans, and right now, it makes more sense for us to remain on the inside."

I lean in the stone archway, gathering my strength. I'm going to have to walk the rest of the way on my own. "Callum is going to come for her. He's not going to let her get away with this."

"He will be sorely outnumbered," Meri warns.

I nod, trying to make sense of the conflicting thoughts whirring through my brain. I need to warn him, but I know it's highly likely he isn't going to trust my word. And why should he? I have done nothing but scheme and betray him. I broke his heart and got his sister killed, and yet, as I consider our options, where we might go where Andra will be safe, there is only one place that comes to mind.

If what Callum told me is true, Harold is there, and if Andra's vision is true, he's alive.

Rosa deposits Andra on her feet, slinging one of her arms around my neck and the other around Bianca's. I have no idea how we are going to manage escaping the grounds without being seen.

"We cleared the way for you, but you don't have much time," Tes instructs. "Get as far away as you can, as quickly as you can."

I nod, looking between the three women I consider sisters. "I don't like leaving you here."

Meri shrugs. "She needs us."

"When she realizes we are gone, she will know it was you who helped us."

"Then perhaps when you see that prince of yours, convince him to make his move sooner rather than later."

I doubt that prince will be listening to me anytime soon, but I don't say that out loud. "We'll come back for you."

At once, we fall into each other's arms, an embrace with too many limbs and too many words still left unsaid to be much comfort. But it's a start.

"Go." Tes points the way.

Bianca and I support Andra's weight and head out into the darkness, moving as quickly as we can. The trees swallow us up and I head toward the only solace I can think of. A man who wants nothing more to do with me, but the only person I trust to keep us safe.

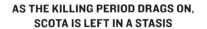

AS THE KILLING PERIOD DRAGS ON, SCOTA IS LEFT IN A STASIS

It has now been several days since King James of Scota died as part of the first sanctioned killing period set in place by the Uprising. According to sources, King James was killed by Harold MacVeigh, the owner and operator of La Puissance, a pleasure club located in Stratford City. Though MacVeigh hails from Scota, he has not lived in the province for many years.

MacVeigh has yet to be officially announced as the Scotan candidate, as the killing period has not yet come to a close. When we reached out to Uprising officials for a statement, our requests were ignored.

Citizens of Scota don't seem to know what to make of the news, with some expressing regret, others dismay. Many others still seem to be confused as to what happens next.

I took a ride through the rolling green hills of the Scotan province yesterday, ambling down the cobblestone streets of the normally bustling villages, stunned by the lack of activity. It is as if the entire province has shut down for the duration of the killing period.

"We just want some answers," one tavern owner mentioned when I stopped in for a beer. I was the only customer at the time.

I think all of Scota, and perhaps even all of Avon, echoes his sentiment.

28

CALLUM

TIME PASSES. THE sun rises in the morning and sets in the evening. I do not have the strength or the desire to count them. To know how many days have passed since I lost everything. My father. My sister.

Cate.

Even as her words replay in my mind, over and over, until they no longer cut me like a thousand knives, I can't make myself truly believe them, cannot fathom a world where the feelings I have for her are not reciprocated.

Which makes me nothing more than a fool.

Harold remains alive, but unconscious. According to Harold, Lady M has been feeding him a slow-acting poison. He's grown thinner and paler as the days go by, but he keeps breathing. I don't think there is much hope for him without a Gifted healer, but I wouldn't know where to find one, even if I had the desire to try.

"I don't think he has much time left," Alex tells me one morning, the clouds outside the one tiny window as gray and heavy as the mood in the room.

I've barely dragged myself from the rickety cot that passes for a bed. I know deep down I should care about this news, but I can't manage to make myself feel anything, content to linger in this state of numbness.

If I let in one tiny emotion, what's to keep the other, much bigger and more dangerous ones from pulling me under?

A knock sounds on the door.

Alex and I exchange a look.

I haven't left the safe house since I arrived back from the fortress. Alex has slipped out a couple of times in the dark of night to gather more food and supplies, but no one is supposed to know we're here.

Did he betray me again? I wonder. But the look of fear and surprise in his eyes is too genuine. He doesn't know who's on the other side of that door.

The knock sounds again.

Alex rises, drawing a knife from his boot. I reach for the dagger I keep under my pillow, joining him at the door. I flatten my back to the wall next to it, ready to spring into action if need be.

I give him a nod, and he cracks the door.

Whatever he sees on the other side must not give him pause, because he throws it open wide, and three bodies fall into the open space.

My heart stops. I would recognize that golden hair anywhere.

My body freezes along with my heart, but the room bursts into motion around me.

A redhead rushes to Harold's side, her hands hovering over his body, doing lord knows what.

Alex helps Cate lift another golden-haired woman onto the empty cot.

This must be Andra. She and Cate have the same coloring, though Andra is thin and frail, lifeless except for the rise and fall of her chest. Cate tucks a blanket around her, smooths back her hair, whispers something in her ear. Dark circles line her eyes and exhaustion curves her shoulders; it must have taken them the whole night to make it here, but it doesn't surprise me that Cate managed to find a way to save her sister.

I can't take my eyes off her.

She's here, her presence stinging more than soothing. I had resigned myself to never seeing her again, and yet, now that she's here in front of me, I don't have anything to say. Conflicting emotions wage a war within me and I'm unable to settle on a single one. I don't know what it means, that she came here of all places. I do know that a small part of my heart stitches itself back together knowing at least she's alive.

Cate rises from her position next to Andra only to sink to her knees again, this time next to Harold. Her own war of emotions flits across her face, but she finally gives in, taking his hand in hers. And it becomes clear why she came here. Not for me, but for him.

It shouldn't hurt. There shouldn't be any part left of me to hurt.

Her eyes meet mine and they are layered with so much pain and grief that I long to take away from her, to share that burden even if I am unable to ease it. "You didn't kill him."

My chest aches as I watch the two of them together. Despite everything, I had many years with my own father. Cate thought she had lost hers long ago, but really he was right there with her, protecting her and caring for her, the whole time. How will she react when she finds out the truth?

I pray I won't have to be the one to tell her. I don't think I could.

"I told you he was alive." The words come out harsher than I intend, as if to remind both of us of the division still separating us.

She nods, a million emotions in the small gesture. She opens her mouth to speak, but nothing comes out. Instead, she turns her focus back to Harold.

Minutes pass, bleeding into hours and still the redhead, Bianca I presume, fusses over Harold. I don't know how her Gift works, and watching her isn't making things any clearer. The whole room looks on with bated breath, searching for some sign of change in his condition.

He comes to with a start, a violent cough racking his lungs.

Bianca calls for water and Alex darts into the kitchen, returning with a glass of it seconds later. She holds it to Harold's lips and he sips, barely taking in more than a few drops at a time.

Harold's eyes flit around the room, searching for something, or someone. They linger on mine for a second before they land on Cate. He sits up, moving quite well considering the state he was just in, and wraps her in his arms.

Cate resists at first but finally acquiesces, her arms finding their way around Harold's frail body.

"We have much to talk about." His voice is so weak I can barely make out the words.

"We'll leave you alone." I gesture for Alex to head into the other room with me to give them all some privacy.

"No," Cate says. "Whatever it is he needs to tell me, you need to hear too."

I don't know if it's supposed to be a peace offering or a sign of trust. I almost refuse, heading into the small bedroom if for no other reason than to not have to see her face.

"Please, Callum. I need you to hear." She turns to Harold. "If that's okay with you."

He nods, adjusting his position, gratefully accepting the pillow Bianca offers to put behind his back.

I stay rooted in my spot, unable to deny her anything, even still.

Harold opens his mouth to speak, hesitating as if he isn't sure where to begin, but once his tale starts to unravel, it doesn't stop. He speaks for maybe an hour, spinning the story of his childhood friend, the woman who became his wife. The woman who became the mother of his children.

Cate pieces it all together before he says the words. "It was you all along."

Harold nods, his eyes brimming with sadness. "I thought it was the only way. Diana told me we needed to send you girls away from Grecia if you were to have any chance of surviving. It killed me to say goodbye to my daughters, but I would have done anything to guarantee your safety. I would still do anything to guarantee your safety, Cate."

Her grip on his hand tightens. "Why didn't you say something sooner? We could have had a whole life together, as a family."

He reaches for her cheek, patting it the way one would a young child's. "We did have a whole life together as a family, and I wouldn't change anything about it if it meant no harm would come to you or your sisters."

"Sisters?" Alex questions, the first time one of us on the outside has dared to speak.

Harold nods, his eyes never leaving Cate. "There were—are—three of you."

Cate sucks in a breath. "We have another sister? Where is she?"

"I'm not sure. But before Diana died, she assured me that she was safe. That she would come into our lives when the timing was right."

Cate's fist clenches. "I can't believe Diana never told us."

Harold gently unclasps her hand from where it grasps the blanket. "Such is the way with Seers. Sometimes they know too much."

"So your Bond with this Lady M, it really can't be broken?" Alex watches the group with sympathy shining in his eyes. But underneath that there's a calculating edge to his question. This isn't over. We might have escaped the fortress, Harold might have survived the poisoning, but Lady M isn't going to rest until she secures the candidacy for herself.

"It seemed to be, for a while, after we lost the girls. But I'm afraid I triggered it when I went back to her. I don't know that anything now is strong enough to sever it, save for one of us dying."

"It won't be you," Cate says, the fierceness in her determination stoking a flame of pride deep in my chest. It's an unwanted feeling, and yet I can't seem to force it down.

"She's your mother, Cate," Harold reminds her gently.

Cate shakes her head. "No, she's not. She might have given birth to us, but that woman is no mother. She is evil, Harold, capable of so much more harm than you can imagine."

"She will be ready for you. Between Diana and Andra, Grecia knows what to expect. She will know you are coming, and she has the Gifted on her side. I don't know that we can stop her."

"What is her end goal?" I ask. Maybe if we know what she is really after, we can find a way to put a stop to it. "Does she want to be the Scotan candidate? Does she have plans to try to win the election?"

Harold hesitates, but after everything that's been revealed, there is little use for more secrets. "When we were younger, Diana told us we would amass power, live in prosperity. It didn't mean much until Andra came along. Her visions are more attuned, more specific."

"What did she See?" Alex asks quietly.

"She Saw a crown, and a Gift, and a pair of golden eyes," Cate answers.

"That could be Lady M," I concede. "But it could also be you, or Andra."

"Or our other sister," she says quietly.

Alex clears his throat. "I think it would behoove us all to focus more on the here and now, rather than looking too far ahead. We need a Scotan candidate, and I don't think it should be you, Harold."

"I do not disagree with you. I have no plans to be for much longer." Harold shoots me a look, both of us remembering my promise, uttered what feels like a lifetime ago. "Unfortunately, Grecia seems to agree with me on that much at least. I know she is planning to end me, claim the candidacy for herself. Hence the poison."

"We can't let that happen." I'm not even sure who says it, because it comes from more than one voice in the room.

"More importantly," Cate inserts, "we can't leave the rest of the Gifted there to be used by her. Look what happened to Andra; she could drain any and all of them. Next time she could end up killing someone. They aren't safe with her. We need to find a way to get them out."

"Once the Gifted are free from her clutches, it should be easy enough for Callum to take her out. What is she without her army?" Alex crosses his arms over his chest, ready to go to battle.

"You should not underestimate her," Harold warns. "I fear I might be the only one who can get through to her, to find a way to put an end to all of this."

"Will your Bond allow you to do that?" My eyes flit to Cate's. I can't imagine ever being the one to hurt her, let alone end her life, even after everything she has put me through.

Cate rises, coming to stand by my side, like the brief eye contact between us was enough to stir her need for me. I itch to take her hand in mine, but there is still so much we need to say to one another. She is here, but I don't know that it's enough.

"I don't know." Harold watches us, and it's hard to tell if that's concern in his eyes, or hope. He pushes up from the cot. "But I don't think we should wait too long before we find out."

Bianca reaches out a hand to steady him, but he doesn't need her help. "I don't think you should be going anywhere near her right now, Harold, you need to heal."

"There isn't time for that." He turns his focus to me. "You're coming with me, I presume."

I nod. Even though I no longer have plans to kill him—there is no way I could do that to Cate at this point—I need to see to it for myself that Lady M doesn't come anywhere near the candidacy. Her, I would have no problem killing.

"I'm coming too." Cate holds up a hand to stave off the arguments coming at her from all sides. "Our only chance against the Gifted is to reason with them, to make them see who Lady M truly is. I'm the only one who can get through to them. And I'm not letting you go in there alone." It's unclear if her final words are for me or for Harold.

Harold nods, like he knows there's no point in arguing with her. "We should meet there tomorrow morning, at first light."

"Why not tonight?" Alex asks.

"I need to go back to the club. There is something I need to do there before I go to see her."

"Will you go with him?" I ask my uncle. He might be the only one I trust to protect Harold.

Alex nods, heading to the bedroom to gather his meager pack of things.

I cross the room to where Bianca sits, having shifted her attention to Andra. "I'm going to take Cate to another location for the night, closer to the fortress. I think it might be safer for you if we are not here. Do you know how to use a dagger?"

She nods, her eyes weary as they dart to Cate's.

I hand her the knife tucked in my boot. "Don't leave the safe house, and don't let anyone in."

She nods again, taking the dagger from me and setting it at her side.

Cate waits for me to cross to the door before she heads toward Bianca, whispering something in her ear before embracing her. She sends a last worried look in Andra's direction before joining me at the front door.

She didn't argue when I said the two of us needed to leave, whether that's to protect her sister and her friend, or because she knows we have much to discuss, I'm not sure. But even with the inches of space separating us, I can feel the heat of her. It licks at my skin, and the urge to take her in my arms, to meld our mouths together, to enter her and claim her, is nearly overwhelming.

I take a deep breath, steadying my nerves before speaking. "We should go."

She nods, reaching for my hand instinctually.

I pull it out of her reach.

Her mouth flattens into a straight line, and there's hurt and determination shining from her eyes.

I swallow thickly, open the front door, and head out into the darkness of the night. The air is cool, but the stench of the river is thick. I don't check to see if she follows me, but I can sense her presence, trusting me as I guide her through the shadows.

I thought the girls would be happy to see me when I showed up at La Puissance. I knew—of course I knew—from the moment I saw them that they were my daughters. Well, two of my daughters anyway. I spent the past years of my life collecting Gifted girls with nowhere else to go as if they could replace my babies, and my own little Gifted girls were right there all along.

But my reception wasn't exactly warm. I suppose I can blame that on Andra. She saw too much, right from the beginning. It's clear why Diana wanted to keep her away from me, though it doesn't make her betrayal sting any less.

Andra is useful, but weak. Cate, on the other hand, is strong. Formidable, even. Too bad she's found herself Bonded to that waste of a man. At least it will make it fun to toy with her. It'll be almost poetic. Harry and I were separated for so long, we'll see how well Cate deals with being apart from her one true partner. I had hopes of working alongside both of my remaining daughters, but Cate has made it clear she wants no part of my plans.

I'll have to make her regret that.

—FROM THE JOURNAL OF GRECIA MACVEIGH

29

CATE

CALLUM LEADS US to a ramshackle building on the opposite side of the river, much closer to the stone fortress we'll have to deal with tomorrow. Calling it a cabin would be generous, it's more like four wooden walls with some slats piled on top, but inside there are some blankets and a potbellied stove and plenty of wood and outside there's a water pump and a bucket.

Cal fills the bucket with water and lights a fire in the stove and all the while neither of us says anything, the unsaid words between us like a companion on this little trip.

"I should have thought to bring provisions. I don't think there's anything around here we can eat," he says after checking the space, not that there are many places a stockpile of food could be hiding. "We stopped keeping the safe houses stocked once the Uprising ended."

I shrug, curling up on top of one of the blankets and pulling another one over me. "I don't think I could eat anyway." My mind is racing, full of secrets revealed.

Harold is my father. Not just in the sense of being the man who raised me but in the sense of being one half of the parents who created me.

And my mother, I can barely begin to think on it, let alone let the truth sink into my brain. Lady M is my mother. According to Harold, she has no idea who Andra and I are to her, but I can't help but wonder if she hasn't somehow figured it out. I think back to that first day, the knowing smirk when her eyes landed on Andra. Harold and Lady M may be Bonded, but that doesn't mean she hasn't been keeping secrets of her own.

Callum lowers himself to the floor across from me, wincing with the movement.

I sit up, happy to have something else to focus on, though I hate seeing him in pain. "Are you all right?"

His eyes meet mine, a kaleidoscope of emotions. "How could I possibly be all right, Caterine?"

I tug my gaze away from his, even though it hurts to break this single point of contact between us. "Right. It was stupid of me to ask."

He runs a hand through his hair. "I didn't believe you, you know."

My heart stills in my chest. "What do you mean?"

"When you told me you don't love me. I didn't believe you." He hooks his arms around his knees, pulling them close as if to keep me away.

"But you left."

"I figured if you were trying that hard to convince me of something we both know to be false, you must have had a good reason. But then . . ."

If my heart stilled before, now it freezes completely. "Callum, I . . . I was scared. For my sister, and for Harold. For what we still have to do." I fill my lungs with a steadying breath. "But mostly I was scared that you wouldn't forgive me. That you would realize that you are better off without me."

His posture softens, but he doesn't move toward me or unclench his arms. "I have spent every second we were apart wishing for nothing more than a chance to kiss you one more time, Cate."

Tears fill my eyes, but I don't deserve to shed them. "I'm sorry. Of course I didn't mean what I said in that hallway. Lady M told me the only way she would let you go is if I made you believe I never loved you. And I would have done anything to save your life, even lie to you."

He takes in the information with a furrowed brow. "Why? What did she have to gain by sending me away?"

"I don't know." It's something I've thought on often since that fateful moment. "I think she likes hurting people, liked that it devastated both of us equally. Maybe it was some kind of sick retribution for the time she and Harold had to spend apart. I also think she didn't want to kill you if she didn't have to. Whether she wants to admit it or not, you are popular with your people, and if she hopes to win their vote, it's better for her to leave you alive."

He lets his legs fall, extending them in my direction. "I fear there is likely more to it than that."

I know in my heart he is right. But I also don't want to expend any more energy talking about Lady M. At least, not tonight. I scoot myself closer to him, letting his woodsy sage scent calm me, and steady me. "I'm sorry for all of it, Callum. If I had known, had any hint of an idea, that this is how things would turn out, I never would have gotten you involved in this."

He doesn't reach for me, but he also doesn't turn away. "I am responsible for my own decisions. I knew the risks I was taking."

"I'm so sorry about Dom."

He swallows, his throat bobbing as he attempts to choke down his emotions. "Me too."

I tentatively cup his cheek in my hand. "There is no force in this world that could make me stop loving you, Callum Reid."

He leans into my touch, his eyes fluttering closed for half a second. He doesn't return the sentiment, but for right now, this is enough. It might take some time for him to process everything that has occurred, but I would give him all the time in the world if he needed it.

"It's been a long day." He lies back on the pile of blankets. "We should probably get some rest while we can. Want to be as sharp as possible when we go back in."

I nod, though I don't see how I could possibly sleep, not with all the wild thoughts running through my brain. What I've seen and what happened, but also what's to come. I want to believe that my sisters will see what Lady M is truly doing—not just to them, but to all the Gifted she's essentially trapped. But I know what fear can do to your mind, and I don't know that I could fault them if they aren't able to see past their own.

When I lie down next to him, he tucks me into his embrace and the physical contact warms me from the inside out. And I know that no matter what else happens, we will always find our way back to each other.

WHEN I WAKE, slivers of sunlight break through the walls, shining through the hastily put together wooden slats. I'm warm and comfortable, my back pressed into Callum's front, his arm tucked around me.

Sleepy instinct has me pressing the curve of my butt into his hardness, shifting closer to him, searching for the familiar grunt he releases.

His lips drag along my bare shoulder, lingering on the spot where my trio of freckles lives. "Cate . . ."

I turn my head, meeting his gaze. The blue of his eyes is bright in the morning sun, but emotion shadows them, darkens them.

His mouth drifts closer to mine, seeking silent permission. I give it to him, pressing my lips to his, sighing at the pleasure of it, the instant sense of peace his touch instills in me.

We shouldn't be doing this—there is so much at stake today—but I can't make myself care. I lose myself in the kiss, in the heat of his lips, the strength of his hands as they grip me tight and pull me closer.

If this is the last moment we have together, I will not let it go to waste.

He licks at the seam of my lips until I part for him, his tongue sweeping into my mouth. One of his hands curves around my neck before reaching down to brush gentle fingers over the swells of my breasts. The other delivers the same treatment to the bare skin of my belly, drifting slowly down to the patch of curls at the apex of my thighs.

His hardness thrusts against me as his fingers part me. I'm already slick with wanting and he makes quick work, stroking my clit exactly how I like it, exactly how I've taught him.

"You have ruined me, Caterine," he mumbles into the curve of my neck, his teeth dragging along the exposed skin. "I will never be able to live without you."

"Good," I manage to choke out, breathless as the tension rises deep in my core, even though I don't really mean it. Callum deserves to live a long and happy life, with or without me.

I fumble behind me, shoving the fabric of his undergarments out of the way, wrapping my hand around the thickness of his cock. He groans, thrusting into my hand as his fingers bring me to the brink of release.

"I need you inside me, Callum," I pant, dizzy with wanting. Dizzy with needing this, needing him.

He obliges, pushing into me from behind with one smooth stroke that leaves us both gasping for air. Shifting my leg over his hip, he strokes into me, slow and long and so deep it takes my breath away.

He turns my head so our mouths can come together, the stroke of his tongue mirroring the delving thrusts of his cock. It's somehow better and deeper and just . . . more . . . than anything I've ever experienced before. It makes sense now, knowing about the Bond, knowing why he fills me to completion. But I think even without the Bond uniting us, Callum Reid would still feel like home.

I don't want the sensation to end.

Callum doesn't seem to want it to either. He takes his time, moving slowly inside me, driving me to the edge of the cliff and pulling me back again.

We both know what happens after this and if this delicious coupling can delay the inevitable for even a minute, well, it's a gift I plan to receive fully.

"Touch yourself for me, my lady." The words rumble out of him, dancing along my lips.

I oblige, my fingers finding the swollen bud of my arousal. Callum's mouth returns to mine and it doesn't take long before a climax unlike anything I've ever felt is barreling through me. His mouth never moves from mine, even as we both cry out a release that leaves waves of pleasure rippling through me long after the orgasm passes.

The air in the cabin explodes in a shower of sunset, pinks and oranges and golds, the most beautiful colors I've ever seen. There's nothing there for me to twist or manipulate, no emotions I need to ease or amplify. It's just a breathtaking cloud of pure bliss.

Callum holds me together until my breathing steadies and my heart calms. When we part, tears line both of our eyes.

We both know what the day might bring. We dress in silence.

"WHAT'S THE PLAN?" Callum asks as we push through the trees and make our way back to the stone fortress.

I look at him, searching for some sign of his joke. "What do you mean, what's the plan? You're the planner here, not me."

"We have no hope of winning this if the Gifted remain with Lady M. You said yourself, you are the only one who can get through to them, Cate. Do you know what you're going to say?"

"I think the Gifted from the club are already convinced." Even if they wouldn't leave with us, they helped me escape. They know Lady M has been lying to them, and I don't think they will stand against us. "But I don't know any of the others she has recruited to her sick little army. I don't know if I there's anything I can say to get through to them."

"I'm sure you'll think of something."

His faith in me bolsters me, but I can't help but feel it might be more than a little misplaced. Callum is the one with the leadership experience here, not me. Having our fate rest fully in my hands borders on terrifying.

Harold isn't there waiting for us in the copse of trees, and I try not to linger on the bolt of fear his absence sends through me. Maybe his business at the club took longer than expected. Maybe he's decided not to come after all.

Or maybe he's already inside, the Bond between him and Lady M too strong to fully break.

"Should we wait for him?" Callum asks.

I shake my head, not wanting to accept that Harold might have turned against us. "I don't think so."

We don't bother sneaking in a side door this time. We march up to the front entrance and let the guards escort us in. I don't recognize the two men, but Callum sizes them up quickly and if it comes to a fight, I'm sure he can handle it.

But I don't think the fight is upon us. At least, not yet.

We're shown into some kind of dining room, where Lady M is sitting at the end of a long table. My heart sinks as I take in the women surrounding her. My sisters. The only one missing from the group is Bianca. I hope she's still doing okay, that she hasn't burned herself out healing Harold and watching over Andra. I hope we don't end up needing her Gift here today.

I hope the rest of Lady M's Gifted stay where they have scurried off to.

Harold's absence is a small bit of relief. He hasn't betrayed us. At least not yet.

Callum nudges me forward, letting me take the lead. I raise my hands in surrender, needing them to know we didn't come for a fight.

We can't win a fight. Not all of them against the two of us.

I force a smile to my lips as I stare down my mother. "Lady M."

She stares at me from the end of the table, the distance not enough to dull the coolness in her sharp gaze. "I'm surprised you came back, Caterine. You've stolen your sister from me. I let your boyfriend walk away from me unharmed. It would appear you've gotten everything you were searching for. What more could you hope to take from me?"

"I did not *steal* my sister. She is a human being, not an object." I tamp down my rage, knowing it won't help. "You have no claim over her."

She arches one sharp eyebrow. "Don't I?" She leans forward in her seat. "It would seem I very much have a claim over her, the same claim I have over you. I sat back once before, as my babies were stolen from me. I don't intend to make the same mistake twice."

"Thank god Diana had the foresight she did, to take us away from you." My stomach twists at the thought of a lifetime raised by this woman. "You are nothing to us."

"I am your mother, Caterine. You might not like that fact, but nothing you say can change it."

A quiet gasp echoes around the room. I'm not sure which of my friends it came from, but clearly Lady M chose not to fill them in on this bit of family history.

"A mother does not use her children for her own personal gain." My fists clench at my side. "If you ever truly loved us, cared about us, you would end this now."

Lady M dismisses my request with a wave of her hand. "Why have you come back? Surely you know I don't plan to let your boyfriend leave here alive a second time. Surely you know I have great plans for you, plans that you don't seem to want to be a part of."

"You are right about one thing, I have no desire to be a part of anything you are doing here."

A sick smile pulls on her lips. "Andra's vision was correct. I had my doubts about letting you leave, but she assured me you would come back, that both of you would come back."

I suck in a deep breath, ignoring the implications of what Andra could have Seen, turning my attention to the women gathered around her. Helen and Meri and Rosa and Tes. These women have been in my life for more than a decade. They are the only ones I need to convince.

And if I can't, then I'll have to rely on Callum to get us out of here.

I focus on Helen first, her Gift maybe the most useful in this situation. I open my mind to her, letting her see all the things that have happened to me and to Andra since the day Lady M arrived at La Puissance. I push the memory of finding Andra unconscious and curled up on the cold stone floor to the forefront of my mind and I know by Helen's sharp intake of breath that she's seen it. I let her see the Gifted choking the life from Dom. I show her Harold, slumped over and poisoned. I show her the truth. I don't know if it's enough, but the furrows of her face show me she's at least listening and taking everything in.

Tes cocks her head when our eyes meet. She arches a single eyebrow at me, and I fight not to breathe a sigh of relief.

Just because they are standing at her side doesn't mean they are standing against me. I pray they have some kind of plan, and I keep talking, not wanting to let on to Lady M that anything has changed. "I may have been raised with only one twin, but from the moment Andra and I moved into La Puissance, the four of you have been my sisters. I know that things have been rough, and that times have looked bleak and that having Lady M come in and revamp our home may have seemed like a good thing."

Lady M pushes out of her chair. "We don't need to listen to this."

Rosa glares at her, and Lady M's mouth clamps shut against her will. Her eyes widen, shocked at this first hint of betrayal.

I pull my shoulders back and continue on. Just because the other Gifted, the ones I have never met before, aren't visible doesn't mean they aren't listening in. They deserve to know exactly who they are aligning themselves with. "The contracts that Lady M forced us to sign require us to meet impossible demands. We would never have been free of them because they have been designed that way."

"You signed one the same as we did, Cate," Meri points out, keeping up the ruse that I still stand alone.

I nod. "I know. Because even though I had misgivings from the beginning, I wasn't ready to give up on my home, and my family. But the things Lady M has done since we all signed—guards at the doors, forcing Andra to work herself to death, chaining Bianca to a wall—how can you not see that how she is treating us is wrong?" They don't interrupt me and so I keep going. "The whole purpose of the Uprising was to bring us to a place where everyone is treated equally. How can that exist when people like Lady M treat us as expendable tools? Use us for our Gifts and care nothing for the people behind them? She is using us because she thinks we can help her take power. But what about taking power for ourselves? Why should we fight for her, when we have the opportunity to fight for us?"

Tes glares over my shoulder at Callum, hiding her smirk at my triumphant tirade. "So what, you would rather we put our faith in him? A man born with a silver spoon in his mouth, who has never known what it's like to struggle?"

"Callum may have been born a royal, but that does not mean he hasn't endured struggles." I gesture to him, fighting every instinct not to take his hand in mine. "He is a good man, one who will make a fair and just leader."

Callum steps forward, standing next to me. "I feel certain that if you gave me the chance to explain my positions, listened to what I hope to accomplish, you might change your mind." He presses his palm to mine, linking our fingers, and a wave of peace washes over me.

"Enough!" Lady M rises from her chair once again, throwing off Rosa's hold over her.

Rosa stumbles back, her hands flying to her forehead. "What did she just do?"

My hands immediately reach for my dagger. "She can block your

Gifts, just like she can amplify them when she wants to use you and drain you, like she did to Andra."

"And do you know what your sister Saw for me, my darling daughter? She Saw me becoming more than the Scotan candidate. She Saw me becoming Queen. I had no intention of ever harming poor, sweet, malleable Harold until Andra told me what she Saw in my future." Lady M crosses around the table, her movements slow and deliberate. "We all know Andra's visions are never wrong."

The shift in the room is immediate, even if Lady M doesn't seem to notice it. She stands in the center of the room, Callum and me in front of her, the rest of the La Puissance Gifted behind her. She thinks they have her back, that they will move on us with a single word from her. She hasn't realized she is alone in this fight.

Meri's eyes narrow on Lady M's back. "You assured us that Harold was going to be fine."

"And he is," Lady M spits. "Your little friends managed to save him, though he won't be around for long if I have anything to say about it. He was always weak. To think I Bonded with someone so fragile. Once I am free of him, my Gift will be limitless."

I watch Meri gear up, preparing to throw some kind of illusion over Lady M, something to give us time. And I watch her realize she no longer has access to her Gift, though that doesn't stop her from trying.

Callum and I exchange a look. Now is our chance to take Lady M out, but whether the rest of the Gifted are on our side or not, it doesn't much matter. None of us have access to our Gifts. We'll have to do this the old-fashioned way.

Cal strikes out first, and either he's still feeling the lingering effects of the events of the past few days, or he underestimates Lady M, because his punch is weak and slow. Lady M dodges easily, and from that one movement alone, I can tell this isn't going to be an easy fight. Callum is the only one of us with any formal training—I learned the basics of defense during the Uprising, but my skills are weak and I'm out of practice—and it appears he and Lady M might be evenly matched.

She knocks him to his knees after just a few minutes of sparring. "Rosa!" she calls as she circles him.

Rosa looks to me, eyes wide.

I shake my head, silently begging her not to oblige.

Rosa crosses the room, standing shoulder to shoulder with me. Her hands immediately fly to her forehead once again as Lady M reinforces the block on her Gift.

"We have to do something," I whisper fiercely, standing back and watching Callum and Lady M go blow for blow, strike for strike, feeling so utterly helpless.

And then the doors of the dining room fly open.

Before I have the chance to count how many more Gifted are joining the fray, my body is lifted clean off the floor. I fly across the room, colliding with one of the stone walls and landing in a heap.

My lungs seize and I fight to inflate them, wondering if this is the same woman who killed Dom. But I don't think I'm being strangled, I just had the wind knocked out of me when I hit the wall with such force. I regain my breath, struggling to my feet as I take in what's happening.

Meri has picked up a chair, using it as a shield as a Gifted throws sparks of lightning at her face. Tes is on the ground, straddling another woman, delivering punch after punch to her stomach. Her opponent gets her weight under her, toppling Tes so their positions are switched and now Tes is at the mercy of her fists.

Callum and Lady M are dancing around one another in the center of the room. A gash on his cheek is bleeding profusely, but he's still standing.

And I've been still for too long.

A pair of arms encircles my neck.

I immediately grab at them, but it's fruitless trying to break the Gifted's hold. I dig an elbow into her side, aiming for the ribs. I connect with enough force to loosen her grip slightly. Ducking away, I reach for Callum's dagger, holstered at my thigh. I shove the woman against the wall, pressing the knife to her neck.

"I don't want to hurt you."

She struggles against my grip. "Go ahead and try."

I dig the knife in a little deeper, enough to draw a line of blood. "How can you not see that she is using you? Lady M is manipulating your Gifts for her own benefit, and you're letting her."

"My parents sold me to a brothel when they found out I had a Gift. And not a brothel like La Puissance, *Lady* Caterine," she says with a sneer. "The kind where you don't have a choice. Where you are forced to do things so depraved your head would spin."

I unconsciously loosen my hold on her. "I'm sorry that happened to you. That's what the Uprising has been fighting for, a way for us to regain our rights."

She laughs in my face. "If you believe that, you are even more naïve than I thought. The Uprising is out for themselves. Everyone is."

"It doesn't have to be this way," I say quietly.

"It's always been this way." She pushes my hand away from her throat.

I take a step away. When she lunges at me, I bring the butt of the dagger down on the back of her skull, knocking her out. I don't stop to see if she's still breathing because I don't know if I can handle it if she's not.

My dearest Grecia,

I know it has now been many years since we last saw each other. That doesn't mean you haven't been very much present in my heart, and in my mind.

I am writing to you today because La Puissance is in trouble, and I think you might be the only one who can save her. I know there are many conversations we need to have. So many words have gone unspoken because it would have been too painful to say them, and to hear them. But I think now is the time.

Despite the distance between us, we are Bonded, Grecia. A piece of my heart has always belonged to you, and I hope your heart still belongs to me.

With your permission, I would like to come visit you, so we may have those conversations and perhaps give our Bond the attention it needs to flourish once more.

I will not lie to you, Grecia. There have been many nights when the loneliness nearly overwhelmed me. I have often reached for the comfort of another's arms. But I have never been unfaithful to you. You are the only one for me, and I have felt the need to be back in your embrace growing in recent days.

Please allow me to come visit.

All my love,

Harry

30

CALLUM

I WAS HOPING THIS wouldn't come to a fight for obvious reasons, and my list did not include the fact that Lady M seems fully equipped to kick my ass as thoroughly as Dom usually does. As Dom used to. The reminder of her absence, not just in this battle but for the rest of my life, doesn't help me concentrate on the fight before me.

I spin out of the way of one of Lady M's strikes, only to be hit from behind and knocked to my knees. I look up just in time to see Cate knocking a woman unconscious.

"Behind you!" I call out, watching her turn just in time to block a strike.

All around me, Gifted are fighting Gifted. Powers burst across the room. Lightning bursts fling from one woman's fingers; another lifts Meri off her feet with just a wave of her hand.

This is exactly what we have been afraid of for more than two hundred years. The Gifted banding together and creating an unstoppable army.

No, my mind argues. That isn't what's happening here. Because there are Gifted fighting on both sides. Cate and her sisters want to do this the right way, work with the Uprising to regain their rights. It's this Lady M who has created this toxic group.

I sense her at my back, springing to my knees to deliver a blow to Lady M's stomach that should knock the wind out of her.

Lady M grunts but doesn't fall, a wicked smile tugging on her lips. "You are not going to win this, Your Highness."

I watch through the corner of my eye, keeping tabs on the women around me. Cate and the others are holding their own, all of them still standing, still fighting. The unconscious bodies of several other Gifted litter the ground, but Lady M doesn't seem to care much about her fallen soldiers.

"I will die before I let you win, Lady M." I move to strike her, feinting, spinning to her other side as I rip a dagger from the sheath at my waist. I bring it down, slashing.

She moves just in time, the knife grazing her arm, leaving a bloody gash in its wake. "Are you going to kill me, Your Highness? How will your Bonded feel if you are responsible for killing her mother?"

I dodge her next advance, but just barely. "I think she will thank me for it."

Lady M whistles, the sound sharp and harsh. Two Gifted move immediately to her side, their eyes locked on me.

I raise my knife, not sure where the attack is going to come from, or if a knife is even going to do me any good.

A pain unlike anything I have ever experienced before rips through me, knocking me to my knees. A strangled cry escapes my throat, my eyes watering as I fight to stand.

"Callum!" Cate is at my side in an instant, her arms looping through mine as she tries to help me stand.

"Leave me," I choke out. "They will turn their Gifts on you, Cate. Leave me, get out of here."

She helps me stand, then spins on her heel and rushes at the Gifted abusing me with her power. The move is graceless but effective; Cate and the woman fall to the floor and the pain leaves as quickly as it came.

As soon as I've regained my breath, I lose it again, as Lady M's other minion chokes the air from my lungs without laying a single hand on me.

I know in this moment this is the woman responsible for killing my sister, that it was her Gift that stole Dom's last breath from her lungs. Rage coats my vision and all logical thought flees my brain.

It's enough to stir me to fight back. I close the distance between us in two large steps, my hand gripping her throat, tightening enough that her eyes widen and bulge. "How do you like it?" I growl at her.

She claws at my hand, useless without her own powers.

Air fully fills my chest, and I squeeze harder.

The woman's lips are starting to turn purple when a hand lands on my shoulder.

"Let her go, Cal." Cate's voice is the only sound that could penetrate my haze of anger. "This isn't you. Let her go."

I come back to myself, and the feeling of the woman's flesh under my hand suddenly feels wrong.

I drop my hand from her neck, and she collapses on the floor. She doesn't get up, but her chest still moves up and down.

Cate's hand finds my cheek. "You're all right."

It's not a question, but I nod anyway.

Meri cries out and Cate's face blanches as she turns to take in the rest of the room. She runs to her friend's side, heedless of the combat still raging. Lady M has retreated to the far corner, as if she can avoid the bloodshed she caused.

I take Meri's place, fighting off yet another unknown Gifted, trying to pull the fighting away from where Cate crouches over Meri, whose hand is pressed to her thigh and covered in blood.

"Rosa!" Cate calls. I shouldn't be paying attention to her, should be focusing my full attention on the woman whose strikes keep on coming, connecting with my ribs and my knee and the side of my head. But I keep one eye on Cate at all times, unable to fully break away from her.

Rosa hoists Meri to her feet and pulls her from the room, escaping the fighting, but leaving us even more outnumbered.

Cate looks down at her hands, the blood covering them stark against her pale skin, and it takes everything in me not to rush to her side.

The fight rages on. Cate, Tes, Helen, and I are the only ones left. Several of Lady M's Gifted have been knocked out, maybe even killed, but there are enough of them to keep me occupied, my eyes constantly flitting between my current opponent and Cate.

Lady M takes advantage of my distraction, moving back to the center of the fighting when she sees that her side has the upper hand. A swift blow to the back of Tes's head and she collapses. Lady M continues, shoving Helen hard into the arms of one of her soldiers, who quickly knocks her to the ground with a single punch to the face.

She's upon me before I have the chance to ready myself for her attack, the other Gifted at my back requiring my full attention.

"I think that's enough for today."

Her dagger swipes across my stomach and a second later, I'm folded in half and falling to the floor.

"Callum!" Cate cries, her anguish echoing around the room.

She rushes for me, but Lady M steps in her path. Gritting my teeth, I force myself to my feet. The pain is blinding and unbearable, but not nearly as unbearable as watching Cate single-handedly grapple with Lady M.

Lady M, who has handed me my ass despite my training. Cate doesn't have a chance against her, and I can't watch her fall, not after everything

Cate launches herself at Lady M, with strength and determination but not a lot of skill. It doesn't take long for Lady M to knock the dagger from Cate's hand, sending it skittering along the cold stone floor.

I will my feet to move, shuffling closer to the fight.

Lady M strikes Cate across the face and I growl. Cate gets one good swipe in, knocking Lady M back a few steps, her dagger clattering to the floor. But Cate also dropped her weapon. Her eyes search the floor for it but are quickly pulled back to Lady M as she recovers and moves to slash at Cate with her second knife.

"Cate!" I find the right moment to call for her, when the distraction won't cost her her life.

Her eyes immediately lock on mine, and I toss her a dagger, the red jewel embedded in the hilt smeared with a streak of blood the same color. I hope she can use it to fend off Lady M until I can make my way across the room. My stomach rips open further with every step I take, and the few feet separating us feel like miles. I know deep within my bones that I won't make it to her on time, that Lady M is too strong and too quick for Cate to make it out of this unscathed.

The thought only pushes me forward, my stomach ripping in agony with every move.

Cate catches the dagger, using it to block the next strike aimed at her.

The next part seems to happen in slow motion.

Lady M punches Cate in the stomach, causing Cate to stagger back, gasping for breath. Her back hits the wall, the only thing keeping her upright.

I lunge toward them, but I stumble, falling to my knees. My hands are slippery with blood, as is the floor, and I can't force myself back to my feet. She is so close, yet the distance between us is insurmountable.

Lady M raises her hand, the one holding the knife, its tip aimed right for Cate's heart. I don't know how a mother can take the life of her own child, but I know that she won't hesitate to steal Cate from me.

I call out a useless warning, my gut burning fury and fear.

Cate blocks the strikes with her forearm, grimacing as the knife slices through her flesh. A trail of red blooms on her skin.

Lady M moves to try again, the knife rearing back with such force I'm surprised it doesn't fly right out of her hand, finding a home in the heart I've come to cherish so deeply.

But someone blocks her. Even as a guttural cry rips through me, a shadow moves in so quickly it takes a minute to realize Harold has finally made it. He grabs his wife's wrists with a strength I didn't know he had. Lady M drops her knife, but she brings her knee up, striking Harold right in the groin.

He drops his hold on her, staggering back. Whatever energy he entered the fight with seems to have already been depleted. Cate lunges, aiming for Lady M once again, her dagger finally back in hand. Lady M waits until the last minute to dodge the blow, but the force of Cate's strike is too much to pull back. She stumbles forward under the weight of it and her knife makes contact.

Cate's dagger finds its home, inside Harold's chest.

Her eyes widen in disbelief, in horror, her hands covering her mouth, though it's not enough to dampen her scream.

I push myself further, but she's still so far away.

Harold falls, the knife still protruding from his heart. Cate watches, frozen and unmoving for a minute before she kneels by his side, takes his hand in hers. She leans over him and his hand drifts up to cup her cheek.

I'm too far away to hear the words whispered between them, and I'm glad for it. His final words will forever be embedded in her heart.

Harold smiles, though it's pained. His eyes fall closed. His chest stops moving.

I listen for Cate's cries, but they are drowned out by the wail coming from Lady M. Her mouth drops open in shock, though I'm not sure if it's due to her husband's death or the fact that it actually emotionally affects her.

She staggers, like some force has physically knocked her back. Her chest heaves with uneven breaths and she has to brace herself against the wall. She pushes Cate out of the way, her body draping itself over Harold's as if it could shield him from what's already come to pass. She seems to forget in this moment that this is what she planned for all along, that she was poisoning the man her soul is supposed to be bound to.

For a single, solitary click of a second, I feel sorry for her. With the agony of losing her Bonded husband, even her cold heart must have shattered.

Before any of us can move, before any of us have the chance to use this moment of her grief to our advantage, she rips the dagger from his chest and pushes herself up from the stone floor. "This isn't over," she whispers to Cate, ice coating her words. With one final look at her dead husband, she stumbles from the room, her keening cries echoing through the halls, the bloody knife leaving a dripping trail in her wake.

Cate doesn't move, doesn't try to leave Harold's side. Until her eyes meet mine. Hers are full of tears.

She staggers over to me, collapsing in a puddle next to me. Her arm is bleeding heavily, but she comes for me, her hands pressing to the open wound at my stomach.

"I'm sorry, I'm sorry, I'm so sorry," she mutters the refrain tearfully, over and over and over. "You should have been the one. I'm so sorry, Callum. What have I done?"

I grasp her cheek with my hand, wincing at the smear of blood I leave on her skin. "Stop. You're alive. That's all that matters. I love you, Cate, so much."

"I love you too, Cal. I need to get Bianca." The words come out as barely a gasp, her face going scarily pale. She tries to rise but can't get her feet under her.

My vision blurs, but I try to help her stand. I search for the source of her bleeding to stanch it, but it's hard to tell whose blood is whose, and where it's all coming from.

"Hang on," she tells me, her voice faint and garbled.

Her face is the last thing I see.

I COME TO with her name on my lips, it croaking out of me before my eyes are fully opened.

A glass of water is pressed to my lips, and I sip gratefully.

My eyes flutter open and it takes me a minute to recognize my surroundings. I'm back in my suite at Scotan Castle, tucked into the same bed I've been sleeping in since I was a child.

I search for her, and my vision finally focuses on the hand holding out the glass of water.

She smiles down at me, though it's strained. Dark circles paint her under eyes; she looks too pale, too thin. The arm holding the cup of water is wrapped in a bandage. "Welcome back, Your Highness."

I take the glass from her and set it on the table next to the bed before pulling her into my arms. One hand works its way into the long waves of her hair, the other pressing flat to the small of her back, holding her close enough that I can feel the echo of her heartbeat.

Her heart is still beating.

"I'm happy to see you too," she murmurs against the shell of my ear.

"Is everyone okay?"

She pulls away just enough to nod. "Bianca was on her way to us before we could even go to her. She healed everyone. She's been asleep ever since." Worry for her friend mars her face.

"Lady M?" I'm scared to ask, but I need to know that she's truly gone.

"Disappeared. No one has seen or heard from her." The distress on her face echoes my own. *Disappeared* doesn't mean gone forever, especially considering her parting words.

"And Harold?" I grip her hand in mine, knowing the truth before she voices it.

"He's gone. It was an accident, but you killed him, Cal. I know it's hard to imagine, but he would have wanted it this way, I'm sure of it." She pulls away from me.

My brow furrows. My head still feels like mush, but I'm aware enough to know that's not right. "What do you mean, I killed him?"

She sits up, putting space between us that I don't want. "I mean, as far as anyone outside this room is concerned, you killed him."

I reach for her hand. She lets me lace our fingers together, but hers remain limp in my hold. "We both know that's not what happened."

She shrugs, avoiding my gaze. "It's what should have happened.

You were meant to be the leader of your people, Callum. And now you will be. He told me, before he died, that the poison was still in him. He was going to die anyway, and he meant for you to be the one to do it."

"Cate . . ."

She returns her eyes to mine and they are determined. "I already told everyone that's what happened. The newspapers have reported it. The killing period has ended. You are the Scotan candidate for the first presidential election of Avon, Callum." Her smile is weak and a bit sad. "You are going to be the president this country needs, Your Highness."

She tries to pull away again, but I keep a tight hold on her hand. "I don't think I can do this without you. I almost lost you, and even the thought of facing a single day without you was too much for me, Cate. I need you. And I know you need me too."

She studies the wall as if it's the most interesting piece of art. "I do."

But it doesn't sound like she means it. I search for the Bond, the tie that has linked us since our very first meeting. There's still a heat there, deep in my veins, and if I focus hard enough, I can feel the itch. But it's strained, like one of us is resisting the connection.

I know it's not me.

Somehow, with all the loss of the last week, this is the one that hurts the most.

Alex,

When you first approached me and we discussed the plan, you promised me your nephew would be a perfect candidate. Forgive me for my bluntness, but how is being involved with a courtesan a representation of a perfect candidate? I don't think it's an issue that she's Gifted; if anything it only speaks to his willingness to uphold the ideals of the Uprising. But she works at a pleasure club, Alex. You need to do something about this.

If he insists on staying with her, at least ensure they get married.

Let me know his decision.

August

31

CATE

THE HOURS AFTER I killed Harold passed in a blur. At some point Bianca arrived. At some point Alex showed up. At some point I was moved to another location and reunited with my sister, who was awake and on the road to recovery herself. Bianca stitched me up, providing the bare minimum since my injury wasn't life-threatening and she was expending her Gift saving the others. She told me Callum was going to be fine, he just needed rest. At that point, I finally allowed myself a moment to relax. He'd fallen back asleep shortly after our conversation, but just seeing him open his eyes assured me of the truth of Bianca's prognosis.

I sit with Andra in the room she's been given at the Reids' castle—already she's looking better, her color improved and a hint of light returned to her eyes. She doesn't bother to ask me how I'm doing.

"Do you think the rest of the club is going to be okay?" I ask her, partly because I want to know what she thinks and mostly to distract myself from the thoughts that have been plaguing me since my knife found its way into Harold's chest. Our last few whispers to each other run on a constant loop through my mind. At least he died knowing that I loved him. At least we got to have a few short moments with both of us knowing the truth.

Andra rests her head on my shoulder. We're sitting side by side on her bed even though there are plenty of more spacious and comfortable options in her opulent room. Somehow, we seem to blend into one when the situation calls for it. "I don't know, Cate," she says. "I don't know what happens to La Puissance without Harold there to take care of her."

I fight back the sob that threatens to leap from my throat every time I think of what I stole from this world, what I stole from Andra, who never got to even speak to him as his true daughter. "I still can't believe so many chose her side. How could all of those Gifted not see what she was doing to them?"

She searches for my hand among the pile of blankets crowding the bed. "Lady M was there for them when they needed someone most. It can be scary to leave the only real home you've ever known, Cate."

I scoff, not so willing to excuse their violent behavior. It's easier to place some of the blame on them rather than face the truth that I am the one who caused all this. "You don't have to tell me that. I did it. You did it."

"It's different for us." She pokes me in the side, hitting my ticklish spot like a bull's-eye. "You have the financial resources and I have the knowledge that we're going to be okay. And we have each other. Most of the girls at the club don't have that, let alone the other Gifted. Besides, our friends came through for you when it really mattered."

I poke her right back in her own ticklish spot, though I make sure to keep my prod gentle as she is still looking frailer than I would like. "They know we would help any and all of them if they asked for it."

"You of all people should understand how difficult it is to ask for help."

I let her comment simmer for a minute before I respond. "I suppose that's fair."

"We have another sister," she says softly. It's not the first time one of us has uttered the sentence. First in wonder, now more in awe tinged with apprehension.

"We need to find her, as soon as you're feeling up to it." As much as I want to learn about this third one of us, as many questions as I have about Lady M's intentions for the future, the last thing I want is for Andra to strain herself when she's finally on the road to healing.

"We will."

We sit with a comfortable silence for a few minutes before Andra pulls her head from my shoulder so I can see her eyes, mirrors of my own. "Don't push him away, Cate."

I toy with a thread on the blanket covering the bed so I don't have to look at her. "I don't know what you mean."

I don't have to be looking at her to know she is rolling her eyes. "Cate, you are my sister, and I love you more than anything on this earth. I also know you better than anyone on this earth. And you are incapable of letting yourself be loved without either holding some part of yourself back or running away from it."

I raise my chin stubbornly. "I let you love me."

Her eyes narrow and for a minute she looks more like me than herself. "When was the last time you let me take care of you?"

"I'm the older sister, it's my job to take care of you. Besides, we both know that you've always been in a more precarious position than me."

It's her turn to scoff. "Because I was born two whole minutes after you?"

"Because your Gift is much more valuable than mine. Much more valuable than just about anyone's. I've taken care of you because it's my job and because I love you." And because the thought of losing her, of ever not having her by my side, is too much to bear.

She softens her voice. "I love you too, you know that. Just as you know somewhere deep down inside that stubborn old soul of yours that I don't need you to take care of me." She knocks my shoulder with hers. "And don't try to deflect. This is about you and Callum."

"Callum and I had a week of fantastic sex, but it was all merely an arrangement. We both know we can't be good for each other in the long run." It stings just to say the words, to pretend like what's between the two of us is merely physical, like our Bond no longer exists. I've been trying to convince myself of that for days now, pushing down the urge to touch him, to be with him until the itching need for him dies down. I doubt it will ever fully dissipate completely, but for now, the lingering pain of missing him is bearable. I know that he needs that space from me if he is going to figure out what's truly best for him, best for this election and the country.

"He's a good man, Cate, and you would be wise to give this a real chance. Open yourself up to him. You're so wrapped up in everyone else's vulnerabilities that you forget to show your own."

I brush off her words with a roll of my eyes, pushing off the bed and heading into the other room with a mumbled excuse of needing to check on Callum. Andra's eyes bore into my retreating back and

I think even if we weren't twins, her telepathic message would be clear: *You're running away again.*

I ignore her. But her words are not so easy to forget. They run on a loop through my brain as I pace the hallway in front of Callum's suite. Of course it's hard for me to let people in; I've been fending for myself—and for my sister—for as long as I can remember. Aside from Andra, everyone whom I've loved, especially those who were supposed to take care of me, has abandoned me in some way. Our parents left; the societal structures meant to help us failed us at every turn. And Harold, one of the few people in my life I thought I could trust, kept the biggest secret of all from us.

How could anyone open themself up to love after everything we've been through?

And yes, Andra is a grown woman fully capable of taking care of herself. But she is also too valuable for me to just trust that she is going to be okay. I need to make sure she is going to be okay. I could never survive if something happened to her.

"Do you hate the carpet that much? You're about to wear a hole in that rug."

I spin on my heel, catching Bianca hovering behind me, a tentative smile tugging on her lips. I know she's probably still exhausted and I should be gentle, but I can't help it—I launch myself at her, practically tackling her in a hug. "Thank god you're okay."

She laughs, patting me on the back. "I'm fine. Still a little tired, but I'm fine."

I loosen my hold around her neck but keep her arms grasped in mine. "Thank you, B. I don't know how I'll ever repay you. You saved all of us."

She shrugs, but there's a hint of pride in her emerald eyes. "You don't have to thank me for that. I'm just glad I was there and able to get to everyone in time." She cocks her head toward Callum's door. "How is he doing?"

"Good. He woke up for a few minutes earlier, but he's back to sleep now."

"How does he feel? About officially being the Scotan candidate?" Something about the way she poses the question—the tilt of her head, the knowing look in her eyes—makes me think she knows what really happened in that room, knows the secret I'm determined to hide for as long as it takes to fade into nothing.

"We didn't talk about it much." It pains me to lie to her, but right now, no one can know the truth. "But I know he's going to be a great leader."

"Now he just has to win the election."

"Right. Any word on when the next period is set to begin?"

Bianca shakes her head. "I'm sure the news is out, but I haven't seen anything about it yet."

I gesture to Callum's door. "I think I should go check on him again. I don't want him to wake up alone."

"Cate."

I pause in front of the door, my back facing Bianca. If I look at her, she will be able to read everything on my face, so I don't turn around.

"Callum has proven himself to be good and honorable. But just because he is a good man doesn't mean he is the right person."

"You mean you don't think he's the right person for me?"

She takes my hand and tugs, forcing me to face her. "That's not what I mean at all, and you know it. I think if you can get over your own bullshit, the two of you could be truly happy together."

"Should I be offended by that?"

She ignores my question. "What I mean is, just because Callum looks like what we're used to leaders looking like doesn't make him the only choice. Or even the best choice."

"The rules of the game were very clear, Bianca. Callum has been named the candidate. The selection period is over." I spin back around. "I'll talk to you later."

"Count on it," she says in a tone that I know means she isn't going to drop the subject.

I sigh heavily, pushing through the door. I can deal with Bianca later.

32

CALLUM

THE DOOR TO my suite opens and I hope to see Cate on the other side. Instead, Alex peeks his head in, hovering in the doorway until I nod for him to enter.

His face relaxes slightly when he sees me sitting up in bed, a tray of food perched over my lap. A servant delivered it a few minutes ago, advising me to eat slowly. I've been trying to heed her word, but when the scent of the soup hit my nostrils, the hunger of the past few days caught up with me and I inhaled every morsel within just a few minutes.

"Glad to see you're back to normal." Alex wipes a few crumbs from the covers on the bed, his voice careful, like he's afraid I might kick him out any second.

"Uncle."

"You gave us all quite a scare, son." The word slips out, echoing around the room, highlighting the loss.

"We will need to plan a memorial for Father," I say quietly. "And for Dom." I still haven't come to terms with the loss of my sister. I prepared for weeks to lose my father, was even prepared to take his life myself, and I was still a mess when it actually happened. I never expected my sister to be a casualty in all of this. I would have made many different decisions had I known.

"Already working on it. I know you're going to be busy in the coming weeks."

I shift the tray of food to the other side of the bed. "I won't be too busy for this. I owe it to them. I owe it to her."

"I know there is nothing I can say to ease the pain or assuage the guilt, but I know what it is like to lose a sister, Callum." Alex's throat catches on his tears. "What I can offer you is the reassurance that she would be proud, and so would James." He crosses to the side of my bed, placing a comforting hand on my shoulder. "Your mother would be proud too."

Now is the moment when I should tell him the truth—that I'm not the actual candidate, I wasn't the one to put the knife through Harold's heart. But I can't seem to make my mouth form the words. I can't start this campaign with lies, even if it is what Cate claims she wants. But I allow myself this moment to bask in the false praise, imagine the looks of pride on the faces of my parents and my sister.

"Thank you for saying that." I shift my weight, subtly causing Alex's hand to fall from my shoulder. "I know that you had the best of intentions, joining the Uprising. I know who you are, and I know you would never do anything to hurt me or this family."

"But it is going to take some time before you trust me again."

I nod. "I'm sorry."

"Do not apologize, Cal. I made my choices, and I stand by them. But I am not ignorant of their consequences." He opens his mouth to say more, but hesitates.

"Please don't hold back, Uncle. Now is not the time to keep secrets."

"It's Cate."

I raise myself off the bed. "Is she hurt? Why didn't you say something as soon as you came in? Where is she?"

Alex pushes my shoulder, keeping me in place. "She's fine." His eyes darken with what feels like foreboding.

I clench my fists in the blanket covering me. "Whatever you have to say, just say it."

"We've been having some meetings, early strategy sessions," Alex says.

"How long have I been out?" I ask sarcastically. I know it's only been two days. I shouldn't be surprised that was plenty of time for him to start scheming without my input.

Alex ignores me. "The bottom line, Cal, is that everyone agrees on one thing: Being with Cate is going to be a major hindrance in the election."

A wall of hot anger crushes over me. "Because she's a courtesan or because she's Gifted?"

"I know how much she means to you, but it wouldn't be wise for her to be by your side during your candidacy, Cal. It's not her Gift that is troubling, but how she chooses to make her living. It's the one thing a whole room of strategists can agree on."

"I don't care." I cross my arms over my chest, not caring if I sound like a petulant child. "Cate isn't going anywhere. I'm not doing this without her. Besides, things aren't like they used to be. Aren't we supposed to be building a more equitable world? Does that not include courtesans?"

"Of course it does." Alex sighs wearily, the stress of the past few days clearly visible on his face. "There is another option."

I eye him warily. "What is it?"

"You get married."

“I’m sorry, what?”

The words don’t come from me, but from a voice in the doorway.

Cate.

Not exactly the way I would have chosen to propose.

She crosses to the bed, standing on the opposite side from my uncle. Her eyes rake me over, taking in the empty tray of food and the way I’m able to sit up on the bed. She offers me a soft smile before turning her attention to Alex. “What was that you were saying?”

Alex shoots me a heavy look.

Cate bristles, pulling her shoulders back and schooling her face. “You don’t have to hide it. I know that my relationship with Cal could potentially damage his campaign. I told him the same thing myself.”

Alex lets out another long sigh. “Good. Then we’re agreed that the best course of action is for you to end this relationship. The sooner the better.”

Cate’s eyes narrow. “I didn’t hear either of us agree to that. I already tried to convince him, but he was kind enough to remind me that I don’t get to make his decisions for him. Just like he doesn’t get to make mine for me.”

I reach for her hand, buoyed by her defense of us, and intertwine our fingers together. Maybe there is a chance of earning her forgiveness. “I choose Cate. And as long as she continues to choose me, we will remain a couple.”

“So option B, then,” says Alex with a grimace. “You get married.”

Cate’s fingers tighten around mine, and I feel it again, the itch. It’s a little less persistent, but it’s there, buried under my skin. “Those are our options? Never see each other again or tie ourselves to one another for life?”

I would be lying if I said her reaction didn't sting, just a bit, but I know where it's coming from, and I understand her hesitation, even if we both know we're already connected forever.

I turn to Alex. "Can you give us some time alone?"

Alex looks like he's going to protest, but he sees my glare and decides otherwise. He turns on his heel and strides for the door, shutting it gently behind him on his way out.

Once he's gone, Cate shifts the empty tray to the table and climbs into bed next to me. She doesn't say anything, just burrows down under the covers and tucks herself into my side. I take her willingness to touch me as another good sign.

"We don't have to do anything you don't want to do, Cate." I run my fingers through the long golden waves of her hair, entangling them around my fingers before releasing them to fall in a shiny curtain.

"I don't know if I can get married, Callum." She mumbles the words into my chest. "Not just to you but to anyone. Look what it did to them, being Bonded." She doesn't have to say their names.

"We are not them, Cate. There is something rotten inside Lady M that has nothing to do with her Bond to Harold. Neither of us would ever be capable of doing the things she's done." I press a kiss to the top of her head, letting her familiar citrus scent fill my nose and stir a sense of longing deep inside me. I hesitate before asking the question I know I need an answer to. "Have you felt the Bond lessen?"

She stiffens in my arms, pulling away ever so slightly. "I don't know what you mean."

I sigh, though the sense of relief that it wasn't all in my head is short-lived. "Why are you pulling away from me? Why are you fighting this?"

"There are so many things, Callum. So many reasons for us to not be together. This election, the strength of our Bond and what it could make us do. I'm not good for you."

I cup her cheek in my hand, raising her face so I can look her in the eye. "I told you that I would always choose you, Cate. And I meant it. You're not helping me by pulling away. You're only causing both of us unnecessary pain."

Tears spill down her cheeks. "I'm scared, Callum. Of so much."

I wipe her tears with my thumbs. "I am too. But we can face whatever the future has in store for us, as long as we do it together. You've had my heart from the moment I first saw you, Lady Caterine. And I'm not taking it back. If you would rather not marry me, I understand, and it won't change my love for you. Nothing ever could."

She presses her lips to mine, the kiss soft and sweet, though tinged with the salt of her tears. I deepen the kiss, letting us linger in it, but make no move to take things further.

She sighs as the kiss breaks, the sound full of longing and resignation. "I'll do it," she says, her voice quiet. "If it will help you win, if it's what you need, then I'll do it. I'll marry you."

"I'm not going to marry you unless it's what you want, Cate." She starts to speak, but I press my lips to hers. "We don't have to make any decisions tonight."

Her eyes search mine, the golden amber darkened with worry. "I don't want to lose you."

I tighten my hold on her. "You won't. Ever."

She starts to pull away. "You should probably get some more rest."

I keep her pressed close to me. "Stay with me?"

She smiles, but it doesn't fully reach her eyes. "Of course."

We settle into the comfort of the mattress and the warmth of the blankets, and together, fall into a restful sleep.

I'M AWAKENED BY the press of her lips against mine. No light shines through the many windows of my room, nothing outside but the purest black. It must be late, or very early, but I still don't have my bearings on time.

I also don't care much, my lips finding solace in Cate's as she perches over me. Her golden waves tumble down her back and spill over her shoulders. There's a calmness, a surety on her face that has been missing since I first awoke. She's never looked more beautiful.

She pulls away from me, as if seeking permission to continue. I cup the nape of her neck in my hand and bring her mouth back to mine. I lose myself in her. Our tongues mingle and our hands explore, like this is the first time all over again.

Cate sits up, pulling her sleep shift over her head. I rise as well, scooting my back to lean against the headboard so I can cradle her in my lap. I'm already shirtless and the brush of her skin against mine sends a shiver racing down my spine.

I want to tell her that we don't have to do this, that I'm happy to wait as long as it takes for her to be truly ready, but with the exchange of one simple glance, I know I don't need to voice the words. This is what she wants. What we both need. To find our way back to each other.

She tugs on my cotton breeches, freeing me from the material, wrapping her hand around me. I cup her breasts in my hands, my thumbs stroking while my mouth moves between her nipples, sucking and nibbling while her hips roll and her fist pumps.

I'm on the verge of exploding, her touch enough to bring me to the brink, but she knows the exact moment to hover over me. I guide myself to her entrance and she sinks down so slowly I think I might combust.

When I'm fully seated inside her, we release matching sighs of relief.

"Cate?"

"Callum?"

I cup her cheeks in my hands, bringing her eyes to mine. "I want you to use your Gift."

Her breath catches in her chest and her eyes search mine for the truth. "Are you sure?"

I nod. "I trust you with my heart, and I trust you with my mind. You've already seen me at my most vulnerable, at my lowest moments, and you have handled that vulnerability with nothing but love and the utmost care."

"Callum . . ." Her eyes fill with tears, but she takes in a deep breath to steady herself. "I've dealt in vulnerabilities for so many years, but I never allowed myself to have any."

"You don't have to be strong for me, my lady."

She presses her forehead to mine. "I know."

We're already as intertwined as two people could be, but I pull her even closer, bury myself deeper inside her. Matching groans escape us and her mouth finds mine once again as she begins to move.

Being with Cate has never been anything less than incredible, earth-shattering, life-altering. But this moment between us, this strengthening of a Bond that could have so easily been broken, it fills my soul close to bursting.

We hold each other tightly, arms locked as if we plan to never let go, as we move together as one, as the release overtakes us. My chest tightens and I have to fight for breath, but I don't break the kiss. Couldn't even if I wanted to.

I don't know what to expect when I open myself up to Cate. She never breaks contact with me and a second after I come, I'm enveloped in lightness and warmth and comfort. I don't forget about my sister or my father, but somehow the loss of them feels settled, the wound scabbed over, no longer raw and bleeding in my chest.

It's peace, and happiness, and nothing short of pure bliss.

My forehead falls to her chest and her hands work themselves into my hair. I don't realize I'm crying until I see the tears sparkle against her bare skin. It's cleansing and purifying and my entire being feels renewed, and whole.

After several minutes of heavy breathing and no need for words, she climbs off my lap and settles into the crook of my arms.

The whole encounter would almost feel like a dream, were it not for the familiar itch returning to my skin in full force. I welcome it, burying my face in the waves of her hair, entwining our limbs as we fall back asleep.

ONE KILLING PERIOD CONCLUDES, ONLY FOR ANOTHER TO BE SET TO BEGIN

Now that the first killing period has successfully concluded, the Uprising's experiment seems to be moving full steam ahead. The Scotan province has chosen its candidate, the former prince of Scota, Callum Reid.

Now the date has been set for the next province to determine its fate.

The province of Talia will see its killing period begin next week, though it is interesting to note that the Uprising has shortened the period, from a week to only one day.

Let us hope things go as smoothly there as they reportedly did in Scota.

33

CATE

BIANCA CINCHES ME into a brand-new dress. It's violet and high-necked with sleeves that go down to the tips of my fingers. It's suffocating and nothing I would ever choose for myself, but today isn't about me.

It's been a week since Callum and I reignited our Bond, and with it, decided to get married. The thought still makes my stomach spin.

The anxiety has nothing to do with him. Callum has been steadfast and true since the moment I met him. The man was meant to be a partner and a father and a leader.

It's me that is the problem.

I don't want to let him down. I don't want to cost him this election. But when it came down to the choices presented to us—marriage or nothing—I was too selfish to make the smart decision. I couldn't bear the thought of losing him, and so now, we'll be legally bound together for the rest of our lives. There will be nothing he can do to shed his association with me.

Andra tucks a stray curl into place. "You look beautiful."

I study our reflection in the mirror. Andra is still not back to her usual weight, but her color has improved, and she no longer looks like she might faint without notice. She looks happier and healthier than I've seen in a long time. I take one of her hands in mine, grabbing on to Bianca with the other. "I can do this."

They both hear it for the question it is.

"You can," Bianca affirms.

"Am I ruining his life?" I ask on a whisper, unexpected tears filling my eyes.

Both of their hands tighten around mine.

"Do not talk that way about my sister." Andra reaches for a handkerchief, dabbing at my eyes. My face has been left bare so at least there's no makeup to ruin.

"Do you love him?" Bianca asks.

I nod. "You know I do."

"And does he love you?"

I roll my eyes. "You know he does."

Bianca shrugs, straightening my sleeve as she drops my hand. "Then let that be enough, Cate. Let yourself have this."

I nod again, not entirely convinced.

There's a knock at the door. Alex enters with my permission, smiling as he takes in the conservative dress Callum's team chose for me. "It's time to go."

The four of us file down the long hallway of the Scotan Castle like little marching soldiers. Callum waits for us at the bottom of the stairs, looking devilishly handsome in a perfectly fitted three-piece suit. He offers me his arm when I reach the ground floor, and I tuck my hand into the crook of his elbow.

"You look stunning," he tells me as we make our way to the carriage out front.

"Thank you."

"You hate it, don't you?"

I tilt my head up to catch the gleam of a smile in his eyes. "It's terrible."

He chuckles, opening the door of the carriage and helping me inside. "After today you can wear whatever you want."

"Let's wait and see what your team has to say about that."

Callum folds himself next to me, sitting close so our thighs are pressed together. "You are my team, Cate. It's you and me, that's all I care about."

I reach for his hand, lacing our fingers together. His thumb traces soothing circles over my palm and I lean into his comforting weight.

We arrive in Stratford City sooner than I would have liked. What I wouldn't give to stay locked in here with Callum for the rest of the day. There are several ways we could put the small space to creative use. But now isn't the time to think about that.

Our Bond hasn't wavered since the night we made love in Callum's room, the night I agreed to marry him, the night he let me use my Gift. Since then, we haven't been able to keep our hands off each other. Every moment not locked in campaign work is spent wrapped up in one another. The longing I feel deep in my bones for him hasn't abated; if anything it's only intensified.

Just the thought of it is enough to stoke the fire in my blood.

"How long do we have?" Callum mumbles, his lips finding the sensitive spot on my neck, and I know he's thinking similar thoughts to mine.

"Long enough." I hoist the heavy skirts of my dress and clamber my way onto his lap, our mouths tangling around my clumsy maneuvering.

Within seconds, his hard cock is in my palm, his fingers are stroking my folds, and I sink down over him with a sigh of relief.

"We don't have more than a few minutes." His hands slide under my dress, latching on to my thighs and assisting my hips as they roll over him.

"Then you better make me come quickly, Your Highness."

He does, because he always does, chasing his own release seconds later.

The wheels clatter over the cobblestones as we right ourselves, rolling to a stop right as I manage to get my skirts back in place. Next time I will insist on wearing something less restrictive, if for no other reason than it wouldn't be prudent for the fiancée of the future president of Avon to be caught with her skirts around her ears.

Callum exits the carriage first, reaching back to help me down the rickety steps of the carriage. My feet hit the ground and I sway, leaning into him to keep me upright, the sudden rush of blood and fear making me queasy.

The carriage has stopped right in front of La Puissance.

I haven't been back here since we lost Harold, and the sight of my former home brings on a rush of emotions.

"Are you all right?" Callum tightens his hold on me, pulling me into his side.

I sink into his warmth, but only for a second. I force myself upright, force myself to be the kind of partner he needs right now in this moment. Callum needs me to be strong and so I will find a way to be so.

Callum's worried eyes never leave me, even as we're ushered behind the building to the back entrance. He guides me into a chair in the kitchen where I've spent more hours of my life than I can count and crouches down in front of me, the fine material of his suit pulling across his thick thighs. "Cate. Talk to me. What's wrong? If you don't want to do this, now is the time to tell me."

"Why are we here? Did you know this is where we were coming for the announcement?"

Callum hesitates, his blue eyes hiding emotions that send a tingle of fear down my spine.

Bianca cautiously creeps over to us, as if she doesn't want to interrupt our conversation. "Cate? Do you have a minute before the announcement?"

I look to Callum, who nods.

"I'll give you a minute," he says, planting a soft kiss on my cheek before turning to walk away. "We can talk later."

"You should hear this too." Bianca stops him before he can get very far, a calm hand on his forearm.

I stand, linking my arm with Callum's. "What's going on, B? You're scaring me a bit."

She smiles and it's genuine and calming. "Nothing to be scared about." She turns to gesture behind her. Many of the Gifted club members join her, coming from around the side of the building to clump around her. Meri and Tes and Rosa and Helen, a few faces I haven't had the chance to get to know very well.

Bianca takes a deep breath. "We have been talking over the past few days, and we've come to a consensus."

I raise my eyebrow, trying to hide the hurt that comes along with being excluded from these talks. I understand why, but their rejection still stings.

"And we all agreed, voted unanimously in fact, that you should be the one to take over leadership at La Puissance."

Bianca's words hang in the air for several long, quiet seconds.

"I'm sorry, I think I misheard you?" My stomach spins once again, but this time, there's no grief or sadness. Only excitement, and some disbelief, and an overwhelming feeling of this being exactly right.

Meri grins, but it's Tes who says, "We want you to take over for Harold. And we think that's what he would have wanted too."

"Actually, we know it is." Bianca holds up a piece of paper, full of Harold's scratchy handwriting. "He left this on his desk, a note leaving the club in your and Andra's names."

The rest of the group nods.

Callum's hold on my arm tightens and I turn to him, the bubble of happiness in my chest on the verge of popping. I can't take over the club if it means damaging his campaign.

But there's a smile in his eyes as he asks me, "Is this what you want?"

"I think so," I whisper, afraid to latch on to this possibility if it's only going to be snatched from me. "But I won't, if it means—"

"Don't even think about turning down something you want because of me." He cups my cheek in his hand, his thumb running along the line of my jaw.

I lean into his touch for a brief second before turning my attention back to the women in front of me. Some of them are watching Callum and me with expressions bordering on sappy. Some, like Tes, look like they want to throw up. But all of them grin when I tell them I accept, enveloping me in a stifling hug that I never want to end.

The hug breaks apart only when Alex comes to tell us Callum is about to be announced, and the girls head out to the main lobby.

I start to walk toward the grand staircase, where Callum will deliver his first speech as the Scotan presidential candidate, ready to stand by his side, but he pulls me back, his brow furrowed. My heart sinks. Despite the impending disappointment, I still feel like taking over the club is the best decision for me. "I can stay back here. We can delay the marriage announcement, or cancel the marriage altogether." For some reason the thought of losing something I don't even know for sure I want makes me incredibly sad.

"Cate. How many times are we going to have to have the same conversation?" The corners of his eyes crinkle with an exasperated smile.

"I don't know. Several, I'm assuming."

He takes my face in his hands and kisses me softly. "Are you happy? Is this truly what you want?"

I nod, the movement breaking his hold on my cheeks. "It is. And I am happy. But only if my decisions don't affect your future."

He takes a deep breath. "I had something different planned for my announcement, you know."

This time it's my brow that furrows.

He continues without giving me time to interrupt. "I was going to tell everyone that you are the one who killed Harold, and that you not only earned the candidacy, but you had my full support. That's why I chose La Puissance for the location to deliver this address. This place is what made you the person you are today, and the person you are is someone who would make an incredible leader, Cate."

My heart softens, squeezing inside my chest. "Callum. You are wonderful and perfect, and so incredibly misguided sometimes."

He frowns. "I don't know about that."

"I have no desire to be president of Avon. That is a job you were born to do. Just as I was meant to be the head of the club. You are exactly where you're supposed to be and I can't wait to stand by your side." I loop my arms around his neck, pulling him closer to me.

I've already heard the speech he will deliver to his people in a few moments, have heard him speak about how he has plans for a future where everyone in Avon has equitable resources, where the Gifted are no longer treated as second-class citizens. He is going to do great things for the people of this country.

He leans in and kisses me, soft at first, and then deeply. Warmth shoots through me and I rise up on my toes, pressing my body to him. His heartbeat pounds in his chest, and mine syncs with his.

A throat clears. "It's time."

We break apart and turn to see Alex waiting for us, a frown creased on his perpetually tense face.

I fix Callum's hair, taming those gorgeous copper-colored curls. "You ready?"

He nods, his hand slipping down to lace his fingers through mine. "Are you?"

"I'm ready for anything if you're there with me."

He tugs on my hand and we start a slow walk through the kitchen and out toward the grand staircase, waiting to hear our names announced to the sound of raucous cheers from the large crowd. "My lady, that comment was downright sappy."

"This is what you've done to me, Your Highness."

He lifts our interlocked hands to his mouth and kisses the back of my hand. "I wouldn't have it any other way." He pulls us to a stop just out of the sight line of the crowd of people. "I love you, Cate."

"I love you too, Callum."

Alex calls our names and a swell of applause greets us as we walk to our place front and center on the grand staircase of the pleasure club that raised me. We stand next to one another, solid and proud, ready to face whatever the future holds.

A WEEK LATER, we gather in the courtyard of the Scotan Castle. In two days' time, it will be turned over to the Uprising, and so our timeline was pushed up a little.

Alex wanted to make sure our wedding was a grand affair, something for the papers to write about, for the citizens of Scota to partake in, but we decided instead to keep it small. Bianca, Tes, and Meri. Andra, of course. And Alex. Callum's side would feel noticeably empty, so we decided to do away with sides, our friends and family circling around us, surrounding us with love.

We take a moment to remember Harold and Dom and James, and Callum's mother. The grief hasn't passed, for either of us, and I don't know that it ever will. But each day it's a bit easier to breathe. Luckily the club and the campaign are keeping us plenty busy.

I wasn't so sure about marriage, but when we stand and face one another, our hands linked, smiles bright, I know this is where I am meant to be.

We pledge our love and faithfulness to one another, and when Callum slips a ring, his mother's, on my finger, he brings my hand to his lips, kissing my palm.

"I will love you until the day I die, my lady," he whispers, too quiet for anyone else to hear.

"I will love you forevermore, Mr. President."

He grins, his blue eyes sparkling. "I think it might be bad luck to call me that before the election has even truly begun."

I shrug, leaning in to kiss him even though the ceremony isn't officially over yet. "We don't need luck. We have each other."

It has been a long time since I've had a vision of Caralia. I don't know if it's the distance separating us, the fact that I have never been as close to her as I have been to her sisters, but she manages to evade my Sight.

Sometimes I think back to those initial visions, the ones that forced me to separate Grecia from her daughters, and I wonder if I made the right call.

I know I was right to remove them from their mother's influence. And clearly, Andra and Cate are thriving in this life they've created for themselves.

But Caralia was always the wild card.

Sometimes I wonder if I was right to let her live.

—EXCERPT FROM THE JOURNAL OF DIANA BRAHAN

ACKNOWLEDGMENTS

I STARTED WORKING ON the first version of this book way back in 2020. *Lease on Love* was about to go on sub and I was following the age-old advice of writing the wait. Things in publishing were obviously very uncertain at the time, "romantasy" wasn't even a term yet, and I had no real hopes of this story ever seeing the light of day. Cate and Callum went through a lot of changes between that initial draft and what you are reading today, and I am so so thankful I had the opportunity to bring these characters to the world. It wouldn't have been possible without a whole lot of people.

First and foremost, this book is dedicated to my agent, Kimberly Whalen. The first time I mentioned this book to her and asked her if I should try writing something totally different, she told me to write whatever was calling to me. Thank you, Kim, for always encouraging me to follow where my passion leads. You are the epitome of a badass heroine.

To my entire team at Putnam, I truly have no words. I never in my wildest dreams thought this book would find a home at the place I am lucky enough to already call home. Thank you for taking a chance on me and this book, and for always being so solidly in my corner. This particularly applies to my editor, Kate Dresser, who has embraced the unknown right alongside me, and Tarini Sipahimalani, who is a literal superhero. Huge thank-yous also to Katy Riegel, Leah Marsh, Sanny Chiu, Lindsay Sagnette, and Ivan Held.

This book made its way to your hands thanks in large part to my publicity and marketing teams, who are top tier! Thank you Kristen Bianco, Jess Lopez, Brennin Cummings, Alexis Welby, and Ashley McClay.

Adelle Kincel, and the entire Putnam art department, thank you for the cover of my dreams. Cassandra Lynn, thank you for the gorgeous map.

I had a bunch of incredible beta readers for this book, who gave me so much impactful insight. *Something Wicked* would not be what it is today without guidance from Emily Shannon, Nicki Webber, Vanessa Valdez, Jessica Schlangen, and Emily Waller.

To all the bookstagrammers, book-tokers, booksellers, librarians, and everyone else who shouts about books they love to the world, none of this happens without you. I am endlessly grateful for your support.

Thank you to India Holton and Nisha J. Tuli for their early love and support.

Sonia Hartl, you not only showed so much enthusiasm for this project, you gave the best feedback—thank you for your care with my words. Jessica Parra, you gave me confidence when I needed it most. Ashley Hooper, you continue to listen to me blather on about plots and characters and all my anxieties. Brianna Mowry, you continue to show up for me and send me the best TikToks.

When people ask me for my best writing/publishing advice, my answer is always the same: Find your community, find your people. I am so lucky to have nestled my way into the absolute best circle of people. You know who you are, and I love you.

Courtney Kae, this book wouldn't exist without you. Literally—because you talked me through the biggest plot hole in the history of plot holes. Figuratively—because I don't think I could survive publishing without you by my side. Thank you for being Romance-landia's brightest light.

Thank you, as always, to my family and friends.

Canon, I love you—put this book down immediately.

Matt, you remain the gold standard. Thanks for being my emotional support husband—no one could do it better. Love you the most.

Finally, I am writing these acknowledgments on February 5, 2025, and things are looking all-around pretty bleak. To everyone who is fighting the good fight, keep fighting. It's all worth fighting for.

ABOUT THE AUTHOR

Photograph of the author © Brianna Mowry

Falon Ballard is the *USA Today* bestselling author of several rom-coms and the cohost of the *Happy to Meet Cute* podcast. When she's not writing a romance book, reading a romance book, or talking about romance books, you can probably find her at Disneyland. Ballard lives in the Los Angeles area.

VISIT FALON BALLARD ONLINE

falonballard.com
FalonBallard
FalonBallard